Feeling Etienne's Love
Bad Boys Book Eight

I0553993

Christine Young

Chapter One

Paris 1824

    Elisa Moreau stepped inside the brothel in Paris with her delivery in hand. She turned at the doorway, shaking out her rain stopper, water sluicing into the alley even as the wind gusted around the corner sending the door banging shut behind her. The hard fast drops pounded on the roof above. It was truly a nasty day outside. She hoped inside the environment would prove to be a bit warmer.

    She inhaled deeply enjoying the smell of freshly baked bread linked with other delicious, tempting aromas filling the kitchen. The cook, Francois, was a particular friend of hers, so he tolerated her presence in his kitchen like no other. She supposed it was so because she'd known him from birth, played with the pots and pans along with the measuring cups in his kitchen. Vividly, she recalled his thinly veiled curses when he couldn't find a utensil he needed.

    Once a year she handed over the completed books for the madam in this Paris brothel as well as those for her mother in her brothel in the city of Bordeaux. Her mother saw to her education even while she protested the need for such a thing. Now she appreciated her particular skills, realizing she was a very lucky woman.

    Elisa always entered Margaux's establishment through the servant's entrance behind the building before making her way through the kitchen. Angelique, her mother, insisted that no one see her entering or leaving the brothel to protect her reputation. Anyone who knew her, everyone she cared about understood she was the daughter of a notorious and wealthy Madame. What difference did it make whether she entered through the back or the front door? Still, she never argued with her mother or her mother's best friend.

The two women had known each other for years, Margaux beginning her career with Angelique in the bordello in Paris until Angelique moved her business to Bordeaux leaving the brothel in Paris to Margaux. Both women spent the years keeping Elisa from seeing the seamier side of their business all the while failing miserably in their attempts. It was just too difficult to keep a precocious child from exploring and seeing things she shouldn't. Despite the lectures coupled with dire warnings until Elisa was sent away to the small cottage in the Bordeaux region of France, she continued to do and go as she pleased within the buildings owned by both her mother and Margaux. In the country her behavior changed little. However, she had fewer opportunities to find trouble. Her bodyguards kept a constant watch over her, steering her away from her curiosity, turning her life into one of avid boredom.

She stopped in the kitchen, sampling some of the delicacies that would be served later this evening when the business was at its prime hours. Madam Margaux prided herself in her kitchen as well as the food along with the very expensive wines she served her clientele. At the moment, except for the ladies chatting about the evening to come, the house was very nearly empty. A small game of chance was going on in a backroom. Other than that, only the people who lived in the brothel were about.

"*Bonne journee*, mademoiselle Elisa. How is your day? It's not so beautiful out there but at least you did not get a soaking. That rain stopper of yours must be doing a good job." Francois greeted her with a broad grin holding his arms out for a hug.

"I like the rain," Elisa said with a smile and a wink, searching the platters already heaped high with mountains of food. "What have you got here that warrants a taste before I bring these documents to Margaux?"

"Ah, I see you've been keeping yourself busy with your work. Seems as if a lady as beautiful as you with such sparkling and unusual blue-violet eyes would have a man by now. You spend too much time burying your nose in your books and not spending time with your friends."

Her heart had been with one man since she was six-years-old, when he kissed her on the lips, twirling her in a grand circle while she told him she loved him. Remembering that hot summer day, as well as his sudden appearance near her small cottage with his friend Gil. His smile was a quirky half-smile with a dimple showing on the other side of his mouth. Whenever she thought about that gorgeous dimple, she wanted to kiss him there. Her mother as well as Margaux would have an absolute fit if they knew the direction of her thoughts.

The two young men had been riding bareback, wild and free, shouting and yelling their pleasure as they wove their way through the vineyards of the Bordeaux countryside. Neither wore a shirt. Their skin was bronzed from the sun, sweat sliding down their well-muscled chests. She didn't know why she recalled that so vividly but nonetheless she did.

"What are you grinning at, *mon amie*?" Francois asked. "A special young man who will whisk you away from all this boring everyday drudgery? *Oui*, I hope it is so."

Having been caught in her dreams, a wave of heat rose to Elisa's cheeks. She waved her hand in the air not really wanting to divulge her secret desires to Francois who would most likely tease her incessantly. "Nothing." She popped a small delicacy into her mouth and rolled her eyes at the incredible taste. "*Tres bon.* I'd ask you for the recipe but I know you'll refuse."

"Ah, *oui*, you change the subject quite handily for a young woman. Your verbal skills perhaps are too sharp for a sensible man. You must change your ways. Stop intimidating the masculine species." Francois laughed as he pulled a tray of tiny lavender cakes from the oven, the icing sitting nearby waiting to decorate the delicious morsels. "I will not pursue the question. It seems you keep secrets from me, *non*? That is not well done of you. I would know everything," he sighed softly. "I suppose you share those secrets with Margaux. Should I be jealous?"

"Some," she reluctantly admitted, knowing there was very little anyone except her mother knew about her.

Margaux was a woman who would never judge or criticize nor would she relay her most inner thoughts to her mother. She was a sounding board for her even though her mother never judged either. She always wondered what Angel, the Madame, was thinking versus Angelique her mother. When she spoke, she would always have to figure out which persona was listening to her.

She enjoyed Paris as well as her friends from school even though she was growing bored with the endless parties along with the secret dalliances she didn't want to find herself caught up in. None of those people would stay friends with her if they knew what her mother did for a living, yet many of the young men she knew frequented this brothel as well as her friends' fathers. The ties of home linked with the small cottage where she lived tugged at her heartstrings. Perhaps it was time to leave the city and return to a place where she felt more comfortable.

"You going to see Margaux? Bring her this tray of snacks, this pot of tea also. Both of you enjoy with my blessings. Don't leave without saying goodbye. I will give you a little something to take with you to your apartment."

"I will. *Merci beaucoup.*" Elisa kissed his chubby cheek before she swept up the tray and headed for the lavish suite of rooms where Margaux lived, her heart racing. She knew Margaux would ask her questions about her love life. All her answers would be the same as the last time she was here. For many years, she tried to keep the mention of Etienne Dubois from the talks they shared. It was useless. Eventually, she gave in telling the madam all about him along with that day she fell in love with the young man.

On her way upstairs, she stopped several times to chat and say hello to the women she'd befriended over the years. She understood these ladies as well as why most of them sold themselves. Her mother had been in the horrible position of having a baby coupled with having no husband when she first entered the business. At that time, Angelique had no way to support herself let alone her child other than to sell her body. When she rose to the position of madam of her own bordello, she vowed that any lady who wanted out of the business she would help them find their way.

With her foot pressed against the hardwood, Elisa tapped on the door. "Margaux, it's me, Elisa. May I come in? I cannot open the door. My hands are full."

A few seconds later the door swung open. A beaming Margaux with open arms awkwardly embraced her before kissing her on both cheeks. "*Bonjour*, and how are you this fine day?"

"Happy to have all your books completed. You made a fine profit this year, enough to take a vacation although you never seem to want to do that. You should find some time for yourself, even if it's just to visit Bordeaux and my lovely mother." Elisa brought the tray to a small table in the parlor of the suite of rooms Margaux occupied.

"I do not like vacations. They are a horrible waste of my time. Who would run this place if I wasn't here? Tell me. Francois? Bah," she paused thoughtfully, seeming to realize any number of people could keep it going for a few weeks. Then with a heavy sigh, "Do you want to chat first or talk business first," Margaux asked, pouring the tea. "Sugar?"

"*Non*. Let's talk business then you can grill me on all my nonexistent beaus. My status has not changed since last I was here." Elisa laughed thinking suddenly her status might never vary. She'd never had a beau. Still, she only thought of Etienne coupled with that one chaste kiss so many years ago. It seemed she relived that moment over and over again.

Margaux would berate her for still feeling love for this young man she never truly knew. Despite her attempts to do just that, she couldn't help the emotions sweeping through her whenever she thought of him. Every time she closed her eyes at night, she would see the wild young man and the debonair smile flashing on his handsome face as well as his dark brown eyes sparkling with some unknown joke.

Elisa picked up the box containing all her work before settling down on a comfortable chair. She quickly brought out the ledger, which she carefully designed so Margaux could easily read the results of her business this past quarter.

By the time they finished, the sun was beginning to go down. The crowds outside the madam's door had become more boisterous, the music livelier. The night was clearly going to be busy, but Margaux didn't show any signs of wishing to visit the customers.

Margaux reached forward, touching the back of her hand. "Now it is time for you to tell me about yourself as well as what you've been doing for the past months since last I saw you. I pray it has not been all work and no play."

"That's what I was afraid you'd ask. I've not really done anything you would approve of or for that matter disapprove either."

Elisa looked to the window and the last dying rays of the sun which managed to peak out from behind dark gray clouds. No, she'd pretty much kept to herself, distancing herself from the people she'd met at school before they would find out who her mother was, and in the process, shun her themselves.

"So, you have not found a young man to replace your Etienne Dubois. You need to look farther than the end of your nose, young lady. Eligible men don't just fall out of trees, you know."

At her look of surprise, Margaux cleared her throat. "I spoke with your mother a few weeks ago. It was a vacation of sorts as Bailey drove me to Bordeaux for a long-needed visit, a much-needed visit for both of us. Between the two of us we decided your young man must be Pruitt Dubois' son. We put together the things you told us. It was not too difficult to come to that conclusion."

"I didn't know his name at the time." She was just as surprised as she supposed the look on her face told Margaux. "I was only six when the rogue kissed me. Since then, I've been in school in Paris. Mother thought it best to send me away. Now I understand why."

"She didn't want you that close to the young man who stole your heart when you were just a little girl. He was way too old for you at the time. Could have taken advantage of you," Margaux was laughing but the humor suddenly vanished.

"As you point out, he is or was too old for me then, nevertheless. He would not have found a six-year-old interesting or appealing in any way. I don't believe for one second he would take advantage of me."

Elisa thought on the lost years and wondered why she was still so enamored of someone who didn't know or care that she existed, a man she'd known for one brief moment in time. It was with great difficulty that she tried to push thoughts of Etienne Dubois from her mind, telling herself she didn't even know what kind of man he was. He could be cruel or hateful. He could be a womanizer.

"Until now."

"I suppose, until now. Don't know how old he was then so I certainly don't know his age in the present."

Margaux leaned back in her chair, her hands clasped together beneath her chin. The pose was one of her favorites. "He frequents my place from time to time. I heard he has been to several other countries over the years. It seems he always returns with rumors and gossip about his adventures on his heels. He is not the sort you want to be acquainted with, especially not a man worthy of your love. I've heard he is a very dangerous man. Not the sort you would want as a husband even if he was amenable. By his actions here, in this establishment, Etienne Dubois is far from amenable. Mark my words. He is not for you, Elisa. Not good enough by far. You need to forget him, put him in the back of your mind. Find a man who will treat you with respect."

Elisa felt her heart sink at Margaux's words. She wanted his behavior to be heaped with praise, not liking the fact that now she was discovering Etienne was a bounder and a cad of the worst sort. What exactly made him a dangerous man?

"What were the rumors about?" she blurted the question she really didn't want to know the answer to.

"From what I've heard mostly fathers searching for him so he would marry their daughters. He's obviously not the marrying kind." She sat up as a knock on the door caught their attention. "Come in."

It was Francois personally delivering dinner. "Your assistant, Gabriella, is not feeling well today. She asked if I could bring this to the both of you and not to have any worries. When the new girl arrives, she would personally see to her and make sure she is comfortable. A room is waiting for her along with a list of possible clients."

"I had wondered where Gabriella was, but I was so lost in conversation this afternoon with Elisa I didn't think to ask. I can see to the new girl when she arrives."

"No," he laughed, "she made me promise to insist you visit to your heart's content. You see Elisa so seldom. In any case, one of your bodyguards will be at the front door. He will let Gabriella know when the new girl arrives."

When the cook left, "Would you like me to pour the wine?" Elisa rose, examining the bottle and the writing on the label. "This bottle comes from the Dubois vineyards. So, you do business with the older man, with Etienne's father?"

"I do and when Etienne is in town for his usual short visits, he handles the sales personally. After the deliveries are seen to, he partakes of a night of pleasure, on the house. Otherwise, his friend Gil takes charge of the shipments of wine. I suppose it must have been Gil with him that day Etienne made such an impression on you."

Waving her hand in the air before sipping the wine she'd poured, "It must have been. I've heard that except for his travels they were always inseparable. Do you know why he is always travelling?" Elisa couldn't stem the curiosity she still felt for this man. It was something she could not vanquish from her heart.

"Gil would have made a much better man to lose your heart to. I don't suppose he kissed you too?"

"Unfortunately, he did not dismount before sweeping me into his arms for a quick thank you kiss along with a lasting impression."

"How is your mother?" Margaux asked seeming to think it necessary to change the subject. "Last I heard she was doing better than ever. Thriving actually."

Elisa let out a long-drawn out sigh, unsure of how exactly to answer the question posed to her. Her father showed up last year, demanding a part of the business, a business he had nothing to do with over the years. Angelique's lawyers were the best and kept the unwilling partnership from happening, but he'd shown up several more times at the brothel, drunk and demanding free service.

"Mother is feeling her age. At least that is what she would tell you. Father has visited the bordello several times expecting full use of any woman he finds attractive. Each time the girl he was with was severely beaten. Mother's guards have standing orders to throw him out if he ever comes again, however his presence has served as a painful reminder of her past. A place she does not wish to visit or recall."

"No, I suppose she doesn't. Vividly, I recollect her story. With you just a wee babe, she ran from him in the middle of the night. If not for the kindly madam she met, the two of you would have starved. That single moment changed her life for the better, although I realize many condescending people would not see the circumstance in that light."

Leaning on her elbows with her chin resting in the palms of her hands. "Tell me about Gil. Does he also visit here? Perhaps he would be a better more responsible choice for my heart. I could always try to meet him. See if there was something for me." Elisa laughed then, wishing for what she wasn't at all sure. "But I wouldn't know how to go about meeting him."

"Gil is more responsible," Margaux paused for a moment still smiling, "He is still a rake. Not someone for an innocent like yourself. Neither Gil nor Etienne are anywhere close to settling down. It has been suggested that when the right woman comes along, the man will change. From all the circulating stories I've heard, I doubt if Etienne will ever differ from the path he's on. He seems to like the danger and intrigue he's surrounded himself with. Some men just don't have it in them to be satisfied with only one woman. Even if that woman is as lovely and precious as you are." Margaux stood then, walking to the window and staring out at the city. From her vantage point Elisa knew she could see some of the landmarks that people visited Paris to attend. The view from her window was quite picturesque.

"How are you doing besides monetarily? Have you ever wished that you could leave this work and find an honest man to keep you in the lap of luxury surrounded by children?" Elisa asked, half grinning half knowing the answer.

"So, you change the subject from you to me. You do that quite handily." She stayed at the window. "The lap of luxury. I think this is the best it gets. I've got everything I've ever wanted coupled with more money than I can ever spend. Why would I want a man to beat me down? To command and order me?"

"They are not all like that." Elisa was determined to see the best in men.

She had to or she would give up on her dreams of a home and family. Children were part of her dreams.

"Name one who is not," Margaux challenged.

Elisa sipped her wine, the silence echoing in the small room while she tried to think of someone. She could not. In any case, she didn't know enough men to even consider suggesting one.

"I didn't think so," Margaux said sarcasm coating her voice.

"There must be some. As you well comprehend, I don't know many men. Actually, only a few boys from school who have tried to steal kisses a time or two. I've told them *non*. They are not interested in me as a person, just what they can glean from me."

"Good for you. We both know and I'm sure your mother has told you more than once, kisses lead to other things. Things we don't want to deal with. If you ever get into trouble, I want you to come to me if you don't feel your mother will understand."

"Since there is no one I'm interested in, I'm sure that will not happen. No kisses... I could only hope for one more from..."

"Do not dream of that man any longer. He is not worth your time." Margaux shook a finger at her. "He is incorrigible. Where women are concerned, Etienne has only one thing on his wicked man's brain."

"Wicked man's brain?" Elisa laughed understanding the drama of the moment. "Whatever does that mean?"

Margaux poured them both another glass of wine. "You should clear your mind of that man and..."

"And what?" Elisa challenged, wishing for more information. "I don't know anyone in the city. Heaven knows you cannot introduce me to any of your customers. They would think the wrong thing. How am I to meet a man who will take my heart away from Etienne? Tell me that."

"We have many of the best in the city who come here. There are dukes and earls many wealthy bankers along with lawyers." Margaux turned from her view, "I would have to figure out some way for them to meet you outside this building. I'm afraid I don't have any idea how to go about that. Perhaps Bailey can figure something out."

"No, I don't suppose there is any way for that and I'm actually grateful. I'm not in a hurry to marry or meet a duke. That could prove to be very boring. Duke's tend to be stuffy. Don't you think? There are plenty of years ahead of me."

"What are you planning?" Margaux asked appearing suddenly

wary.

"I'm going back to the country. Mother has promised security for me. I miss the home I grew up in the countryside with it rolling hills. I like to walk down the rows of grapes as well as watch the sun set behind the hills. The moon is bigger there, the stars brighter, so brilliant sometimes it seems one can reach out, touch them with their hand. When there is a storm, one can feel the excitement as well as the energy to their very bones." She held up her hands a chuckle following. "I'm not giving up on finding a husband. Maybe a nice vineyard owner would take my mind off the elusive and roguish Etienne Dubois."

"Perhaps one would. Now, I'm not trying to get rid of you but would you like an escort home tonight? The hour does grow late. I would make sure you get through this part of Paris safely. At night it can be dangerous for a woman alone."

"I'll hire a cab right in front of your door. I promise to keep my hood over my head so no one will recognize me. Should we finish the wine then call it a night?" she asked feeling a sense of relief now that the conversation about her love life appeared to be over.

"Of course, a cab would be perfect. I deposited the money you earned in your bank account. Do you have enough money with you for the fare?"

"Just enough and not a penny more. Mother taught me not to carry a lot of coin with me while I'm in the city."

Elisa closed her eyes as she drank small sips of the wine, feeling the effects of the alcohol as it seemed to warm her while making everything a bit hazy. How many glasses did she drink? Perhaps she should see if there was an empty room so she could stay the night. It wouldn't be the first time she spent the evening in a brothel. It most likely would not be the last.

Her mother used to let her stay at the one in Bordeaux during the week when she was younger. She had seen things young women should not. Still, she was fairly innocent in the ways of men and sex. The lectures from both Angelique and Margaux had been numerous as to what she shouldn't do, but they'd never told her what to expect if she wanted to have sex with a man. From what she'd seen in the brothels along with what the two women told her that the knowledge was all a jumble in her mind.

"What has you grinning?" Margaux asked setting her glass on the table. "You have this strange look in your eyes."

"I was thinking about what I do know coupled with what I don't know about sex. What I've seen and what you and mother have told me. None of it makes senses. It's all a confusing tangled mess in my head."

"It's best we keep it that way until you are betrothed. When that happens, I will be more than delighted to explain everything as I'm sure your mother will also. At that time, not a moment sooner, will either one of us enlighten you as to the ways of a man and woman in love. It is much different than what goes on beneath this roof."

She sighed softly, the sound a small whisper in the evening air. "I've changed my mind and thought I might ask if I can stay the night. If there is an empty room that is. I'm tired and it seems the wine has crept up on me. I'm a bit dizzy headed."

"Yes, of course. I'll call Bailey. He can escort you to one of our vacant rooms upstairs." Margaux rose from her chair, a small groan as she kneaded her back. "Just as with your mother, age might be getting the best of me. Sometimes it hurts just to stand up if I've been sitting too long."

"I can find my way. Is it the room on the third floor? The one I stayed in a few months ago?" She placed a kiss on Margaux's cheek.

"No, at present the only empty one is on the second floor, first door on the right. Do have a nice rest."

"Thank you. I'll see you in the morning then."

Elisa felt a strange exhilaration. It was a feeling she couldn't put a word too. She didn't understand the sensation as she felt as if something momentous might be about to happen, something that would sway the course of her life.

"Perhaps. I don't get up so early any more. If you are up and need to be on your way, then go, don't wait for me to rise."

"I won't. I'm awfully tired. I'm not sure how early I will be up. I know I've got until the afternoon." Thought of lazing the morning in bed appealed to her vanity. She'd not thought to do anything of that sort in ages. Mayhap she was the one who needed a vacation. As everyone important to her insinuated, she spent too much time working.

Elisa walked from the room then into the main hall. Looking around, the scene in front of her was much different from when she arrived. Music played loudly. Men along with scantily clad women were scattered around, sitting on couches, kissing and doing other less platonic things. Over the years, she'd become used to this panorama as she visited Angelique as well as Margaux. She grinned, despite her mother's best efforts to keep her away from this. She felt at home in this environment.

Second and third thoughts assailed her as she thought of the pros and cons of staying the night. At the front door, she stopped for a moment before realizing she left her cloak in the kitchen when she came in through the back. Perhaps she should leave that way too. She didn't want to walk in the dark alley though. Most of all didn't want to wait for Bailey to escort her. No, she would go to the room Margaux spoke of.

Second floor, first door on the right.

She didn't make it very far before a large hand, settled around her arm roughly stopping her. "There you are. Been looking all over for you. Where do you think you're going?"

"I don't know what you mean. You need to let me go." She was surprised as she felt a moment of discomfort but was sure this could be easily explained.

"You the new girl. I've got to get you settled then find some work for you. A possible client list for your inspection is at the front door," he replied. "Customers are waiting. Come along."

She tried to brush the hand away, which seemed to have tightened over the last second. Panic set in, "Let me go." She wasn't the new girl. She wasn't going to peruse a client list nor did she intend to entertain any customers.

"You having second thoughts about this job? Can't do that. You signed a contract for a month. Have to fulfill it."

"I don't know what you're talking about."

She summoned as much force as she could. For Elisa this was a shattering scene, something she'd not expected. The man coupled with his arrogance along with the wine left her with a loss for explanatory words. The Neanderthal probably wouldn't believe her anyway. Where was Bailey?

"Let me go. If Margaux knew I was having second thoughts, she wouldn't force me."

He turned her, shaking her slightly. "Can't do that. The madam would have my hide if she found out I let the new girl leave without fulfilling her contract. I'd lose my job. Can't have that. While it's no matter to me, why did you sign something you weren't willing to fulfill?"

Elisa understood arguing with this man wasn't going to get her anywhere. After all, his point was well taken. The man didn't know her, would of course assume she was something she wasn't. She just needed to find a familiar face. "I want to see Margaux."

"New girls don't get favors. You need to learn to call her Madam Margaux. Now I'm going to take your cloak for you. I'll hang it up right here by the door. Do you have a valise? Where is it? Then you are going to behave yourself, do as you're told. Everything will be fine if you do."

He let her go of her arm then. Momentarily, she thought to dart into the kitchen. Francois would defend her. Tell this man she was hardly the new girl, however when she turned, her gaze rested on the stairway, her breath catching in her throat as she stared mesmerized at the picturesque view in front of her. The sight was something she dreamed of almost every night since their first kiss.

"Etienne..." she whispered softly, staring at the man wide-eyed who seemingly heard his name stopped and was now looking over his shoulder straight at her. His dark brown eyes melting her right where she stood.

Inside her chest, her heart thundered, beating so rapidly she thought she might swoon. She couldn't be sure this was Etienne. Still, he looked as she imagined him. He was taller, his shoulders broader than she recalled. His dark hair was disheveled, a thick strand hanging rakishly across his forehead in that charming way the six-year-old girl remembered. She wanted to get close enough so she could see the sparkle in his deep brown eyes as well as the quirky, dimpled smile she remembered.

Etienne pointed at her. "I want that girl."

~ * ~

Earlier that afternoon, Etienne wiped the sweat and blood from his face. Gil landed a few solid punches to his face. His friend was an established boxer and he'd spent the night before drinking and gambling. He touched his nose, grimacing a moment while at the same time, hoping it wasn't broken again. The women in his life would of course, appreciate the slight flaw fawning over him to get his attention. He grinned.

"You're getting old," Gil said with a chuckle as he wiped sweat from his body then dipping his towel into a basin of water, he repeated the process. "I didn't used to be able to best you so soundly or so quickly."

"Just as old as you." Etienne shot back without hesitation, thinking he needed to spend more time with this type of physical activity rather than those with the ladies. "Just a bit rusty on my boxing skills. With a little time, I'll be back to my old pace."

"It's your lifestyle. You should think about settling down with a good woman."

"Don't suppose you know any? I certainly don't," Etienne laughed, looking in a mirror and dabbing at the blood over his eye. Where women were concerned, he was more than slightly jaded. No one would believe him but his heart had been broken several times during his younger years. Besides, his life at the moment didn't lend itself to serious dalliances. Working for the French government took all his concentration. Distraction was not an asset to his work. Now, he vowed to never lay his heart on the line again. He poured water into a basin before splashing the liquid on his face, feeling the cooling droplets slide across his body. "Need a bath before tonight. Want to come with me?"

"For a bath, no. You seeing a lady or are you going to the bordello?" Gil asked, grinning at him as he also cooled his body with the water.

"No, gave up on good ladies. Present me with a naughty one anytime. Get into too much trouble with the good ones. Seems they expect certain things I'm not willing to offer. Going to Margaux's. Might do a little gambling beforehand. See how my luck is running."

Etienne thought on the last girl he bedded. When her father

discovered him in her bed, he had to go out the second story window without his boots to escape a marriage. That was the last time he would put his life in jeopardy, especially when he knew of a respectable brothel, a place where he could have a night of pleasure without being worried about his life and limbs or losing a perfectly good pair of boots. He walked away from that night with a turned ankle and he was just glad nothing had been broken.

"Guess I'll join you. Don't have anything better to do. Madam Margaux's establishment is usually quite the thing?" Gil asked grinning.

"Heard there was a new girl coming tonight. Perhaps I'll give her a try." Etienne was toweling his hair knowing he needed something new in his life even if it was a whore. Perhaps she was new to the business, not just to Margaux's establishment. A virgin, *non*, he didn't want to dally with an untried lady while having to worry about hurting her.

"Heard she's a virgin. Personally, don't want anything to do with virgins," Gil said as he towel dried his golden hair.

Two hours later the two men entered Margaux's establishment. Etienne grinned, planning his night. He had profits from the delivery of wine this morning. Now he was going to relax and enjoy the games as well as the spirits. If things went his way tonight, he would enjoy more than the gambling. A night spent in a willing woman's arms was just what he needed before he left on his next mission.

Bailey led them through the rooms to one in the back with a cluster of small tables. Brandy as well as wine flowed freely. The stakes were high. They sat with some other gentlemen. A few minutes later the cards were dealt. He leaned back in the chair, a cheroot in his hand, smiling. When his funds were plenty, he rarely lost. It was only when he was desperate for money that he would come out of the game with less than when he entered into it.

Tonight, he was restless though. He didn't know why. Gil presented new ideas, ones he needed to consider. His father was after him to settle down and provide grandchildren, an heir to the Dubois vineyards. He didn't know where to find a good woman, one who his father would approve. Certainly, he wouldn't find that type of respectable woman in this house of ill repute.

Possibly he was tired of playing the games of love. Maybe he was looking in all the wrong places. If he found someone, he would settle down, become a decent human and father he hoped. Problem was he seemed to gravitate toward women who, well, women who were less than ladies. They either wanted him for the sex or for what he could give them. He decided the next country he visited, he would lie about who he was then maybe, just maybe, he could find a suitable woman.

"You in or are you just going to stare at your cards?" one of the players asked with a smirk, apparently sure of his hand.

"In," he said, fingering his cards, still acting distracted yet he was fully alert and sizing up the expressions on every man's face. Perhaps this was as good a hand as any he was going to get tonight.

The games continued for a few more hours until Etienne tired of the sport. He'd won a sizable amount. Luck was with him. Most of his winnings he planned to lavish on the prostitute he was going to spend the night with. He smiled to himself thinking of the night to come; of soft breasts, a sweetly curving hip, the soft velvet between the woman's legs.

"I'm done," he said, stretching his gaze to Gil with a silent question. "You coming or staying?"

"Tired of cards. So..." Gil stood seeming a bit confused, running his hands through his hair, his expression one that told Etienne he wasn't sure what he wanted. "Not really in the mood for a woman. Think I'll go to the apartment. See you tomorrow afternoon for another boxing lesson."

Etienne let out a long chortle wondering what Gil was truly up to. "I will be giving you the instructions, *mon ami*."

"You can hope."

They spent some time in the foyer, chatting and watching the women as they showed themselves to the two men. "Change your mind?" Etienne asked as he saw the slow smile of appreciation cross his friend's face when a certain woman with huge breasts and swaying hips approached them.

"Perhaps the little red head is appealing tonight. Seems she has all the necessary assets." Gil stared at her while she stepped closer, her hand on his shoulder, her breasts pushing against his chest, her silver-blue eyes twinkling. "Guess I'll stay."

Etienne watched his friend leave with the woman. Searching the room, he didn't find anyone especially tempting. He leaned against the wall, his arms crossed in front of his chest. Perhaps he should just leave. Maybe what he sought couldn't be found here tonight.

"You need a woman?" A blond with sparkling brown eyes pressed against him, running her hand along his chest, pushing her ripe full breasts evocatively against him.

Her lips were too red, her face too made up, but, "What the hell?"

"I can ease your stress," she murmured softly taking his hand. "Along with whatever else ails you. Don't ask questions. Don't judge."

He realized she must have seen the money he won. Once again, the lady wanted what he could give her not him. The fact didn't help his jaded heart even when he reminded himself he was in a bordello. Lord but he wanted someone who wanted him. "You could give it a try," he told her, thinking once more what the hell. She was a warm willing body to relive his baser needs. That was all he needed tonight.

Warm and willing.

Scotland called to him. He was going to be sent there on a secret mission. His operatives were on their way. He'd yet to receive the details. Next week, after seeing his father and saying his goodbyes, he would head to Glasgow. He'd never been to the land of kilts and bagpipes. Perhaps that country would give him a new interest, some lady he could call his own. Yes, he would go to Glasgow. Tonight however, he meant to have sex with the woman standing next to him.

"I will do more than try," she murmured as his hand slipped around her waist before moving higher to rest just below her breast. He felt the small shiver of passion as her pliant woman's curves molded against him. She tossed her head sending a wave of blond curls around his arm.

"Where is your room?" He started forward, matching her small steps as they headed up the stairs while he explored more interesting spots with his hands.

A whisper of his name in the noisy room caught his attention. Halfway up the steps he stopped, turning to search the room. His heart caught in his throat as his gaze rested on a woman near the door. Her back was stiff as were her shoulders. There was something intriguing about the provocative face, the soft lips as well as the tilt of her regal chin. She met his gaze, moistening her lips with the tip of her tongue then slowly closing and opening her eyes. For a moment, his heart forgot to beat.

He had never seen a woman as beautiful or one who had him lusting after her with just one look. The darkening of her eyes spoke of passion. Her sensuality seemed to take over every part of her, calling his name as no other woman could. What the devil was this woman doing in a bordello when she could have any man she wanted? His actions now might impact the rest of his life, but damnation, he couldn't resist.

"I want that girl." He didn't know if she was the new girl but the talk around the table tonight had revolved around a new woman coming to the brothel. He'd never seen her here before. He understood the price would be higher. As he also knew the madam would indulge him in this, simply because it seemed Margaux had a soft spot for him, spoiling him when others scorned his ways.

"*Mais non,*" the blond said.

"Sorry, sweetheart. You can find someone else." His full attention turned to the young woman staring at him wide-eyed from the bottom of the steps.

The manager standing beside her placed his hand on her waist before whispering something he couldn't hear. She nodded as if accepting his request. Slowly, they made their way up the steps toward him. Her lips were parted invitingly even as he saw the flush paint her cheeks along with the slight trembling of her petite frame. She was everything he could ever hope for.

He met her halfway, taking her hand in his. Before bending over, he caught her gaze with his, "*Enchante mademoiselle.*" He kissed the back, felt the shiver pass from her into him, and knew he'd remember this night forever.

"*Bonsoir,*" she spoke softly, her words whisper thin as he sensed the potent surge of energy sweeping between them. He felt the soft flutter of air as she let out the breath she'd been holding. Then she looked upward, their gazes meeting his in a haze of powerful desire he could read clearly in her eyes.

She wanted him.

He watched as she seemed to try to inhale a large dose of air, her bottom lip finding purchase beneath her small white teeth. He thought of tasting that full lip, putting his teeth where hers touched. Beside him her body trembled. "You have nothing to be afraid of, mademoiselle." His voice was soft and throaty from the rapid rise of passion. "Come, we can talk first if you'd like. Don't have to rush anything tonight."

His hand was on her tiny waist, his thumb rubbing gentle circles. He was guiding her upward to her room, but he wasn't sure where to go. She seemed to sense his hesitation then she looked at him with wide vividly unique blue eyes rimmed in violet. "Where are we going?" Then she paused again for what seemed an eternity as she looked around.

"To your room. You have been assigned a room, haven't you? Or is it too soon?" He didn't want to wait or go downstairs until something could be arranged.

"Oh!" She sounded surprised, her eyes widening with sudden comprehension. "My room, I thought. Second floor, first door on the right."

"Good, now that was not so hard." He felt a small chuckle rise from his belly as they turned down the hallway to stop at the first door. *She is delightful.* It swung open. He waited for her to walk inside before he closed and locked it behind them, leaving the key in the door. Clearly, she was nervous. He wanted her to relax.

She stood in front of him, her hands clasped tightly in front of her, wispy strands of nearly white, blond hair falling in soft very touchable curls around her face while the rest was piled intricately on top of her head. Her uniqueness stole his breath. Did she have any idea how beautiful she was?

"What do we do now?"

She looked to the floor then back to him, her blue-violet eyes shimmering with some emotion he craved to discover. For a moment, her hand fluttered upward and toward him before she drew it back.

"Take all our clothes off."

He watched the expressions flit across her face then thought better of his statement. While that was his intention and hers to be sure before the night's end, perhaps this was too soon. If she were the new girl, this would all be uncharted territory for her.

"Do we have too?" She looked up, startled wide eyes staring at him. "I mean..."

He kept his laughter behind his teeth. "*Non*, but it would be more fun as well as easier if we did."

Now she looked down, plucking at her skirts and before he could say anything more, she touched his chest with her small hand. "If you say so."

He placed his hand over hers, enjoying the pressure. Perhaps something else to speak of would be prudent at this time, "Do you have a name?" He spoke gently in a fervent attempt to ease the way for her.

"Do you?"

She sounded defensive. He wasn't too sure why. He only asked for a name.

Perhaps she wasn't as nervous as he thought. He would have to proceed with caution before he could see just what was going to transpire next. He bowed low, "Etienne Dubois at your service."

Turning her head away for a moment then looking at him and with a few blinks of her eyes, "Elisa."

"A pretty name for a pretty lady. Do you have a last name?"

"Just Elisa."

Realizing she would give up only so much, he granted her the omission for now. In the scope of things her last name was hardly important. After tonight, he didn't plan on seeing her again.

"Just Elisa, are you the new girl?" he asked, suddenly wondering just how new she was to all this.

If she was still a virgin, Madame Margaux would charge him double. He realized he didn't care. All his previous notions coupled with his reservations about bedding a virgin vanished as he watched her small, pink tongue moisten her bottom lip. In that instant he was fully aroused.

She was shaking her head then, seeming to deny the fact but everything about her actions described a novice. "No, well, yes, I suppose I am new to all this. Don't understand what is expected of me though. Never been with a..."

Once again, her moist tongue swept across her lips leaving them wet, enticing and very pink. She invited him to intimacy with such delicate gestures.

The knock at the door surprised him, momentarily averting his attention from Elisa. When he opened the door, a man was standing in front with a tray of food along with a bottle of wine.

"This is for you and your lady friend. Enjoy," he said, handing the gift to him before backing away a step then holding out a parcel wrapped in tissue paper. "This is also for the lady so she is more comfortable this evening."

"Thank you," he said as he backed into the room turning to Elisa. Surprised, "Do you know what that was all about?" Etienne asked as he set the platter on the table before giving the package to her.

He returned to lock the door again. It was unusual for food to be served to the guests unless they paid for it in advance, also unusual for packages of any sort to be delivered to the prostitutes.

This time she was nodding her head in what seemed to be a continuous motion, "Madam always sends food and wine to my room when I stay the night. Since my remaining here is usually spontaneous, she sends me a peignoir to wear. Comfortable, yes."

Those were puzzling words; ones to think about at a later date. Right now, he didn't really care. The night was looking better with each passing second. He hadn't eaten since breakfast that morning. He was hungry for food as well as the so very beguiling young woman standing before him. He didn't plan on taking her strange words at face value.

"You must be special," he said, studying her closely for some clue as to what was rattling around inside her head.

She shrugged her shoulders slightly, giving him a wobbly smile before she spoke. She opened the gift, pulling out a dark blue negligée and robe. "I suppose I am."

"The madam doesn't do this for her other girls. Do you wish to change now or later?" Etienne wanted her to change now, wishing to see her in the silky confection.

"Later. I wouldn't know," she sighed softly stepping forward as she seemed to watch him from the corner of her eye. "I'm not really hungry, but you go ahead and eat. I'll pour the wine."

He rummaged around on the tray heaping two plates with food then accepted the wine from her shaking hand. Evidently, the arrival of food did not make her any less nervous.

She ate sparingly while he used the time to satisfy his belly before moving on to the second part of the evening, which would inevitably satisfy other parts of his needy body. He did have the entire night with her having paid for it beforehand while making sure the extra money he gave the attendant would go directly to her.

Now, Elisa peered at him over the rim of her glass. Seemed to be staring at his mouth. He adjusted his position in a feeble attempt to calm his eager man parts, the lust for this enchanting lady beginning to take over his body along with his mind. Well, hell, he never responded to a silent invitation such as she was sending so quickly or so intensely.

"Is there anything you'd like to tell me about yourself?" he asked pleasantly, hoping she wouldn't turn into a chatterbox, but it would be nice if she said something, anything.

She lifted her tiny shoulders in a hesitant shrug. "Not really."

That was what he thought. He set the plate down and with a pleasant voice, he asked, "Should we get to it then?"

"To what?" She moistened her lips before following suit, her eyes crossing. Setting the glass down, her gaze roamed the length of his to settle on his rapidly hardening crotch.

What the devil did she think she was doing? Those were the actions of a practiced courtesan.

Blood rushed to his groin. "I'm sure you know as to what I'm referring. Why don't you change into that lovely confection that was sent up to you?"

He couldn't help the slight tinge of frustration he was sure she heard. Being blunt was not his usual way, nor had he ever needed that aspect.

"I still don't know what you expect. What I do understand is that you mean to have sex with me. Just not really sure what all that entails. Madame Margaux did tell me when the time..."

She stopped just when he was getting interested, a becoming rise of color to her cheeks following.

"When the time?" Lifting a dark eyebrow in speculation, he queried hoping to pursue this line of conversation more thoroughly, his mind spinning with too many fascinating scenarios to settle on one.

"It doesn't matter." She waved a hand in the air, some of the wine in her glass spilling out. "Oh, my..." She looked at him, growing even redder then set the glass on the stand taking a cloth and wiping away the red drops, her hands pushing against her breasts as she cleaned her gown.

He took her hands in his, "You don't have to be nervous. I'm not going to hurt you. Never hurt a woman in my life."

But he'd never had a virgin. He was becoming increasingly sure Elisa had never had sex before even though her previous statements confused him countering that very thought. He'd never seen anyone so skittish and unsure of herself before the sex act, one she'd agreed to.

What to do?

He certainly wasn't going to walk away.

"I didn't think you would." She paused. "Hurt me. I've wanted this with you for so long."

"Go, change into the negligée. We can proceed from there." He inhaled long and hard. What the devil was she talking about? To his recollection he'd never seen this woman before.

"Fine." She rose, striding into a dressing room. He heard a small curse. She was back, turning away from him. "I need help."

He chuckled softly as he brushed the long silken curls that had fallen loose from her chignon away from the fasteners. Deftly he undid the dress then her corset. The gown as well as the other garment fell to the floor.

"I will be right back."

He sat, waiting for her return, thinking on all that had been said between them, still puzzled. When she appeared in the room her hands clasped in front of her, his breath caught in the back of his throat. She looked so tiny and frightened. He needed to erase that look of fear from her eyes.

"What do we do now?"

"Perhaps a kiss would relax you. We can take this slow and easy, one small step at a time. After all, we have all night. Promise to tell me what you like and don't like."

"I'm sure I'll like your kisses as much as your smile and the little dimple." She touched the side of his mouth with a fingertip. "Right here."

Etienne couldn't help but groan. She was a provocative little minx and she didn't even know it. He held her hand in his, the protruding finger now resting on his lips. Nibbling then sucking it into his mouth, he smiled anew at the surprised gasp of pleasure that followed.

"Did you like that?" His question in any other case would sound insincere but now and with the pleased expression on her face he was glad he took the time to ask.

She nodded several times before a veiled sigh escaped her soft pink lips, "Oh, yes. It makes me feel things in places I've never thought of before. There are butterflies flitting about in my stomach, lower too."

"Good, I'm glad." He slowly began removing the pins from her hair, watching as the silken tendrils fell around her shoulders, lightly touching her ear with a finger then his lips, the column of her neck then following with tiny little nips of her flesh. "Your hair," he paused thinking and remembering another time very long ago, "is unusual. I've only seen its color one other time. I'm trying to remember."

"Wh-where," she stammered, her eyes wide an emotion he didn't know how to interpret.

He brought one of the loosened pieces to his cheek, letting the softness caress him. "It is nothing."

He remembered Angelique's white-blond hair. That thought gave him a pause in his memories. There was another time. He searched his mind. It seemed the image would not resurface.

"No, tell me," she whispered, reaching out a hand to rest on his chest before spreading her fingers wide. While she'd been changing into the negligée, he partially unbuttoned his shirt. Her fingers rested tantalizingly on bare skin.

"Then you tell me something about you?" he asked. "It seems only fair."

"Alright then. You're right of course. If you share then so should I." She played with the lace around the neckline of the robe she wore, inadvertently lowering the bodice slightly to reveal more alabaster skin.

He wanted to take her hands in his, slow the nervousness but he didn't think anything would help at this point. "I saw your hair color on a madam in Bordeaux. I believe her name was Angel. Now it's your turn. While I'd like to learn your last name," he wasn't sure why he had a change of thought on this, "tell me anything you like, something you feel comfortable sharing."

She stiffened seeming to think better of a reply that he knew almost blurted from her lips. For a few seconds she ran her tongue across them.

The silence seemed to echo in the room while she appeared to be thinking about what to tell him. "While I've never been in a room alone with a man, I've spent time in a brothel."

Those words shocked him. By her actions, he would have never guessed such a thing would be true. Yet her innocent shyness delighted him. Deciding it was time to end the conversations, determined though to take them up later, he placed a gentle kiss on her neck then higher, taking her earlobe between his teeth and tugging gently, one hand cupping the back of her head. Tiny sounds rippled from her throat. At that moment he knew everything would work out.

Shivering beneath his touch, she turned in his arms then leaned into him, her back against his chest while he continued with lips teeth and tongue to trace the line of her neck and along her collarbone.

With a wistful sigh, "Do you do this often? You seem to know what you're about?"

A low belly laugh rumbled from his throat. She turned toward him again, a puzzled expression on her face, lips slightly parted in question. "Probably more than I should. I'd like to know what you're thinking but I'd rather kiss you so I can show you there is only pleasure to be had in what we are about to do here this evening. Do you trust me?"

"You told me earlier to take my clothes off but I don't want to, not... Do you mind? Don't believe I can make my fingers work to do something like that. Are you going to remove your clothes too? I'd like to see your chest. I saw it once a long time ago." Her fingers rose before softly caressing his cheek. The wistful expression as well as the revealing words left him in a state of stunned shock. A long time ago, perhaps that was when he saw her.

If only he could remember.

He groaned at her simple words when they registered in his mind. Pursuing this line of conversation was not something he could do right now, not when she was softening under his tutelage, relaxing beneath each gentle kiss. He knew in minutes he would have her naked beneath him. He would be deep inside her velvet warmth.

Velvet fire.

Long enough to remove his shirt he stopped kissing her. He began again, her hands resting on his shoulders. They were soft, touching him. Her nails were well trimmed, not overly long. He tugged on her bottom lip then soothed it with his tongue, pressing inside and meeting the sultry warmth of hers while her hands rose to the back of his neck, tugging him closer. She tasted sweet, tasted of the wine from his family's vineyard.

"I'm going to take your robe off now," he said as he pulled away, his brows drawing tightly together.

"Do you have to?"

"We spoke of fairness earlier. If my shirt is off then..." He intentionally left the words unsaid and hoped she would fill in the blanks.

"... my robe should be off. Still, I can't do it." Her words were so quiet he had to lean forward to hear her. "My fingers..." she sighed as she held up her shaking hands for him to see.

"Not a problem." He wanted to undress her slowly. The undoing of each tiny bow down the front was followed by a soft kiss along her collarbone. Tenderly he pushed the fabric from her shoulders. Again kisses, gentle kisses, nipping kisses followed the semi-unveiling of her white flesh.

Her soft sigh of pleasure gave him reason to grin, yet his patience was slowly coming to an end. When he entered the room with her, he'd thought to have her beneath him in a matter of minutes. At least an hour had already passed. Even now, this slow seduction was making progress. He guessed by the time he was inside her, she would be hot and exciting, wild and passionate.

She sat in front of him now, her thin negligée all that stood between their lovemaking. Her tight puckered nipples pushed beguiling against the silken fabric, enticing and tempting every part of him. He set her against the headboard before coming between her slightly parted legs.

He sat back, looking at her kiss-swollen lips loving the tangle he'd made of her hair. Her eyes were wide with what he hoped was desire coupled with passion, raw hunger that could make a man hard with the ecstasy. While he undressed her, she'd said very little. Now, her breaths drew in and out in short wisps of air. When he tenderly sipped at a pulse point, he felt the rapid beating of her heart. He had no doubts she would be ready for him.

"I'm going to remove the rest of your gown now." He stopped staring at her, his gaze slowly raking the length of her, intrigued by the darkening of her eyes. "All but your stockings. Now, help me out and lean forward."

She did as requested. He slowly undid the tiny bows at the top of each shoulder as he watched the silken fabric slide the length of her to pool around her hips. Her scent was lavender mixed with vanilla. *Mon Dieu*, a man could get used to this.

Her legs were spread for him, the dusky rose tips of her breasts responding to his gaze, tightening without even being touched. To his jaded heart she was a vision of desire and passion. He believed for the first time in his life she might want him, not just what he could give her.

That remained to be seen though.

He wanted to laugh. It was all she could do not to try to cover herself, but she didn't know where to put her hands.

"What about you?" she asked.

"You thinking of what's fair along with what is not?" He sat on his bed, pulling off his boots then stood. His wide grin seemed to give her a reason to return the sentiment. He found the fastening on his pants and slipped them off. He stood in front of her naked.

Her gasp of surprise coupled with the widening of her eyes startled him. "I never thought..."

"Thought what, sweetheart?" He was still grinning pleased with her innocence.

"Don't laugh at me."

"Never. Thought what?"

She caught her bottom lip beneath her teeth. Then she whispered, "That you would be so large."

While he expected those words at her startled look, he had no idea what to say in response. In all his life, he'd never bedded someone who was so unknowing in the ways of the flesh. It was truly a shame. She was destined now to spend most of her life in a brothel. He was almost tempted to whisk her away from this place. He didn't. As he well knew the madam would have his hide if he attempted such a foolish thing. This lady would prove to be a gold mine for Margaux. Either that or he would have to pay a small fortune for the privilege to make her his mistress.

Perhaps... Perhaps that is what he should do.

He came down on top of her, kissing and caressing every tender erotic spot he could find. He left no part of her untouched, reveling when her hips began to rise to meet him, her back arching imploring him for something more, twisting beneath him. Her breasts, the hard tips, her navel he left nothing unattended. Higher and hotter, he felt the same enchantment. Kisses, nibbling caressing, tasted the sweet essence that was Elisa.

"Etienne..." her softly uttered words touched his soul. "Please."

He understood all too well what she was saying to him but she didn't. Another moment of remorse or hesitancy snaked through him. He'd never been a man to wallow in remorse or guilt. Someone would have her first. Why not him? She had not said *non*.

"Elisa," he whispered, his voice hoarse with need.

She was an unknowing enchantress, white magic in a dark place. This exquisite joining that hadn't even happened yet was bewitching. Sweat beaded on his forehead. A soft sheen of moisture covered her body. His lips seduced the satin hard tips of her breasts while his fingers found the swollen velvet knot of ecstasy that would bring her more gratification than she'd ever felt before. Sending her to a place of sweet satisfying delight was his only thought.

He didn't know what to expect when he came inside her tight sheathe. Slipping a finger inside, he moved slowly. He touched her maidenhead. Sucked in a huge draught of air. Once more, he almost stopped, not wishing to cause her pain.

She's a whore. It makes no difference that she has never done this before. Someone has to be her first. This is what her life will be from now on.

Truly, he didn't know if he should take this slowly or just get it over with.

Well, hell.

With a long deep breath in his lungs, he pushed inside, drove into her then stopped at the constricting of her muscles linked to the small cry of pain. Her nails bit into his shoulder. She beat at him with her tiny fists, pushing at him even while he understood she wanted him to leave her be. He wasn't going to do that.

Couldn't.

Minutes ticked by so slowly he thought he'd rip the clock from the wall. For too many seconds to count, he held his breath, waited for her pain to subside. Held it until finally her nails biting into his shoulders relaxed. He found that her hips were rising to meet him once more.

"You said you wouldn't hurt me," she said accusingly, a lone tear slipping down her cheek.

"I didn't think I would. Didn't know you were a virgin when I said the words. This pain only happens once. Is that what Margaux was going to tell you my sweetheart?"

Slowly, he was moving, the velvet softness within, her fire compelling him, taking him deeper and deeper into her wet velvet core.

"Etienne..." the one word slid out slowly.

His name on her lips was heaven. "What?" He smiled at her as she reached out to him, gently touching the side of his face.

"Open your eyes. I'm going to make up for the pain inflicted. Going to help you forget everything but the honeyed joy."

His lips closed over hers while his fingers danced evocatively in all the places that would give her the greatest pleasure.

"I love your half-smile and the dimple," she murmured softly.

He pushed her words aside thrusting into her, needing release himself but waiting for her to feel the tremors sweep through her, the mindless blast of ecstasy that would last only seconds in the process changing her life forever. Finally, the spasms seemed to envelop her as she cried out his name, reaching for him as he drove deeper and harder into her. He didn't stop until she began to calm and her body seemed to slow.

"Did that hurt?" he queried, hoping her answer would be what he needed to hear.

"No, but it was somewhere between pain and pleasure, something I've never thought could exist."

He pulled her to him, caressed her back, letting his hand rest on her derrière, thinking the next time might be even more pleasant.

~ * ~

Pruitt Dubois sat in the lush apartment where Angelique Moreau resided in Bordeaux. The cold January temperatures had changed to warmer spring like weather. It was March. The daffodils were poking their heads from the grounds while the trees were blossoming with leaves and flowers. Angelique thought for a moment this was her favorite time of year.

"Etienne quit looking for Elisa?" he asked, one white eyebrow arching upward.

"When he couldn't find her in Paris, he came here, but you already know that," Angelique said, her voice soft with the pain she felt for her daughter.

Everything she tried so hard to avoid happened anyway. "It's for the best. The way in which he lives now, he would not make a suitable husband for my daughter. In any case, I'm sure he does not wish to be a husband. It appears to me, he is much enamored of bachelorhood."

"Is it for the best?" Pruitt waved his hand in the air in disagreement. "I have judged Etienne in the past but to imply he cannot change, does not sit well with me. He deserves to know the truth of the matter. It is not right to keep such an important secret from him. Something that could change his life forever."

Angel knew that look well. She also understood how much Pruitt wanted his son home, hoping for a grandchild and an heir to his vineyard.

This time when Etienne showed up here, Pruitt thought it was for good only to discover he left for Glasgow as soon as he understood Elisa was not planning on speaking with him.

"I believe so and so does my daughter. She is not ready to take on a husband of such experience. She is still very young. I believe she made a grave mistake by giving herself to Etienne as does she."

Angelique did not want to hand Etienne the news, but he would discover the truth soon enough. What mattered is what he would do with the knowledge. In truth, she acknowledged begrudgingly he deserved the complete facts. Just before Pruitt stopped by three months ago, she received a message from Margaux, explaining what happened on that now infamous evening. Now, three months had passed by.

Elisa knew the truth.

Etienne did not.

"Why is that? There is something you are not telling me. I don't believe Etienne has asked for her hand or for anyone else." His voice grew harsh and agitated as he asked the question, his gaze riveted on her.

Angel squirmed a bit under his intense scrutiny. She didn't know what to tell Etienne's father. "We both hoped for something more between our children. However, it won't happen anytime soon. He's gone. She's somewhere between Paris and here. When she comes out of the self-imposed hiding, I'm sure she will go to the country home. We both know how much Etienne detests the country and the tiny villages. Perhaps if Elisa had stayed in Paris, there would be hope for them."

"There is something you aren't telling me. Your eyes have never lied. What is it?" He leaned forward picking up her hand in his. Focused on her, Angelique did not want to meet his gaze but she understood she would have to do just that.

"True, but tonight is not the time. I need to speak with my daughter first." She withdrew the hand then walking to the window, she stared out at the city, feeling guilt swamp her even while she gazed at the twinkling lights. "It is getting late. You will want to stay the night. I'm sure the ride home would not be wise in the dark. There are bandits, you know."

"Perhaps with dinner I can discover what you have been keeping from me all this time. It is not too difficult to make assumptions. Secrets are hard to keep, Angel. You have never been good at hiding your thoughts from me. Never."

"This secret is not mine to tell." She wondered at her daughter and her actions. The note from Margaux said very little. She would need patience. Coming to conclusions now would just not do for either Elisa or herself.

Pruitt stood beside her now, a hand on her shoulder, gently massaging her tight muscles. "You need to relax, *mon ange*."

His angel. She was really no one's angel. Under the circumstances Angelique was afraid relaxing was impossible. It was just like her intrepid daughter to get herself into trouble of this sort, trouble with a man she'd wanted since she was six years old. Angelique was sure this was the first and only time Elisa had sex. There had been no men in her life. For some reason, she thought herself in love with a man she knew from a single encounter years ago. It was just like Etienne to take advantage of an innocent. She could tell herself that over and over again but the fact remained Elisa had been in a whorehouse. She presented herself to Etienne as a prostitute, never telling him who she was. *Mon Dieu*, what was he to think?

She turned, stepping back at the same time to put a meager amount of distance between them, a bit of anger rising inside at Pruitt's words. "You know very well I'm not an angel."

"Just because you were forced into this business by necessities you had no control over does not make you a fallen woman or change your basic nature. To me you are an angel. Look at yourself. You made the best of a horrible situation managing to thrive in the process." Pruitt walked to the sideboard to pour himself a whiskey before sitting down. He crossed his legs, watching her. "You need to share whatever it is you are hiding from me as well as the rest of the world. Now I understand the world should not know, but I've been your friend when you've needed one. It will make all things better for you. Someone to share the burden with."

"Perhaps you are right." She let out a deep breath of air, treating herself to a glass before sitting down across from Pruitt. Second and third thoughts assailed her as the seconds passed slowly. She tried to form the words in her mind.

"Well?" His eyes brightened when she gave him hope that she would relate her secret.

She inhaled several breaths of air, listening to the clock along with the soft patter of spring rain on the window. Closing her eyes, she thought about holding a baby again, running a finger along its soft cheek. She would be a grandmother sooner than she expected. By that title, she shouldn't have to change too many diapers, but she would. She waved a hand in front of her face as if she'd spoken the words.

Don't get ahead of yourself and don't surmise what might have happened after one encounter. It was, after all, only one encounter. I must have patience and wait for news or confirmation. Elisa still refuses to say anything. By the way Elisa acted, she was sure.

What to do? Did she truly believe she had the right to tell Pruitt the truth about his changing life? The facts were all that she could relate despite the feeling deep in her belly that her daughter was with child even as the soon to be doting grandparents discussed their children's sex lives.

"Well?" he prompted again, seeming to begin to lose any semblance of patience. His grin changed to a frown.

Angelique smiled at him, understanding she would have to swear him to secrecy. He could not under any circumstances divulge a word of this to anyone, especially not Etienne until Elisa told him herself or until she left the telling of the truth so long it could not be avoided.

Once again, she was getting ahead of herself. She needed to speak with Elisa She prayed her daughter was on her way here and didn't plan to remain in seclusion. Margaux had not spoken to that bit of information so perhaps she didn't know. She wondered if Elisa even knew or thought she might be with child. It had only been a few months.

"You must swear that you will remain silent. Nothing I say here can leave this room." She cleared her throat, knowing he would say the necessary words to gain her confidence. If anything, Pruitt Dubois was a man of his word.

"Very well. I swear that whatever you divulge here today will remain here and that I will not say a word to anyone."

"Even Etienne?"

"Yes, even my son."

Slowly, she sipped the whiskey she poured herself almost an hour ago, watching the leaves on the tree outside her window rustle with the breeze. His tapping fingers on the crystal brought her back to the present and the fact he was making another attempt at patience, something that didn't suit him.

"I am only guessing. I have no proof. It is just a feeling in the pit of my stomach. September sometime, you will be a *grand-pere*."

A rush of guilt swept inside at the revelation she should have avoided at all cost. This was not her story to tell.

When she looked up, however, it was amusing to her how his eyes began to light up as the words registered in his head. "I assume that night they spent at Margaux's is the cause. It couldn't be anyone else?"

"It was and before you ask, I've never been more positive even though it happened only a couple of months ago."

She felt a flame of anger spark inside. How dare he question the morality of her daughter when his son... She swallowed hard. When his son tossed skirts at whim.

"You're angry. I should have never even thought it, but I'm excited to finally know that another Dubois could be on the way as we speak."

"You cannot say anything. Unless Etienne comes home and marries my daughter, the *bebe* will be a Moreau. Not a Dubois."

Chapter Two

Elisa woke up exhausted, her eyes feeling as if they were glued shut. She'd had too much to drink at Etienne's encouragement. Yet she'd had all her wits about her. She could have said no at any time. They had made love several times over the course of the night. She supposed she'd had too much sex too. It was a night of overindulgences, something new to her. Her normal conservative self never overindulged. She didn't actually know what to call what they did. At her mother's brothel, she'd heard vulgar terms as well as several other terms. What they did together could not be called making love. Perhaps they just had sex and there was nothing more to it.

She pushed herself to a sitting position, the covers falling to her waist. Good Lord but she didn't have a stitch of clothing on her body. Heat surged throughout her thinking of all the things they'd done and the places he touched, where his fingers roamed. She let him do anything he wanted. Swinging her legs to the side of the bed, she glanced at Etienne, relaxed in his slumber. At the sight her breath caught in her throat. He was so handsome, more debonair than she remembered.

He was on his back, one arm across his eyes as if he was warding off the coming daylight. His half-smile graced his face and she wondered what exactly he was dreaming about. The dimple she loved so much, the small indentation was there too. Today there would be no reason to stay here. She could not. Didn't want to see him awake, his eyes burning with desire. The gray skies told her rain would fall most of the day if not all of it.

She needed to leave now before the house woke and Margaux discovered what happened here. She would be angry, furiously so. Before

Etienne woke and asked questions she didn't want to answer. An explanation was not something she could do coherently. From impulse born of years of thinking about him, she reacted emotionally with no thought to the consequences. What would the madam, her friend do and think? Elisa supposed there was nothing that could be done. She was a willing participant. *More than willing.* Etienne even offered to pay her, leaving the money on the bedside table. She would never take the money. Still, he had no idea who she was and Elisa hoped to keep it that way.

Moving away from the bed she found her clothes, dressing in everything but the corset, which she would have needed help with. She found her cloak draping the warm fabric over her shoulders hiding her back where she couldn't fasten all the tiny buttons. Looking once more at Etienne, she was tempted to brush a light kiss on his forehead but wisely refrained from doing so. She didn't want to wake him either.

When she gazed outside, no one stirred. The scene was exactly what she expected. It wasn't even six o'clock yet. No one save a few servants would be about until after the noon hour. Francois would not even be in the kitchen. Inhaling a long deep breath along with one last look at the sleeping Etienne, she stepped into the hallway.

The need for secrecy was something she didn't understand. Numerous times she'd left at this hour or a bit later and never felt as if she had to explain what she was doing. She had no reason now. Hours would pass before Etienne stirred from his slumber or Margaux came to her room to see if she was still there to kiss her goodbye.

She stifled a tiny laugh then a gasp at what Margaux would discover. She hoped it would not go bad for Etienne, but there was no way she could think of to leave a note for the madam. He would need to talk fast because Margaux would be furious when she discovered him in her room coupled with the evidence of her lost virginity.

Trying to tread lightly she made her way down the steps to the front door then changing her mind, it was light after all, she headed through the kitchen toward the backdoor. Familiarity helped her move quickly through the large space to the back door, glad that polite conversation would not be required. Reaching the alley, she strode purposefully to the front of the building before walking down the street looking for a carriage she could hire to take her home. After several minutes, luck was with her.

At the apartment, she paid the driver before making her way to the second-floor loft she'd called her home for the last two years. A bath was what she needed. It seemed muscles she never knew she had were sore from her activities last night. She set water on the stove to boil and pulled out the small tub she used. Rinsing herself off with the meager water in the basin would just not do in this case.

Minutes later she was soaking in the hot water, her cat curled up on one end of the tub. She always wondered how the cat kept from falling into the water. Closing her eyes, she slipped farther into the soothing liquid heat while she remembered. That night was one she would hold close to her heart forever.

"Well, young lady, you did get what you've been dreaming of the last eleven years," she murmured sleepily to herself, recalling the night and all the magical and intriguing sensations.

The cat's purring was the only comment.

The feel of his hands caressing her shoulders then her breasts startled her, yet she wasn't awake. At least, it didn't seem she could open her eyes. Deep inside she knew he wasn't in the room with her. The mercuric heat linked with all the enchantment she felt last night in Etienne's arms came rushing back to her in a blind rage.

She moaned, wishing she could open her eyes and see him leaning over her, climbing into the water with her. There wasn't room for him, barely room for her.

A loud noise by the window, jerked her to a sitting position. Her breaths hard and fast she looked for something that caused the noise. The cat was no longer curled on the edge but on the windowsill. A flower vase had been knocked over and now was shattered on the floor into hundreds of tiny pieces along with the dirt from the pot.

The lump in her throat vanished as she finished washing. Standing, water sluicing from her body, she reached for a bath sheet. Hot water still boiled on the stove. A cup of hot tea would warm her insides and perhaps calm the strange emotions twisting through her with each ragged breath.

Elisa found her nightgown then slipped the soft linen over her head. With her cup of tea and a slice of bread in hand, she curled up on her bed. So many thoughts filled her head. Now that she'd played, there might be repercussions.

She had no regrets. She would deal with any consequences that came her way.

Etienne might look for her. While she needed to figure out how she felt about that, she wasn't going to do it this moment. The man didn't love her. It was one night in a brothel. Nothing more. Nothing less. Why would she think the future would bring anything different? Setting her food and drink aside, she settled her hands on her belly, smiling. A child would be nice but a responsibility she might not be ready to handle. Her mother would tell her that when you sleep with a man and don't take precautions, you have to grow up fast. She already felt old beyond her years.

She wondered about her future, thinking for the longest time. This would be something she would have to plan carefully. To the best of Etienne's father's knowledge, his son had sired no children. Pruitt Dubois would have taken care of any babies sired by Etienne.

So, why didn't the man take precautions with her?

What to think? At this point, she certainly had no idea. Perhaps it didn't matter with whores. Maybe prostitutes took all the precautions. She certainly didn't know.

Unable to concentrate on anything but Etienne, she slipped beneath the covers, pulling them to her chin. The tick of the clock seemed to calm her as she drifted in and out of sleep with erotic dreams. She was entangled with his big hard body, his warmth permeating through her. At times she thought of his hands and the way his body fit so perfectly to hers. Then her mind would travel in other directions.

Pruitt, what would he do and say when he discovered her truth? For that matter, what would Angel say and do?

During her pregnancy as well as after, her mother would see that she wanted for nothing. Angelique would never say a harsh word, neither would she judge. At least Elisa hoped that would be the case. She didn't know why but she was sure she carried Etienne's child. She didn't intend to look backward and wish she could replay the past. She would not change anything.

Elisa stayed in bed the rest of the day as well as the night only rising to make tea and find food. The need to leave the city overwhelmed her. Earlier she toyed with the idea. Now it was an incessant throbbing ache in her head. In any case, there was nothing for her in Paris except perhaps Etienne. If she saw him, she had no idea what to do or say. To him, she was a whore fit only for his use, never his love. It was a huge price but one she was glad she paid.

With the first rays of sun pouring through her window, Elisa was up, her valise and trunk packed to the brim. Arrangements were made for the rest of her belongings to be picked up and sent to the cottage her mother owned in the Bordeaux countryside. She was ready to leave Paris behind her. All she needed now was to find a way to put Cat into the carrier she always used when she traveled. Finally, small pieces of fish leftover from a few nights ago tempted the feline inside the small box.

"Got you," she said with great relish and a grin when she closed the lid on her cat. Now all I have to do is keep you content for the next few days.

The knock on the door told her her driver was here. She'd sent a message with a boy passing by on the street before she started packing. Taking a last look at the room, she drew a deep breath. Ready to get on with the rest of her life she opened the door.

"I'll take my valise if you can get the trunk," she told her driver, the same man who always took her back and forth from Bordeaux to Paris. This might be the last time because she never wanted to see Paris again.

The ride to Bordeaux was long and boring. The nights spent at the inns worse. She passed the time talking to her cat while wondering just how long she would stay with her mother. Maybe a small apartment near the brothel would be in order. She could visit when she wanted. However, she would also have her much needed privacy. Margaux paid her generously for the work. She could go to her home in the country, but if Etienne was looking for her, he would undoubtedly find her there. If she stayed in the city, she knew her mother would never tell anyone where she was.

If he figured out who exactly she was. If Margaux told him.

Problem was she wasn't sure if she wanted to be found or even if he would look for her.

"Why would he look for a woman he thought was a virgin whore?" she muttered under her breath, pushing errant strands of hair from her face while also attempting to blow the unruly strand away with a puff of air when it fell back. "Not because he kissed you when you were six and your shared your body with him too many years later to count." When she saw him on that staircase in the brothel, she'd lost all ability to think.

It seemed to her the trip lasted longer than usual. Perhaps it was the ever-present rain as well as the snow that fell on the last day. Maybe it was the nerves that seemed to center in her belly, radiating outward. The driver was constantly stopping or veering to one side of the road to go around potholes. He stopped more often than usual to change horses.

The sun was beginning to set when he finally pulled to a stop in front of the bordello and helped her from the carriage. He carried the trunk to the door for her. When she reached inside her small coin purse to tip him, he waved her off.

"Your mother pays well and the extras are always appreciated, if you get my meaning. I'm sorry the trip was so long." He shrugged, "The weather didn't want to help."

Elisa knew her mother paid with favors from her worker's favorite ladies as well as the coin she gave them for their work was more than most employers. Once she told her it was the best way to keep the people who work for you loyal and happy.

She watched him stride back to the carriage. The front door opened. Eric, her mother's bodyguard stood in the middle of the entrance. The man came from Ireland or so he told her one day when she was still a little girl. At the time, she thought he was a giant. Actually, she still did; his bright red hair attesting to his heritage.

"Your mother has your room waiting for you as well as a hot bath," Eric said, easily lifting the trunk to his shoulder.

"How did you know...?"

"Didn't you know? Your mother keeps her eyes on you, always

has. There is very little you can do that she doesn't know about." He chuckled, his teeth showing beneath his well-trimmed red beard. "If I had a daughter and if she was as striking as you, I'd do the same thing. Wouldn't let her out of my sight, not ever. Never know what some young man might have in mind for her."

A shiver swept through her at his words, sure that was what Angelique would do. Keep her eye on her. Well, mother might know she slept at Margaux's brothel, however she didn't know what happened in her room that night which now seemed like an eternity ago. At least she prayed she had at least that much privacy. Still, she would most likely learn it was Etienne she'd slept with.

"Well, she's always been afraid of my father and what he might do. I thought that threat had passed. The man has been dead and buried for the last two years."

Margaux would have gone to see her if she rose early enough to say good-bye. She would have found Etienne in her bed as well as the evidence of her lost virginity.

When she left and she saw Etienne lying on the bed, the sheets in a disheveled mess around him with one leg resting on top, she tried to ignore the too obvious signs of her lost innocence. The evidence couldn't be ignored. Margaux would notice. She felt heat rush to her cheeks.

"What is it *mademoiselle?*"

"I-I," she stammered, swallowing hard, wishing to vanish into the air.

Her mother would have found out. She could not pick and choose when she wanted to tell her what happened. Margaux would have sent a message. Of course, her missive would travel faster than the lumbering carriage.

"Angelique would like to meet you in the parlor as soon as you're settled," Eric informed her. "I hope everything is as you wish it to be."

Nothing was as she wished it to be.

Elisa followed him up the steps, her insides churning while her knees wobbled. With one hand she kept herself steady, hanging onto the railing. She didn't understand the nervous energy snaking through her insides or the very real terror pushing into her heart. Her mother had always been proud of her along with the fact she was well schooled and competent made her smile even more. Many times she spoke of a husband for her as well as the fact her life would not be influenced by what happened in a whorehouse or the things she learned and saw while she was growing up.

This would be the first time she disappointed her mother. The thought didn't sit well with her.

Eric opened the door. Walking into the room, he set her trunk near the armoire. "There is a tub with hot water in the dressing room waiting for you. I'll tell Angelique that you will be down in an hour, sooner possibly?" he asked, one eyebrow raising a fraction.

"Probably sooner. I'm tired and would like to get the gist of this meeting done sooner than later. I'd like to have something to eat before I go to bed."

Not one doubt entered her mind that her mother knew what transpired in Margaux's brothel. The two women were like sisters. They shared everything.

How she would confront her was the question.

She didn't take a lot of time in the bath even though her muscles were sore from the swaying carriage. She did, however, take more time with her dress and makeup. A servant appeared to help her lace her corset as well as fasten her clothing. The thought of her corset reminded her of the one she left behind and the erotic way Etienne unlaced it before he seduced her body and mind. At the vivid memory of the backs of his hand touching her bare flesh, her breath caught in the back of her throat.

Her knees buckled, suddenly sending her to the floor. Her eyes closed. She nearly fainted. Etienne could be sitting in the parlor waiting for her, ready to tell her... tell her what? That he wanted her.

None of that was likely.

It was just wishful thinking on her part. No, she was confused by what she thought she wanted coupled with the reality of what actually happened. When she agreed to go with him that night, which now seemed an eternity ago, she had not thought her actions through. Had not considered anything except that she would be with the man she'd thought she loved for so many years. She had always longed to feel his arms around her as well as a second kiss, perhaps one more intimate than the first. Well, it appeared she got what she wished for. Having grown up she understood the first one didn't really count although the one sweet gesture by a young man molded her life.

Except to a six-year-old. It was a simple thank you for a ladle of water.

"You hurried so you could get this over with. So..." She lifted her full skirts heading for the door. "Quit thinking of things that need to stay buried until someone else brings them up. If you're lucky your mother won't know anything."

It was a fool's dream.

As she walked down the steps and hallway of her mother's private apartment, she was amazed at the lavish décor. She'd never really looked at it before. Now every item stood out in stark relief. Before now, the furnishing had just been there. This was a profitable business. Now it pretty much ran itself. It was a rare occasion Angel showed herself in the main part of the bordello. Many years had passed since she sold her favors.

At the entrance, Elisa stood for several seconds gathering her thoughts as well as her courage. Her mother's back was too her. Elisa assumed the setting was staged. With Angelique it always was. Air didn't want to come into her lungs.

"It's nice to have you home, Elisa. Come in and pour yourself something to drink." As usual, her mother's voice had a calming effect on her yet the underlying current told her not to let down her guard.

"I've missed you. The last year in school was anything but fun. Some of the other students found out about this business," she murmured, unsure why she shared this with her mother. After all she'd spent two years avoiding the topic of her mother's work as well as what the others knew about the bordello. It wasn't something she enjoyed speaking of.

"You've never said anything of that nature before," Angelique said tilting her head a bit sideways as if studying her. "You look very nice this evening. The color of your gown suits you, brings out the color of your eyes." She had no choice but to smile at her mother's words. The color of her eyes as well as her hair was an exact replica of her mother.

Elisa thought her mother would pursue the information about the business. What transpired within these walls was their livelihood. However, the other topic was probably closer to the forefront of her mind, sure that she wanted to know her version of the occurrences at the bordello.

After a few more seconds, she lifted her shoulders slightly then with a small smile, "I never thought my friends were an important topic, actually they are more like non-friends. We never had anything in common except money. Theirs was earned in a more conventional if not more moral way. I'm sure many of their fathers cheated and lied to move ahead in the world while they obtained the wealth they now flaunt."

Angelique set the crystal glass of brandy on the table before straightening, her brows drawing together. "You sound sarcastic. Why are they, er, non-friends?"

"Because they ceased to be my friends when they discovered where the funds for my tuition came from. I'm glad I don't have to go back there. They are all such huge hypocrites. Initially, they thought Margaux gave me the money, tainted money even though many of their fathers and brothers frequented the establishment. I was supposed to be a lady and the money just did not come from anything reputable."

The blue violet of Angelique's eyes sparked with anger. Elisa understood her mother would never act on what she was thinking. Perhaps she would but she would inevitably do it in her fashion. No one receiving the impact of her vengeance would realize Angelique was behind the retaliation.

"It doesn't matter anymore. I've moved on. In doing so I will follow my life as I see fit." She hoped her mother would understand her reference to her past indiscretions and realizes that night with Etienne was hers alone to deal with.

Seconds ticked by while her mother studied the liquid in her glass. She sipped it slowly once more, her mouth forming a tiny circle before she spoke. "Then you won't mind working here in lieu of an allowance now that you've reached your maturity and have shown a penchant for whoring."

The ensuing gasp startled her more than her mother's unkind

words. Angelique was going to use blackmail in order to wrest the truth from her. She was certain of the fact. "I already do your books. I have other clients as well. I don't need an allowance. What more could you ask that I'm proficient at? It's certainly not sleeping with men. I can't believe you actually presented that option to me after all you've done to keep me away from the business. I'll be happy to do my duty but I won't see men."

"Will you? Or won't you? I'm confused." She motioned at the door. Two of the women who worked for her downstairs entered with garments draped across their arms. "How long do you think you will be able to," she paused, "do your duty?"

Elisa sat in the nearest chair, her hands folded in her lap, trying to calm her racing heart, unsure they were speaking of the same thing. A drop of sweat trickled down the side of her face. Of everything she thought might happen tonight, this growing fiasco was not among them. If her mother was confused, she was more so. What the devil did Margaux tell her? Neither Angelique or Angel were ever cruel.

"You need to explain your thinking, Angelique. Is it time for me to repay you for my schooling or is this just some sick joke? You've spent my entire life shielding me from the going ons in this house. Why do you change your mind now?" She'd never spoken to her mother quite like this, but Angelique had never implied that she should be a part of the bordello. That she should sell her body to men. Her mother had always put her daughter's interests ahead of hers.

"I did not succeed. Did I?" She was motioning for the women to set the garments on the sofa. "You can pick from any of these. I'll make sure these girls receive new ones. They will be compensated for their loss."

"No." She stood quickly, her hands fisted tightly then just as suddenly as an afterthought sat down again.

Once again, the silence seemed to settle in the deepest and darkest part of her soul. This truly could not be happening to her, yet Angelique might just be attempting to make a point. If she acted like a whore, she would be treated as one. This was just not like her usually protective mother.

"Tell me." Her voice was harsher than she'd ever heard it. "Tell me what went on at Margaux's place. Perhaps then and only then I'll reconsider. The truth, Elisa, speak only the truth. The letter she sent left many gaps. It seems I need to have them filled in." Angelique poured herself another drink while she watched her carefully.

Elisa understood she was trying to see inside her head, knew her mother was adept at reading expressions while looking into one's eyes and knowing what was in their heart. She was amazing at cards.

"What do you know?"

"Pretend Margaux did not send me a message about your exploits that evening." Her voice was even harsher than before. The last words were edged with anger. "Start from the beginning. Don't leave one detail out."

Elisa downed the first drink then poured herself another, feeling she would need this and possibly more liquid courage if she were to get through the next hours relatively unscathed. She ran her tongue along her teeth, thinking. The chair seemed too far away but she slowly made her way there.

"I brought Margaux the ledgers along with the other paperwork for the year. We talked about the business. I explained how well her business was going coupled with the profits she earned," she said in a rush of words.

Angelique's frown grew broader and deeper. "Go on."

"That wasn't what you wanted to hear, but you did say start from the beginning." She was still rushing her words. If she wasn't careful, they would all come out in a jumble with no meaning. She tried to keep her hands still but that didn't seem possible. Her fingers wove in and out of the fabric of her gown.

"What happened next? I can only assume Margaux wanted to hear about your love life."

"Non-existent love life," she corrected her mother, her gaze solidly fixed on Angelique.

"So, you decided to fix that in one fell swoop. Why ever would you decide something so drastic?"

Her questions and voice sounded more like her mother. The tone was laced with concern as well as empathy with a tiny bit of sarcasm thrown into the mix, but at this point Elisa didn't know if she would change back.

"I was leaving. I forgot my cloak in the kitchen. I always go through the back and talk to Francoise. He gives me lots of samples. He also wants to know if I've found a special young man."

"Yes, well, Margaux stole Francoise from me. I've never forgiven her that transgression even though I know it's not entirely her fault. He wanted to live in Paris. Do continue."

The change of subject for only a few seconds gave Elisa a reason to smile and to weigh her next words more closely. "After I returned for my cloak, I headed back to the front door. A man I didn't know grabbed my arm. He thought I was the new girl who was supposed to arrive sometime soon."

"And you meant to oblige him?" Her voice now took on a severe sarcastic edge from earlier. "This does not sound like you. Why didn't you tell him who you were?"

"Not at first. I searched for the words to tell him who I was but he wasn't listening to anything I had to say."

The man had been so sure, so assuming. Still, none of this would have happened if Etienne had not been there walking up the steps.

"You could have screamed and someone would have come to your defense," Angelique said.

"Margaux would have fired the man for his insolence even though he was doing what he was trained to do. He had no idea who I was."

It seemed Angelique wasn't going to speak again. She drummed her fingers on the armrest. Her gaze riveted on her so fiercely Elisa squirmed in her chair. Her mother had not scrutinized her so sternly since she was a little girl when Angelique caught her watching two people in an intimate act.

"I caught sight of Etienne on the stairs. He was with one of Margaux's girls. Although when he heard his name whispered," Elisa paused, running her tongue across her lips, her gaze moving upward in an attempt to avoid her mother's piercing scrutiny, "he turned, pointing at me then said that he wanted me, the new girl."

"He crooked his little finger and you obliged?"

Now there was no sarcasm or harshness in Angelique's voice. All Elisa heard was anger. Elisa didn't know if that rage was directed at her or Etienne.

"I didn't think," she said, not wishing to explain her actions or her reasoning. Still, she understood her mother would not let her leave the room until she said everything.

"Apparently true."

"I don't regret anything," she said in her defense. "I've always loved him. In my mind it was what I'd wanted my entire life. Didn't believe it would ever happen. There he was looking at me and telling me he wanted me. In my mind it was what I wished for most of my life."

"There is a huge difference between wanting and loving. He doesn't love you," Angelique said her voice soft now as if the mother Elisa expected had finally returned from the grave it had been buried in.

"I understand all that and more yet at the time that fact made no difference in my mind. He didn't recognize me. In any case, that didn't matter either. I knew who he was. I wanted him to make love to me. It was my chance and might be the only opportunity I would ever have."

Her mother nodded, a tender smile creasing her lips, her brows no longer furrowed together in a ferocious scowl. "You will have to deal with the possible consequences."

~ * ~

With a groan, Etienne rolled over, trying to block the meager light coming in through the window. Slowly, he pieced together the events of the last night and early morning. She had been insatiable, as had he. The thought left him with a smile. He didn't understand what exactly had come over him. In truth, one bout of love making with any woman was usually enough. He rarely if ever stayed the entire night. He realized then she was not beside him in the bed. More than a little disappointed, he wondered if she'd just chosen to take her leave after their last session of lovemaking.

The door suddenly slammed against the wall. Etienne sat up, startled, his gaze shooting to the doorway.

"What the hell are you doing in Elisa's room and where is she?" Margaux stood in the opening, her hands fixed on her hips, Bailey behind her.

He blinked a few times. When he started to stand, he realized he was naked beneath the covers. He wasn't sure if the madam was going to give him a chance to explain or if she was going to have Bailey kick him out right now. In any case, her expression told him she might be pleased if he was tarred and feathered then run out of the city on a rail.

He drew in a long deep breath of air as he tried to think of a suitable answer to the furious question she posed. The only answer was the truth. "Elisa is or was the new girl. She came with me last night to this room. Quiet willingly, I might add. There was something about her that intrigued me, touched a spot in my heart I thought long dead. As to where she is now, I've no idea. I just woke up as you can clearly see." He emphasized his last words with the fury he was feeling at the moment. "She is not here."

"Elisa is not the new girl, never was." Margaux was pacing the tiny room, clearly agitated by what happened. "She is dear to me. You violated her. Took her innocence without even blinking."

"I had no way of knowing that. She could have told me no. She told me nothing about herself except her first name and that she'd never been with a man. Hell, I just thought you'd charge me more," he said, a half-hearted response at best, wondering just how dear Elisa was to Margaux as well as what the upcoming repercussions would be. Then, with a slight arrogant shrug, "Not my fault, she was more than willing, enthusiastic..." he stopped at the change of Margaux's expression.

"Of course she was enthusiastic."

"Of course?"

Margaux's words surprised him. He searched the woman's expression; in addition looked into her eyes for a little more meaning to the words she spoke.

"Never mind. The fact is that much information is more than I'm willing to share with you."

He pulled the sheet from the bed before wrapping the length around him, not thinking of anything except he no longer wanted to be naked. The vulnerability put him at a disadvantage. She gasped even though she must have known they had sex on the bed. He should have realized the evidence that he took her virginity was also clear and apparent now.

"You know her well. However, it seems I was mistaken in my assumptions. If I may, I'd like to make apologies to the lady."

She was not a whore even though he'd used her as such. Still, he didn't understand how he suddenly understood that fact. The lady touched a jaded part of his heart. This young woman wanted him, not his money, which he saw was still on the nightstand.

"You can search for her, young man. Although I'm pretty sure you won't find her."

Listening, he heard what Margaux said. Also heard what she didn't say. *It would be a cold day in hell if he ever found her.*

"I'll turn Paris upside down until I learn who she really is. Need to talk to her one more time. I have the resources as well you know."

"You can try," Margaux said before exiting the room. Then turning, "You can collect your winnings from yesterday anytime. You are still welcome here. I hope you will choose your lady from now on with more discretion. Elisa will never be available for you again."

Etienne had the distinct feeling that at least for now, he really wasn't welcome at the brothel. He usually left his winnings in a safe place in the house so he would have funds the next time he wanted to gamble. Margaux never asked him to collect the money.

With a last look at the bed, he dressed quickly before making his way to Gil's lodgings. He needed a friendly face to talk to so he could bounce what happened last night to a friendly ear. A lot had been said, but Etienne wanted to figure out was what had not been said.

When he walked up the steps Gil was busy with some paperwork, which he quickly set aside.

"Didn't expect to see you this afternoon. When I left Margaux's, you were still in bed. Must have been a pretty good night with the new girl." Gil chuckled as he set the pen back into its holder.

Etienne's body stiffened suddenly, tired of referring to the woman he bedded thoroughly as the new girl. If he'd had his wits about him, he would have recognized the fact she was anything but a whore. Her innocence screamed at him from the first hesitant kiss until he burst through her maidenhead. Firsthand knowledge of the trade should have yelled at him that there was something wrong here. Perhaps it did but last night he hadn't been willing to listen to his instincts. Now he craved information.

"That's just the thing. She's not a whore and Margaux wouldn't tell me why she was there or anything else about her. The strangest thing is that I've this gut feeling that I should know who she is."

"You should listen to your gut more often or at least think beyond your cock. The girl is someone, you know. I'll let you think about it for a few minutes." Holding up his hands, "Before you ask, I caught a glimpse of her early this morning as she was leaving," Gil said, a wry smile on his face. "We both know of her."

"You're going to torment me too?" He just didn't want to deal with all this intrigue. Needed answers. "You knew she wasn't a whore. Still, you let me take her to her room and bed her?" He was astounded by the revelation. "Take her virginity?"

"Didn't know she wasn't a lady working at Margaux's when you left me. Remember, you started up the steps with someone else. Nothing I've learned about her and her mother over the years while you were dancing from one country to another led me to believe she was different from Angelique."

That name stopped his thoughts cold and sent a shiver up his spine. "Angelique?"

"Yes."

"That's the little girl..."

"You kissed that day and twirled her around in your arms as if she was a princess. Suppose you made a lasting impression on her although her not on you." Gil was chortling now, almost hysterically. "Sometimes it doesn't pay to be debonair. You would have been much better off with a *merci beaucoup* then left it at that."

Etienne had to admit the laughter was at his expense. Had to admit he deserved it. If he wasn't embroiled so deeply in his thoughts, he might be laughing too. If feelings for the girl weren't something he never felt before. Then confused, "How did you remember?"

"You forget I stuck around while you were gone. I watched her grow up, albeit from a distance. Her mother guarded the home diligently. Made sure she knew of everyone who ventured within a few hundred yards of it. I was shocked when she sent her to school in Paris. I was sure she would be secluded in that cottage for the rest of her life."

"I haven't been home in years except for a week or two. Each time I returned, I spent the hours with my father rather than traipsing around the countryside," he said in his defense. "I don't think I've seen her since that day I kissed her."

"You don't need to justify your actions. I understand what you do. While I would never take the chances or the risks that seem to excite you, I suppose someone must do just that." Gil was still grinning. To Etienne it seemed he had this perverse sense of humor that was grating on his nerves. Gil was the only person who really understood him. Knew what he did when he was gone. Not even his father comprehended the complete truth about his life.

"Do you have any idea where she lives now, an apartment nearby?"

He needed to minimize his life and concentrate on Elisa's. While he'd always taken precautions with the other women who entered his bed, he had not done so with this girl.

"Most of the time in a small two-story cottage a little way from Bordeaux. As to her lodgings in Paris, I've no idea, might be somewhere near the school she attended. What I am sure of is that after this encounter she will be called home if she doesn't go there on her own."

"The cottage?" he queried still trying to figure out how his friend knew so much about the tiny woman who graced his bed last night.

"No, the bordello in Bordeaux." Gil told him.

"I'm going there," Etienne said becoming more determined than ever to set this to rights.

He needed to see Elisa again, talk to her. If there was a baby, he wanted to know so he could do his part.

"If, Elisa is there, if... Angelique will never let her see you. Your reputation precedes you. What is said about you is not good where it concerns women. Even if the little lady in question wants the opposite, well, I've my doubts she will win out over her mother."

"I have to try. I'm unwilling to waste more time," he smiled at his friend. "I'll make my way to Bordeaux then on to the vineyard. I'm sure my father would not mind seeing me for a few days."

He turned then, refusing to look back or even acknowledge Gil's laughter.

Several days passed before Etienne could make arrangements to leave the city. He had few belongings that needed packing but he had obligations that revolved around the vineyards that needed tending to. His father's vineyards to be exact. This time he wasn't willing to leave any of his responsibilities untended.

At night when he closed his eyes, he saw Elisa, felt her sweet and so innocent response to him. She was an enigma to him. Now, he had no idea how to handle this situation. All he knew was that he had to see her again, make love to her one more time so he could get her out of his thoughts. As it was now, he lost sleep every night dreaming of her and the days weren't much better.

With everything taken care of in Paris, he set out for Angelique's brothel in Bordeaux. When it appeared in front of him, he reigned in his horse, stopping for a few minutes to rehearse the words he planned to say to the madam. This time the eloquent phrases he planned were no different from his first thoughts. She would throw him out on his ear if he said the things that were scrambled in his weak man's brain.

This was the first time since he was a lad that he failed to protect the woman he bedded from his seed. The reasons eluded him. In any case, he had no excuse except the intensely crazy notion Elisa bewitched him linked with the fact he'd been cast under her sweet innocent spell. On second thought, he supposed that was no excuse, no excuse at all. He was a grown man. He knew better.

A man he knew well, Eric, stepped from the imposing building. "The madam is waiting for you. Thought you would be here sooner."

In her eyes he was already lacking, needing to make up for the lost time. A winter storm slowed him down as well as a lack of horses along the way to trade. "In light of what happened, I suppose I should be grateful

I have an audience at all."

"You should be," Eric said in a stoic voice that ended with a chuckle. "You should guard your manly parts, young man. I doubt if she is above castrating you. By now you realize the gravity of your actions. Angelique Moreau is a powerful and resourceful woman."

"I deserved that," yet... Hell he deserved that and more even though he knew she would threaten but not carry through. Did everyone she employed know what happened? What he needed though was to discover how Elisa felt about what they did that evening on the second floor first door to the right. Also, he needed to learn if he had more responsibilities.

"The madam wanted to know if you would like to freshen up or see her now."

In his mind, he weighed the two different scenarios. After a few seconds of thought, he decided the best course would be to see her immediately. "I'll see her now." The weakness he felt was tangible. While he tried to breathe evenly, the attempt was futile. He had no idea how he'd be received. He also wasn't sure of his intentions if she asked him. Marriage was out of the question.

"Good choice," Eric said, as he watched Etienne tie his horse to the hitching post.

Etienne followed the man inside, through hallways he'd never seen before. He expected to be ushered into Angelique's private quarters. Nothing prepared him for the lavishness of this home. Elisa had grown up here as well as the cottage in the country. She took all this for granted as a way of life. No wonder she'd not been shocked when he asked for her in Margaux's bordello.

He stood, framed in the doorway while Angelique sat as if she were a queen watching him. For a moment, he wondered if he should bow and kiss her hand as if she were truly the royalty she appeared to be. The breath he drew was ragged and shallow. He didn't want to admit to the fact but he was terrified of this woman.

"Angelique?" He did bow before he entered.

"Help yourself to a drink."

She spoke quietly even while Etienne sensed the underlying

current of anger in her well-practiced sultry voice. He had defiled her daughter, stole Elisa's innocence yet he reminded himself Elisa had been a willing participant. Hell, if she had told him who she was he would have never touched her. She was Elisa, just Elisa. Would not proffer a last name.

He poured himself a whiskey before taking a seat across from Angelique. "Thank you."

"You have a lot of accounting to do, Monsieur Dubois. I'd like to learn of your intentions where my daughter is concerned." Her voice was steady and strong, unyielding.

This was what he wasn't prepared for. "My intentions are honorable. It's your daughter who fled leaving no address where I could find her. Until I spoke with Gil, a friend of mine, I had no idea who she was."

He leaned back, watching his adversary with a steady eye. The lines creasing her forehead were etched deeply there.

"So, you came here immediately." It was not a question but to Etienne it seemed a threat.

"I'd like to speak with Elisa if she is here. We have private matters between the two of us to discuss." For a few moments he held his breath realizing this mother was not going to let him anywhere near her daughter.

"Truly, I don't rule over my daughter with an iron hand. She is an adult and can make her own decisions. Elisa has told me that if you showed up here, she does not want to see you."

"Why?"

For the briefest of moments, his heart stopped. If she was with child, with his child, he deserved to know. But then it was too soon for her to know.

"Your question is blunt as well as to the point. However, all I can tell you is that I don't really know. Where you are concerned, she is confused about her feelings. This, what she did at Margaux's, is new to her." Angelique lifted her shoulders a bit. With a tilt to her head, "She needs time to think. If you care for her at all, you will give her the time she needs."

"How much time?"

He had employment in Scotland waiting for him, people who expected him and counted on his skills. He could not wait forever.

"I can't tell you that."

He rose then, pacing the room, feeling as if he was caged with no way out. "I can give her three months."

"You have a pressing engagement somewhere?" Angelique asked pleasantly. "Something more important than my daughter?"

He stopped swirling to meet her gaze seeing the anger rising, "I don't know how important Elisa is to me. I've not had the chance to know her. If we could be together, talk, learn about each other, maybe then."

"You bedded her."

He downed the drink he just poured in one swift gulp. "I thought she was a whore. That fact is at your daughter's feet, not mine. Living here, she should understand that her pretense was not well done of her."

Angelique grimaced at his words. Defensively, she shot back, "But you know now that she isn't."

"I don't know anything of the sort. It could have all been an elaborate ruse, a scheme between you and Margaux, perhaps even your daughter. She came to me, walked up the steps and allowed me to take all her clothes off."

He was goading the madam now. The only reason for it was the silence as to Elisa's whereabouts coupled with his escalating fury.

A slight flush of color-stained Angelique's cheeks. Etienne wondered how long it had been since she felt any embarrassment.

"You will not win my good graces by speaking of my daughter in that way."

"I will be back. Hopefully, she will see fit to speak with me."

Etienne set his glass on the table and left. He wasn't sure where he would go at the moment, but he did not plan on staying under this roof.

~ * ~

Almost three months later Etienne was sitting in the parlor of his father's home, sipping brandy and still thinking about Elisa. He waited three months just to speak with Elisa. She wouldn't concede even a chaperoned meeting. The one night he spent with her had been like no other in his lifetime. The magic and energy surrounding them astonished him. When he thought of her, which was often, visions of her remained vivid in his mine. His father watched him, frown lines etched on his forehead.

"You are going away again? To work?" Pruitt asked, watching his son pace the room. Pruitt understood his son was agitated. While he'd never seen him quite like this, he hoped the restlessness revolved around Elisa. He'd never thought it possible the two would wed. Their age differences had been great, until now that she was growing up.

"Before I leave the country, I will stop at the bordello on my way to Paris. Take one last chance to see if Elisa is up to talking to me. That is the real question you're asking. I have my new assignment. as far as I can see If Elisa still wants nothing to do with me, there is no reason to refuse the job. If she has changed her mind, I'll go to my boss to tell him he needs to find another person to take the mission." He stopped at the window, his hands clasped behind his back.

Pruitt knew the answer to that but he'd promised Angelique he wouldn't renege on the vow. The young couple would have to figure this out on their own. From what he'd seen in the past, Etienne's assignments usually lasted no more than a year then he'd be off somewhere else on another adventure from the government. He most often returned home between missions. There would be another chance for their reconciliation.

"You will refuse if Elisa will talk to you?" he asked wondering at his son as well as his stubbornness.

It wasn't as if Etienne needed this work. There was plenty for him to accomplish at home. At the moment, it seemed Etienne would be leaving. Everything he heard from Angelique was that the girl was still confused and unwilling to accept his son into her life. The one night they had together must have left her with too many questions that needed answering. Perhaps she was feeling ashamed by her actions that evening. Angelique had not brought her up to succumb to seduction. Ah, but in matters of the heart one could never be sure how they would react. Pruitt couldn't be sure either. He certainly recognized why it might be difficult for her to look at Etienne.

Etienne lifted his shoulders, a half-smile on his face as he turned to reply to his father, "Depends on what she says."

"What if she wants to see you?"

"I've an open mind."

That was just like his son, confident and sure of himself in every way. He wasn't going to put a hold on his life if the reason didn't please him. However, Pruitt was pleased his son was willing to listen. He was sure if he learned of Elisa's condition, he would do right by her.

"I see, of course, and I understand."

Pruitt waved a hand in the air as he moved to stand beside his son, looking out over their land. The valley was green the vines thriving. He wished with all his heart to share this land with his son. Someday soon, he prayed.

"You don't, not really but I appreciate the fact you, too, have an open mind where my assignments are concerned."

"You crave excitement as well as adventure to see new lands. What would it take for you to settle down? A good woman, one who loves you?"

He prayed it would be Elisa, but his son's call to her wasn't strong enough. She intrigued and fascinated him, that was all. Ah, but Pruitt thought that same fascination might grow into something more permanent.

"The right woman," Etienne spoke slowly. "A woman who wants me just for me. Not for what they think I can give them." His heavy sigh drew his father's attention. "I thought, for a small moment in time, perhaps Elisa was that woman, but she won't even talk to me. What can I think? That she most likely used me too?"

"That is hard, I'm sure for a man who has to control everything."

"Control everything?" Etienne chuckled, the sound rumbling from the back of his throat. "Am I that bad?"

"Promise me you'll try one more time."

Chapter Three

Elisa and Pruitt sat on a bench in the back of her cottage, watching Masson play with the wood horse his *papi* brought him. Masson would be four years old in a few months. He'd never seen his father. He made squealing noises that Elisa was sure he thought sounded like a horse. His father didn't know he had a son. She smiled at him wanting to ruffle his hair. She sighed softly. Her little man was outgrowing that sentiment, especially in public. Thankfully, he still wanted a kiss and hug before he went to bed.

It was spring, almost four years after Masson was born on a fine autumn day in September. He was the light of her life. She now understood the overprotective nature of her mother. She wanted everything to be perfect for her son but without a father, she wasn't sure that could happen. Perhaps that last time Etienne came to see her she made a mistake by refusing him. She didn't know. If she had a regret, that was the one. When she thought on that day there were so many what ifs in her mind.

"He's a fine boy. You've done a wonderful job bringing him up." Pruitt ruffled the little boy's hair, receiving a scowl in response. "Are you sure you want to let him go for a sleep over?"

She rose. "I can use the time to get a few things done. He loves visiting you. Asks about you all of the time and when he can go to see you."

Still, she didn't regret anything about that night in Paris. Perhaps if she'd had the courage to speak with Etienne that last time he visited Angelique before he left, things would be different. Mulling over that notion was not good for her.

Just because she was in love with the man and always would be didn't mean he would ever return the sentiment. Binding a man to her because she bore him a son was not her way. Elisa wanted a man to love her because of who she was, not because she gave him a son.

No, she did the right thing by refusing him entry into her life. She would have never been certain if he'd decided to stay that he stayed because he cared for her or felt obligated to be a father to his son. She laughed softly. Etienne had been gone for so long.

"What is so funny?" Pruitt asked, turning his attention away from the little boy to her.

"I was thinking of your son and how I would never want a man to feel obligated to me, but from all accounts Etienne Dubois rarely feels obligated to anything save his own amusements. He is always off and about doing this and that for the French government. He doesn't need the money. He has the vineyard. He does it just to entertain himself."

"I'd like to argue with you but I can't. From how he's led his life, you are absolutely right in your assumptions. Although I don't believe that has ever been his intention. As of yet, the right woman has never presented herself to him." Pruitt grimaced.

Elisa wondered at the thought behind the expression. Once she wanted to be the right woman, the woman who he changed his ways for.

More than once she felt sure the man held information about his son back from her. She could never be certain. One eyebrow rose a fraction as she studied the man, wishing she could read his mind and understand his thoughts. Most of all she wanted to grasp what kept Etienne away from home. What was the nature of these assignments Pruitt spoke of?

She should have spoken to Etienne the last time he visited. Terror of the unknown coupled with indecision about what she would tell him kept her from talking. At that time, she would not have told him about the baby. She didn't show yet so he had no reason to assume anything. Angelique even encouraged her to talk to him. Still, she adamantly refused.

"I received a letter from him two days ago. Thought you should know he's coming home."

Her gasp startled her while her heart leapt to her throat. "Home? Here?" her voice squeaked. "For how long?"

"Mama, what's wrong?" Masson was tugging on her skirt

"Nothing. I think you and your *papi* should go now. It will be dark in a few hours. I'm sure he wants to get you settled before dinner."

She needed to come to terms with the arrival of Etienne along with what she expected. One look at the boy and he would know. Masson was the very image of his father.

"Besides, a thunder storm might be brewing. The clouds on the horizon are looking like a storm. Wouldn't do any good to find ourselves caught in the middle of a tempest." Pruitt extended his hand to his grandson. "Are you all packed?"

The middle of a tempest, I'm afraid that is what is going to happen here when Etienne returns.

"I am. Mama packed my favorite pillow. We forgot it last time, remember?"

His dark brown eyes sparkled with excitement. Rakishly, his black hair fell across his face, just like Etienne's. Masson bore the same quirky half-smile and dimple. Even if she'd wanted to forget about Etienne Dubois, she would have never been able to do that. Every time she looked at her son, she was reminded of Etienne and the one unforgettable night together they shared.

"Good, good, go on and climb in the carriage." Pruitt turned to her, his arms open wide for a hug. "Take care. We both know that as soon as he sees the little boy, he will know the truth."

"I understand. I won't deny it, would never do that. If he wishes, a father should know his son."

She felt her breaths grow ragged just as they did every time she thought about this meeting as well as the inevitable outcome. She should have written to him, told him about the baby. He deserved to know he had a child, deserved to be able to make his decisions about what he wanted and didn't want.

Pruitt touched her hand with his. "I wrote to him, imploring him to come home just before the birth. I would have told him why but I was sworn to secrecy. He chose not to come."

"Angelique?"

Pruitt nodded. "I knew from the very beginning, from the first thoughts of the child, this baby would be his. Your mother was also sure from the moment you came home from Paris, telling her what happened. She said as much to me."

"You kept the secret all these years." She pushed hair from her face. "I almost wish you hadn't yet in more ways I'm glad you did. Now there will be a reckoning. I don't know what to say to him."

"He's going to want to be part of the boy's life," Pruitt warned her again touching her shoulder before quickly giving her a hug. "He will also demand to know why no one told him, including me."

"I won't deny him."

By not telling him the truth from the first moment she knew, she had deprived him of knowing his son. He would be angry, should be furious with her. There would be no feasible reason to forgive her.

Gil even weighed in on her silence once before the baby was born, admonishing her for it. Several times he lectured then offered to send a message to Etienne. She told him no every time, understanding the truth needed to come from her.

"What is it?" Pruitt asked.

"I guess I've been warned by the only two men in my life who mean anything to me that I've been dishonest with Etienne. Suppose that's the truth of it." Would it be days or weeks before Etienne realized what had gone on under his nose before he confronted her with his demands? He lost four years of his son's life. She was so very sure he would have many?

"Hurry up, *Papi,*" Masson leaned out of the window in the carriage, waving his hands. "Time to go."

"You better get in that carriage before he falls out and hurts himself," she said, smiling at her son and waving.

"How long?" he asked.

"Let him stay as long as he wants or you have the energy to entertain him. Won't be more than a day or two. He can come home when he misses me."

"Fine. Sweet child, you best spend your time thinking about what you're going to say to my son."

With the wind blowing the lose strands of her hair, she watched the carriage until she could no longer see even the dust the wheels created. When it disappeared from view, she stood on the road for a few more seconds before she turned for the front door. Melancholy settled over her.

An hour later she finished sewing the jacket she was making for Masson, setting it on the bed in his room. He would be so pleased even though she knew he'd rather have a new rag doll or a gift from his *papi*. Restless, she put another log on the fire, sitting back on her heels and watching the bright, warm flames lick upward.

Pouring herself a glass of wine then taking the bottle with her she sat on the porch swing in the front of the house. Lightening lit up the darkening sky while a harsh crack of thunder followed. She shivered as the night began to take on a decided chill. A tempest indeed was brewing.

Idly, at loose ends with herself she wandered inside, collecting an afghan before she walked back to the swing. Pulling it around her before bringing her feet up to get comfortable, she watched the storm seethe around her. The tempo as well as intensity increased as rain now pounded the ground, turning to hail.

She still loved Etienne, that much had not changed over the years. While she didn't think it ever would, she wouldn't make the same mistakes again where he was concerned. Not that he would ask to be in his bed. When he discovered the truth of what she did, he might despise her.

A gust of wind sent hail sluicing inside the small sheltered porch. The pellets lying on the floor like snow, unwilling to melt just yet. It wasn't strong enough to reach her but the tiny pellets startled her out of her musings.

"Elisa?" The strong masculine voice surprised her more.

Wine sloshed from her glass. Quickly, she set it on the floor.

When she looked up, a tall dark figure stood in front of her, his coat covering him from head to foot. She swallowed hard, recognizing his voice. "Etienne? You startled me."

"May I?" He stepped farther onto the porch not seeming to care if she gave permission.

"Looks like you don't wait for an answer." She smiled at the audacity he always showed. He was arrogant as well as so very sure of himself. The man of the world returned to see what waited here in Bordeaux for him. Would he stay for a while or would he leave again?

He slipped the hood of his cloak off, his black hair falling rakishly across his forehead, his half-smile coupled with the dimple still just as compelling as it was four years ago, fifteen years ago when she was a child. She ran her tongue across her lips.

"May I?" He picked up the bottle of wine then her glass and handed it to her. Once again failing to wait for her answer.

"There are more glasses in the kitchen."

If she rose, she would not be able to walk on her shaking limbs.

He didn't say anything. She understood he must think her horrible to make him wait on himself. In any case this was happening sooner than she anticipated. She needed time to think, had not expected him to show up tonight at her doorstep. Lord, but she thought she had more time to figure out what to say to him.

When he sat down beside her, she gasped startled once again by his sudden appearance. She was only used to Masson's noisy encounters. "You move too quietly."

"In my profession a necessity to stay alive." He sat next to her then, sipping the wine he poured for himself. "From my father's vineyard I see."

"Pruitt treats me on occasion," she said before she realized that would create more questions she didn't want to answer.

"Pruitt?" One dark eyebrow arched toward the heavens. His smile changing to a slight frown as if he devoured everything she said while creating hidden meaning. "When did his name change from Monsieur Dubois?"

"Since I've been here by myself."

She didn't have to answer his question. What he insinuated left a sour taste in her mouth.

"That must be nice for you."

His words implied many things, none of them pleasant.

She stood quickly tossing the remnants of her glass in his face.

Using the afghan, he slowly wiped the droplets away.

"Suppose I deserved that. Come, sit down again. I'll play nice."

"Not if you believe I'm a whore or your father's..."

She could not speak, her breathing turned ragged. All she wanted was to rush inside then bar the door. This was not the beginning she'd imagined. He thought her a whore when the only man she ever slept with was him and she only slept with him once.

"Mistress?"

The smile was not pleasing and the dimple didn't appear.

Grabbing the bottle of wine along with her glass she marched into the kitchen. Leaning on the counter she tried to inhale a breath of air then another. Her lungs wouldn't fill. Sobs wracked from her body but there were no tears. No tears for this man who marched into her life unannounced and made ludicrous assumptions that just were not true. How dare he assume she was his father's mistress? How dare he?

He was standing beside her, leaning on the counter when she finally inhaled enough air so she could speak. His hand rested possessively on her back.

"You know nothing."

"Then tell me. You didn't want to talk four years ago. Even while I gave you several chances, at that time we could have hashed out our differences. Don't suppose it was that important." His voice held a dangerous edge she didn't recognize. He was not the same gentle man who bedded her. No, this man was different, dangerous as she'd been told.

"I didn't know what to say to you. I was confused. There was nothing to tell." She shrugged her shoulders then and by the change of expression on his face she knew he misinterpreted the gesture. He would think she was flirting.

She wasn't.

"I'm sure your agile mind would think of something. You literally lied to me when you came to the room with me. There were two things I deserved to know that evening. You kept your mouth shut. Why?" He mocked her now with his smile as well as his words. Then, "You do know what those two things were."

She was shaking so hard she thought she would surely end up on the floor. Needing him despite his apparent dislike for her, she would not give in to this man. "You should go home. There is nothing here for you."

"In this storm?" He pushed away from the door, walking toward her before placing a hand on her shoulder. "You would toss me out to drown? Now, answer my questions. What were the two things you didn't tell me that night?"

"I don't want to talk to you."

She did but she wanted him to listen to her, not judge or criticize. Right now, he was doing both. It would be worse for her when he discovered her secret. Blurting it out might be for the best.

"What if I don't want to talk either? What if I have something else on my mind, a bit of unfinished business between us?" He ran his hand down her bare arm. "I found that one night with you was just not enough. I've dreamt about you, recalled how your hot, naked flesh felt against mine. I can't seem to forget no matter how hard I tried how you twisted and arched against me, silently begging me to give you your woman's pleasure."

One night was not enough for her either, but the second was not going to be tonight. He was too confident, too arrogant and imposing.

Heat suffused her body even while she trembled with the need only he could evoke. Quickly, she distanced herself from him. His presence so close to her created havoc in her mind as well as her body. She couldn't think. Had no idea what she should say.

"Don't touch me." She was backing away from him, knowing that only distance, a great deal of distance between them would keep her from allowing him liberties she wasn't prepared to give, not unless he cared for her, loved her as she did him. If he cared for her even the tiniest bit, she would give him anything he asked for.

Because she loved him with all her heart.

"That's not what you said before. How you acted. You wanted me. I felt the passion deep inside my heart. Saw it in the violet shimmer of your eyes. To me that night was a magical enchantment I have carried with me for years now. How many has it been?"

She backed herself against the wall. He held her there with the intensity of his gaze, nothing more. She could move away anytime. Yet, looking into his eyes she couldn't will her feet to move, maybe because deep inside she didn't want to leave him again even if it was to walk into the next room. Still, she couldn't find the words to tell him about Masson.

He deserves to know.

For her the sooner the better.

"What are you hiding?" he asked suddenly, running a gentle finger along her jawline before exploring along her neck to her collarbone.

She shivered with the caress, wishing she dared touch him. If she did, she would be lost. "Why did you stop here? Why didn't you ride to your home?"

She needed to change the subject, was looking to figure something out to say when his lips touched a tender spot behind her ear then his teeth tugged gently. She inhaled a quivering breath of non-existent air.

"We've unfinished business. Don't you think?"

His lips followed the curve of her neck, softly evocatively. He would coax her to his will. She couldn't allow that to happen. Not this way. Yet, the sensations were just as she remembered. They had been ever-present in her dreams. As her lashes lowered for a second, tiny little sounds hovered in her throat.

"No."

She pushed away walking back to the counter for her glass of wine then proceeding to the parlor where she sat stiffly in a chair as if her posture could prevent his seduction of her. The sofa was across from her. She tried to think about her mother and how she would handle a situation such as this.

Her mother would call for Eric. Would have him tossed out on his ear. Or she would give him what he wanted.

Neither choice was viable.

"No?" This time when he smiled the quirky smile was back as well as the endearing dimple. "I think you want me, Elisa. Are you going to add a third lie to the list?"

"I don't want you to seduce me."

"You could seduce me. I've no objections. Suspect your bed is soft and warm just as I remember you. Yes, soft and warm. Velvet heat."

His voice was sultry and husky with need, just as she recalled. He could seduce with his voice as well as his body. She didn't know how to defend herself or her heart from his roguish ways. If she allowed it to happen, he would bed her then leave her. Ah, but that was not fair of her. He didn't leave her until she refused to speak with him.

"You're not going to be in my bed tonight."

She needed to stay strong but when he smiled at her... She was shaking her head and walking away from him, hoping he would understand the reality of this moment.

Blue-white lightening flashed again just as she sat down on the porch swing once again curling her legs beneath her, sipping from her glass of wine.

"I don't remember asking." He sat down beside her, touching a strand of hair that came loose from its bun. "I should have realized who you were just by your hair." However, he paused long enough to rub the strand between his fingers. "I was so mesmerized by you, by the energy between us that I didn't think. I thought..." He brought the strand to his face. "So soft."

"What did you think?" she asked, wondering if he had some story just like her that needed to be shared but was uncertain.

Etienne did not strike her as a man of uncertainty.

"It's nothing. What about you? What have you done for these past years?"

Just then Cat jumped on his lap, purring and rubbing against his chest.

She almost laughed. Cat had no reason to distrust the man even though her mistress did. Maybe she distrusted herself more than Etienne.

Then it seemed he became distant, staring at the landscape as well as the constant flashes coming from the storm. No longer seemed to care what happened here.

She could hardly tell him she'd been spending her time raising his son, couldn't tell him they looked so much like each other that except for the age difference they could be twins.

"It's really none of your business what I've been doing."

She lied too easily. He would most likely call her out when he saw the little boy that didn't carry his last name but hers. It was his concern as to what happened almost five years ago.

Without looking at her, "I'm exhausted from the ride. I'm not going out in the storm. Is there anywhere I can bed down?"

His eyes sparked and once again he grinned lopsidedly. She felt her insides flutter helplessly when she felt the heat of his gaze. Pulled inexorably into the desire he displayed so clearly, she needed to think quickly.

She understood he wanted her to invite him into her bed. It couldn't happen. If it did, she'd be lost to him and his irrevocable charm. "In the barn. There is a nice pile of hay. It will be warm and dry."

Her actions were uncalled for as well as rude but she was too afraid of her feelings and what she might allow if he were to stay inside.

"I don't mean to frighten you. I just thought perhaps there was another bedroom in the house. The barn seems a bit extreme, don't you think? But if that's what you want." His shrug was only half indifferent. She understood she'd hurt his feelings. The fact shouldn't matter to her but it did. She was not naturally this rude.

There were two extra rooms. They were both too close to hers and one was their son's. "The barn will do fine. It wouldn't be proper for you to stay in the main house."

He ran his hands through his hair until it seemed to go every which way. Disheveled, he looked more rakish than ever. "Elisa, if you haven't noticed, there is nothing proper between us." After a lengthy pause, he continued. "I suppose the barn will have to do."

She nodded, "Yes, the barn will have to work."

He rose. She followed, walking into the house. She collected a quilt and a pillow. Handing it to him, she watched as he turned, walking through the kitchen then out of the house using the back door to the barn, his back stiff and clearly angry with what transpired. Compliance had been unexpected. For the moment, she didn't trust what she was seeing.

A wave of guilt swept through her, curling deep inside the pit of her stomach. He didn't deserve this treatment. She did have another bedroom. If she wasn't such a coward, she would have sent him there.

This was not well done of her. She could not undo it, would not change her mind as she was too terrified to do anything else.

For a few more minutes, she watched the backdoor, her hands clasped beneath her chin fully aware of the compelling magnitude of the man. She wanted to run after him in order to bring him back to the house. It wouldn't do. Trusting herself with this man so close to her was not feasible, would never be realistic. The long deep breaths she was trying to inhale, just didn't happen.

Beneath her breath she swore, dashing upstairs she retrieved another blanket. She did not want him to be cold. It was still early spring. The nights could be chilly. She promised him warm and dry. If nothing else, she would make sure he was warm.

Inside the barn, he was curled up beneath the solitary blanket. Slowly, she walked to him, extending the second covering. "I didn't want you to be cold." Her voice shook with emotions she had no control over as she felt the heat as if it emanated from him and into her.

Now she was standing over him. His eyes were closed. He couldn't possibly be asleep. Suddenly his hand snaked out, grabbing her wrist. She gasped.

She toppled down, finding herself lying beside him, her body pressed against his. "I thought you would never come to me."

His voice was deep and husky, ripe with desire she remembered from that night when she gave herself to him.

His mouth slanted over hers, his hand holding the back of her head. His tongue moistened her lips. Remembering what he taught her, she wanted to open for him. She was seconds away from losing herself to him.

Pushing away, "No, no, I can't do this. I just brought you another blanket. I didn't mean for this to happen."

He let her go. "I'm sorry. I misunderstood, *mon bijoux*."

His treasure?

~ * ~

After that brief encounter, Etienne lay awake for several hours. He'd thought she had a change of heart when she came to him with the blanket. Evidently, he'd been a fool once again, mesmerized by her fragility and innocence. Intrigued by her beauty and the simmering passion she couldn't deny that he saw in the blue-violet of her eyes when she looked at him.

Still, he wondered what exactly she was hiding from him. He knew women well. She was indeed keeping secrets. He had hoped to find a place to rest in the house. Once she fell asleep, he could look around. Perhaps discover her unspoken truths.

Elisa was just as beautiful as he remembered, her feminine curves molding deliciously against him. His breath had caught in his throat this evening when he discovered her sitting on the porch swing sipping wine during a thunderstorm. That moment he wanted to reach out to her and draw her into his arms. Energy danced between them. Energy that was just as potent and violent as the storm. He didn't dare act on his desires. It was obvious from the start, she didn't want to talk to him now, any more than she did years ago. He needed to know why.

Over and over again he told himself she was a willing participant in their lovemaking. He had not coerced her in any way. Yet after the fact coupled with the unspoken messages she sent him this evening, they were opposite in their thinking. He would have asked her forgiveness if she had given him the opportunity. She refused every gesture of goodwill.

He punched his pillow again then again, lying on his back and staring at the rough beams above him. The last few weeks had been spent sleeping under the stars, escaping Scotland only because the lassie he'd thought to give his heart to covered for him. Ah, but she'd been sweet on another man. He understood at that moment there was only one woman he truly craved.

Elisa.

She was beautiful and sweet. He had no illusions she would still be unwed by the time he reached home.

When he woke the storm had passed, clearing the air. Sunlight filtered through the open barn door. Birds filled the peaceful morning with their songs. A soft humming came from somewhere close by. He sat up, looking around while he grabbed his pants before slipping them on.

He found the basin of water she must have left for him. Quickly, he washed then pulled his shirt on over his head. When he found Elisa, she was milking the cow and singing. Her voice was clear, the notes she reached a fine soprano.

"Didn't expect to find you doing chores? Thought you would have staff that would do things like milking the cows." He watched her with bit of fascination and a lot of disbelief.

"Why? Someone's got to do them. Do you see anyone else around here? It's just you and me. Unless you know how to milk a cow, I suppose I get the job."

She sounded angry to him. Once again, he found himself trying to think of the right words to say without offending her. When he came here, he didn't think he'd be dancing around his words and tip toeing just to make her happy. He came to talk, that was all, as well as see if his memories of her were real. The first moment he saw her sitting on the porch swing during the thunderstorm, he understood all that he recalled about Elisa Moreau was real.

Merde, what did he think? *That she would take one look at you and fall into your bed as she did that night at Margaux's.*

"No, my apologies. Doesn't seem I know what to say."

He leaned against the stall door, arms crossed in front of him. Keeping his gaze from her was impossible Watching her long slim back as she did her chores gifted him with other ideas best kept in check. She was not his. Yet, he paused in thought, if the way she melted into him last night gave any indication, he could easily coax her into his arms.

"I'm just about finished here. Are you hungry? I've breakfast warming."

Her tone changed quickly as if she didn't like the way she spoke to him.

He was hungry for a lot of things. "Famished," he told her. "Anything I can do to help?"

"No, I've people who do the majority of the chores as you thought earlier. Not sure why I took exception to your assuming the truth," she told him a bit apologetically.

"Seems you took exception to just about everything I said last night. So, this morning most likely won't be any different." He was ginning as well as enjoying the color rising to her face. From everything she told him last night she was not immune to him. For a moment, when he kissed her, he felt the beginnings of a rise of passion. Maybe she wanted him as much as he did her. He didn't intend to give up on Elisa.

"I did. In my defense your sudden appearance last night shocked me. I didn't have time to collect my thoughts before you were challenging me in little ways. Frightening to some degree." She stood then, reaching for the bucket of milk. "I..." she began but turned away before finishing.

"I'll get that," he said, taking it from her hand before she could start walking. "What's for breakfast?"

"Nothing fancy, eggs and bacon, bread with strawberry preserves if you like something sweet."

"You fix breakfast every morning?" Or is it just for me?"

"I do but not this much. Most of the time the morning meal is oatmeal and fruit when I can get it fresh."

"Coffee?" he asked, needing that instead of tea. "The good people of Scotland like their tea. It was rare to find a cup of coffee.

"Lots of it."

She'd been walking ahead of him. She fell back to his side and smiled.

It was the first real smile she'd given him. It sent his jaded heart into a tailspin, melting it in the process. He decided he would try to arouse more smiles. At the table they ate in silence. She would steal furtive glances at him every few seconds. Amused for the time being, he decided to let this play out at her speed. He wasn't sure if he had the patience though.

Satisfied, he set his fork on the plate then picked his utensils and plate up then took them to the sink, returning for her dishes. "I'll wash. You can dry. Don't know where anything goes."

"You don't have to do that," she was quick to say. "Men don't..." she quit before she finished the sentence.

"Of course I do. I appreciate your hospitality. For your information, I've been washing my own dishes for a very long time."

"Really, it's not necessary."

She had planned ahead and had water heating on the stove. As an afterthought he should have asked to dry. He could think of nothing better than to have her at the sink, her hands in soapy water. Looking at the nape of her neck, he was tempted to hold her again, place tiny kisses along the tender spots revealed and enjoy her reactions. Perhaps she would be willing to give him more this morning than she had last night.

Maybe she would think the same, wishful thinking old man. As far as you can tell, she doesn't want anything to do with you and your advances. Doesn't want to be coaxed into surrendering her body to you. For Elisa the first time was most likely one time too many. *Mon Dieu* but he'd never felt this insecure when it comes to winning a lady's approval. They usually fell into his arms.

"Consider it payment for the accommodations." He chuckled at the glance she shot him.

"You will go home now," she said as she dried and placed a dish in the cupboard. "I'm sure your father will be thrilled to see you."

"My home is not my father's. I'll send a message to my father that I will see him in a couple of days. I plan on seeing to my château as well as the vineyard father wants me to take care of. Going to spend a day with Gil catching up." *Perhaps he can shed some light on what you are hiding from me. Behind that elusive smile I know you are keeping some secret from me.*

Looking over her shoulder, he caught a glimpse of a smile. "I'm sure that will be nice for you. Are you planning on leaving again or are you here to stay for a while?"

"I've quit that line of work. I'm staying put. At least until I get bored. How soon that will be, one never knows."

"Etienne..." she began but was cut off by a noise out front.

"Sounds like you have company." He continued to wash dishes and wondered why she stayed in the kitchen instead of greeting her new guest. "Would you like me to see who it is?"

"No, I'll go."

She didn't seem to be in a hurry. In fact, she held back so long he almost changed his mind and went to the door himself. Nothing she'd been doing for almost twenty-four hours made any kind of sense to him. It was just like their first encounter. Her words coupled with her actions didn't align.

"Gil, what brings you here?" When she spoke, her voice was whisper thin.

He heard the quivering and wondered if she was afraid of Gil or afraid he would find out she was seeing his best friends. *Merde,* but he didn't have any claim to her. What if she and Gil were involved with each other? She would have some explaining to do. He wasn't about to make it easy for her either.

Etienne dried his hands then walked into the front room, scowling, his gaze moving between Gil and Elisa. He was holding both her hands in his as if he was comforting her. Jealousy rose fast and furious. "I'd like to know the same thing. Just what has you stopping?" he snarled at his longtime friend.

"Just checking in on Elisa to see if she needs anything from the village," Gil grinned seeming to understand what Etienne was thinking and trying to goad him into staking his claim to Elisa. "Do it on occasion, but now that you're home, I guess I won't be needing to stop by any longer. Suppose you're going to take care of her now. About time you stepped up to the job."

"I don't know why you would assume that," Elisa said, her voice tight with what sounded clearly like anger to him. "It so happens I enjoy your company. Gets lonely here. A girl needs someone to talk to every once in a while."

"Alright then if you like, I'll keep stopping by when I'm on my way into the village."

He was looking at Etienne when he spoke, seeming to wait for some sign from him. If she wanted Gil to stop by so be it. He would just make sure he came to see her more often so Gil would have nothing to do for her.

"I would like that," Elisa stepped close to Gil, putting her hand on his arm, reinforcing her words. "You've been a dear friend to me the last four years."

"You won't need to while I'm here," Etienne's words were a low growl meant to give warning to Gil.

There was no way he could be as compliant as he wanted to be. She would not take aid from Gil as long as he was around.

On further inspection and despite her brazen words and actions, Elisa appeared visibly shaken by Gil's appearance at the house. It seemed she was saying one thing while at the same time her face was the color of ash. Etienne wanted to get to the bottom of the woman behind the lies. She stopped talking. He doubted if she would say anything more as long as Gil remained at the house.

"Can I pick anything up for you today?" Gil's smile was too broad for Etienne's liking even though he knew his friend was goading him.

"No, Pruitt stopped by yesterday with some fresh fruit and vegetables. I've enough to last for several days."

Once more, Gil looked from Elisa to him then back. Again, he was struck with the notion there was something significant Elisa was not telling him.

"Coffee?" Etienne asked as he set the towel across his shoulder now hoping that the longer Gil remained, the sooner he would discover more about Elisa.

"You look comfortable, settling in?" Gil asked thoughtfully eying the two of them.

"For the time being."

Etienne grinned watching Elisa's reaction to his words coupled with the play of emotions across her face. He stepped up to her and wrapped an arm around her shoulder, pulling her close as he made sure Gil knew he was claiming her as his own. "Not planning on leaving for the château for the next couple of days."

She whirled on him, her eyes flashing with energy, her tiny fists clenched at her sides. "I..." but she didn't finish, deciding to look at Gil as if he could provide the words she needed.

He followed her gaze until he was also staring at his friend. "Either of you want to explain what is going on here?"

"No," they said in unison.

Gil tipped his hat. "Guess I'll be on my way. Seems more than prudent at the moment to leave the two of you to sort this out. Appears there's a lot to be said by both of you. Wouldn't want to get in the way."

When Gil was gone, he sat down on the sofa. He patted the spot beside him. "Best you sit down and start talking. It looks as if I've lost what little patience I had when I saw Gil at your doorstep as if he's your lover. Don't like him coming around here." He didn't want to admit to the jealousy eating at him as well as the lost years with her.

"I don't know why that would bother you. You've no claim on me." She stood her ground, her hands still damp and with a few soap bubbles lingering. He tossed her the dishtowel. "You could have come here any time. I never kept you in other countries doing whatever it was you did."

"Actually, Elisa, I don't plan on going anywhere until I've found out what secret you and it seems Gil are harboring. No matter how long it takes. I'll wait for the clarification."

He couldn't explain his anger when he saw his friend with her, offering to help her out. It was something he should be doing. He didn't want to think of the very real possibility Gil had slept with her. That thought caused his stomach to turn sour.

"We have no secrets," she protested wiping her hands dry.

"None but you do have at least one secret. Don't appreciate the fact Gil knows what it is while I don't?"

Etienne was convinced Gil knew more than he was letting on. He was holding that information close to his chest because he cared more for Elisa than he was willing to admit possibly even to himself.

Elisa's full mouth thinned just a little as she addressed him, "All true but I don't understand why you of all people think you should be privy to that secret. It's about me. The truth doesn't concern you and has nothing to do with Gil. It's something from my past I'd rather not share with anyone."

"Even your first lover?"

"Yes." She sounded contrite.

"You're lying." Etienne held himself perfectly still waiting for her to reveal something more of her thoughts. "It's not hard to see the truth of that in your eyes and the way you can't look at me when you say the words. Gil would tell me but I'll wager you swore him to secrecy. Can't blame the man for keeping his word. From my experience, it's something most women folk have a difficult time doing, telling the truth."

His thoughts travelled back to the Scottish lass he left behind in

Glasgow. Daryl MacTavish had a way of spitting out the truth even when she shouldn't.

It appeared, despite his confrontation with her, she hid the truth she didn't want to talk about. She picked up the broom by the door. Started furiously sweeping outside. Her back to him she worked diligently for at least ten minutes before she finally walked back in and sat down blowing flyaway hair from her eyes. "I wish you would go away."

"When it's time."

"My mother threatened to castrate you if you didn't do the right thing by me," she blurted.

He knew that. Knew also that wasn't a secret. Everyone understood what Angelique would do if someone harmed her daughter. She was a mother bear when it came to Elisa. "That's a nice diversion but it doesn't tell me anything I don't already know."

She rose again. This time she was in the kitchen doing something. He couldn't quite be sure. He heard pots and pans rattling around. By the time she was finished, the clock told him it was past noon. He spent the time perusing the living room, staring upstairs thinking he should go to the second floor and see if there was something there she was hiding. She certainly didn't want him up stair last night.

"You're truly not going anywhere?" She stepped into the room. Her hands were settled on her hips. "You can't think to stay here. People will think..."

"Nope. I don't give a damn what people will think."

"I didn't invite you to stay the night."

"I'm staying."

She appeared utterly defeated and dejected; her shoulders hunched forward. "Even if I don't want you to stay."

"Until you tell me the truth." He shrugged his shoulder in indifference. It didn't make much difference to him where he stayed the night.

She seemed to get ahold of her emotions, straitening, fire flashing in her blue-violet eyes. "Then you might as well have some lunch. A couple of days ago Gil brought several types of cheese from the village. I don't like to go there myself so he has been kind enough to bring me things I'd like or need. Your father does the same only with him it's his servants who make the trip. Would you like a sandwich? I've freshly baked bread."

"I could eat but the breakfast you served was large and satisfying. Perhaps we could put food off until..."

"You already know everything about me," she said quickly, too quickly for him to believe her. "There is nothing more for me to tell you."

"I do know a lot but not what I'm looking for. I know you don't lie well even though your mother is the best. I know the two dimples on your back at the base of your spine. I don't even have to close my eyes to remember how sweet the tips of your breasts taste..."

"Stop it." She rose quickly this time disappearing into another room, clearly agitated by his words.

Putting her off guard was what he hoped for even though everything he told her was the truth. He followed her. The room held a few bolts of cloth along with some fashion plates. She was rearranging things, seeming to try to cover up the fact she'd wandered in here.

What he saw stole his breath then he realized there could any number of reasons she might be sewing children's clothing.

"What are you doing with these?" He held up a pair of tiny britches. "I'm sure they won't fit either of us."

She snatched them from him, quickly folding them before placing them in a cubicle. "I sew for the neighbors. It keeps my hands busy. Also brings in some money."

She was breathing hard. He noticed moisture beading on her forehead before slipping down her cheek. If she was telling him the truth, the words would not have affected her that way. Nor would she continue to look so charmingly guilty.

"Of which you don't need." He pulled out the pants, examining them. "They are very well made. Didn't take you for a seamstress. Thought your skills lie in another direction."

"That was uncalled for."

"Possibly. Time will tell."

"There is a lot about me you don't know." She turned from him again as she walked back to the main room leaving him in the sewing room with even more questions.

"A spoken truth." He poured himself a whiskey before sitting down. "My father's favorite brand. Does he come here often?"

Jealousy rose again. He tried to tamp it down by watching her and sipping the drink.

"He's welcome here anytime but no, he doesn't come often."

She told him sitting down near him again then seeming to think better of it she rose and poured herself a drink. This time she sat in a chair across the room from him.

"Keeping your distance? Afraid?"

"Not afraid of you."

"You never told me why you didn't want to see me that last day I came to visit. I'd like to know. Can that be too hard? A few moments of honesty from you would be nice."

Pursuing this, he knew first hand, was a waste of time. Nothing short of an earthquake would shake the words from her lips.

She sighed softly, almost mournfully. To Etienne the simple gesture was meant to be dramatic. "I was a coward. I couldn't come to terms with what..." she swallowed and looked away. "I was terrified of seeing you again."

"With what we did in bed together?" He was shocked by the revelation. This was a new experience for him. Women were never terrified while in his presence, especially in bed. "Need I remind you that you were willing? Nay, even eager."

"The way you made me feel. I didn't know what to think of myself and how I reacted even though mother assured me I wasn't a *putain*, I thought that I might possibly be."

"You're no whore. I'm sure Angelique would not have let you believe that of yourself. Your responses to me were all very real as well as innocent. A whore is not that way."

He had wondered at that. Sure, Elisa would have come to terms with what happened that night by now. It looked as if she had not.

"When I first came to my mother, when I ran from the city to seek solace in her arms, she treated me as a whore. Intimated that I could go to work for her. Never before had she judged me."

There was a catch in her words then a sob. Her shoulders were trembling.

His heart went out to her. All he wanted now was to pull her into his arms, comfort as well as protect her. At this moment, he wasn't sure if she would accept his offer. He also wasn't sure if this was a ploy to change the tenor of the conversation to something more to her liking."

"I'm sorry for that. She surely didn't continue in that vein. You don't have the skills to be a *putain*."

He meant that as a compliment, however by the look on her face, she perceived it otherwise.

"By the time you came to see me three months later, I didn't know what to say to you. Didn't know what you would say to me." She tried to smile but her eyes were watery and her lips didn't stretch that way. "I thought you might call me names also."

He saw the effort and applauded her but, "If you'd chosen to see me, you would have learned I only had your best interest at heart." He did so want to reach out to her, pull her into his arms to comfort her.

"What would that have been? My best interest?"

"I wanted to know if you were pregnant with my child before I took the oversees assignment. I supposed you were not since you chose not to see me. From my experience, women want their children to be born with their father's last name." Her expressions ranged from shock to anger then she smiled and laughed outright.

"What would you have done, *monsieur,* if I had been pregnant. Change your life completely for something that happened one night and really had no bearing on your future. It wasn't as if we were courting or if we even knew each other. You didn't love me and truly had no responsibility to something that happened in a bordello." She spoke so fast the words tripped over each other.

"I knew I was your only lover. Even though the possibility was slim a pregnancy would happen with just one encounter, I needed to make sure. I don't take my responsibilities lightly. It's rare for me not to use protection when it comes to sexual encounters."

He watched as heat rose to her face to color it beautifully.

"You didn't answer my question."

This time she had the feather duster in her hand and was sweeping it across the shelves and figurines in the house. She kept herself so busy he was getting dizzy watching her.

"Do you ever sit still?" he asked, meaning the words to be humorous, but at this point he just wanted her to stay in one place.

"Not when I'm nervous," she told him frankly.

He grimaced, "Didn't mean to make you nervous but the topic is invasive if it were true. Is it? Did you have my child and if so...?"

He wanted to know what she'd done with the child. Perhaps the *bebe* was at Angelique's.

"What would you have done?" she persisted her lips thinned in what he thought was a good imitation of anger. "That's why I couldn't talk to you. I didn't know and... You do deserve an answer I suppose since it's all hypothetical anyway."

He leaned forward beginning to suspect that perhaps she had carried his child and perhaps miscarried. "Is it?"

"Hypothetical?" she squeaked.

The reddish color no longer graced her cheeks because now she was ashen.

The dusting continued until she finally set the duster down. She wandered into the kitchen. Once again, he heard the obvious noises of a woman preparing a meal. He wasn't sure why she bothered, thinking neither one of them would eat until the air was cleared.

"Hypothetically pregnant."

The pause in his mind was poignant. He'd never really thought she was but now he was tempted to investigate upstairs and perhaps discover why he was sent to the barn last night. No, none of that made sense. The child would be here playing if indeed there was a child. He could see for himself. How old would the baby be? He thought backward for a few seconds then inhaled sharply, almost four years old.

Had he really been gone for so long? It seemed one assignment led to another then another. The last one had very nearly cost him his life along with his freedom.

In the kitchen, he leaned against the doorframe, watching, his arms crossed in front of him. She was busy, moving from one place to another, her movements frantic. It seemed she was undoing everything she'd done before.

"Do you want help? Someone to undo what you're inadvertently doing?" he asked, knowing she would refuse but wishing she would find some way for him to occupy his hands other than what he wanted them to be exploring.

"Are you hungry?" She was bent over now, her bottom in the air, searching for something in a low cupboard.

The sight entranced him. For a moment, he thought he could get used to this, a home and a wife. If she was his wife, he would find other ways to make sure she told him what was in her head.

"I could eat something as well as drink a glass of wine."

Perhaps it would loosen her tongue although it did nothing last night. Figuring out ways to get to the truth was becoming more difficult. It seemed to become harder as she sidestepped everything he asked with questions of her own or silence.

"Me too, food will give me something to do with my hands."

He pushed away from where he was standing. "I can think of things you can do with your hands."

Feeling the enchantment of her body beneath his was something he yearned for. "You should understand that I don't plan on sleeping in the barn again tonight."

"Then you are going home."

The pan she was holding crashed on the stove.

"No. I know you've more than one extra bedroom. I'll sleep in one of those."

His hand was on her back now, lightly touching each tiny bone that lined the length of her body. He meant to explore more of her after they ate. There was much more to his feelings than sex, although that was huge.

"We can discuss where you are going to sleep after we eat." Her voice was thready and weak. "As long as you don't intend that place to be with me, in my bed."

He understood she was struggling with herself. He smiled. "If that is what you want."

He was willing to give her every concession she could think of, but nothing she said or did would change the outcome. He would either sleep in her bed with her or in another one of the rooms upstairs. A second night in the barn was unacceptable.

"I'd like that."

His voice was smooth. He meant to do everything in the realm of possibilities to coax her to his way of thinking tonight. So far, he tried everything he could think of to discover her truth. Nothing worked. Once she wanted him, and he knew she still did.

"Fine." She brought out a ham and began slicing it. "You can get the bread and cheese. There are pickles on the shelf if you like."

He did as she said and cut the bread into four pieces assuming she meant to make sandwiches. A few minutes later they were eating and sitting on the porch with a glass of wine.

She was not making this easy. He smiled as he watched her breathing as it began to grow ragged when he touched her cheek with his knuckles before running a fingertip along her neck. "This doesn't have to be so hard. Just give into me as well as your feelings for me, *mon bijoux*."

Tucking her lips beneath her teeth she looked at him, her blue violet eyes seeming to lose some of the fight he'd seen earlier. If he were to guess, she appeared defeated. Her food was half eaten. She played with the glass of wine, whirling the liquid around in tiny circles.

"You're not hungry after all. Drink the wine and I'll pour you a second glass."

"No, I suppose I'm not. The food seems to stick in my throat."

She closed her eyes, leaning back on the swing.

He wanted to tell her that the truth, whatever it was, would make everything easier. Having come to suspect there was a child somewhere, not that it would be his, but that would be the only reason she persisted in her silence that he could think of.

"Have the wine and perhaps the food will go down easier." *Perhaps it will loosen your tongue.*

She drank then coughed, some of the wine splattering on the porch in front of her. Surprised, he looked down the road to see a carriage.

His father's vehicle, it seemed, he was coming here.

Anger swept inside as he watched it come closer. He'd hoped to have the evening to himself. Now he would have to share some of the time. He was sure his father would stay into the night.

At the sight of the carriage, she downed the entire glass and poured another. "Your father is here."

"He causes you distress. Why is that?"

He had not expected that reaction. Too many questions and scenarios swept into his head. Earlier he'd thought Gil was her lover and now this. Why would his father show up early in the evening if it wasn't for one thing? Dinner and sex.

She choked on the wine again. When she looked at him her eyes were wide with fear. Those blue-violet eyes told him she was terrified of his father or what his appearance here would tell him.

Finally, the carriage rumbled to a stop. The door swung open. A tiny figure leapt from the carriage racing to Elisa. "Mama, I missed you so. *Papi* was fun but it wasn't home."

Masson stopped just short of throwing his arms around her. Then he pointed at him, "Why do you look just like me?"

Etienne heard the small gasp then watched as Elisa crumpled to the floor, her wine spilling, sending a blood red stain on the boards around her. He wanted to throttle his father. How could he do this to a woman he knew his son cared about?

His hands fisted at his sides. The need to lash out at his father twisted inside.

~ * ~

Pruitt knew the instant he saw the set of his son's jaw coupled with the narrowing of his dark brown eyes that Etienne's mind traveled to the wrong place. Etienne didn't think the boy was his but his father's. Pruitt had not expected that scenario. He would have to think quickly, and Elisa would have to tell Etienne the truth. Obviously, she'd been delaying that.

It was not well done of her but he was not surprised. Elisa was terrified of the truth coming out. She should have written to Etienne as soon as the boy was born, nay before the birth. She had not done so.

For a moment, Etienne let his attention return to Elisa. Gently lifting her from the floor he held her close. To Pruitt that was a good sign. Perhaps he misread his son's expression.

She moaned softly when Etienne touched her cheeks.

"Is Mama alright?" Masson asked, standing beside his mother, his eyes watery.

"She will be. It seems she was surprised."

"Surprised? Why?" Masson asked.

Slowly Elisa opened her eyes, a weak smile forming on her lips. "I guess you know the secret I was keeping." Her voice was thready and thin. "Truly, I was going to tell you."

"Mama, you didn't answer me." Masson was tugging on her hand. "Are you all right?"

It would all be out in the open now. Pruitt knew it was best for everyone involved.

"Good afternoon," Pruitt said as he followed his grandson at a more sedate pace up the walkway to the porch. "I suppose I should have sent word ahead of me that I was coming."

Etienne looked up, "Yes, it might have been nice to know ahead of time. Obviously, this was not good for Elisa."

With his gaze directed at Elisa, Pruitt asked, "Are you going to answer Masson's question or do I need to?"

"Whatever needs saying I want to hear it from Elisa," Etienne said with a low growl, his eyes flashing with suppressed anger.

Many seconds seemed to tick by before Elisa closed her eyes then opening them, "Masson is your child, Etienne. He looks like you because he is yours."

Etienne's expression changed. A softness Pruitt had never seen before gathered around Etienne's eyes. "My child." His voice was filled with awe as he looked at his son then to Elisa. "For a moment I thought..."

"I conceived that night at Margaux's. I was terrified and confused. I fancied myself in love with you, you see and everyone told me I could not be. So... over the years, well, I figured out they were correct in their assessment. What I felt was a childhood fascination for a dangerous although intriguing man who would never love me in return." She paused then, inhaling a short soft breath of air. "You certainly don't love me. It was just sex for you. At the time I didn't know what to call what we did. Now I do."

"You should have told me." Etienne's words were laced with the fury he must be feeling at being duped for all these years.

To Pruitt the conversation between these two was long overdue. This was the first moment everything was out in the open, all that stood between them still did but at least now Elisa could no longer run from it. She had been hiding for nearly four years. He needed to leave these two alone to sort out their feelings for each other. Unfortunately, they would not be alone because he wasn't going to take Masson back to his home.

"I didn't know how." Her breath caught in her throat. "I tried but the words just wouldn't come."

Masson climbed in her lap, looking from one person to the other. "Do I have a papa now?"

His little voice broke Pruitt's heart. He should have always had a father. If not for Angelique and her determination to keep these two apart, the little boy would have. Pruitt didn't doubt for a moment Etienne would have stayed in Bordeaux if he'd known or would have returned before the birth of his child had he had the leeway to tell his son what the urgent matter was he wrote about.

For five years he kept his word, sworn to Angelique. Now he was free.

"Would you like to stay?" Elisa asked, a wistfulness in her voice that Pruitt understood to be fear.

"No, I believe the three of you have some catching up to do. I don't belong here now."

Pruitt turned then, smiling. This was exactly what he hoped for. It happened sooner than he expected. Etienne would do the right thing because he loved the girl.

He just didn't know it yet.

Chapter Four

Elisa picked up the wine glass that was still toppled on the porch before walking into the kitchen with it. Methodically, she found a towel and cleaned the drops of wine from her bodice as well as her skirt. Masson followed her seeming a bit weary of his newfound father.

"Mama, is he really my papa?" He tugged on her skirt when she wasn't answering fast enough.

She looked over her shoulder. Apparently, Etienne followed them too. He was leaning against the doorframe, well-muscled arms crossed over his chest, his eyelids lowered, waiting in seeming anticipation of her answer. "Are you going to tell him? Seems we both need to be certain. You've left us hanging for nearly four years now. It would have been nice if you'd written."

"I already said the words, but yes, Etienne is your father if he wants to be." She knelt down beside her son, so they were at eye level. "He is your real father."

"Where has he been? You said he was gone. Didn't he want me?" The boy's eyes filled with unshed moisture while he hid his little face in her apron.

Elisa looked to Etienne for help but received only a shrug of his broad shoulders for a response. "On assignment?" Her voice wavered. "I'm not really sure. Why don't the two of you go play while I get you something to eat? Would you like a sandwich and milk?"

She had no words, nothing to say that would ease the boy's mind. Etienne would have been here for him if she'd told him. She had no excuses now that everything had been revealed. Masson was deprived of a father all these years because of her selfishness.

"Yes, Mama,"

Then he turned to Etienne, the tears seeming to vanish instantly at the notion of playing with his father. "What do you want to play?"

Etienne looked to Elisa for help. She smiled, lifting her shoulders, saying silently it was up to them. "I'm sure the two of you can figure it out. What did you like to play when you were a little boy?"

"Damned if I can remember," he muttered.

"You need to watch your words while you are around him. I understand he will learn soon enough, but for now I'd appreciate it if he doesn't have knowledge of those words just yet," she reprimanded him.

The two left the room, chatting about big red balls and wooden horses that his *papi* gave him. Elisa didn't know what they would come up with, but she meant to take as long as possible making her son a sandwich and pouring a glass of milk.

Inside the small kitchen, her stomach fluttered miserably. She rubbed her shoulder where it hit the floor when she fainted, not being able to recall another time when that happened. For now, she needed to think, comprehending the fact he would press her for more information. In truth, those months so long ago she'd been a terrified young woman expecting a child from a one-night mistake.

So many times she told herself there were no regrets and so many times when she looked at her son, she confirmed that thought. It had not been a mistake, at least not for her.

No regrets.

No mistake.

Yet here and now she did have regrets, not about Masson but about not telling Etienne as well as the way she handled things since he arrived. He'd deserved to know so he could make some decisions for himself. Even though she waited so long to share the news, he was still faced with the same conclusion. She would not marry him no matter how sweetly he put the question to her.

No matter how much she wanted to be his wife.

No, she would not bind a man to her who didn't love her. Could not do that to anyone. Of course, Etienne would be able to see as well as visit with the boy whenever he wanted. She would never deny him that.

After all, he was Masson's father.

Elisa placed the sandwich on the plate after cutting the crusts off. When she reached the porch, she saw the two playing with a ball on the lawn in front of her house. Masson was laughing as was Etienne. Childish giggles coupled with a man's laughter left a warm space in her heart. The little boy looked up as if sensing her presence then waved. She set the plate on the table waving back.

She sat for a while, watching them, assuming Masson would come eat as soon as he grew tired or hungry. It didn't matter which came first. When Etienne looked at her the smile changed, sending a shiver of fear down her spine, her lips thinning in anticipation of his fury. If she wasn't mistaken, she saw the anguish in his face, the repressed rage at her.

Nervous energy raced through her as it was slowly becoming evident things between her and Etienne were not what she hoped. For his son he was projecting an air of serenity and acceptance, even love. For her it seemed she saw determination coupled with a lot of defiance. He would do what he would and everything else be damned. She didn't suppose he would ask her permission.

Now Etienne was lying on the ground while Masson was above. He was tickling his little boy. The laughter was evident while Elisa watched in understanding how much Masson had always wanted a father. Gil played with him like that but Gil was not his father. It just wasn't the same.

Pruitt rarely got down on the ground when he played with Masson. He usually had trouble standing if he sat too long. She inhaled a long deep breath reveling in the sight in front of her. Having longed for this moment, it was now bittersweet.

The wine was still on the table so she poured herself a glass, staring at the evidence of her fainting spell on the porch. What was in store for the future, still remained to be seen? Etienne could demand many things. There was very little she would refuse him, pertaining his to son. Pruitt once told her, he could take her son away from her if he chose. She didn't believe he would do something like that.

Still... the thought troubled her.

She was glad there was no sign of a tempest tonight. The sun was fading but there were no clouds on the horizon, which was painted with wonderful shades of oranges and yellows with a few pinks thrown into the brilliant mix. The sight gave her hope. Probably something she shouldn't take much stock in. She loved this country, the rolling hills all lined with grapes, the small villages doting the countryside and the people, so friendly.

Etienne would go to the family's second winery. The grapes were different there, sweeter. They left them until the fruit dried to get the most sugar from them before they were picked. The Sauternes were a different color, some even yellow and orange. Pruitt had always made sure to bring her both the Bordeaux and the Sauterne to keep in her pantry.

Over the years both men, Pruitt and Gil, pampered her. Now, now she didn't know what to expect. Her life was in upheaval. She had no one to blame except herself.

Suddenly, the two were standing in front of her.

"We're hungry," Masson said. "Can we eat now?"

"Dirty, I see. You're going to need a bath before you go to bed," Elisa smiled at her son. "Go wash your hands and you can eat."

Etienne followed the little boy, returning a few minutes later with clean hands and faces.

Masson scooted onto a chair, "I didn't think he would know how to play but he's almost as good as Uncle Gil."

With that said, Etienne's dimpled smile turned to a scowl. Then, "I promise I'll improve until I'm better than any other man."

He turned his attention to her, lifting an eyebrow in question. "Uncle Gil?"

"We should talk later after Masson goes to bed," was her curt reply. He had every reason to question her but not in front of their boy. She was sure by the time Masson was in bed he would have even more questions.

"It's okay," Masson said when Etienne looked at him. "It's grown-up talk. *Papi* and mama do that all the time. I have to go to bed first."

"You had discussions with Pruitt." Etienne's voice was a low growl, his eyes darkening angrily.

"About his upbringing. We can talk later." Elisa sipped her wine trying for an air of tranquility even while her hands shook. She didn't want her son to see how agitated she was.

"Can Etienne..." Masson began.

"Father," Etienne corrected him.

"Father," the boy said. "Can he give me my bath then put me to bed tonight? I want him to read me a story too."

"If he's agreeable but you need to remember that I will have to come in to kiss you goodnight."

They both looked at Etienne. "I would love to."

This time if she wasn't mistaken there were tears in his eyes. He turned away as if he didn't want her to see but the emotion pleased her. She'd had no idea how he would view his child, this little boy who looked so much like him even to his half-dimpled smile and dark brown eyes. There was nothing about Masson that even remotely resembled her.

For the rest of the meal, she kept silent, enjoying the chatter between father and son, realizing so intensely how much Masson missed out on over the years. As well as Etienne, he never heard his first words or first steps. He never saw the charming baby smile that made her feel as if the sun was shining, "sunshine."

When they were finally finished, "Is it bath time now?"

"The water is heating and perhaps your father will pull the tub from the scullery," Elisa said, looking to him, unsure if a man with so much wealth would be comfortable doing daily chores such as this.

He nodded, rising from the chair and extending his hand to his son, who eagerly grasped hold. They disappeared into the back of the house.

"Will you take a bath with me?"

She heard her son's words and chuckled softly, remembering Etienne's body so lean and hard. She recalled other hard parts of him, too vividly for comfort. Swallowing the lump in her throat she cast her gaze over the land toward his home, trying to vanquish the thoughts of Etienne from her head. He would probably leave in the morning. She had not one doubt he would return.

The two were singing now. His voice was a deep rich baritone melding with the childish voice that caught her off guard. She'd never expected him to sing with her son.

His son also.

Now Masson was laughing and Etienne was making low growling noises. She would have liked to go and watch but just the thought of Etienne naked inside the tub with her son was enough to send heated waves through her. Waving her hand in front of her face, she stared at the countryside for the longest time. Now that he was in her life, she didn't know how long she would be able to resist any advances he might make toward her.

He might not, might not want her.

Unable to listen any longer, she brought her wine to the front porch. Sitting down she watched as the darkness slowly took over the sky. Stars twinkled in the night, casting a feeling of romance and pleasure. The soft scent of Daphne lingered in the air coupled with a warm flower-scented breeze. She'd never known romance, had never been courted, only bedded. Since that night her existence had been lonely.

No regrets, she reminded herself. Don't dwell in the past, just look to the future.

Lust for the young man who kissed her and twirled her around in this very yard, formed her life molding her into the woman she was now. It was time to take that into account accepting who she was as well as the choices she'd made.

No regrets.

"Mama?"

There was a question in his voice as he stood in front of her in the pajamas she had laid out for him. The two of them surprised her but the sight of them together gave her many more reasons to smile. She wanted to reach out, ruffle his hair. Masson wouldn't like it though. He was almost five.

Etienne stood behind him, his hair damp, his shirt open. Her fingers curled tightly. His feet were braced apart yet he smiled at her despite the underlying current of anger still emanating from his eyes. For his son Etienne was hiding his emotions.

Mon Dieu but he stole her breath. An inferno seemed to build inside nearly sweeping her from her feet. She tried to hide what she was feeling, but his grin grew wider the dimple deeper until she turned away, hearing a soft chuckle of recognition. He knew what she was thinking, how he was making her feel. She could not hide anything from him. He must know she wanted him.

"Etienne..." Masson paused, a huge grin on his boyish face, "no, *pere* is going to read me a story now."

"Call me when you are finished, Etienne" she paused, "Don't let him talk you into more than one story. He has this way about him and he has just returned from his *grand-pere's* home. He's usually a lot spoiled even if he's only stayed a day and a night."

"I don't mind spoiling my son. Since I haven't seen him in almost five years."

The meaning was made clear to her, impossible to miss. Now that Etienne was here, he would dictate his son's upbringing. She wondered just how much say she would have. Perhaps none if the scowl on Etienne's face meant anything.

"I see."

Her words were strained. She looked away unable to watch the two as they walked up the steps to the second floor, Masson riding on his father's shoulders, his hands gripping Etienne's hair, squeals of boyish laughter echoing down the stairs.

Once again, she was left alone with her thoughts linked with her very real fears. The clock on the mantle ticked slowly. She heard an owl's voice in the sultry night air. A soft breeze swept around the corner of the house. A half-moon sat near the horizon casting golden warmth across the land. The night began to take on a decided chill while she sat on the porch swing sipping her wine while waiting for the conversation that should have taken place five years ago.

He must be reading four or five books to Masson. She hoped the little rascal would be able to sleep tonight. A great deal happened today. His miniature world, as he knew, it was changing quickly.

She wrapped a blanket around her, unwilling to come inside, enjoying the chill of the night snug in the soft warmth of the quilt. Somehow, she needed the solace of the darkness to soothe her racing thoughts. Not only was her son's world evolving but so was hers.

Angelique made it clear to her he would be able to dictate to her when he discovered her treachery. She would be left to do his whims. It was up to him whether or not she stayed in her son's life. She hoped he would allow it to stay the way it was, prayed he would not make huge changes. Masson was happy here. She didn't want her son uprooted.

The wine was gone so she walked into the kitchen intending to open another bottle. She understood it would be wise to keep all her senses about her, but tonight the wine seemed to go down like water. Perhaps there was a hole in the bottle, she laughed to herself.

Etienne's demands would start tonight, as soon as her, their, son was asleep. He would return with the sole purpose of telling her how things would be from now on.

He was sitting on the swing beside her before she heard him. She wasn't sure if she had just closed the sounds of the night off or he was really that silent.

"I didn't hear you," she told him pleasantly while trying to mask her obvious terror. "Is Masson asleep."

"Don't think so. When I finally turned off the light before closing the door his eyes were still open. We should wait to talk. I suspect he will be down soon, begging for a story from you."

He placed an arm across the swing, behind her allowing his hand to rest possessively on her shoulder.

"That's fine with me," she told him, unable to look at him while trying valiantly to ignore the gentle movements of his thumb on her neck.

"You'd probably like it if we never talked at all." His voice was soft and gentle yet it held an underlying current of control with a hint irritation.

He would mandate the following events, the rest of her life. "You're right. I don't want to talk. I want everything to stay as it was before I looked up to see you standing before of me."

Suddenly, Masson was standing in front of them. "Mama, you didn't come kiss me goodnight."

Relived for a few more minutes reprieve, she swept her son into her arms and carried him up the steps. She set him on the bed then hugged him tight.

"I love you."

"I love you too, Mama. Thank you for bringing my papa to me today. Would you read me another story? I liked it when Papa read to me but it wasn't you."

More time before the inevitable talking, she knew she wouldn't like what Etienne was going to tell her. Elisa read two more stories before she kissed him on the forehead. He was soundly asleep, his eyes closed, gently snoring. It was a soft childish sound. One she would remember for the rest of her life.

She was tempted then to do what she usually did and retire to her room for the night. If she did, he would come and either crawl into bed with her or... she wasn't sure. He would probably make sure she would join him to talk even if she was only wearing a nightgown. What difference would it make? He'd seen her wearing absolutely nothing.

It was a risk she wasn't willing to take. If he joined her in her bed...

The night was young and perhaps she could deflect most of his questions as well as avoid any mandates he might try to make.

When she sat down beside him, he was still on the porch swing. He filled her glass then with his dimpled smile, he asked. "How many books did you read him?"

Once again, he settled an arm across her shoulder. Laying claim Elisa was sure.

"He fell asleep half way through the second book, but he has this way of waking up if I close the book before it is finished."

She sighed then, suddenly feeling exhausted from all the stress of last night as well as today. For herself she grabbed a few seconds to close her eyes.

Etienne tightened his hold slightly. Strange that she suddenly felt protected. Elisa didn't understand the simple gesture, but she gave into the stress and accepted the comfort he gave her. She let her head find a place on his shoulder.

"Are you always this tired at the end of the day?" he asked, as his finger gently released the pins holding her hair in place, the strands slowly falling one by one around her shoulders.

She drew in air, feeling the comfort of his arms. "Yes, most days. Masson, although he is a very good child, has more energy than I possess. Along with the chores..."

It felt so good to have someone think of her needs. Since she left Angelique's bordello a few months after his birth, she had not felt that. "I stayed with my mother until he slept through the night."

"It was difficult."

His words as well as his hands were soothing while she reminded herself she could not give in to whatever it was he planned.

"No more so than for any other mother. Perhaps in ways I had more help than most."

She didn't want pity for her choices. She chuckled softy. No, pity would not be an emoting Etienne would ever feel. He was just finding out things, searching for information in his own way and time.

"I see. So, you had servants here helping you."

For the first time since she returned his words were noticeably harsh, accusing.

She pushed away from him, needing the distance. "You have no idea."

"That's what I'm trying to discover. I want to know if my son needed anything, if he was treated as he should be treated. He should never want for anything."

Without hesitation, she stood feeling her anger with intensity. She didn't understand him or the insinuations he made. "It's been a long day. I need to go to bed. You can pick a room or the barn. I don't care." She stopped on her way into the house, "Any room but..."

"I pick yours." His voice was warm and thick with passion.

She heard no anger. She understood what he wanted despite her lack of experience. The memories of that first night were starkly clear in her head.

"That's not a choice." Her voice was thin and shaky.

Unable to think straight, she now regretted the wine she consumed.

"Not what you just said. So, what is it? Pick a room or not?" He held on to her wrist, tugging her onto his lap, refusing to allow her to leave.

"Please." She inhaled several times searching for the word. "Please, you know what..."

"What do I know, Elisa? What is that you can't say to me right now? I'd like to please you as I did when we created my son."

Still, he didn't touch her intimately, didn't kiss her. Still, his breath whispered against her cheek, sending a wealth of shivers skidding through her body.

"I cannot. You cannot. Please..."

"One goodnight kiss?" he asked as his lips settled lightly on hers. "I won't' take anything you aren't willing to give."

She felt the gentle brush of his lips across hers, the touch of his tongue along her bottom lip. Tasted the wine. The tender sensations more than she could resist, she didn't hesitate but she opened for him. "Just one," she spoke softly but the words were absorbed into his mouth.

What am I to do? I cannot refuse this man despite my will. He has come back into my life. I want him just as I did so long ago, just as I have since I was a little girl. She discovered suddenly that he'd unfastened her dress loosening the ties of her shift as well. His fingers closed over her breast, his palm sweeping across the quickly hardening bud. This was so much more than one good night kiss. It was her life. She wanted to give herself over to this man yet she didn't dare be so brazen.

It didn't matter that he didn't love her. She had enough love to give for both of them.

For a moment he pulled away staring at her, his dimpled smile creating more havoc within. "You are just as I remember. Your lips are swollen from my kiss and your nipple is hard and tight waiting desperately to be suckled. You melt in my arms tonight just as you did then."

She could do nothing more than nod her head as his lips took hers in a deep searing hot kiss filled with heated passion that reached all the way to her soul. At that moment, she knew she had let this go too far. He would take everything she fought so hard to deny him simply because she couldn't say no.

"Etienne." She touched his chin with her fingertip, wanting to tell him how much she loved him.

Then, his low growl surprised her. "You are mine, Elisa. I want you. Want you now. Don't tell me no. Not ever."

Suddenly, she was shaken from the stupor she found herself in. "I'm not yours."

"Of course, you are. I'll prove it to you."

He kissed her again and again. With the ever-deepening contact, she had no will, no way to tell this man she needed to be heard. That she would be his but he had to give her something in return.

"No... Perhaps you should." She let her head fall back and his lips and teeth found the hollow at the base of her throat, touching, exploring tender flesh, sending heat waves through her. Higher, ever higher, sensations seeming to reach into the sky, enchanting her while he gave no chance to deny.

"What should I do?" he queried as he continued his assault on her emotions.

"I don't know." Her voice was thin and made no sense to her when she tried to replay in her mind all that had gone on tonight.

She was going to tell him to sleep in the extra bedroom, or he could pick the barn. It was up to him. Now it seemed that conversation had never happened.

He picked her up, tenderly cradling her in his arms. "We're going to go to bed now and we'll discuss all the other things that need discussing in the morning."

"Other things?" she asked, her eyes opening for a moment.

"Tomorrow."

He kissed her again while he carried her up the stairs.

"I don't want to go..."

She did want him in her bed. Did want him to do those magical enchanting things to her again. But she couldn't even think right now. Her mind was in a terrible muddle.

"Don't worry, I'm just going to sleep with you. When I make love to you, I want you to remember what we are doing. Tomorrow we will all go to my home."

"I don't have a choice?" she queried even as she tried to claw herself out of the self-imposed alcohol-induced haze.

"Always a choice."

~ * ~

Etienne helped her from her dress but left her shift on her to sleep. He stood back, gazing at her, realizing why he made love to her that night even though he guessed she was a virgin. Virgins had always been off limits to him. He laughed softly, a self-imposed rule until then and afterward as well.

Ultimately, she would come around to his way of thinking. If she wanted to see her son, she would have to agree to live with him, perhaps even marry. Marriage or not would be left up to her. There was no other way for the three of them to move forward unless she understood her love for the boy would give her only one choice. He was never going to let either of them out of his life even for one night.

He undressed quickly, slipping into bed with her a slight chuckle on his lips. He didn't miss the desire as well as appreciation in her eyes when she looked at him in the kitchen, his shirt open. He was surprised to see she was already asleep. She might take issue when she woke in the morning. Needing to feel her body pressed against his, he pulled her close, wrapping an arm around her. He was pleased when she pressed into him sighing softly at the warmth or the pleasure she found with him.

The morning sun was just slanting through the window when he looked up to see dark brown eyes, an exact replica of his, peering straight at him. He smiled then placed his finger to his lips, motioning for his son to be quiet. Silently he rose then finding his pants and shirt, dressed. He pulled on his boots, all with Masson staring at him with those huge expressive eyes.

Placing a hand on the boys shoulder they left the room. "I think she needs more sleep. What do you think?"

"You weren't wearing any clothes. Do you do that all the time? Mama makes me wear pajamas to bed.

"Think we should talk about what you want for breakfast."

His mind went to pancakes, something easy for him. While he

could make do in a pinch, he wasn't that great in the kitchen.

"Was Mama naked too?" he asked continuing in the same vein seemingly unwilling to quit until he got a satisfactory response.

"No, she wasn't. I just don't like to wear anything when I sleep." Etienne ruffled the little boy's head as they took the last step to the first floor. "Don't want to mess up the kitchen too much. Are pancakes alright with you?"

"Better than oatmeal. That's what Mama usually makes. Sometimes we get bacon."

Masson sat down at the table, his chin in his hands watching him as he puttered through the kitchen.

Etienne rummaged around in the cupboards until he had all the ingredients he needed for the meal. Setting the bowl on the table beside Masson, "You can stir this if you like." He handed the boy a spoon as he added all the ingredients to the bowl.

"Mama never lets me do this. Says I make too big of a mess," Masson said as some of the contents ended up on the kitchen table.

"Well, I don't care about messes. We'll clean up whatever spills together. A man has to learn how cook so he can eat when he doesn't have someone to do it for him."

Etienne fired up the stove. He set the pan on a burner before dropping in a dollop of butter.

"That's hot. Mama won't let me do anything on the stove."

"You're right. You might burn yourself." Etienne wondered what he would ask next, realizing that he could stir the batter but he'd still never eat if he didn't learn how fry the cakes. He was pretty sure Elisa would have his head if he let Masson anywhere near the hot burner, but in his mind the boy was old enough to do this with help.

"So, you think I should eat this?" He dipped the spoon in the batter letting it slide back into the bowl.

"No." Masson laughed at the question, his eyes twinkling with mischief.

Etienne was willing to take the chance with this endeavor. "Bring a chair over here."

Masson did and Etienne lifted him so he was standing on it in front of the pan. "You're really going to let me fry the cakes?" he asked, his voice filled with excitement at the unexpected opportunity as Etienne handed him the spatula.

"I am but you have to promise to be very careful not to touch the pan. Your mother will never forgive me if you burn yourself. I'll help with the more difficult parts. A person learns to cook one step at a time. As you get older, you'll have more responsibility." He was hopeful this would go well with the boy.

His mother as well.

"I promise. I'm going to be a man."

"Yes, you are."

Etienne smiled lovingly at his son who he was just getting to know one little second at a time. It was about time the boy had a man in his life other than uncle Gil and his grandfather. "Now I'll help you hold the bowl. We'll pour a little of the batter into the pan."

With that accomplished, "I'm glad you came back to us," Masson said his eyes still bright with the excitement of doing something his mother would never allow.

"I am too," Etienne smiled.

Yes, he felt more than ready to settle down with this instant family. He'd had enough adventures to last him a lifetime. Now he wanted a bit of peace and quiet.

They managed to cook most of the pancakes before Elisa entered the kitchen,

"Good morn..." then, "What are you doing?"

"I'm cooking pancakes, Mama. I'm a man."

When she looked at him, her blue-violet eyes blazed with anger as they turned a darker shade of violet. Her fists were clenched tightly by her sides. Etienne understood she wouldn't say anything with the little boy present. He reveled in that fact, hoping that when the other things he was going to tell her after breakfast were revealed it would set this particular anger aside.

"You are doing an excellent job," she told him appearing to keep her seething emotions in check as she walked to him and wrapping her arms around Masson gave him a quick hug. "Why don't you let Etienne finish? You can help me with the berries?"

Adeptly, she lifted him from the chair, quickly setting him on the floor, one hand on the top of his back leading him to the table.

When Etienne watched them, cleaning and sorting the berries, she would shoot him looks across the kitchen that would make a lesser man weep. The anger she bequeathed him with pure and hot. Admittedly, he might have overstepped his bounds but he would never apologize.

His son needed someone to teach him how to be a man and cooking if not a simple task was important along with an array of other things that were not so unusual. There were any number of times he would have gone without a meal if he didn't know how to cook simple things.

He set the plates and forks on the table while Elisa fetched the coffee along with the milk for Masson. The stack of pancakes appeared next as he dished up Masson's plate arranging the berries on top.

"What are your plans for the day?" Elisa asked, eyeing him critically, her brows still furrowed together.

Her shoulders and neck were stiff. He was sure she was worried about the things he was going to talk to her about in privacy. As well she should be, "I'm going home. I'm taking Masson with me. You're welcome to come along if you like." He tried to keep his voice pleasant and unassuming. "The choice, of course, is up to you."

He heard the swift intake of air, watched as she stood quickly, her fork clattering on the floor. "No." It seemed she tried to remain calm, her voice anything but. "No, you are not going anywhere with my son."

"Our son," he gently reminded her, his arms now folded in front of him. "My son, one I haven't seen his entire life. Might I remind you? I mean to make up for lost time beginning this morning."

She looked to Masson who was wide-eyed listening to every word even. His tiny fists were clenched as it seemed he understood what was being said. "You can't take me away from my mama."

He lifted his shoulders keeping his gaze focused on Elisa. "Like I said, she's welcome to come with us."

"Is it just for a sleep over like when I go visit *Papi*? I'm fine with that."

"No, this is for good, for always. The Dubois winery will be your new home until you are grown, Masson. I do want both my son and his mother to live there. I can't force your mama."

Her jaw was clenched tight while the rest of her was shaking. She nodded her head toward the other room. "We need to talk, Etienne." His name was spoken with such fierceness he was surprised at the intensity.

"I'm going to finish my breakfast first." He smiled at her then pointed his fork at her uneaten plate. "You should too. It might be a long day. While my father said he would arrange servants to be there when we arrive, I can't say for sure which ones or if we will have to manage our own dinner."

She sat down, staring at him across the table. "Etienne, you have no rights here. He is my son. I will decide where he lives."

It seemed she chose to talk even with Masson nearby. "Of course I do. I'm his father. We both know that to be the truth. There is no question as to paternity. I was your only lover."

"We are not married."

"I know. Doesn't change a thing."

"You've no rights!"

Masson's gaze drifted between the two soaking in every word, much of what Etienne was sure he wouldn't understand, but they did need to curtail this discussion to a more private time.

He realized she was losing any semblance of control. "Mores the pity but lack of a marriage certificate can be remedied. Just say the word."

Also appearing to think privacy was necessary, she tossed her napkin to the table before she left, marching from the room, head held high with shoulders squared. Etienne heard the front door open then bang shut. It made no difference. Her things would be packed and moved even if she didn't lift a finger. He understood she would come, angry or not, fairness notwithstanding. Elisa would follow Masson.

"More pancakes, Masson?" he asked pleasantly, keeping a partial gaze on the entrance to the kitchen.

"You should really go after Mama. I've never seen her that angry, not even when I came home with all my clothes muddy."

"She needs time by herself to figure things out. There is nothing she can say that will change my mind."

For a moment he felt sorry for her. He barged into her well-ordered life. Now, he was changing it to suit him. It was from his experiences people didn't like change but this, in the end, would be good for all of them.

Well, that was too bad. She'd brought it on herself after all. If she'd told him anything, he would have listened to her and granted concessions where the boy was concerned, but she lied by omission for too many years. Lied when she first saw him, two days ago. Lied to him yesterday before Masson showed up on the front porch, unexpectedly. He would make all the decisions now. She would make the adjustments to her life.

"When are we leaving?" he asked, more eager than his mother to be on the way.

"As soon as the carriage arrives," he smiled picking up the dishes and setting them on the counter. His servants would see to the dishes as well as the packing. "Should be here in less than an hour."

"What if Mama hasn't come back by then?"

"She will." He was very sure of that fact. There was no way she would let him take the boy without her to accompany him.

Once they were living in his home all he needed was to figure out how to convince her to marry him. She seemed against the notion. That fact puzzled him. Just about any other woman he'd been with would have jumped at the chance to become his wife. Daryl MacTavish being the one and only exception he could think of.

He stepped outside, Masson by his side. She was walking across the hill, her movement's jerky, her steps inconsistent. He watched as she stumbled, her knees hitting the ground, her hands following. She was hunched over. A very real concern for her washed over him.

"You stay here. I'm going to see to your mother."

He raced out the door unsure of what he would find. When he reached her, huge, terrifying sobs wracked her slim body.

He had done that to her by his careless words and assumptions yet he regretted nothing. Kneeling beside her, he placed a hand on her back as he searched his mind for words that might lend some measure of comfort.

"A hint at what you planned would have been nice," she said through the sobs. "It's not right."

"And given you a chance to leave here with my son. I don't think so. You could have disappeared in Bordeaux, at Angelique's. I would have never found you. I've already missed too much time with him. Don't intend to miss any more." He was more determined than ever to press his point.

"I wouldn't have done that," she said, moving away from him while trying to wipe the tears away with her hands. "Why can't you just settle into the château by yourself then visit him when the whim hits you?"

"You have the resources, still do if I give you the opportunity to send a message. As I just said either Angelique or Margaux would be happy to help you escape from me. Hell, even Baily and Eric would do the same. Besides, I've missed too much of his life. I intend to see him grow to a man." He wasn't about to take the chance of losing his son again.

"I didn't think of any of that. You can't rip him away from the only home he's known. He will be devastated." She was clutching the lapels of his shirt, begging him with her moisture-laden eyes. He wasn't unmoved but he wasn't going to change his mind.

"Masson will come to love his new home and family. All his things as well as yours will be brought there. It would be nice for the boy to have a real mother and father. Then he would no longer be a bastard. Will you marry me, Elisa?" He thought the fact her son was a bastard would move her to accept the invitation to become his wife.

"No." She rose then and once more her back was stiff. Slowly, she walked toward the house. "No, that's not a reason to place my life in your hands."

He didn't think it would be easy. Hoped she didn't have any more resistance in her. Suddenly she stopped, whirling her skirts flying around her ankles. "Why? Why would I marry you? You don't love me."

"I thought I just gave you the reasons." He smiled at her knowing full well that his motives were not enough for her. He wasn't about to tell her that he did indeed love her. Laying his heart out for her to trample on was not going to happen.

"We don't suit," she said as she pushed herself off the ground with a little help from him. "You are nothing like me."

Thank God we are so very different.

His hands at her waist he tried to steady her. He was grinning at her now. That seemed to make her even angrier, but she remained silent. He enjoyed this prickly side of her. How the devil could he love her when he barely knew her? He didn't know how. His feelings went far deeper than just wanting her. In his life, he'd wanted a lot of women. This was different.

"Are you going to come with us?" He wanted to laugh at the expression on her face and the way her lips thinned at his suggestion.

"I don't have a viable choice so yes."

"Best you get back to the house. It seems the carriage has arrived and Masson is already headed for the carriage as well as eager to discover his new home."

For the first time as he watched his son racing to the transport with a pillow in his hand, he had the feeling of a proud papa.

"The carriage won't leave without you."

She shot out, simply not amused by his words.

"My things are already packed and unless you want to be a little bit nicer, I don't have any reason to wait for you. You can always come later, tomorrow or the next day. Whatever suits." He baited her, was ever eager learn her reactions.

He knew she would reply to him, also understood he was just waiting for her to make a commitment. She picked up her skirts marching to the house ahead of him. Sighing heavily, he understood the long road ahead of them would not be easy.

She strode up the steps ahead of them, to be met with men bringing her trunk downstairs and loading it on a cart. Masson was leaning out the carriage door and waving his arms excitedly.

"Mama, you don't have to pack. They are doing it for you."

"You overconfident bastard."

"I know you, Elisa, understand where your heart lies." He did in his own way understand her. One thing he did well was understanding women.

Her hands fell to her sides as she stared at everyone scurrying about in her home. She would be leaving the house, making a new home coupled with a new life at his château. He prayed they would find some measure of peace together because he meant to have her for his wife in every was and at any cost.

Surprisingly, Pruitt was there beside her. He was helping her into the carriage. They said a few words then his father tipped his hat before heading for the horse he'd ridden from the vineyard. His new family sat inside his carriage waiting for him.

For the short trip he decided to ride his horse, which his father brought. The conversation inside the vehicle was not something he wanted to endure. He and his father rode together for a couple of miles before the two roads forked.

"She has come to your way of thinking then?" Pruitt laughed as the time passed.

"Hardly. She's stubborn. Refuses to listen but she does love her son." Etienne wasn't used to having his orders disobeyed. For a moment he was sure his father would tell him what he thought of his decision.

"She is that, stubborn as well as determined to have everything her way. She will not give in easily. You should understand it was not Angelique that kept the news from you. In the end, she felt you should know. It was Elisa. She was terrified of what might happen that you might disavow your child. It was easier to make sure everyone kept the secret," Pruitt said.

"I've never been with a woman who didn't fall into my arms. Granted most wanted me for what I could give them. Ironic, isn't it. Now, the one woman I want doesn't want me. No, Elisa doesn't want to admit to wanting me, but I will make sure she learns I won't hurt her."

He looked over his shoulder at the lumbering carriage wishing things here had been different. He supposed he could have been gentler, more understanding. Impatient to get on with his life, he barged on ahead with no concern for her sensibilities. Since he'd been denied his son for four years, he now wanted everything taken care of yesterday.

"Perhaps if you had found her before she reached her mother's place you would have had a better chance of persuading her to your way."

"She was so different. In my arms, it seemed as if we were a perfect fit but she disappeared. No one knew where she lived in Paris. I spent too much time there searching for her as well as finishing family business rather than heading for Bordeaux."

"If you had found her in Paris then maybe you would have had a chance with her," Pruitt spoke thoughtfully.

He remembered his first look into her eyes. He was lost the moment she whispered his name. Along with the instant, he turned to the sound. "Can't live the rest of my life thinking that way. I have to make sure our future is so much different. Now, Masson comes first."

They reached the fork. Pruitt was heading in a different direction. "Don't hurt her, son. She as well as the child mean everything to me."

Etienne laughed softly. "I don't intend to hurt her, only love her."

"Perhaps you should tell her that."

He wasn't sure if he could ever trust his heart with her. All she'd done with it so far was break it. Suffice it to say, he would keep her close protecting her from herself as well as their son.

At his château, Elisa's trunk was placed in the master chamber while Masson was allowed to pick out a room for himself.

Elisa stood in the middle of the entrance, her hands clasped in front of her, her gaze drifting upstairs, the telltale signs of insecurity and fear shaking her slight frame. Her face was white, her eyes sunken and dark.

"Come, this is not so bad. You will grow to like the château. You cannot stay in the entryway forever. Let me show you around." His hand was pressed lightly on the small of her back, urging her forward. "Would you like a look at your new home?" he asked again. "It seems Masson has already perused the entire east wing. Next he'll be sliding down the bannister."

"I would sleep in a different room from you." Her breath whispered out in a silent rush.

Against his larger frame, he felt her stiffen. "It is presumptive of you to put me in your bed without my consent."

"Possibly the barn would suit you? I'll make sure you have blankets. It is warm and dry, perhaps even hot if I were to join you. Would you like that?" He watched as she seemed to flinch at his words, color suffusing her cheeks. Provoking her might not be such a good idea. He would gain nothing from the harsh sarcastic words.

The rest of the afternoon passed in silence between them while he and Masson carried on a delightful conversation. The boy had questions about what he would do now, how much time he would spend playing with him, along with what chores he would be given. Etienne told him he would hire a tutor for him as soon as he turned five. Told him also about other things he would learn now that he had a father.

Elisa remained quiet throughout dinner, sipping her wine occasionally with seeming caution as to the quantity. One small glass lasted her for more than an hour then she set it aside refusing more.

He took care of Masson before bedtime reading him a book then tucking him in before calling for Elise to give the boy a goodnight kiss.

"I'm tired. I have a headache. I'd like to retire now."

Her voice was soft. She refused to look at him.

"Not yet. I'd like to spend some of the evening with my soon to be wife. I'm sure you have questions that need to be answered."

She looked at him, a startled expression in her expressive eyes. Then she told him quite acidly, "I'm not going to be your wife. You do not have my consent."

He was content she did not use the word never in her statement. "Your denials become increasingly less adamant. If I didn't know better, I'd think you were coming around to the idyllic notion of marrying me." He linked his arm in hers before escorting her downstairs despite her pleas to go to bed. If she were to go to bed now, he would join her and the way he was feeling he would have no restraint where she was concerned. His body and mind were stretched thin, nearly to the breaking point.

They walked through the house then outside to a patio surrounded by trees and spring flowers. The chairs were lavish with pillows. "I'd like to enjoy some conversation and another glass of wine with you. We don't even have to talk. I won't ask you to marry me again, at least not tonight." He smiled at her hoping the gesture would be to her liking.

She inhaled a deep breath before she had enough air inside her lungs to speak. "That's good because the answer would still be no."

~ * ~

Two burley men sat in a *boulangerie* in Bordeaux drinking and eating the fresh baked bread.

"Etienne Dubois has a boy. Did you know that?" Leod asked, needing revenge, thinking the child would be a means to accomplish that.

He'd misjudged Etienne when he last encountered him. Didn't expect his honest loyalty to the French government. When he tried to buy his silence, he discovered Dubois could not be bought. "We could make sure he never sees the little one again. Make sure the child is left in an orphanage somewhere. That would devastate the man, exactly what I want to do. Leave him desperate and hurting."

"That's taking a huge risk. Too much for me," Troy told him, leaning back and methodically studying the scene outside the window. "The man is lethal. It would be unwise to go up against him. He has many resources along with dangerous friends, more than either of us."

"Not if he's taken by surprise. I for one would like to see him hurt, a deep dark hurt that he will never recover from. One that he will take to his grave."

As it was the government confiscated everything Leod owned. He was left with nothing except the clothes he was wearing.

You should take the mother of his boy too. Strike twice and inflict the most harm."

"What I know is that Angelique would do anything to spare her daughter or pay anything to get her back. If there is a grandchild involved, the profits will double," Leod said gleefully seeing the possible blackmail that could last for many years. "You might even be able to leech money from Margaux. I would rather have the money than revenge. We cannot have both."

"How do plan on achieving this. I'm sure the château is guarded heavily as was the cottage. The Madams are not fools. Etienne Dubois understands his enemies and just because he has retired it doesn't mean someone will not seek vengeance if we hurt him. True enough the man understands that fact."

"I don't know as of yet how to go about the revenge I'm seeking. I'm sure something will come to me. For now, we need to watch the place, learn everything we can about what they do, day in and day out. If we can find an opening, then we should take it." Leod sat back in his chair, arms clasped across his chest more determined than ever to take everything away from Dubois.

He was unwavering in the notion that Etienne would pay for his lost enterprise as well as his wife and child. While they were still alive, he would never be able to return to them. He no longer had the funds to bring them to him.

Etienne Dubois should suffer the same fate.

"Should we visit Angelique's and see if we can learn something new?" Troy asked. "Wouldn't mind a bit of entertainment tonight."

"You go. I might join you later. For now, I need to think and plan. There is too much at stake to leave to chance."

Leod watched as his friend left the bakery. This had to work or both of them would be dead. Troy was too naïve to think this could end in his death. Etienne would not let anyone who threatened his family escape his wrath.

Chapter Five

Saying yes to Etienne would solve all of Elisa's problems, she was sure of it. She still held back, unsure of herself coupled with the question of his true feelings for her. Sun bronzed, confident of himself, he was everything she was not. He had a way of moving silently and quickly, surprising her when she least expected it. He was an experienced man of the world. Her knowledge revolved around the tiny cottage where she no longer lived. He ripped her from the only real home she'd ever known.

"What are you thinking, *mon bijoux*?"

Her gasp of surprise didn't seem to sway Etienne in any way. She stared into her glass for seconds then some more seconds until she wanted to scream. Speaking her feelings then telling him she wasn't sure of herself didn't work. The wine was dark, rippling gently when her hand shook just the tiniest amount. Tucking her bottom lip beneath her teeth, she changed her attention to him, his brown eyes compelling her to bare her soul, to tell all. There was something about those damn eyes that drew her to him.

She resigned herself to speak. "So many things." Her words were flippant and meant to set him off track, perchance make him question himself, but she doubted if that would work. Did Etienne Dubois ever question himself? She didn't believe it for one second.

"Just one will do." He laughed, reaching out to feather a gentle caress along her cheek before letting his hand glide down her neck. "I can out wait you. Waiting is something I'm very good at. My job as a French spy gave me a wealth of experience in that particular area."

She thought perhaps she could surprise him, change his confident smile to a frown of wonder or concentration. If he didn't expect her to agree to at least one of his proposals, it might set him off guard as well as give her some insight into his plans for their future.

Her glass rested on her lips as a tiny drop of wine slid down her throat. "I have often wondered what it would be like to have you again. We could try this evening after Masson goes to bed," then she paused, still looking at him over the rim, "I never know what to call what we did that night. Was it making love or having sex or making lust? Perhaps it was just a good fuck." She lowered her lashes in what she hoped was a flirtatious gesture.

At her outrageous words, he coughed, spewing wine from his lips. His grin broadened the dimple growing deeper as one side of his lips crept upward. "Most likely a little of all three. We can find out tonight. A second round if you're amenable, as you just implied you were. I for one would like nothing better than to make love to my hopefully soon to be wife. Your education at a brothel has put words in your mouth no lady would utter. I find that I enjoy hearing you use those words. We could even try the latter if that is what you choose."

"You appreciate the candor."

She wondered what he would say to that, other than he enjoyed the words coming from her.

"Sometimes," he shrugged, lifting his broad shoulders while his shirt tightened against the play of his muscles across his back and chest.

The sight mesmerized her. He entranced her in every way possible.

Elisa swallowed hard. She might have just set something in motion she wasn't at all sure she was ready for. "My mother taught me to be honest in all things, but I never bargained on being pregnant before I was married. That one tiny miscarriage of fairness changed my life forever. I haven't wanted to repeat that night. Still don't."

Although she knew that tonight would not end up with her carrying his child once again. Her woman's time was nearly here and she understood from the women in the brothel it was a safe time for a woman to have sex and precautions need not be taken. With no worries, she could have him for one more night.

"You've hardly been honest with me," he reminded her.

"You're right but it was by omission. I never lied openly to you."

She was plucking at the buttons on her dress, the motion giving her a small amount of calmness. It seemed he watched her, smiling. She wondered at his thoughts as she followed his gaze to the bared skin below the fasteners. She drew a long deep breath, shuddering as it seemed just his gaze heated her. He didn't even need to touch her for her to melt under his scrutiny.

"That night, why did you whisper my name and catch my attention when I was halfway up the steps. I've been told by numerous people, perhaps even you, but I'd like to hear the words again. That single moment has haunted me for the last few years almost as much as the reasons that you didn't want to see me again."

His question was fair. Still, she didn't want to answer him. "You know all this. Why go over it?"

Buttons began to pop free as she tried to put them back but he reached out to her, holding her hand.

"I like to look at you. I stopped when I heard my name. You looked so very familiar the rare sight of you caused my breath to catch in my throat. I felt a very real need to have you, to discover more about you. My body trembled with that same need. I never felt anything like it before or since. To me you were the most beautiful woman I've ever seen. Still, I didn't remember you. Never recalled the little girl I met that day in your yard and kissed. Still don't. Gil said you gave us water on a hot summer day."

"Even though I want to, I won't share a bed with you tonight. It's not what is best for me. It's not what I want my son to see. He told me he saw me in bed with you and you were naked. Is that right? He has questions now that I have no idea how to answer. He is too young to see his mama in bed with a man who is not her husband."

"He will have needs. In time, he will have women. You cannot shelter him and protect him from something that is natural and normal. And," the pause was long as she was sure he was thinking, "I want you to be my wife." His words were meant to convince her of something she didn't agree with.

"It's not right."

She turned from him seeking air as she tried for breath along with the understanding he prompted. At the same time, she could not reason with this man. She knew she didn't like to think of her son, older, mature, bedding a woman, any woman.

His soft kiss on the back of her neck surprised her. She closed her eyes, willing him to stop, but the gentle slow caresses continued with practiced ease coupled with his expertise. She did not want her son to be able to seduce so easily, yet she didn't want him to be afraid of a woman's touch or touching in return. She knew she could not have it both ways.

"Come to bed with me, *mon cherie*. We can talk more at a later time. Now is the time to feel and give pleasure to each other. We both want what the other can give to us."

The pull he had over her didn't surprise her. Once again, she was falling under his erotic spell, and truly she didn't see a reason not to succumb to desire and the delicious passion she recalled so easily and longed for every night. So many times she dreamed of him, of his touch, the way he stroked her.

He scooped her into his arms. Before she could barely breathe, they were up the steps and in the master bedroom. He set her on the bed then came down on top of her. The weight of his body pushed her into the mattress, yet she didn't feel confined. Her fingers wound around his neck, sliding slowly into his hair. It was so soft and thick. His scent was of man and spice of the spring air and the vineyards. "Your lips and your hair, so soft," she whispered to him only to hear the manly chuckle.

"And all of you is soft, every seductive part of you. I intend to find every soft part before this night is over." He trailed kisses along the exposed skin where she had unfastened buttons. He continued the process, exploring, nipping enticing her with his proficiency.

He rose above her then on his knees while he unbuttoned his shirt. Her hands slid up his muscular torso, touching him, feeling the amazing heat of his body, pushing at the sleeves, wishing all the while he would get rid of it. "You are just as I remember."

She closed her eyes. He bent close and touched each breast with his lips before tasting and possessing her mouth.

His lips opened over hers, his tongue playing with hers while creating sensations she'd never forgotten. At night had desperately missed. She heard the tiny response spiral up from her lungs as he touched her in more tender spots, more erotic places. Her body twisted and arched again him, pleading for more.

"Etienne," his name was on her lips as well as her mind. "We cannot do this. I'm sure it's not right."

Once more she arched to meet him, tried to give him better access to those intimate places she wanted him to caress. The buttons were all free now. He leaned back to examine his handiwork. His eyes were predatory as he slowly lowered himself to her. Again, and again, she pushed at his shirt moving down his arms then ran her hands along his back fascinated by the rippling muscles.

"Elisa," he whispered her name with such reverence her breath caught in the back of her throat.

He moved with fluid grace. His touch was gentle and sweet, so like the man she was growing to love more everyday despite his stubborn nature where her son was concerned. This was the early evening, pale blue moonlight filtered in the French doors leading to the upstairs balcony and cast a long rectangle of light on the wooden floor before spiraling across the rug.

Etienne lay above her, the tautly carved edges of his chin coupled with the slightly crooked line of his nose were all reminiscent of their past. The centers of his eyes were darkening as he searched her face. There was so much desire in the dark depth of his eyes. There was also a question.

Elisa looked up at him. "What is it?" She let his palm encompass her cheek, turning into his caress with an eagerness that surprised her as she tried to forget all the reasons she had for not allowing this intimacy. His head lowered a fraction. Her hands lifted and slipped behind his neck. Her fingers threaded in the hair at his nape. She raised her face as she urged him forward with her fingertips. The air fairly hummed between them.

"After tonight you will not deny me ever again." Etienne's mouth fit itself to hers. There was a hard and heady hunger sustaining the kiss. His lips moved over hers insistently, greedy for the taste of her, demanding she give back to him in return. His tongue pressed for entry. It wasn't enough for him to touch the corner of her mouth or trace the line of her lips. Just as she craved for more, it seemed he did too.

"I need..." Elisa's hands slipped from Etienne's neck to his shoulders.

At his sweetly urgent stroking, her mouth parted wider. The kiss deepened. She answered the heated sensation, thrusting against him, not only with her tongue but with all of her body. The familiarity of the kiss was being repeated all along her length. She felt his arms coming around her, cradling her. She knew the hard length of his legs by the separation of hers and the broadness of his back when her arms clutched him close. There was no turning back now. She was sure he would not allow her to say no.

"I understand, *mon bijoux*. I need you too."

He shifted, twisting so they lay stretched across the bed. His hard, deep kiss had become a dozen swiftly pressing ones. She felt the imprint of his mouth on her eyes, her cheek, at the base of her throat. His tongue found the sensitive spot just behind her ear. His touch there made her body arch and her fingertips whiten against his shirt. Still, he wore the damn shirt. She wanted it off, needed to feel the naked length of his body pressed intimately against hers.

Etienne had no patience for the remaining buttons. He tore at the ones still fastened intending to replace the gown as soon as possible. He pushed the loosened neckline over her shoulders, along with the straps of her chemise. His hand slipped beneath her bodice as he eagerly pushed the fabric upward.

She flinched not from the intimacy of his touch but from the heat roaring to life within her. Still, he paused and looked at her, his gaze full of raw, hungry passion. She didn't turn away. He held her racing heartbeat in his palm, the edge of his hand cupping her breast. His thumb passed lightly across her tightly puckered nipple. When Elisa's breath caught, he bent his head kissing her again, giving her back the breath she had lost in the moment.

He felt good. His weight. His mouth. The shape of his lips against her skin. Pleasure hummed through her driving her to feel his magic touch more strongly with each stroke of his hand. Elisa's hands slid under the material of his shirt, stroking his skin. Fascinated by the way his flesh retracted under her sweeping touch, she didn't want this to end, not tonight. He sat up long enough to rid himself of his shirt. It sallied over the edge of the bed as she was reaching for him again.

"You are mine," he whispered close to her ear. "Always."

"Only for tonight."

A low growl followed then Etienne pushed the edge of her bodice below her breasts. She watched him, saw his hands upon her. Where his thumb had grazed her nipple, the nub was like a hard pink pebble. He bent. His mouth closed over the tip, worrying it gently between his teeth, touching, pulled gently. She shuddered. The movement that swelled through her felt as if he tugged ribbons of pure sensation from her. Her fingertips trailed upward along his spine, touching upon each vertebra. He raised his head, his dimpled smile catching her breath, reaching into her heart. She tried to say something. The words never came as he gave equal attention to her other breast. Her fingers tightened on the curling ends of his hair at his nape. She longed to take everything he gave into her to savor every moment, keeping in her mind for future loveless nights.

He laid a trail of kisses between her breasts. They traveled upward, ending at the curve of her neck. He sipped her skin. When she moved under him, her thigh was pressed to his groin. Of their own accord his hips thrust against her.

"*Mon Dieu*," he groaned.

Her skin seemed to vibrate against the moist heat of his mouth. He raised his head a fraction. She was watching him, her eyes intent and alert, unwilling to miss one moment of this divine magic.

"Ah, but there is a certain willfulness in your desire. Are you challenging me to something or are you daring yourself? Your sensual maturity has not quite outstripped your innocence. So, I cannot be sure of the emotions I'm seeing in your face as well as your beautifully expressive eyes."

Elisa sensed his hesitation. Was surprised by it. She raised her face and gently touched her mouth to his. Her lips moved over his mouth in the manner he taught her. Her tongue traced the edges before slipping along his upper lip. She let his shudder pass into her as the weight of him cocooned her again. They engaged in a sweet battle where his mouth was a formidable weapon while her hands were no shield at all.

"It is time." His whiskey smooth voice penetrated her heart and soul, reaching into the deepest part of her.

He knelt, looking at her. She understood what he saw. Slowly, her gown was pushed to her hips, then lower, past her thighs, her knees, until it was sliding over the edge of the bed. Her chemise gathered at her waist. Her petticoats were already a tangle about her legs, hiked up to the level of her knees. Her calves lay bare and smooth against the bedcovers. She raised one leg and wound it around his, stretching with feline grace to feel more of him against her. In the back of his throat, he groaned softly as her palms stroked his back and arms. Her fingers edged along his waistband, sometimes dipping beneath it. His skin burned where she touched him.

Etienne rolled away from Elisa making short order of his clothes. He made no attempt to hide his ardent arousal but turned toward her, unashamed by his body's response to her shapely form.

"I don't really remember what you looked like or that you were so..." She couldn't finish.

"I remember exactly how you looked that night. I'll also remember tonight in every minute detail. Little has changed yet you're older, more mature in many ways. You've had my baby. You are no longer coltishly slender but more womanly."

Elisa's flush covered her entire body. It never occurred to her to look away. In truth, she was fascinated, frightened, and a little awed. "I don't remember," she said softly.

She glanced at Etienne's taut features, the creases at the corners of his eyes, the muscle working in his jaw then slowly reached out to him, "Does it hurt?"

He stared at her a moment his half smile along with his dimple transformed his features as he bent over her. "More than you know, more than you could ever guess. There is a remedy though," he fairly growled. Kissing her full on the mouth, he finished with her undergarments until they were both splendidly naked.

Elisa's hands trailed to the small of his back then over his buttocks. The texture of his skin delighted her. She kissed his shoulder. She moved lower. Her fingernail flicked his flat nipple. Her tongue aroused the tight bud. This time whatever happened in this bed, she thought, was not simply being done to her. She was doing it to him also. The power of that knowledge was heady.

Etienne's hand traveled over the length of her thigh. The caress was insistent as a shiver of desire coursed through Elisa. His mouth covered hers while his fingers teased the underside of her raised knee. He drew them across the back of the thigh then the soft inner side. Her lips parted. Her legs parted. He touched her intimately, his fingers making a gentle exploration of the swollen damp folds of her femininity. She was tense now, but not resistant. When he lifted his head to watch her, she drew in a ragged breath.

The response of her body surprised her. She was warm, wet where he touched her. Her hands fell away from the back of his neck before curling in the covers beneath her. His hand was between her legs. As he moved his long fingers, he was watching her. She couldn't look anywhere but at him, feel anything but the heat. It was growing white-hot just beneath his fingers. There was a certain way he would touch her that would make sparks skitter along the surface of her skin. She drew in her lower lip as she sipped her next breath. Sensation started to coil in her quivering and rippling inside ever higher, always stronger than the previous second. She lifted her hips slightly, pushing with her heels against the mattress. Her finger tightened. Her eyes fluttered closed.

He nudged her mouth, kissing her softly. "Open them for me," he said against her lips. "Wider." She raised her lids. Her legs parted more. "Perfect. You are so beautiful," he whispered just before he froze, his dark eyes narrowing.

"What is it?" she asked, suddenly alarmed by his change of expression. The intimacy between them was over more suddenly than she could have ever expected.

"Hush." He placed his finger on her lips pulling what covers he could find across her before he found his pants and slipped them on. "We have an intruder."

"Mama?" The tiny voice so close to the bed shocked and

embarrassed her. It was exactly what she didn't want to happen, what she had feared. She sat up, covers to her breast. "Masson. What is it? What's wrong?" She wanted to hold him in her arms but Etienne picked him up, cradling him gently.

"Is something wrong?" Etienne asked his voice low and soft. There was no censure in it.

"I wanted mama. I was afraid. I couldn't sleep." His voice was small and defeated.

"Then you shall have her," Etienne said but you must give her a moment.

"Were you hurting her?" he asked.

"No, I was not hurting your mama. Never would I hurt her." Etienne looked over his shoulder at Elisa. "Perhaps you should give your mama a quick hug. I will see you to bed. There are things we need to talk about." Then he turned to Elisa. "Is that alright with you?"

Surprised he asked her for permission, she nodded trying to hold the sheets in front of her and hug her son as he ran to her. "Mama, he really didn't hurt you? I heard noises. I didn't know."

"Would I let you go with him if he did?" She ruffled his hair before giving him a quick kiss on the cheek.

"No, I don't think so but what were you doing?"

She looked at her son then Etienne wondering what she could say. Perchance it was best if Etienne handled this situation. She caught her lip beneath her teeth as she watched them in the doorway.

"I will stay with him until he falls asleep."

"Thank you," she murmured.

They were gone then she was left with her thoughts as well as the knowledge that but for her son's appearance, she would have given herself to Etienne again. She melted in his arms. His lovemaking was impossible to resist. All it took was a kiss to surrender to him.

He knew that. To get what he wanted, he would always capitalize on that knowledge in the future. Wrapping one of the covers around her, she rose from the bed. Looking through her things she found a nightgown and slipped it over her head.

The covers were warm around her but not as warm as his hard

body pressing hers to the mattress. She thought it would be hard to fall asleep, but it seemed it was easier than she expected.

When he slipped into bed pulling her gently to him, she sighed softly pushing herself against his hard body. Protectively he wrapped an arm around her then with a heavy sigh pulled her close.

~ * ~

Etienne had not counted on a child interrupting their lovemaking. This was something new he would have to take into consideration in the future, including a lock on the door. He couldn't blame Masson for being afraid in the night. The home was new to him. The little boy still didn't have all his precious possessions in bed with him.

Crawling back into bed, Elisa was just as warm and giving as he remembered. She was asleep though. He didn't want to wake her to resume their lovemaking. There would be tomorrow night along with many more after that. It seemed he waited a lifetime to have her in his arms again. Then, well, he was sure it would not be the last time the little boy stood over them when they were making love. Explaining what he was doing with his mother was another challenge all together. He would have to work on that aspect and as Masson grew older, formulate the right words. Tonight, his explanation had been brief with few to no details. All he truly did was reassure the boy he wasn't hurting his mother.

He closed his eyes then and knew he slept for a few hours before the sun shining in through the window woke him. Before he fell asleep thoughts of seducing her again flitted through his head, but he understood Masson would need her or him in the morning. If she was as exhausted as she seemed, he would let her sleep all day if she needed to. He would be there for his son.

He heard the low moan of pain. She was curled into a tight ball, a soft sob emanating from her as she tried to push away from him. He had no idea. No thought as to what could possibly be wrong. This was not something he anticipated.

"What is it?" he asked concerned, pushing damp hair from her face, trying to understand.

"No..." She closed her eyes. "Go away. Just go away. Don't you have something to do?"

His heart caught in his throat having no idea what was causing this reaction. Thought of the night before. Perhaps she was mortified that he had so easily seduced her when she wanted to refuse him. He'd known that from the beginning, but it was only fear that caused her reticence.

"Tell me what is wrong?" He needed to let her know he was disturbed. She couldn't get away with hiding her feelings from him. He wouldn't allow it. "I'll get you whatever you would like. Should I send for the doctor?"

"Just need for you to leave me alone." She pulled a pillow over her head. "I'll help myself. Used to this. Nothing you can do. I'm not sick." Her words were uttered into the pillow.

He wasn't going to allow her to lie by omission again. She was going to tell him what was wrong. If she needed assistance, he meant to give it to her. With the back of his hand, he touched her forehead. "No fever, but you are a bit warm."

"Please." She looked at him, the lines around her eyes strained with pain and her blue violet eyes hazy with what he assumed was the discomfort. "I can deal with this. Just go. If you want to help, see to Masson for me. You can bring me a cup of tea when you get a chance. Masson will show you the kind I like." She paused then, "If you brought it from my house."

"Alright. I don't like this." He was backing away, watching her as he stepped slowly toward the door, his mind racing with possible scenarios. The control he was used to vanished in these few moments. He didn't like the helpless feeling coursing through him. His plans now taking on a new shape as he watched her curled in a tight ball. Despite her efforts, she could not keep the groan inside.

"You don't have to like it. I just want privacy that's all."

He was confused more than a little frightened. She seemed to accept whatever was happening with her body. Then he realized what was happening, everything coming to the forefront of his mind. "I will leave you alone for now and bring you the tea as soon as we can make it. Rest assured when you are feeling a bit better you will explain yourself. You will not keep secrets from me."

His last words were not well done of him. He needed to know everything if he was to asses this the best and the most intelligent way possible. She also needed to learn to trust him with her most private thoughts. Best she get used to it now.

Leaving the room, he strode downstairs wondering what he could learn from Masson. He grinned, probably more than Elisa would think. She said he knew what tea she liked but yesterday she drank coffee not tea. This was not a normal occurrence.

Masson was sitting at the table, a scone in hand with strawberry preserves spread on it. "Where's Mama?"

"She's in bed. She doesn't feel well this morning," he said, watching the little boy closely for any sign that he knew what was wrong with his mother.

He lifted his tiny shoulders. "It happens. Are you going to cook some bacon? I want bacon. You don't have to tell Mama."

The boy reinforced his earlier guess. "How often?"

"That we have bacon. Not so often. Mama always says that it's only for special occasions."

He knelt down beside the little boy. "No, that your mother wants her special tea."

Somehow, he felt as if he was pulling teeth but what did he expect. This was a four-and-a-half-year-old. He knew life as it appeared to him.

"I don't know. Every so often I suppose. What does it matter? Can we have bacon?"

Etienne smiled, his guess was probably true. He was sure Elisa would take exception to his knowing. She was very private and shy, innocent with no experiences dealing intimately with a man. He reminded himself he had been her only lover, of that he was sure. Her reactions last night were hesitant as well as untried even though she responded so completely and with deliciously raw passion. He felt her hunger for him. For the first time he wondered how old she was, twenty-two or twenty-three. She had taken care of their son with no thought to herself. His admiration for her grew.

"Yes, today you can have bacon, tomorrow also if you can show me your mother's favorite tea," he smiled at the boy, hoping the incentive would help him.

"That's easy, she always kept it on the shelf."

He stopped looking around the kitchen at all the different and very empty shelves then turned to him, shaking his head his disappointment clearly showing. "I don't know where it is."

"Would you recognize the jar if you saw it?" He was pulling jars from the unpacked boxes that had been loaded into the kitchen yesterday evening.

He shrugged again, "I don't know. I still want the bacon."

"I know. I'll make sure you have it as soon as we find the tea. Your mama needs it now not later. She's not feeling so well. You do want to make her feel better. Don't you?"

"Yes."

Painstakingly, and too slow for Etienne's peace of mind, they went through each box, pulling every item and placing it on the shelf, Masson telling him no every time something new was inspected. By the time they reached the third box, Etienne was wondering if the little boy had any idea what the jar of medicinal tea looked like. Frustrated to the tips of his toes, he was losing patience. When his cook walked in the door, he set her to work on the bacon. Even if they didn't find the right jar, the boy deserved the treat.

"That's it." Masson was pointing at a jar. "Right there. I know it is."

There were two small packets of tealeaves left in the jar. Etienne breathed in a huge breath of air, relieved that at least this part of the ordeal was over. He wondered if Elisa would chide him for taking so long to bring her the what she asked for.

Handing the tea to the cook, "Will you make this? As soon as it is brewed, let me know."

His cook looked at the jar and the label. "You know what this is for?" she asked, her brows pulling together.

"I believe so."

"Perhaps you should let me take it to her. She'll be more comfortable if a woman—"

"No."

This was something he needed to speak with Elisa about. He wanted to know every detail as well as how often she needed the tea. He wanted her trust in the future as well as in every aspect of their lives together. From the look in his cook's expression this was no ordinary concoction.

She set the jar down then continued her work with breakfast. Before he sat down beside his son, the water was on the stove. He would wait for the tea to be ready.

While he was watching the water, he went over everything he needed to talk to Elisa about. She wasn't going to like the conversation. Of that he was sure. So be it. They would have it. He wouldn't take no or silence to his questions.

"Here you are. You sure you don't want me to take it to your..."

"My wife soon," Etienne said with a half-smile. "No need for you to worry about the living arrangements here. They are what they are, as they should be."

He kissed Masson on the forehead. "Don't eat all the bacon. You need to leave some for your mother. If she has a piece or two, she might not get as angry with us."

"She won't want anything. Never eats when she's sick," Masson told him as he happily chewed on a piece of bacon.

"I will see that Elisa eats."

He left the kitchen with more information rumbling around in his head. The cook had added a piece of toasted bread spread with a generous amount of butter on the plate with the tea.

She was still curled into a tiny ball. She must have heard him walk inside because she rolled over. Her hair was damp against her face, her eyes vague. She tried to sit up but fell back. Good Lord, this was worse than he previously thought.

"Just wait a moment. I'll help you." He set the tray down before arranging the pillows behind her then helping her to a sitting position.

She pushed hair from her face. She'd never looked so small and helpless to him as she did now.

"Thank you," she whispered a small moan escaping with the

words. "I don't mean to be so much trouble. You don't have to stay. I'll be fine."

He heard the pain in the tenor of her voice, saw the exhaustion in her eyes. "Does this stuff help whatever is hurting you?" he asked as he poured her a cup. "Be careful, it's hot."

She didn't answer but held the saucer in one hand, the handle of the cup in the other. She sipped slowly then as it cooled, she drank more deeply. "It will help for a few hours."

"Then you'll be in pain again." He meant to ask the same questions he asked Masson, but this time he hoped he would hear better and more detailed answers.

It seemed she was searching for tealeaves she stared so hard into her cup. Silence continued but he could wait. He had a lot of practice.

"You should go now. I don't need you here." Obviously, she didn't want any part of the very beginning of the inquisition he planned.

"Not until I learn a few things." He sat down on the side of the bed then leaned against the headboard. Staring at the ceiling, he rested his hands behind his head. He was taking a few minutes to clarify his thoughts.

She picked up the piece of bread then set it down again. "If it means you'll leave then, yes." Her voice held a wealth of indignation coupled with a lot of irritation as well. "How I feel is none of your business."

"Since you're living with me, as long as you're the mother of my child, I'm making it my business. Your well-being is important to both of us. He needs you to be healthy."

Etienne was still staring at the ceiling while thinking of things to say that might put her at ease but his thoughts kept returning to the problem at hand.

"I'll move back to the cottage."

"Suit yourself but Masson stays here." He heard the indignant sigh, felt the need to laugh but wisely held it back.

He was beginning to know her well enough that she was fumbling in her head for something she could tell him. Short of a lie, there was nothing but the truth in front of her. He wasn't going anywhere. He recognized Bessy as soon as she walked in the door. She came from Angelique's place. While he didn't understand exactly why she was here, he was pretty sure it had something to do with Elisa and the monthly pain.

Finished with the brew, she set the cup back on the tray, her hands folded neatly in her lap. Her brows were drawn tightly together leaving crease marks. She pulled her hair back then smoothly wound the mass of it into a tight bun on top of her head with only a few strands falling softly around her face. She was beautiful even in this moment. He thought then she would always be beautiful to him.

"Yes, you guessed right. In a couple of hours, I'll need another cup. Too bad the effects don't last very long." She closed her eyes with the effort those to sentences caused her.

"But you feel better now, so I'm assuming you are up to answering a few of the questions I have. Since you have the tea and Masson knows about it, I'm going to guess that this happens frequently. Why?"

"Not so often," she looked away from him, studying the patio outside the French doors as if she'd like to vanish there.

"I can carry you outside for some fresh air if you'd like that. How often?" He offered searching her face and seeing the immediate withdrawal from him.

"No."

"Very well, how often?"

"Do you have to keep asking that?" She was clearly disturbed, her fingers clutching the covers until her knuckles were white.

"Yes."

He was pretty sure she wanted to get away from him. He was also sure he knew why she wasn't moving. There was moisture in her eyes. He was having a devil of a time ignoring the tears and walking away. This conversation was important for their future. Walking away would set the wrong precedence.

"How long?" he asked again when she didn't say anything.

"Once every month or so." Her words were so low and soft he could barely hear them.

In any case, it was what he expected her to tell him when she finally spoke.

"Mama, are you alright?" Masson poked his head in the door. "We've saved bacon for you. I told Papa you wouldn't want it."

"I'm fine. Come here." She patted the opposite side of the bed where he was sitting.

He ran over to his mother for a quick hug. "Bessy is going to play with me until you need more tea."

Then he turned to Etienne. "You can play too if you want."

"I will as soon as I finish speaking with your mother." This conversation could last well into the morning and well past the second cup of tea. Her solid reluctance now spoke volumes to him.

With those words Elisa's expression changed again. He understood she was embarrassed but still...

"I'm done."

"Then I guess I won't be playing with you this morning because I'm not leaving until your mama decides to enlighten me about the tea." He ran the back of his hand along her cheek, "Until she talks to me."

They were silent until the door closed behind Masson and they heard the last remnants of his footsteps down the steps.

Then she turned on him, "How dare you? You cannot waltz into my life after years and years of absence then presume to be the ruler of me expecting me to tell you everything you ask. I have nothing to tell you." Her eyes were blazing while her shoulders were shaking with the same passion he saw in her last night.

"I've only been absent because you never told me about my son." Then, "It's your woman's time." He decided the torment he was inflicting by his silence had gone on long enough. "Correct me if I'm wrong."

The mutinous look along with the rising color on her face told him he wasn't wrong. Her chin rose slightly once again she stared out the window. "It's not your business."

He chose to ignore the ridiculous statement and continued. "Bessy comes once a month to help you with Masson. I'm assuming she usually arrives a day or two early just to make sure she is with you on the worst day. This month she was a bit late, wasn't she?"

He paused to see if she would acknowledge his words or deny them. She gifted him with a quick nod of her head.

"The first day is the worst," he continued, "but the pain subsides after a day or two."

He picked up her hand in his, rubbing the back with his thumb. "I'm sorry you have to deal with the discomfort. I wish you could talk to me about personal issues such as this one since you are a part of my life now. These are things I need to understand, a husband should know."

She coughed then turning, her eyes alight with the spirit he liked to see, "Don't patronize me. It is not discomfort. What I'm feeling is real pain."

"Some emotion. Thank you. I thought I was talking to a statue."

Her fingers clutched his hand, her jaw tightening. "Bastard."

He stood then, knowing she would truly need some privacy in the next few minutes, pushing her too fast to accept him completely in her life would be a mistake. "I'm sorry for the pain. I should not have belittled your condition. I'm merely a man and truly have no idea as to what you are going through. I would like to know. I'll bring you more tea in another hour and we can continue the talk. Perhaps it's time you found out something about me and where I've been."

In the kitchen he ate and poured himself a cup of coffee, wondering how to proceed with Elisa. This would not be easy for her. He tried to understand the embarrassment. Couldn't. Bessy would never speak a word to him about his soon to be wife and her condition. From what he understood, Elisa's pain must be more severe than most. He wanted to know how to take care of her at these times. Now he was sure it would take much more than one conversation to gain her trust in this matter along with the knowledge he desired.

On the lawn he watched Bessy, her skirts lifted, showing a wealth of ankle as she chased Masson around on the lawn. He wanted to send her home, back to the brothel. He was sure, however, that Elisa wouldn't appreciate the gesture.

~ * ~

Pruitt sat in the plush apartment Angelique called home, sipping the fine Bordeaux he brought from his vineyard while Angelique walked around the room, her nerves on edge.

"You say Bessy was upset when she returned the other day from Etienne's château." Pruitt watched Angelique as she spun around, her fists clenched tightly at her sides.

"He dismissed her. Told her she needn't come again and that he could handle everything from here on out. He thanked her for her service and kindness." Angelique nearly spit the words in his face she was so furious.

Clasping her hand at her chest she gasped for air that didn't want to enter her lungs.

"As her soon to be husband, he has every right to dictate to Bessy. As the boy's father even more." Pruitt spoke calmly one silver eyebrow lifted higher than the other, which goaded her even more.

"They are not wed yet. Bessy tells me she is still refusing matrimony to that man. With good reason, I might add. He is not suited to be wed to anyone least of all my daughter. She deserves a better man."

Pruitt stiffened at Angelique's words. "That's my son you're speaking of. He is a good man. Now that he is retired from service for the government, he'll make a remarkable husband and father as you well know. I do take exception to your hatred of him even though I understand why."

"He took my daughters innocence."

"She gave it willingly," he countered.

"You well know this is not the conversation we need to be having. From the information I've received, Etienne has enemies, ones who might well want revenge. This is all true. She will be forced to be in the middle of feuds that happened over the last ten years, but Etienne will protect her and the boy."

Angelique waved her hand in the air, her anger and fear spilling from her. "If he's made enemies, then let him deal with them. It's best we keep Elisa and Masson out of this. If I have to, I'll barricade them in the brothel where Etienne will never reach them."

"Unless you can find a way to extract your daughter from Etienne, then she is a part of it as is the boy. We both let this go on too long without telling Etienne he had a son. Now the ultimate price might be asked of all of us. As well you know, he would have never left again if he'd been told the truth."

"What was it he did for the government? These assignments?" she asked unsure now.

Pruitt was so calm yet determined. She needed to understand better.

"Etienne is capable of protecting those he loves but you have to cooperate also. If he is fighting you on this front in addition his enemies on another side he will be distracted."

"I see. You won't tell me what exactly he did. It might not have even been legal." She was pacing once more thinking over everything Pruitt was willing to say, furious that Pruitt was sipping his wine as if this was not the conversation they were having as if he didn't care.

"No one save a few people know Etienne's assignments. He has never divulged anything about their nature to me. I'm just as much in the dark as you are. They all involve governmental secrets. He has never been at liberty to divulge." He rose then, walking to Angelique. He turned her, massaging her shoulders. "You need to relax my dear and trust in my son. All will be fine. I do believe he loves your daughter."

She wasn't so sure about any of what Pruitt said. She had been sure when she summoned Pruitt Dubois to her place he would bring more information with him. He told her pointedly he would not be summoned again. He came this time out of respect for her and her daughter.

"Pruitt, I'm sorry. It's just that I've been worried about Elisa."

She had always been worried about her. Perhaps she had overprotected her and that was what caused all the complications now. If she had not kept her sheltered most of her life, perhaps she would not have fallen so easily into Etienne's arms that night. Living in a brothel many people would not agree with her that Elisa was sheltered and innocent. They would be wrong in that.

She turned in his arms, touching his cheek. "Would you like a woman tonight?" she asked him knowing who he would prefer.

"Only if Rubie is free. I wouldn't want to impose on your business or hers. I will pay her, you know." He sat down again as she left a few minutes later returning with his request.

"You will send a crate of your finest."

"You know I will."

"Goodnight then," she told him as they disappeared into another part of the brothel.

Angelique sat down with a glass of wine, her fingers trembling. She would listen and learn more from the men who frequented her place. The ladies were willing to tell her everything they overheard. Perhaps some pieces of information about Etienne could be put together to make sense.

She was sure she knew more than Pruitt. Everything she'd heard had something to do with the King of France, Charles X.

Chapter Six

The events of the last week haunted Elisa. She couldn't look at Etienne without turning away, a flush of color staining her cheeks, her body heating. She didn't know if it was because he knew of her woman's time or because of her wantonness the night before. He treated her solicitously while he said very little after that first conversation but he'd insisted on waiting on her, had dismissed Bessy.

If she could change everything she would. At first, she felt positive he thought she exaggerated the pain. Eventually though, she believed he realized that what she felt was real.

Now the three of them were walking hand in hand through the grapes to a grassy knoll a little way from the house. He told her it would make a perfect place to eat and for Masson to play. She knew he had other motives. She just wasn't sure what they were

When they reached the spot, she was surprised to realize she could see forever in all directions when she turned in a circle. The view was as spectacular as the sun shining down on them. He'd insisted she bring a hat to shade her face from the rays. She hated hats. Now it dangled uselessly on her back. Tomorrow she would regret not taking his advice but for now she loved the feel of the marvelous heat on her face.

He spread a blanket on the ground then set down the basket. "What are you up to?" she asked him, waiting for the next surprise or embarrassment that might come her way. With Masson here he wasn't going to coax her into his arms.

"Masson, go on and play. If you can't see us you've gone too far," he shooed the boy with a laugh.

"What are you up to?" she asked again, tapping her foot

impatiently as if that action would spur him to tell her even though she understood better now, knew he would speak to her when he was good and ready.

He didn't waste any time but pulled her into his arms. "I want to kiss you where all the world can see."

She felt secure this time because he could hardly do more than kiss her with Masson playing a few feet away. Even if she melted in his arms, he would not take advantage of her weakness with more sweet coaxing. Watching as his lips moved closer to her coupled with the whisper of his lips against her cheek sent a shiver of well-remembered pleasure up and down her spine. Unable to resist, she pushed herself closer to him, her fingers gripping his shoulders.

His lips pressed against her, his tongue dancing across her mouth. She opened for him. He touched inside her upper lip then traced the edge of her teeth. The tiny sounds coming from the back of her throat seemed to please him. As much as she tried, she could not stop the response then she realized she didn't want to stop anything. Perhaps her surrender was inevitable.

He pulled away. Masson was tugging on his pants leg as well as her skirt. He wanted the same attention. Well, perhaps not the same but he wanted Etienne to play with him. She acknowledged to herself that she wanted Etienne to play with her.

She inhaled a long deep breath of resignation, smiling at him. "Go on."

He touched her lips with his thumb. "This will have to wait until tonight, don't you think? We can begin where we left off a few days ago." Then he tossed the ball and chased after it with Masson close beside him.

Elisa brought her knees to her chin, making sure her legs were covered and watched them play together. Where Masson was concerned, Etienne was like a little boy. She wished with all her heart that someday they could be a real family. He asked her to marry him. She wasn't sure why she said no. But she did, even when she wanted him for her husband more than anything in this world. There were too many things about him and his life that terrified her.

There were times during the last week where she almost said she would be his wife then she remembered the real fears that festered in her heart. She recalled the stories her mother told her about her father along with the abuse. While she didn't think Etienne would hurt her in any way, she didn't know how she could be sure. Men changed. She heard women in the brothel telling others that their husbands had been sweet and kind until they wed, until the men thought they owned them. She didn't want that for herself. Didn't want to be tied to a man who might beat her or abuse her in other ways.

He told Masson he would never hurt her.

He was quick and fierce. At times she thought of him as a predator. She knew he had secrets he didn't want to speak of. He'd done things not many would be proud of, but she also didn't know what those things were or what prompted him. They were assignments.

Assigned by whom? He'd never said.

Trust worked both ways she decided. When she'd been in pain, he implored her to trust him, but he shed no light on his activities over the years. He didn't know she'd heard stories at the brothel. Even though she understood most of tales were gossip and not based on hard fact, there was probably some amount of truth in the stories.

Rumors always contained a shred of truth.

"What are you thinking about? You look lost in thought."

He settled beside her stretching out his legs then leaning on one arm. Running a finger along her arm, he tilted his head a bit sideways staring at her as if he was seeing inside her mind.

"Watch me." Masson was hopping on one leg then the other, proud of his abilities.

"That's wonderful," she called out to him while Etienne continued his exploration of her, taking advantage of the moment when she was distracted.

"What's in the picnic basket?" he asked, his investigation taking a new path along the bodice of her dress, dipping lower as he passed the shadow between her breasts.

She batted his hand a way, looking toward Masson and hoping he wasn't watching. He was chasing a butterfly at the same time trying to catch the poor winged creature as she was sure Etienne knew.

"If you stop distracting me, I'll look," she told him with a slight shrug.

"This is more fun than eating."

He was watching her breasts, which were now rising and falling as she tried to suck in air.

"We were going to wait for later," she reminded him as his lips found that sensitive spot behind her ear that always seemed to send shivers coursing through her. She closed her eyes as she struggled to find the tiniest bit of air.

"Don't know if I can." He touched the tip of her earlobe with his tongue then bit gently, leaning back to enjoy watching her. "You taste wonderful and smell like vanilla."

"We need to eat and we should probably get Masson home. There are thunder clouds on the horizon."

The first night he was home the tempest raged outside as well as inside her. She had the feeling there would be more than one storm tonight.

Those words stopped him, as she knew they would. He cared for his son more than his life, as did she. At least they had that much in common. She decided then she would not melt in his arms again, not until he divulged at least some small piece of information.

"I see. It seems I lost track of time."

He reached inside the basket bringing out the sandwiches cook packed for them as well as the bottle of wine. There was also a bottle of milk for Masson.

"Come eat," he called to the boy who had now lost interest in the butterfly and was digging in the dirt with a stick.

Masson looked up then ran to them, a grin on his face, hands dirty. He would need a bath before bed again. Elisa knew if Masson had a say in her choice, he would tell her to marry his father. She didn't understand why the decision was so hard for her. Yet she did. Too many secrets surrounded this man. Ominously, she had a feeling she was some part of those secrets.

They finished their meal making their way back to their home before the storm broke, running the last few yards to the back door and laughing as the rain started falling in big fat drops. Masson was doubled over from the merriment. Etienne was in about the same shape. Before they stepped inside the two males shared some joke choosing not to include her.

Lightning flashed though the sky while the brilliance lit up the surrounding area as more and more huge drops of rain pummeled the ground. Elisa set the basket in the kitchen before she shook her cape out in the scullery. For a few seconds she watched the storm, breathing in deeply as she thought of the night to come. If he didn't tell her something about his life, she meant to refuse his advances. She just didn't know how she was going to do that.

"You okay?"

He stood beside her, one hand rested tenderly on her shoulder, massaging sore muscles.

She turned to smile at him. "Define okay."

He shoved both hands through his hair as he stepped away from her, his back straight as he too watched the storm. "I understand you're afraid but you shouldn't be afraid of me. I will never hurt you. I promise you that. The things I've done are in the past as I was in the service of our government. It is my intention they're going to stay there."

She knew his words to be true. What she didn't know was if the people he went up against over the years would hurt her or if they believed their part was in the past also. "I have more than myself to think about as well you know. Don't lie to me just to make me feel better."

"You don't think I know that?" There was a hint of anger in his voice. "I'm not going to lie to you. You should understand I'm more than capable of protecting both you and Masson."

Hearing the tone, she almost apologized "I believe you've done things you might not be proud of as well as things that might come back to haunt you, us. Perhaps they already do, haunt you."

"Why would you think..." then he stopped as if he realized where she heard information about him. Erroneous as it most likely was, he couldn't fight the gossip.

"Angelique's," she finished for him. "Many of the ladies are my friends. Knowing what you meant to me, when they visited, they would bring stories with them, rumors or gossip at best. We both know there is always a shred of truth in any rumor."

"Is that why you don't want to marry me?" he asked tightening his fists as she watched.

"No."

"Then why?" He sounded angry and curious as well.

"Because I'm afraid of my feelings for you, terrified they might harm our son. He is everything to me. Masson means more to me than my life."

There were tears in her eyes as she finally spoke the words she needed to say. It wasn't her response to him that frightened her, well, in many ways it was, but the fear for Masson was the catalyst for all her actions and choices from the very beginning.

"Papa, I'm ready for my bath." Masson was standing on one foot then the other, grinning just like his father, the little dimple growing larger as his smile also grew.

They jumped apart, both looking to Masson then back "Good, I'll..."

Etienne interrupted. "Let me give him his bath and read a story. Take a bottle of wine upstairs to the balcony. I'll join you as soon as we're finished. Put on something," he paused pushing hair behind her ears, "comfortable. Something perhaps silky."

She was going to ask if he was sure but the look on her son's face told her everything she needed or wanted to know. The bond of love between the two was so evident it stole her breath. It seemed the love blossomed from the moment they first met.

"Give me a kiss then," she said to Masson.

"*Je t'adore* Mama," he said as he left the room with his father holding hands.

"Very well," she collected a few things on a tray before heading toward the patio. Without looking back, she wondered if she would survive these two men who held her heart in the palms of their hands. If she were to survive, she needed to put up every guard possible.

In the bedroom, she changed her clothes into some lingerie he'd given her wondering if that was what he meant by silky and comfortable.

Then she wondered if it was wise. Perhaps she should wear one of her old nightdresses. The act was probably braver than wise because she understood why he gave the silken lingerie to her. Still, she hoped they could talk before they finally made love. For so many years, she had thought it was only a matter of time before she was in his arms and under his spell again.

Now it was that time.

She prayed every night he was away that he never found anyone else to love.

If they didn't talk first, perhaps afterward. With the clothing pressed close to her, she inhaled deeply, thinking and praying she was doing the right thing. She decided tonight she would agree to his proposal of marriage. In any case, it was what they both wanted. Didn't see any other way to make herself whole again. Marriage was the only means where that could happen.

Her mother would not be pleased but she was twenty-two. How long could anyone be under their mother's thumb?

How long indeed?

When he appeared on the balcony, his shirt was partially unbuttoned, his hair was a disheveled mess with droplets of water still dripping from the locks. Her breath staggered in her lungs for several seconds then caught at her throat before she let it out in a whispered sigh.

"It seems you lost the bath time battle." Trying to recover, she smiled while holding out a glass of wine for him. She was sitting in a single chair, no room for him to settle down next to her and change her mind before she was satisfied with what she hoped would be spoken between them. This was safe yet she was still sure he could find a way.

"I did lose but the skirmish was worth every second. He splashes half the tub of water onto me as well as the floor playing with his toys."

Nonchalantly, he tossed a piece of cheese in his mouth as he sat down in a chair beside her and put his feet on a low table in front of him.

He appeared relaxed, confident in every way. "But you loved every minute as do I. I wouldn't change anything for the world."

She smiled at him, her son's father, the man she loved with all her heart. If she'd tried to find someone like him, she could have never been so fortunate.

He leaned close so he could whisper, *"Voulez vous coucher avec moi, ce soir?"* As if he didn't just ask her to go to bed with him, he said, "You are very lovely tonight, Mademoiselle Moreau. Your hair is picking up the light from the moon, changing colors with the soft caress of the moonbeams. It shines..." He sipped from the glass, his long fingers twirling the stem when he brought it away from his lips. "I don't know if I can wait to have you. I need to feel you beneath me, in my arms. I yearn to be deep inside you, giving you a woman's pleasure."

"Of course, you can wait. I recall just how well you can wait."

She ran her hands along her arms to warm herself. The chill of the evening seeming to find its way through the thin clothing she wore.

He rose finding a quilt and covering her with it. "Protection for you as well as from me. You have questions. I suppose it is time I answered a few, the ones I'm able to at least. I will still have to have secrets but I will tell you what I can, what is admissible."

His statement pleasantly surprised her. She had thought... "What do you do when you have an assignment?"

"That one is easy. Many different things, it depends on who is paying me."

"You do things for hire?"

"Yes, as well as for the government, mostly for the government."

He looked so at ease she truly didn't believe for a moment that anyone would want revenge against him. "So..."

He laughed a soft chuckle, his face shadowed by the encroaching storm. "Once I stole a painting that had been pinched previously. The original owner was very pleased to get it back and in appreciation paid a tidy sum."

"So, you are a thief."

"I was doing a favor for the museum. They truly did not like the fact that someone could find a way inside to take something so valuable from them. Security had been breached. Security they thought was the best in the world. I brought the painting back to its original home."

"But the original thief took exception to that fact. Now he probably wants to steal something of yours in return."

"There are only two things I have worth stealing."

She gasped as his look pointed directly at her. "What?"

"I think you should know."

"A woman appreciates hearing those words."

"Perhaps." He leaned forward finding more food, chewing thoughtfully or to waste time, she couldn't be sure. "The original thief was not pleased that she lost the painting, but she has been overjoyed that she did not go to jail. The painting was restored to its rightful place in the Louvre."

"So, this man..."

"Woman."

"So, this woman has no reason to be angry with you and seek revenge."

She was studying him closely willing now to overlook the fact he didn't answer one of her questions, at least for the time being. His smile as well as his dimple grew. He enjoyed his work, the danger and the constant threat to his life, but he was willing to put it aside for her and his son.

"Of course she does, but she will not waste her energies on me. She will find another painting or some piece of valuable jewelry to steal."

"Then you will steal it back."

"Only if I'm hired. Now that I find I have a son and hopefully a wife soon the game does not intrigue me as much as it did. I find I enjoy the skirmishes with my son much more. I have better things to do with my time."

"So, it is a game you play."

"It was." He sighed. "The painting is not what has the gossip mills fueled. I worked for Charles X. As his assistant while he employed me, I did things for him. I also have his protection. However, he's been distant as of late. Not so sure I can count on him for anything."

"What else have you done?" she asked but she wasn't' sure she wanted any more answers.

"You sure you want to know?"

"No."

He waited, hands on his hard abdomen watching the storm while giving her the time she seemed to need to decide, sipping his wine. She understood he was waiting her out, his patience exceeding anything she could ever imagine.

"Yes."

"One more tale before we retire for the night. I find I'm very interested in uncovering what lies beneath the fragile slip of material you are wearing." His low whiskey voice haunted her while stirring emotions only he could bring to life.

"Then... tell me or it will be even longer before you find out what it is you want to know."

"I, well, this is delicate. One of the members of the Scottish parliament found out his wife was cheating on him but not before she found out about his mistress. There was a huge fight. It took a lot of negotiations to bring about a solution. Eventually, everyone was pleased. A divorce was not tangible."

His half smile told her he was finished. When he held out his hand toward her, the gesture confirmed what she thought.

"Perhaps you will tell me more on another night."

She placed her hand in his. Instead of leading her to the bed, he scooped her into his arms.

"It's been a long time. I pray that tonight we will not be interrupted by our son or anyone else for that matter."

He settled her on the bed. She rose, moving away, staring at him for the longest time. "Are you positive tonight? This is it you know. If we do this, if I make love to you, you are going to marry me. Giving yourself over to me is a different way of saying yes, but that's exactly what I'm going to take it to mean."

Even if she wanted, she couldn't refuse him, not when he spoke in that gentle, amused voice of his, not when the tone hinted at an urgency he didn't show in any other way, not when his eyes darkened with rising passion. She responded to the choices he gave her all of which she'd overthought for too long.

"*Viens ici*, Elisa." He held open his arms for her. "Don't deny us any longer. Together we have unfinished business."

She shimmered as she walked, as if she were moving through a waterfall while moonlight filtered in behind her. When she stopped in front of him, within arm's reach, the transparent fabric pressed against her. She watched the way his eyes were drawn to her. His dark brown eyes were filled with desire charmingly hinting at delights to come. The wide centers reminded her of polished onyx as they studied her. She raised her face to him, inhaling the scents, wary of the night but wanting it in any case.

It was time.

Past time.

As his hand tenderly threaded in the strands of her hair, his fingers were washed with color. His thumb brushed her cheek. She closed her eyes while turning her face into his palm, placing her lips slightly against the flesh of his hand. Leaning forward he kissed her closed lids then his mouth gently settled over hers, the gentle pressure exquisite.

She tasted his lips again, the shape and texture the same as she remembered from the night before as well as the years before that. The memory of how easy it was for his tongue to raise a shiver from her when he touched her just so, heated her. Her mouth parted beneath his, her lips eager against his. She explored tentatively still somewhat unsure of herself, her tongue meeting his, teasing in the same way he taught her.

Etienne leaned against the bed. His splayed, outstretched legs captured Elisa between them. She allowed herself to be pulled closer, to be nestled against him. She felt his hard arousal at the juncture of her thighs. The kiss deepened. There was an inferno now. Hardness. A sense of demanding that had been missing a second ago.

It seemed he was drawing on her air, forcing her to share his. The intimacy of the kiss stunned her senses surpassing anything she'd felt in the past. She felt as if she were completely open to him, her soul bared, that she was giving him the right to know her in a way no one had ever done before, that ultimately, and most frighteningly, he would come to understand things about her that were a mystery to herself.

If he drew on her air, he also drew on her heart. Its steady beat quickened. When his mouth touched the cord in her neck, she knew he could feel the wild pulse vibrate against his lips. Her throat arched when his mouth slipped to the base of it. His tongue tasted the hollow. He sipped her skin in the curve.

Elisa's fingers curled in his thick black hair, stroking, holding him to her. Her own sounds of pleasure rocked her as his hand caressed her breast.

Etienne placed his hands on her waist as he slid off the soft mattress. In the same motion he lifted her setting her upon the quilts and pillows atop the bed. Kneeling at her feet, he removed her slippers. His hands caressed her skin from ankle to knee, sliding under the soft fabric of the thin gown she wore then farther up her leg. As he stood again his hands traveled higher, raising her gown while he moved beneath it to learn the shape of her thighs. She watched his face, then his hands, then his face again when his finger slipped more intimately between her thighs gently pushing them apart, opening her to him.

She gasped with the sweet pleasure he elicited. Her mouth parted. A tiny sound of pleasure whispered softly in the pale moonlight. A please was mouthed. Then his lips covered hers, accepting everything she was willing to give and pressing for even more. Now her delight was expressed by a humming sound at the back of her throat as she returned the kiss completely.

Etienne cupped her bottom, pulling her to the edge of their bed. Her thighs were parted even more making room for him. When he leaned into her, she cradled him perfectly. He raised her hips for a moment, letting her feel his arousal between her thighs, reminding her of the shape and strength of a man then he eased back down before taking the gown over her head flinging it to the side.

He moved back slightly looking at her, the half-smile so very apparent as well as the dimple while his eyes darkened then blazed with the need and passion she recognized. Tonight, it was more pronounced than ever before.

Her breasts were full, slightly swollen even before he tempted her more thoroughly with the probing need of his arousal pressed against her. His thumbs passed tenderly over the puckered tops and stiffened them to hardness. His head lowered. He touched her neck first then the hollow of her throat then the curve of her shoulder. He forced anticipation on her as his mouth moved lower, skimming her skin until he reached the curve of her breast. Her back arched. Greedily, he accepted her offering. His lips closed over her nipple, laving the hard puckered tip with his tongue, drawing a response from her with the hot suck of his mouth.

Ribbons of flame traveled from her breast to her thighs. It seemed a spark had been struck in her fingertips and in her toes. No matter how she tried, she could not get close enough to him. Her hands slid beneath his shirt. His skin was hot and smooth. The muscles retracted as her fingers explored. His belly was taut, the muscles defined. She traced the edge of his rib cage with her knuckles. Her fingers dipped just below the belt that held his pants in place. She heard his low groan of desire the pulsing need created by her tender strokes.

Elisa felt the loss when he fell back. Her small gasp sounded loud to her, as if it echoed in their chamber instead of being caught in her throat. Etienne's smile was wicked, pure male eliciting satisfaction. She knew he understood and was enjoying making her experience the pleasure then the absence of it. He was binding her to him more completely than she could have ever imagined.

She held out her arms. *I want you.*

He lowered himself, allowing her to wrap her arms around him. His mouth brushed against hers. "Remember what this means." The husky voice complimented his smile. He pulled up on the back of his shirt removing it, tossing it to the floor. "I'll marry you tomorrow if possible, say our vows."

"My mother," she breathed not really caring anymore.

"She doesn't have to be there. I'm sure she will hear about it. We'll just go to one of the churches nearby and pledge our troth. Then it will be done."

He took her hands away placing them at her sides while he waited for her answer.

"Alright."

She wanted to touch him now, but it was with her eyes that she first covered the breadth of his shoulders and the smooth expanse of her chest. She stared at the firm curve of his arms and the way his waist tapered in clean, strong lines. His nipples were already hard. He let go of her. She placed her hand between them, covering the beating of his heart.

It raced on at the same frantic pace as hers.

She raised her gaze to see into his eyes. The smile had vanished. His features were calm, the brown eyes implacable, yet there was the unmistakable stamp of desire as he returned her stare.

Etienne slowly bent his head again taking her other breast in his mouth, sucking gently. Her fingers clutched his arms at first then moved hungrily over his back and shoulders. She felt herself being eased backward against the mattress. Covers twisted beneath her as he moved across her. He placed kisses on the underside of her breast before he moved lower, down her rib cage across her flat belly.

Etienne raised himself up on the bed in order to remove his boots and pants. He straddled her thighs leaning forward, stretching like a predatory cat, sleek and beautiful above her. He caught her wrists and held them lightly just above her head making her all the more vulnerable to his dancing hands. Her muscles tightened. Her movement was reactive, not intentional. Her head was turned to the side away from him.

"Look at me, *mon bijoux*. You aren't having second thoughts?"

She shook her head. As he claimed her mouth, pleasure coursed through her. She returned the kiss, their shared pleasure increasing tenfold. Her arms looped around his neck as her back arched seeking more and more, moving ever higher, closer to the ecstasy she craved. Her breasts scraped his chest, the tender nipples radiating sensation. She moaned softly and his mouth caught the sound.

~ * ~

He released her wrists needing to feel her hands touching him, discovering everything about him. His hands caressed her arms, her shoulders. They slipped along her back before raising her hips. His knee parted her thighs once again as he adjusted his position. He watched her face as he probed intimately, watched the play of shadows on her features as she gave herself up to him. He was achingly hard for her. While he understood this was not her first time, she was still so small and tight. He was desperately afraid he would hurt her again.

"Etienne?" she said his name softly with so much uncertainty it stole his heart.

He'd waited so long for this moment he desperately craved for the next moments to be right, perfectly right as right as any man could make them. He had no idea about the first time, how she'd felt afterward. The first time they made love, had sex or whatever she wanted to call what went on between them, she left him before he woke. He'd never know her feelings from that day unless she decided to tell him sometime in their future.

The soft echo of his name on her lips was almost his undoing. He raised her hips a little more, felt her body begin to accommodate his as he slowly moved within her sultry dark core. Her velvet sheath pulsed around him urging him deeper. He thrust into her hard as she yielded to him. This time she closed around him like a silk covering.

Elisa moved with him now. The pleasure of his body tightly encased by hers was almost beyond bearing. Every sensation surpassed anything he'd ever felt before, beyond his experience as well as his imagination. This was magical. She was the woman he loved. He'd never felt that way before either, although there had been many women in his life. There were none like Elisa.

Etienne leaned close to her as their bodies rocked in unison. His breath moved strands of her blond-white hair, caressing her face. Her smile sent heat racing through every part of him.

Beneath him, she twisted, stretching, finally cried out as she broke through into white-hot ecstasy while tremors seized her body, uncontrollably creating the same molten enchantment in him. She sucked in great draughts off air as her muscles contracted around him as the heat from her climax spilled from her into him, sucking him ever-deeper inside than he already was. She held him close as his thrusts became quick and deep, heard the tempo of her heart race along with each quickly inhaled breath of air.

His features were taut, his skin pulled tightly across the bones of his face. His eyes closed at the moment of his final thrust. He arched, his body shivering with the force of his release. His cry of pleasure was guttural and harsh. Spent, he collapsed against her. He rested his face in the curve of Elisa's neck while he slowly recovered his uneven breath.

She raised a knee then rubbed her leg slowly against his skin. The sole of her foot lightly caressed his calf. He groaned softly before he rolled away separating himself from her, needing to know things only she could tell him.

"Are you alright?" he asked, his gaze running the length of her then back to see into her eyes. His fingertip touched her softly parted lips. They were wet, fragile as every part of her seemed so delicate to him. He needed to take more care with her.

She nodded, her eyes wide with what he read as contentment. "I don't think I'll ever be alright again."

His rolling laughter caught her attention. With her honestly spoken words, a sense of manly pride rippled through him. "Do you realize exactly what you just told me?"

This time she was shaking her head. "Well, no, but I'm glad I don't see a miniature image of you staring at us right now." She tried to find a cover to pull across her but he stopped her.

"Don't, I like looking at you," he murmured as he bent to lightly kiss the hard tip of one of her breasts before turning the same attention to the other one. "I'm glad of that too. I wouldn't relish another man-to-boy conversation again so soon. The other night was hard enough for me to explain to the little man what we were doing as well as the incredible fact that I wasn't hurting you."

"What did you tell him?" Her head lay on his chest. She was smoothing her hands across his hard nipples. He placed his hand on top. "Unless you want to do this again right now, you should stop teasing me."

"If I remember correctly you used to have more stamina."

Her hand rested delicately on his abdomen, seeming to hesitate before traveling lower, caressing him more intimately.

"We have the wedding to talk about. Are you going to tell Masson or do you want me to?" He wasn't going to let her forget what she promised. Tomorrow, no today now, she would be his wife. With that settled, he would be able to protect her and Masson from whatever storm might be coming their way.

"We should tell him together. As to the next question, my mother, if we marry tomorrow there is no way she can attend. She won't be pleased. Do you want to risk displeasing Angel?"

He smiled at her as he rose above her on one elbow tracing a line along her feathered eyebrows. "That is what I was hoping for. Simply put, displeasing Angel would give me the greatest pleasure. In any case, your mother's presence will only complicate the day."

She hit him. He caught her hand with ease. "That wasn't nice."

"I understand but you know the part when the witnesses are asked if they know a reason why these two shouldn't be wed..."

"Yes."

"Your mother would come up with a reason."

"Perhaps you are right to be hasty. We will have to just ask your father and perhaps Gil will be a witness."

His body tightened when Elisa mentioned Gil. Even knowing he had nothing to be jealous of where his friend was concerned, he didn't like the fact she'd thought of him to attend their wedding.

"You want Gil to be there?" he queried, wishing the answer was no.

She touched her hand to his face. "Not for me but for Masson. He would wonder why Gil wasn't invited as well as why his grandmother was not asked to attend something that is so special. It would be easier to explain why just one of them was missing."

"Do you have something to wear tomorrow?" To him she looked beautiful no matter what she was wearing, but he also understood she would want to feel that way too.

"Nothing special. I've a gown perhaps that would do but, in this haste, I don't think it really matters." She closed her eyes and the smile disappeared.

"A big wedding, is it something you've dreamt about? In our haste, I would hate to spoil any of your dreams." He traced the line of her jaw then her neck, thinking he didn't want to know the answer to that question simply because he didn't want to give in to her if that is what she told him.

The gentle lift of her shoulders vibrated against his chest. "Every little girl dreams of a big wedding. However, I was smart enough to know that I would never have one as I suspected I would never marry." She rose slightly and kissed him on the mouth, her hands winding around his head while pulling her to him.

Her tongue touched his lips, traced the line. He opened for her, yearning for a diversion from the conversation. Before he rolled her to straddle him, he looked to the door, checking for a small shadow or the slightest noise. There was nothing standing at the doorway at the moment and he understood that for the next few years, he would have the same scenario presenting itself every time he made love to his wife. If they were lucky, they would have more children.

He groaned then, realizing this could go on for a very long time. He also realized he now needed to give this woman, his soon to be wife, everything she ever wanted.

Her legs were parted for him. She sat on top of him. He grinned at her, lightly touching the tip of her breasts with the palm of one hand. She bent over, teasing him, letting her breasts touch his flesh, tantalize all his senses while he throbbed beneath her. After only a few seconds of her seduction, he was hard, desperately craving release.

He felt the moisture between her legs yet he needed to make this last longer. She was hot and slick, ready for him. He understood he could take her now, this instant and she would respond wildly. If like the last time, frantically until she found her release.

She rose above him and she found she could take him inside her; that she would have the control she didn't have before. When she looked at him as if asking for his approval, he nodded and slowly she took all of him inside her.

Her smile of seeming delight surprised him. It appeared she understood the power she possessed as she rose slowly then settled down again, at the same pace her hands resting on his chest. The process repeated more slowly than the first time. He groaned. She bent over, touched his nipple with her tongue then the other one.

He tried to thrust further inside her but she didn't move. He was held still by her slight weight. "You are a tease, a beautiful one though."

"You love it."

"I wouldn't have you any other way."

Placing a fingertip on his lips. "Let me do this."

She bent over again and kissed him, brushing her lips against his while the tips of her breast danced gently across his chest. She placed kisses along his neck then found the sensitive spot behind his ear, touching, sipping before worrying the lobe with her teeth.

"Let me do what you've taught me."

"I think I've taught you too well."

She smiled sweetly at his comment. He didn't think he would live through this. His deep satisfied groan of pleasure stopped her for a moment then with her hands on his chest she pushed away and grinned at him again seeming thoroughly pleased with herself. When she lowered herself on him, taking him as deeply inside as possible, a wave of her silken hair brushed across him sending an inferno blazing deep inside. She was cocooned in magic with the mystery of all she was wrapping around her.

His hands tightened around her waist wishing he dared take control and end this heavenly, enchanting torment, but he needed for her to have this moment. He craved for her to understand this was really what making love was all about. This wasn't just sex, it was love.

He wished he dared say the words to her. In time, he would when he wouldn't frighten her away.

"Do you like this?" She pushed away, her gaze boring into him but he saw a moment of insecurity in her eyes.

"More than you could ever know. I don't want you to stop being yourself."

She rose again. It seemed she looked down to see the joining of their bodies. When her gaze focused on him again, he saw the questions in her eyes.

"I never really understood how deep inside of me you are, were, when you, when we make love or have sex." Her words were a breathless sigh whispering across his chest.

"You do now though, and I want you to know before we are married that at least to me this is making love, nothing else. Not any of the terms you tossed out earlier."

She nodded then, arching her back and rising above him, letting him take control of the moment as she leaned back. His hands rose to encompass her breasts to tease them further. In her throes of passion, she had never been so beautiful to him. "Let it come, *mon bijoux*," he whispered as he thrust deeper. She closed her eyes, her lashes fluttering softly against her pale skin.

He felt the tremors take over her slenderness traveling once again from her into him, felt the release she was so innocently gifting him with as her silken sheathe tightened around him. He exploded inside her, crying out her name. Once again, this was something so new to him the sensations stole his breath. She held his heart in the palms of her hands. If she ever wanted to, she had the power to cripple him.

She fell against him, seemingly unable to move. He was still deep inside her as she lay on top of him.

He rolled with her, holding her as close as he could. *Mon Dieu*, he couldn't remember what it was like with anyone else, certainly not like this. When she fell asleep, he knew. Her breathing slowed while her body relaxed completely. He dozed.

When sunlight washed the room, he realized it was time to start preparations for their wedding. Masson was his first visit. His son would be the beginning of the arrangements and after that he would send messages to both Gil as well as his father. He would also pen one to Angelique, understanding the action would please Elisa.

Over the top of her shoulder, he saw a pair of deep brown eyes watching him and laughed realizing he would have to get used to this.

"Can I get in bed with you and Mama?"

For a moment, the question startled him. He had no doubt it was something Elisa permitted in the past. It would not be allowed in the present. Having him in bed with the two of them naked wasn't acceptable to him. He doubted it was to Elisa either.

He motioned for Masson to be quiet, touching his finger to his lips. "I'm getting up." He pushed the covers away making sure Elisa was completely covered. Her head rested on her hand as she snuggled into the pillow. She looked exhausted perhaps from the lovemaking or the stress of what was going to happen today.

She promised. The vow was well done of her.

He slipped on the pants he had carelessly tossed aside last night before heading out the door with his son. Once outside the room and with the door closed behind them, he asked, "Are you hungry?"

Masson looked at him as if he lost his mind, "It's time for breakfast. Can we have bacon again?"

Etienne could not help the chuckle and humming a tune he headed for the kitchen with Masson in tow. "It's going to be a special day so yes, bacon it is."

"And scrambled eggs?"

"Only if you help me gather the eggs then crack them in the bowl."

"Can I?"

Etienne nodded, grinning and feeling happier than he had in a very long time. In the chicken coup they collected what they needed for breakfast before heading back to the kitchen.

His cook was there, the bacon sizzling in the pan. "What's got that dimple showing this morning, Master Dubois? she asked.

"I'm getting married today."

He lifted his son and twirled him around in a huge circle then kissed him soundly. A memory seemed to surface that left him nodding his head in surprise.

"I get to crack the eggs," Masson said excitedly, seeming to overlook what he'd just said.

"And we'll have shells a plenty in them if he does." The cook said, her displeasure directed at him. "You marrying the mademoiselle? It's about time. You got her living here and all."

"I would have married her four and a half years ago but she didn't want anything to do with me," he told her still grinning. "Don't you worry, I'll get all the shells out of the eggs."

"Not after you did what you did. I heard the stories. I'm not going to repeat them, especially not around the little man here but you should have gone after her. Should have been more persistent. Instead, you left the country. Should have told her the truth. Her mother was her only source of guidance."

"You're right." He set about handing the eggs to Masson and fishing out the shells when he was done then he sent the boy to the basin to wash up. Perhaps he should have been more tenacious in his pursuit.

Maybe he gave up too easily. Unfortunately, the call for adventure, the need for danger called to him then. God, but he hoped that craving was out of his heart.

"Of course, I am. Wouldn't tell you otherwise."

"Masson, come here." Etienne's voice was gentle.

He didn't want to frighten Masson but telling him now was of utmost importance. This time he didn't think he could wait for Elisa to rise.

Masson looked at his papa with the half smile and dimple showing, leaving Etienne to look away. The boy was so much like him. When the boy was close enough, he brought him to stand in front of him and between his legs.

"Your mother and I are getting married today, in just a few hours. What do you think?" Holding his breath, he hoped for a positive reaction.

"If that means you're going to be my father for real, I like it a lot. I want a real father. That way, you won't ever go away. Will you?"

"I will always be your real father but now the law will recognize it." *And you won't be a bastard.*

"When?"

He pushed the boy's hair from his eyes. "Well, you have to eat then take a bath. I'll go through your clothes. We'll pick out your best suit. Then, your mother has to wake up and..."

"I'll wake her up." He dashed away but Etienne caught him by his shirttails.

"No, she needs her sleep."

"Why? Mama's always up for breakfast."

He cleared his throat, amusement tickling the back of it, "I might have kept her a little bit busy last night. It was to seal a promise she made me."

"You should not be saying things like that to the boy. It will give him ideas he doesn't need," the cook said, pointing her spatula at him with a tiny shake to emphasize her point.

Etienne roared with laughter. "He is not old enough now to know what I'm talking about and a few words in a kitchen said or not said will not muffle what he and his friends will be curious about when he's older.

He might as well know as much truth as he can handle for his age."

"I'm not stupid. He's already talked to me about that stuff, man-to-boy," Masson said to the cook as he watched his father. "I know my mama likes my father a lot."

"Of course you're not stupid, but I'm more in agreement with our cook right now than your father."

Elisa swept into the room, a bathrobe wrapped around her. "He should discuss his lectures to you with me first."

"Thought you'd still be in bed."

Etienne looked at her with appreciation, wishing they had time for one more bout in the bedroom before the wedding. The messages had been sent and the time arranged. He doubted if it would be wise to change anything now. If he did, it would only put the wedding night off longer than he wanted. Tonight, for the entire night, he wanted her all to himself. He hoped Pruitt would agree to keeping Masson overnight.

"I wanted to eat then I'm going to bathe and dress. Thought you would get yourself and Masson ready in one of the other rooms." She broke off a piece of bacon as she was talking.

"We can do that, can't we Masson?"

He tickled the little boy, loving the boyish giggle and wishing with all his heart he had not lost so much time with him. He'd done little over the last four years he was proud of. Anyone could have accomplished the same results. The missions were simply something to take his mind off Elisa.

She sat down at the table. Eggs and bacon appeared almost magically in front of her. "Thank you."

For a few minutes he watched her. She had time to renege on the promise but when she looked, up she smiled at him, her eyes darkening to a dark violet shade, shimmering with the raw desire he was coming to know. "Did you send a message to mother?"

"That wasn't necessary. I suspected something like this after what Bessy told me when she returned, so here I am." Angelique flamboyantly stepped into the room, her arms opened wide. "You didn't think you were getting married without me, did you?"

~ * ~

"You're not going to try and stop us, are you mother?" Elisa drummed her fork on her plate for a moment before she nervously began pushing the food around the flat surface. "I don't think I'm hungry any longer."

"Everything was going fine until you arrived here," Etienne said, frown lines creasing his brow as if he realized what he said in front of his son who was now running to hug his grand-mere. Then in resignation, "You're here now."

"*Maman,*" Masson cried, rushing to her with his arms spread wide. "I'm glad you are here. Mama and my papa are getting married today. It wouldn't be right unless you watched. I love all of you so much!" His arms were spread wide to show everyone what he meant.

Bessy was standing beside Angelique and the little boy gave her a big hug also.

"Why don't you sit down and eat some breakfast. The rest of us need to get ready. If you want to freshen up, Bessy can show you to her room." Etienne said unapologetically. "Come Masson." He held out his hand for the little boy. "We've important things to do before we get married."

Angelique watched them leave, her body quivering with barely suppressed anger. He had thought to leave her out of one of the most important days of her daughter's life. How dare he? It wasn't even going to be a wedding with lots of friends and family, just a hurried event. "I cannot abide that man."

"You must calm yourself. You will have to learn to tolerate him if you want to see your daughter and grandson," Bessy said as she found the hot water and poured both of them a cup of tea. "You accepted this. That's why we are here. I believed you were prepared to at least pretend you were happy for them."

"Humph... I thought I was but that man manages to infuriate me every time he looks at me. How am I going to let him marry my dear, sweet Elisa? He is still involved you know. I've heard at the brothel from some of my clients that he has not left his sordid business with the king behind him."

"Need I remind you they love each other, even found their way back to each other after almost five years despite what you did. There is nothing you can do now that will keep them a part. Do not make your anger known or you might never see your grandchildren and I'm sure there will be more as sure as I breathe."

"I believed I told Elisa enough stories she would never see him in any other light except a bad one." Angelique sat down ridding herself of her coat and hat. The tea was steaming so she sipped lightly.

"Well, your bad words about Etienne worked for a while but it is done now. They are together. The two of them will be husband and wife in a few hours, Masson no longer a bastard. If you want to keep seeing your grandson, I tell you again that you must come to terms with this wedding."

Angelique grumbled a bit but she was hungry and decided she would wait to voice her objections until the ceremony, wondering if Pruitt would attend the small wedding. She smiled. He would clamp his hand over her mouth if she tried to say anything negative.

She finished the tea along with the food that had been set out for her then, "Come, Bessy let's freshen up a bit. I've dust and grime from the drive here. Heaven's sake, we don't want to look as if we spent the last day and a half on the road even though we did."

Bessy laughed softly. "You won't be telling anyone we spent the night at an inn down the road."

"Now why would I say anything about that?" Angelique smiled, thinking of the wedding of her girl.

If she could have picked, she would have chosen someone other than Etienne Dubois. As for Pruitt, his father, she loved him, had always loved him. It would do well of her to acknowledge that before she lost her daughter and grandson.

Chapter Seven

"Elisa?" Bessy stepped into her room unannounced. "Would you like some help with your dress and hair?"

"You will never know how much." She held up a cream-colored ball gown, shaking it out before holding it up to herself. "I found this. Etienne must have bought it for me to wear. It seems he was confident in my answer. Strange he never mentioned it though."

"The gown is beautiful. You are more beautiful," Bessy breathed softly walking forward to touch the folds of material. "You will look amazing in it. Your eyes stand out when you hold it up against you."

"I don't even know if it will fit. How did he find the time to have this fashioned when he didn't know my measurements?" She was still dressed in only her chemise.

"Men have other ways of telling a seamstress a woman's size," Bessy said having had years of experience with such things.

"But..."

"He's held you and touched you or am I mistaken." Bessy's hands were on her hips, her smile wide and all knowing. "He most likely paid an exorbitant fee to have the gown finished by this morning. He's only been in the area for a couple of weeks.

"Yes, last night," then she paused in thought. "And the night before you visited. That was over a week ago. I suppose he had time to have this made for me."

"Of course he did. We should get your corset on and tighten it then slip the dress over your head. We'll see then how well he knew your measurements." Bessy laughed appearing pleased with the notion.

The bust was a straight line across her front just covering her breast. When she finally put the dress over her head, watching as the fabric settled around her, she saw there was small-embroidered bouquet of spring flowers in the middle. The puff sleeves were ornamented with rows of lace and cream ribbons running through. The bottom was decorated with rows of Parisian roses, attached by bows. A cream-colored ribbon encircled her waist.

Bessy stood back, her hands clasped in front of her. "He will swoon when he sees you. The fit is perfect." Then she stiffened, "You are not all going in the same carriage, are you? He cannot see you in this dress before the wedding. That would bring both of you bad luck."

Elisa felt a bit swamped by Bessy. She had no idea about Etienne's plans. She was sure they were well planned out. "I don't know. Etienne never tells me his ideas."

"Well, he is not going to see you until you walk down the aisle. Doesn't matter if it's a small church or not. It's bad luck. And I for one want to see the expression on his face when you step through that door."

"Bessy..."

"You just wait here and start combing out your hair. I'll be along in a moment after I make sure Angelique and Etienne understand what is going to happen. No one, not even your mother, is going to put a stop to this wedding," she mumbled. "I won't allow it."

"I'm not going to ride alone with my mother. She will take the carriage and turn it around." Her hand on the brush tightened as she watched Bessy take one look at her and march out of the room, her back stiff as a rod.

When she returned, Elisa had managed to comb out her hair and apply a small amount of makeup. She highlighted her eyes with a bit of color as well as her lips. She didn't like the face powder so she didn't put any on. Then she darkened her lashes.

"What happened?" Elisa asked when Bessy returned. "Did you find out what Etienne wants to do?"

"Now you never mind. I set things straight. Everything is taken care of." Bessy brushed Elisa's hair. In a matter of minutes had it artfully arranged on her head, tendrils of hair curled and framing her face. "This is for you."

"From mother?" she asked her breath stopping for a few seconds as she suddenly realized perhaps her mother would behave herself.

"Yes, she wore it at her wedding." Bessy held up her hands. "No, don't think about your father. She was happy then. The sapphire necklace is perfect. It's something borrowed. The dress is obviously something new from your fiancé and I have something blue." She held up a pair of sapphire earrings. "Put them on. They were given to me by a man a long time ago. I never wear them and I want you to have them."

She held Bessy's hands in hers awed by the generous gift. "I couldn't."

"No, you must have them. It's important to me. As I said, I never wear them. If you don't want to wear the earrings save them for a child or a grandchild. They are yours. Now, don't you argue with me."

Tears filled her eyes but Bessy pulled out a handkerchief and dabbed at the moisture. Elisa did put them on. A long with the nearly matching necklace, the jewelry seemed to highlight her eyes. She rose when she heard a carriage moving away from the house. "They are leaving without me?" Her heart lodged in her throat and nearly stopped beating.

"No, it is Angelique and Etienne leaving for the church in Pruitt's carriage. Let us pray they don't kill each other on the way to the ceremony. Etienne would have it no other way. You are going to the church with Pruitt who will give you away. I will also be with you." Then, despite her earlier comment, "See, they were able to work out their differences. I promise you it won't be the first time."

"Masson?" she asked, her heart in her throat.

"He is also with Etienne and your mother as it should be. Your son insisted. He wants to make sure Etienne does right by his mother. He is the best man after all."

"I thought Gil..."

"Well, they are both best men."

Elisa felt the tug at her heart. She loved her little boy so much. He was the reason, most likely the only reason she was marrying Etienne now. If it had not been for that night..."

Her breathing quickened just thinking about that night. Of course, there had been last night. Air didn't come to her even as she tried to gulp it down.

"Are you alright?" Bessy was by her side, her hand resting on her back, stroking, soothing the jitters she was finding uncontrollable.

"I will be as soon as I can catch my breath. A moment, it's all I need." Elisa closed her eyes in a desperate attempt to suck air into her parched lungs. Slowly, second by second, she was able to sip just a tiny bit more air then more until she could finally breathe again.

"You shouldn't be nervous. Etienne will make a fine husband and father, you know. Even though your mother doesn't entirely approve of him, she is coming to accept him."

"You're sure about that." Elisa didn't have any hopes Bessy's words were true. It was Angelique who convinced her so many years ago not to see Etienne; that if she did, he would only cause her heartache and grief. She remembered Angelique's words as if she spoke them now. He was no good, a womanizer and a scoundrel as well. The life he chose to lead was a dangerous one. If she married him, she would be swept into the intrigue whether she liked it or not.

"I am positive."

"What does my mother know about Etienne that she refuses to tell me? She's made many insinuations but she has no details or proof. So far it seems he has been honest with me about his missions. I know he hasn't told me everything, but in time I'm sure he will tell me what he can."

"I don't think she is making anything up. She has her ways, you know." Bessy was now defending Angelique. "There is very little that happens in Bordeaux she doesn't know about, most of France as well. Her clients come from many parts of France because her girls are beautifully exotic and well trained in the arts offered there. Of course, Margaux has her eyes and ears in Paris. Between the two of them, no one important has a secret.

Of course, Bessy would stand up for her mother. Angelique was her livelihood. She would not want to be put out on her ear. "Maybe not." Elisa smoothed her skirts looking to the door.

Anything Etienne told her last night could be embellished and the tale could veer many different directions. Only Etienne knew the truth.

Would he ever tell her everything?

Perhaps she didn't want to know everything. Maybe the missions he went on were better left a secret.

"Come, we need to go. You don't want the bride groom thinking you're having second and maybe third thoughts about marrying him."

"No, I don't because he would run after me and haul me back. I made a promise to him that I mean to keep. Besides, I've wanted this forever, since I was a little girl."

She looked one last time in the mirror then turned to Bessy. "I'm ready."

At the bottom of the staircase waiting in the entrance was Pruitt, a huge grin on his handsome face. "I see why Bessy didn't want Etienne seeing you before you walk down the aisle to marry him." He held out his arms for Elisa to take. "You are lovely. Bewitchingly so."

"Thank you." She smiled, her heart filling with love for this man who had helped her over the last years. She thought if Etienne was only half as loving and thoughtful as his father, her life would be beautiful.

Bessy lifted her skirts, keeping them off the ground as they walked to the carriage. Once inside, she smoothed her gown, spreading the fabric around her so it wouldn't wrinkle. Bessy and Pruitt sat on the other side.

"What made you change your mind about marrying my son," Pruitt asked. "I know it's not my business and you don't have to answer but I'm curious."

For a moment or two she stared out the window. "Etienne changed my mind."

"It was as I suspected. It was time. And certainly." He leaned forward setting his hand on Elisa's, "My son was not ready four and half years ago. He had a lot of growing up to do. If he had been prepared to be a husband and father, he would have never taken that assignment that led him out of the country and into more trouble than he needed."

"Adventures to experience. He told me a lot yesterday. We talked about some of them," Elisa said wondering what troubles exactly Pruitt was referring to. "I doubt if I was ready either. When Masson was born, I was barely eighteen. In so many ways I was still a little girl. Mother sheltered me my entire life. Then I expected Angelique to solve all my problems. I listened to her, every word. Did just as she said. There were no decisions I made on my own, except to move to the cottage. She was not very nice when it came to describing your son."

"I suppose so and perhaps I played a part in that. I confided in her my worst fears about Etienne. He was secretive about everything he did, still is. There was much I had no business telling Angelique but I was worried about him, afraid for his life at times. Much of this happened before your incident in Margaux's Bordello. When we knew who the father of your child was, I said nothing more that could be taken the wrong way. I'm eternally sorry for my part in what happened. The decisions should have been left up to the two of you."

"Do you even know where he was all those years?"

She knew Etienne told her relatively nothing in the scope of his adventures. There was more to tell, but she had the feeling some of it might well put her life in danger, as well as their son's life, if she knew of the more dangerous and secretive missions. She would accept what he was willing to tell her.

"A few things. I have to admit that in the latter part of his career with the government, I quit asking. He's been all over the world on royal assignments, but I don't know what they were. He called them adventures."

"He told me he stole a painting from another person who stole it from the Louvre."

"Ah, that is one of his favorite stories as well as one of his first assignments. It must have happened at least seven years ago. The incident was in the news, and he was rewarded handsomely for the escapade. Many who work in the Louvre still talk about it."

"Then it wasn't really a secret."

She sighed a bit defeated by the fact he shared something with her she could have already known. She needed his trust.

"No, I'm afraid not. It might be best if you didn't know about all of the mysteries. Most of them, as he's already told you, are government secrets. Look, we are here. I'll go ahead and make sure everything is ready for you."

He jumped from the carriage just as it came to a stop. Elisa and

Bessy watched him march into the church.

A few minutes later they saw him striding from the door, Angelique beside him, both grinning. A little soft breath of air escaped Elisa, relieved at seeing the smiles.

He and Gil along with Masson are waiting at the altar," Angelique said. "Would you like me to stand up for you?"

She looked from Bessy to her mother then paused, her gaze focused on her mother's blue eyes rimmed in dark violet so like her own. A few seconds passed then, "Yes, mother, I think that would be nice." Perhaps the gesture could mend some of the rift between her soon to be husband and her mother. Might start the two of them on a healing path where this marriage was concerned. "And Pruitt will give me away?"

"Yes, my dear, if that's what you want."

His hands were stretched out to help her from the vehicle while Bessy waited once more to make sure her dress did not skim the ground.

At the door to the church, she paused a moment to suck in a breath of air. An organ began to play a wedding march. She looked down the aisle to see Etienne, Masson and Gil all standing at the altar waiting for her. They looked so handsome in their black suits and white shirts. Masson and Etienne could have been twins expect for their size and age.

Her heart skipped a beat as she tried to suck in nonexistent air. This was her family now. She wanted this for such a very long time.

Angelique walked down the aisle first, her head held high. Elisa hoped with a smile on her face. Her nerves threatened to snap with each footstep bringing her closer to the altar and her waiting groom. Before her mother began the short journey, Angelique kissed her on the forehead sincerely wishing her the best in the marriage. Elisa thought that was probably all she could expect.

Pruitt solicitously patted her hand in an effort to reassure before he sat down, but she didn't need the gesture. To be with Etienne had been what she wanted since she could remember. Now, in just a few minutes her dream of becoming Etienne's wife was going to come true. She felt as giddy and as in love as she did that day when he picked her up, twirling her around in a circle before he kissed her.

She smiled and nodded at Etienne. When he returned the smile, she felt his love. She wanted to feel his love for the rest of her life. The walk seemed to take an eternity. When Pruitt finally handed her over to Etienne and she gave her small bouquet of wildflowers to her mother, she heaved a huge sigh of relief. He squeezed her hands as she stepped to the side so they were facing each other, the minister back a step and between them.

"You stole my breath," he whispered to her.

His brown eyes darkened to a very deep brownish black.

"As you did mine."

She shifted her weight listening as the minister cleared his throat and the ceremony began. Listening to the man she had trouble staying focused, the time seemed to pass slowly yet Etienne continued to rub tiny circles on her wrist, encouraging her. She wished the ceremony was over and they could return home even though she understood Pruitt along with Angelique as well as Bessy would most likely stay the night.

He said the necessary words then she did, faltering a few times as she stared into his eyes, which seemed to be teasing a hint of amusement in their dark depth. She wanted to know what he was thinking; if he could possibly be as nervous as she had unexpectedly become. Masson stood next to him and when the minister asked for the ring, he reached into his pocket and handed it to him.

Before she understood the ceremony was done, Etienne's finger was beneath her chin, slowly lifting it until she met his gaze with her own. His lips found hers in a gentle kiss at first then it seemed he could not hold back nor did she want him to. He deepened the kiss, his tongue moving softly across her lips in a silent invitation for her to open for him. When she did, he prolonged the kiss for a moment before pulling away.

When he looked at her, he ran his thumb along her slightly kiss-swollen lips. "More later, I promise."

Her knees were weak. She wasn't at all sure she could walk the rest of the way. Thank goodness there were no witnesses to her weakness, only his father and her mother. There was Gil and Masson but Masson wouldn't notice anything and Gil wouldn't care except to tease her about it at a later time.

There was no rice or clapping as they left, but the minister did present them as Monsieur and Madam Etienne Dubois. She was his now. What she'd always wanted.

"Are you better?" he asked, leaning close to her.

The whisper of his breath floated across her cheek.

"If you mean are my legs working now, maybe." She tried to laugh but the sound didn't make it past her throat.

He chuckled softly, pulling her closer and pressing on her arm. "Do I need to carry you? I think I'd like that. You would be closer to me as well as in my arms. Do you want to be closer?"

"I think I'd like to breathe." Her words slipped out, barely discernible as she tried to sip air. "I think Bessy laced my corset too tight."

"In a short while, the corset won't be a problem. Or." He paused in thought, "I could loosen it now."

"Promise," she sighed leaning against him, ignoring his last statement.

He laughed again. When she looked at him, his eyes had darkened even farther. "I don't know if I can wait to get you into our bed."

"I want that too. Don't forget we have guests."

She realized they'd never asked for the guests, just his father. Pruitt would have found a spare bedroom and let them have the rest of the evening to themselves. Gil would have returned home. They should have been alone except for Masson and once he was put to bed, there wouldn't be any interruptions. Unfortunately, that was no longer their situation.

"Only my father, your mother and Bessy. Gil certainly won't be staying the night," Etienne promised, his voice sounding more hopeful than positive.

"If it's late, he will," she told him, touching his face with her hand and wishing for the same things he was.

Lifting his shoulders slightly, "We will deal with this or not. Perhaps we can just leave them alone and they will figure it all out by themselves. There is plenty of wine. Cook promised to stay and prepare a meal," he said kissing the tops of her hands. "Your carriage awaits." His hands on her waist he lifted her inside then followed.

The rest of the wedding party boarded the second carriage.

Inside, he sat down beside her, letting his hand cup her cheek. She leaned into him. His lips found hers once more. She opened for him, needing him more each second. He was her life, his love and she wanted to feel his love for the rest of her life.

His lips closed over hers. Tiny sounds swelled through her as she felt his breath softly inhale hers. He pulled away then, disappointing her. "We should wait. I don't want to ruin your gown or your hair. We do have company at home. For some odd reason, I've a feeling we might have more than we expect."

She sat back, staring at him then crossing her arms beneath her breasts. "I don't want company. I just want you, Masson as well. What makes you think there will be more guests?"

He laughed again seeming to enjoy her words. "That is how I feel. People will plague us all night long until we are ready to ignore them to do what pleases us. I'm sure of it, although I'm glad they did not all come to our wedding, only because there was not enough time. I'm sure they would have wanted to attend."

"Who?"

He shrugged again, his dimple forming on the side of his mouth.

She pushed on his chest with no results. "What do you know that I don't?" She blinked several times moistening her lips, anticipating another kiss yet realizing then he did mean to wait to kiss her again.

"Your mother. Now I don't know anything for sure. It was something in her tone when we were in the carriage. She was not pleased at all that we did not plan a wedding with her along with our friends. You are her only daughter and she did want some say in this day."

"What are you talking about? You know I don't have friends." She knew her eyes were wide with alarm at the tenor of his words.

"All of the women at Angelique's as well as Margaux's are your friends," he reminded her gently.

"I'm not sure they would be included in a wedding."

"Why not? They are people. They are your friends." He sounded surprised.

"I didn't mean it that way." Truly, she didn't.

Over those years the women in the brothel listened to her stories and dried her tears. They all knew just how long she'd been in love with

Etienne Dubois. Unlike her mother they weren't prejudiced against him, they understood her love for Etienne would last a lifetime. Some were slightly jealous while others had lost loves of their own.

His deep sigh settled around her, warming her in some way. Even then she knew she wouldn't like what he had to say.

"I hope I'm wrong."

"Well," she began indignantly, not wishing to create a damper on this day of celebration, "whatever it is you haven't told me, from the sounds of it, I hope you are wrong too."

"I think she closed the brothel and all of the women as well as Eric are here," he told her. "Angelique really didn't like being left out of the planning. This just might be her idea of revenge or mayhap justification. Who knows?"

Shock coursed through her. Then, "Everyone? How did she know?" Her amazement seemed strange even to her because she knew he was right even though she was praying he was wrong.

"My father might have had a hand in this. In any case, be prepared and thankful if I've come to the wrong conclusion." He ran a fingertip along her chin then took her shudder of desire into his big body.

She clung to him then for a few moments her head resting on his arm. His strength and the power of him seeped through her, giving her strength to meet the possible upcoming explosion of their wedding day. They both had people who cared about them, both had people who would want to celebrate their marriage. Was it so awful of them to not want to share this day?

"The château is ahead. Only a few more minutes and we'll know what to expect for tonight."

"I want you to carry me through the threshold then into our bedroom. Don't stop no matter what. Don't say anything to anyone, not even *bonjour*. You can even lock the door behind us. That way we won't have to see any of them. They can frolic and celebrate all they want. I know Masson will be well cared for, spoiled beyond his wildest dreams with Bessy and both grandparents in attendance. If he doesn't go to bed until midnight, so be it."

"I want that, too, but I don't want to bring your mother's wrath down on my head again. Don't want to give her one more reason to dislike me." He kissed her quickly on the lips then directed her attention to the grounds where there were numerous carriages as well as tethered horses. It seemed all the lights blazed in their home.

The groan rumbled up from her belly settling in her throat as she clung to him. "I'm not at all happy that you foresaw this. Can we turn the carriage around then go to my cottage? We could be alone there."

"Only for a little while," he whispered softly close to her ear.

"They would come for us even there?"

"I'm afraid so. I will carry you though the doorway, if that is what you would like. I want nothing more than for you to be in my arms if only for a few minutes before everyone wants to congratulate us." He touched the hollow at the base of her throat gently with his lips, sipped there for a second.

When he set her down, the cheers echoed around the room.

~ * ~

"Kiss her, kiss the bride." The clapping and chanting continued until Etienne, with a huge grin, obliged his guests.

Bessy appeared with two glasses of champagne, handing them to the couple. "Cheers to Etienne and Elisa may they be happy and have lots of children."

The blush on Elisa's face was beautiful. Etienne wanted to tell his guest the sooner they left the sooner they could get started on those babies. Actually, it wasn't the babies he was thinking of, but his true thoughts would make the color of Elisa's cheeks even darker if he said out loud what he was thinking.

The babies would come, as many as she wanted.

In the parlor it seemed couples had already paired off, Etienne's friends with the ladies from Angelique's. He hoped they would wait until they found a bedroom in the west wing to explore each other more thoroughly. For now, everyone seemed polite and respectable.

"My goodness," Elisa said, as her mother stepped toward her grinning. "Is everyone here?"

"All the women you've known since you were a child. They wanted to share in your happiness and saw no reason why they shouldn't. I made sure our cook was here to bake all the tiny pastries you love so well. Along with Etienne's cook, she made the cake while we were at the church."

"You've thought of everything, mother," Etienne laughed, holding up his glass to her sour expression.

He understood she would not appreciate being called his mother, but he couldn't resist the jibe since she had outdone herself to put her stamp on their wedding day.

"You're welcome," she gritted out as Pruitt jabbed her in the ribs with an elbow as if to tell her to behave herself.

"We didn't plan on any of this. Thank you," Elisa said, her voice soft, looking up the stairs as if she wanted to disappear.

Then, turning to Etienne, "The only one of your friends here that I know is Gil."

"The only one of these women I know is Bessy. So, if you are asking if I've slept with any of these wonderful ladies who have come to celebrate with us, the answer is no."

"I would not be so crude as to bring a woman to your house on your wedding day who you have been intimate with," Angelique said curtly, turning then and walking away, her back stiff.

Etienne was taken aback momentarily by her curt words then looking to Elisa he saw she'd grown a bit pale. She knew he was no monk and he'd not been celibate over the last years. Her mother's words should not have elicited this reaction but they had.

He bent as to whisper to her, "Don't let your mother upset you. From this day forward the only woman who will be in my bed and beneath me," he stopped for a moment grinning, "or on top of me is you. Look," he pointed into the dining room. "I think that is our cake. The sooner we cut it the sooner we can leave."

"Is that polite? I've never been to a proper wedding. The few at the brothel were far from the norm." She laughed despite the crease line between her eyebrows.

"It's the way of things, but I'm afraid we'll have to mingle a little bit and thank our guests for coming and wishing us well. After that, we can find our way to the cake and make our way upstairs. No one will care because they will understand just by looking at you why I want my bride to myself."

They stepped onto the side patio. The night was warm, redolent with the scent of spring flowers. The nearly full moon cast pale blue-yellow shadows across the furniture and the people.

Etienne pulled out a chair for her. "I'm going to get us something to eat. Will you be alright here?"

She nodded, watching as some of the guests were dancing then waved at Gil as he walked toward her and sat down.

"Are you finally happy?" he asked, taking her hand in his before slowly bringing it to his lips for a gentle kiss. "I always hoped that in time you would fall in love with me."

She pulled her hand away. "You know I've only loved Etienne and yes, I'm very happy. It is what I've always wanted."

He sat back, stretching his long legs out in front of him, sipping on his drink. "A man can hope."

"Best you stop hoping now and find yourself a woman of your own," she chided him.

From the corner of the room Etienne was watching Gil, deciding he'd let the man play his game. He'd always wondered about Gil's loyalty. Over the last few years there had always been something about the way he spoke, too smooth and perfect. It seemed he always said what he thought was expected of him not what was on his mind. When he found Gil playing with his son, he saw the worst possible side of the man. He understood then that he'd been away too long.

"I see you found my one guest that you know." He set the plate of food in front of her. "The cook assured me this selection has only your favorite treats. I hope she was right."

Elisa laughed a purely musical laugh. Etienne didn't think he'd ever heard her sound quite like that. At that moment he truly knew she was happy. "It is. She knows me well. When I was little and before I moved to the cottage, I used to sneak into the kitchen in order to taste everything that came out of the oven. If I didn't like something, she'd always told me she'd take it off the list of foods she served their clients."

"Did she?"

Etienne picked up her free hand, holding it amazed at the fragility of the bones and the feminine curve of her wrist. She was fragile and delicate. He needed to take good care of her. Thoughts of some of his more intense enemies flashed through his head. Yes, he would have to take great care. Now that he retired, perhaps he would not have to worry.

"I don't know since I was never allowed near the kitchen or the parlor after the twelve o'clock hour. She probably didn't but it appears she remembered my favorites."

"I see someone I need to talk to." Gil pushed away from the table bowing slightly as he left.

"What did he want?" Etienne asked, his voice a low growl, knowing his disapproval was too evident. "I don't like the fact he waited until I left to come congratulate you."

"Is something wrong? I thought he was your friend, "she told him as he stared at her hard, his eyes darkening.

He needed to tamp the anger down, realizing once again the emotion he was feeling was pure jealousy. An emotion he was unfamiliar with except where Elisa was concerned.

Then, following a long drawn-out sigh as he tried to conceal his emotions concerning Gil, "I thought so too. I don't know why but I don't trust him where you and Masson are involved. He is keeping secrets."

"Because he has a relationship with our son?" she asked, touching the palm of her hand to his cheek. "So many times, he was there for me. I can't recount all of them. It seems to me that is, in and of itself a true test of loyalty."

"Yes, and because of what he wants from you. It wasn't just his friendship with me that brought him to your cottage," Etienne admitted reluctantly, watching Gil's back. When he stopped to speak to someone, a jolt swept through him then a lost memory that he couldn't recall. He knew the man who Gil was speaking with but the man definitely wasn't one of his friends.

"Hello, you two," Pruitt said, sitting down with Rubie, her hand in his. "You remember Rubie," Pruitt looked at Elisa.

"I do. She used to braid my hair and sometimes put it into ringlets. It never stayed though, in the ringlets."

"You were such a darling little girl and now a beautiful loving woman who has found herself a handsome man." Rubie smiled at her while she found reason to lean against Pruitt who brought her hand to his lips, kissing the back gently.

"Thank you," Elisa said color rising on her cheeks.

Etienne grinned a besotted expression marking his face, "You should enjoy the compliments. Rubie is right. Now if you don't mind, I'd like to see what Gil is up to."

He waited a few seconds to see her nod then left, skirting the shadows until he was within hearing distance of Gil and the other man.

Little was said but Etienne got the distinct impression the man Gil spoke to was not happy with him and Gil was in agreement. He wasn't sure if the anger was over his marriage or one of his past assignments. Yet he understood he would have to discover the truth. Again, his gut tightened, telling him there was more here than was apparent at first glance.

He gave up on learning anything more when the man left and Gil joined one of Angelique's ladies, as Gil appeared to be planning on spending the evening with her.

"What are you doing away from your bride?" Angelique asked, suddenly standing next to Etienne while sipping her champagne.

"You gave me a start."

It wasn't like him to be so engrossed in what was going on in front of him that he didn't hear someone approaching from behind. He would have to make sure that didn't happen again.

"Well?" Angelique's smile was smug.

"Needed some air and a moment to think," he said trying to stick as close to the truth as he could.

"Away from your blushing bride? Now, why don't I believe that?"

She looked to the table where Elisa was still sitting with Pruitt and

Rubie then to the shadowed figures he'd been watching.

"She looks fine to me," he said, grinning and thinking she looked more than fine.

His body hardened watching the movement of her hands, the graceful arch of her neck as she spoke while he thought of the rest of the night in front of them.

"Of course," Angelique said harshly seeming irritated with him once again. Nothing new here.

"Why did you agree to come to the wedding?"

"Between your father and my daughter's obvious love for you, I didn't have a choice. She was never going to move on to someone else even when she was presented with a chance, and when you returned and wanted her, I knew I was defeated. A mother always wants her daughter to be happy."

"Then you will stand by us and support this marriage? Where you are concerned, I don't want to be always looking over my shoulder." Etienne wondered how much of what Angelique was telling him was truth and how much was a lie. It seemed to him Angelique always had her daughter's best interest at heart.

What did Angelique believe that best interest was?

He watched her for a few more seconds, running over everything he knew about her in his head. She'd done so much to sway Elisa away from him, and now she was in favor of the marriage? This also didn't sit well with him. Ulterior motives of course could be at the front of her mind and there was also Masson to consider.

He didn't think so but perhaps age made her more serene. She couldn't possibly want anything bad to happen to her daughter or her grandson.

"Think I'll go see to my wife. In my mind, it's past time to cut the cake so we can let the rest of you celebrate to your heart's content." He wanted to feel her against him, trace the contour of her jaw and watch her shiver in response. Craved to feel her mold herself flush against his body.

It was, after all their wedding night.

He sat down beside her. She was glowing and smiling. Pruitt and Rubie must still be embarrassing her. He placed her hand in his, waiting for her to finish her conversation and look at him. When she did, he stood and pulled her into his arms.

"Would you like to dance, Madam Dubois?" he whispered close to her cheek.

Her smile was wide and the sight sent a spark of enchantment straight to his once jaded heart. She set a hand on his shoulder then he placed one on her waist.

"I'll tell you a little secret, Monsieur Dubois. I don't dance very well. It would be wise for you to guard your feet."

Her voice was soft and lilting. He could clearly hear the amusement in her voice.

He let out a roar of laughter, enjoying her honesty. She most likely had very little chance to dance. "I will heed your warnings. However, I want you to know you can step on my feet anytime you wish."

They moved slowly to the haunting music brought by Angelique. The musicians she found on short notice were truly very good. Even in public and dancing, he loved holding her in his arms, He enjoyed the sensations of her gentle curves pressing against him despite the fact they should put a small measure of distance between them. On his wedding night, giving in to the morays of society was not something he intended to do.

"Why were you following Gil?" She pushed slightly away from him, looking at him as if he could answer.

"Had a feeling in my gut." He spoke softly yet his voice was low, his heart throbbing faster as he put that scenario behind him and thought of this evening's pleasure. "It's nothing for you to worry about."

"I do though. You are so secretive and your life before was so different. I know you haven't told me much about what you did." Her voice trailed off wistfully. She sighed then, the soft sound touching his heart. "I also know you're going to leave me to figure something out and I'll worry. What I don't know is when."

He was struck by the sincerity of her words as well as the knowledge she seemed to have despite the fact he'd only just decided he would have to seek out his informants. Something was brewing. If he had any sense, he needed to be prepared. Originally, when information was leaked to him, he thought to seek Gil's help. Now after witnessing the conversation a few minutes ago, he changed his mind. Angelique would have to keep her guards around the château. In her eyes, that would be one more strike against him.

He wasn't sure if he should admit his departure to her on their wedding night, but he didn't want lies between them. "Only long enough to go to Paris."

"Then you will take me with you." Her eyes were alight and shining. "While there was very little for me there, in some ways I miss the flamboyant excitement of the city."

He cleared his throat, "I'll think about it."

"I can see Margaux," she said. "I'd like that. We could stay in my room in the brothel."

"Second floor, first door to the right?" He winked at her.

"No, that was just the one night. My usual room is on the third floor."

"Perhaps that would be the safest place for both of us." He traced her eyebrows, wishing they were upstairs in their bed. "I'll send a message in the morning and see what she says. It would be a few days before we hear back from her although I meant to leave as soon as I was sure you were acceptable to the idea. Would your mother take care of Masson while we are gone?" He looked for Angelique in the crowd and once again she surprised him.

"I'd love to," Angelique stepped beside them. "Masson will have so much fun and I'll absolutely love spoiling him."

"Are you always eaves dropping?" Etienne growled, irritated with Angelique in one sense but relieved that she was willing to help. Still, he didn't trust her any more than she trusted him.

"Margaux would love to have the two of you at her establishment. I know when she finds out about the wedding, she will be sad she was not invited, perhaps even angry that the two of you could not wait even a few days for her to have time to attend," Angelique went on to say.

"Angelique is right." Elisa turned from his arms to watch her mother whose smile seemed brighter as she spoke of her Parisian friend. "Margaux would love to have us. I've missed her. That night when..." she cleared her throat. "When we..." She looked away then seeming to decide it was not the right time to speak of the first tryst between her and Etienne even though it was no secret to her mother.

"Then it's settled," Angelique said. "When?"

"As soon as I speak with my father," Etienne said searching the area for Pruitt and Rubie. "Perhaps tomorrow. You can take him with you on your way back to Bordeaux."

"That will have to wait until morning. I believe your father and Rubie have already found a room to spend the night. Rubie always sees to your father's needs when he comes to my place," Angelique said. "I would not be surprised if I lost her to your father very soon. They've always been smitten with each other."

Etienne roared with laughter, tightening his hold on Elisa. "They left before we've cut the cake? How *drole*. Come let us do our duty instead of staying here to make our guests wait when they seem to want to retire more than we do."

Eager to depart, he took hold of Elisa's hand practically dragging her to the cake, picking up two glasses of champagne on the way. Angelique followed at a more sedate pace but reached the table with a glass of her own before Etienne made the announcement.

She tapped on her glass with the handle of a fork as she waited for the guests to quiet. Then she held up her glass. "It seems the newlyweds would like their wedding night. Shall we toast them?"

Everyone held up their glasses cheering. As best man, Gil should have volunteered a toast but he was nowhere to be found. When Etienne searched, he found him once again in the shadows speaking with the gentleman.

"Take a sip," Etienne encouraged as Angelique handed him the cake knife, a precocious smile on her lips.

He groaned thinking of the night ahead that had seemed so near a few hours ago and now when he looked upstairs, he wondered how much longer it would be before they were actually alone.

Elisa looked at him wide eyed, "What now?"

"Put your hand on top of mine." After she did, he grinned. "We cut the cake."

With that accomplished and the small piece sitting on a plate, he held the plate in one hand and the other he broke off a small portion.

"Open for me," he murmured and when she did, he set the piece in her mouth, icing brushing across her lips as her tongue swept across her mouth as well as his lingering fingers. He bent and kissed her, tasting the sweetness. "Now it's your turn."

With the process repeated, he downed the glass of champagne then nodded for her to do the same. "Good night, my friends. Enjoy. Make sure when you bed down for the night you stay in the west wing."

He ran with her then, darting between people until she stumbled. Impatient to reach their rooms, he swept her into his arms and continued to race up the stairs taking them two at a time until he reached the landing. Then more sedately he walked to Masson's room and listened at the door.

"Is he asleep?" she asked, her breath rapid as if she'd been the one running.

Before he answered he placed a kiss at her pulse point needing to feel the beginnings of her passion. Then, "Sounds like it. Would you like to kiss him goodnight?" Etienne nearly groaned when he asked her, afraid the boy might wake up.

"Yes, but I don't want to wake him." Elisa slowly opened the door peeking inside.

"I'll wait here," he told her, a catch in his voice.

If Masson woke up, their night would be postponed until they could get him back to sleep. He watched as she slipped her shoes off and handed them to him before she silently made her way to his bed. She bent over and kissed him on the forehead. Etienne held his breath as Masson made a tiny sound then rolled over without waking. With that accomplished, she turned and walked from the room.

When she reached him, she stood on her toes, winding her hands behind his head. She pulled him close, kissing him, her tongue running along his lips. "Thank you," she told him when she pulled away.

"You don't have to thank me. I'm blessed to have him and he is blessed to have such a loving mother."

Etienne's lips met hers, brushed softly, anticipating more in the next few minutes. His arms held her close. Her fingers wound into his hair. He closed his eyes for a few seconds wishing he could remember his mother. It had been so long since he'd thought about his loss. His father had been a wonderful parent though. He'd never wanted for love. The kiss ended but the promise of so much more lingered between them.

She didn't say anything, just leaned into him, her body pressing against his as they walked to the room. These feelings for her were something he'd never thought to experience.

He opened the door, letting her inside first. He held her slippers in hand as he stepped in behind her then let them fall to the floor.

"Look, Bessy must have a hand in this." A few lanterns lit the patio. On the table outside a bottle champagne was chilled in a bucket. There were glasses along with food.

"Do you want champagne?" he asked even while he stepped onto the balcony and poured them both a glass.

"I suppose I do," her voice wavered. "I didn't think I'd be nervous about tonight, not after last night."

"It's our first night as husband and wife. I'm not surprised," he murmured, taking her hand and gently drawing her toward him. He handed her a glass as he tugged her so she was sitting on his lap his hand resting on the curve of her hip. "Shall we?" He lifted his glass to his lips.

Watching him, she sipped slowly, one hand resting on his shoulder. She caught her bottom lip between her teeth then smiled at him, her palm set lightly against his cheek. He turned into her hand before placing a kiss on the palm.

"Did I tell you how beautiful you are?" he asked as she leaned back, exposing the length of her neck to his kisses. "That my breath caught in my throat when I first saw you at the end of the aisle. I knew I was a man well and truly blessed.

"No, not tonight? Well, yes you did," she laughed softly.

The sound filled his senses. He wanted to hear her laughter every day for the rest of their lives.

"Do you like the dress?" he queried, his lips touching her softly then pulling back as he waited for an answer. "I didn't have time to ask before."

"It's beautiful and," she paused, her hands on both sides of his head, "how? How does it fit so well?"

"Did I have it made just for you, you ask? Yes, and I was very careful with the measurements but it's not what you think. Your mother has a dressmaker who also has your measurements. I just told her what I thought you might like. Do you?"

"Oh, it's not what Bessy told me but then," she placed her mouth on his, teasing him in all the ways he taught her, "it's exactly what I would have picked out."

Pleased with her answer, he reached for the tray of food but stopped. "Are you hungry. I'm sure this will all still be here in a little while." He finished his glass of champagne. "No one is going to interrupt our evening to clear this table. We can eat later."

"Only hungry for you," she murmured as his fingers began to travel down her back slowly unfastening the multitude of tiny pearl buttons. He pushed the sleeves down her arms. When she looked down, her corset was pushing her breasts high, the half-moons obvious to him.

His lips trailed kisses across the tops of her breasts. Her hands wound into his hair pulling him closer as she arched her back as if she wanted nothing more than to be closer to him. He reveled in the ripple of sounds he heard, knowing she was feeling his love.

She pushed his waistcoat from his shoulders, letting it fall to the floor. He unlaced her corset, flinging it aside and out of his way. Her fingers found the buttons on his shirt, swiftly undoing them as she once again arched toward him offering herself to his kisses.

His breath stopped as he tried to inhale. Her fragrance was subtle and sweet, slightly vanilla, partially lavender. Her fingers found his nipples as she ran her hands lightly across them, tantalizing every sense he possessed before traveling lower to his waistband. He sucked in air. Instead of removing her camisole, his mouth closed over her veiled nipple while she ran her hands along his back, his muscles flexing with the sensations she created.

Deep in his throat he groaned and brought his lips to meet hers. His fingers ran through her hair, dislodging pins. The sound of them hitting the floor was, for a moment, the only sound in the silence of the night. Her nails dug into his shoulders as his attention shifted to her other breast and he worried the tight coral bud with his teeth.

"Please, Etienne, don't make me wait any longer." She accepted him, completely, totally.

"Please what?" he grinned.

"Take me to bed." She sighed into his mouth, sucking air from him as she inhaled. "Let me feel your love."

~ * ~

Gil settled back against the post supporting some of the Dubois grapes as he watched Etienne and Elisa leave the patio for their rooms. His gut tightened, thinking if he'd acted sooner, perhaps not been such a coward, that he could have been him. It seemed he'd fallen in love with Elisa. The love didn't happen overnight. No, it was slow and languorous, moving with the speed of a tortoise, but it was real nonetheless.

He wasn't stupid enough to think she would ever stop loving Etienne, but he could be content knowing he was the man in her bed at night. Perhaps he was fooling himself and that would have never been enough.

Etienne had left Glasgow under a shadow. The rumors had it he'd found himself working for a woman, a most unsavory one. There was more to the gossip. Another woman almost died and he'd played some part in that role or deception, he wasn't sure. He plucked a piece of grass, twirling the blade between his fingers, wondering about his next course of action.

"What are you thinking?" Angelique sat down beside him.

"She should have been mine," Gil sighed, his voice vanishing into the late night air. "I should be the one bedding her tonight, not Etienne."

"She still can be." Angelique's voice was smooth and controlled. "I can help make it happen."

Gil was shaking his head, disgusted with the tenor of his thoughts along with the fact this woman could so easily bend him to her will, just as she had her daughter. He would never be in Elisa's heart. He understood that fact. Angelique did not. "You still don't get it, do you?"

"What I know is that you're the better man. Etienne has played games with everyone he knows, even his father. His life has been a constant source of gambles linked to bad choices."

"I understand but—"

Angelique waved her hand in the air, stopping him, "Etienne was a little girl's fantasy, nothing more. She's a woman now and if something were to happen to Etienne..."

Her smile sent a shiver of fear down Gil's spine as he wondered what the woman had in mind. In Bordeaux she wielded a lot of power but how far did it stretch? "Nothing is going to happen to him. I would never instigate anything like that."

"If it did."

"The deed would not be accomplished at my hands."

"You've been pressed with the task of bringing him back to Scotland to stand trial for murder," Angelique said her voice soft.

"How do you know about that?" Gil jumped to his feet, furious that his role had leaked to her somehow.

This task had never been to his liking. The loyalty between the two men stretched back nearly thirty years. The murder was accidental, in defense of another woman. He wasn't going to take his friend anywhere. Even now there were negotiations as to his pardon. The notorious Duke of Southcliff vouched for Etienne. The story was riddled with gossip. If anyone understood what happened it would be the Duke. His sister-in-law was the woman who almost died. Etienne played no part in that except to help save her.

"Angelique's place has eyes and ears within its walls. It is rumored, in any case, as does Margaux's place. If one wants to keep a secret, it's best not to speak when at either establishment."

"You really hate him that much? His death would devastate both Elisa as well as Masson." Gil's words shot out quickly and with more force than he intended. "Even belying the fact, he is married to your daughter and his seed gave you the grandson you love? Would you want the boy to be without his father?"

"No, and yet I find that I love my daughter too much to let her stay with that bounder."

She looked down the hill at the château still bright with lights and the celebration of the wedding.

"You know he's a good man. Charles employs him still. He's the king's assistant. Charles would never allow him to die from a mission he sent him on. What makes you think he is all wrong for her?"

Gil didn't understand Angelique, not at all. She was willing to sell her son-in-law, the man her daughter loved, to their enemies. He would have to think on this. Betrayal did not sit comfortably with him. He didn't plan on betraying anyone but if it became necessary, his loyalty was with Etienne.

"He is." She didn't want to admit anything else. She rose, dusting off her skirts. "I should get back to the house, not that anyone will miss me. I've Masson for the next week or so. Seems they are taking a honeymoon in Paris. They want to see Margaux." She turned to address him again. "Or, he has unfinished business there."

Unmoving, Gil watched her walk down the hill then enter the house, all the while going over her words in his head. The information she gave him was valuable to him and his mission. He might not have noticed Etienne's departure if Angelique had not told him simply because he was sure they would depart either early morning or late night. If he was taking Elisa with him, odds would have it their departure time would be early morning. The question now was if it would be today or tomorrow. He looked to the sky, realizing he needed sleep. With a heavy sigh, he resigned himself to the knowledge there would not be much forth coming for him today.

Slowly, he stood and followed Angelique's footsteps to the house. He picked up a few snacks as he walked up the steps to the west wing.

Chapter Eight

The newlyweds entered Margaux's establishment in Paris as Elisa always did by the back entrance and through the kitchen. Today the weather was warm, sunny for the first time since they began the trip. She lifted her face to the sky, soaking in the gentle warmth.

"*Mon cherie.*" Francoise's arms widened as she ran into them, moisture clogging her throat as she brushed away tears with the backs of her hands. "Has it really been four and a half years? I cannot believe it. In the future, you must come visit more often. I've missed your sunny smile."

"It has been that long." She sniffed, realizing there were people in Paris she missed and loved. Not the people she went to school with but the people here at Margaux's. They were dear to her heart and it had not been well done of her to leave them over the years without visiting. With no thought to their feelings, she had abandoned them.

Etienne stood behind her, watching his hands behind his back. When she looked at him, she flashed him a lopsided grin, her eyes watery. She wanted to touch his dimple, run a fingertip along his jaw, needed to feel the closeness only he could give her.

"Madam Dubois," Bailey stepped into the kitchen, his arms wide for another greeting as well as a mammoth hug. "I thought I heard your voice. It has been too long since you showed your face in this establishment," he admonished just as the cook had done.

Another hug and more tears, Etienne pulled her close as she rested her head against his chest. This was a homecoming of sorts. She was with the man she loved and at home now in one of her favorite places.

"I've missed you too, Bailey. You are just as big as I

remembered."

The lump in her throat seemed to grow larger as a few of the ladies wandered in with hugs and well wishes for her marriage. Margaux, she knew would wait until Bailey brought them to her suite of rooms upstairs. Margaux, what would she have to say about this sudden marriage of hers? Over the years, she listened to her pour her heart out about her fanciful love for Etienne Dubois. Now, that love was a reality that couldn't be denied.

"Would you like to rest up or see Margaux first?" Bailey asked, his voice taking on a low throaty sound as if he was moved by her appearance here at the bordello.

He was the tallest man she knew, his shoulders wide His short-trimmed beard now held a bit of silver-gray. In addition, he was also one of the kindest men she'd ever met.

She laughed, drying her eyes again with the handkerchief Etienne handed to her. "I think you know the answer to that."

"To Margaux's private sitting area then." He turned walking slowly even though he would know she knew her way. She soaked in the ambiance of the place, realizing that for a bordello it was very modestly yet richly furnished. There was nothing flashy or gaudy about the interior. Margaux's establishment catered only to the high-class.

They followed Bailey through the parlor, through a maze of hallways then up the steps until they reached her private rooms. Margaux stood when they entered, her hands clasped in front of her, warmth in her expression as she greeted them. Her hair also was beginning to show her age with white hair around her temples complimenting the blond. Her eyes twinkled with unsaid humor, her ample bosom rising and falling with the breaths she inhaled.

"So, you finally married the man of your heart. It is about time Etienne caught you. You did make him chase you."

She opened her arms to Elisa. Elisa ran into them, wishing her mother would comprehend her feelings as Margaux did.

"I did catch him, didn't I?" Her voice was soft as she shot her husband a wicked glance.

She hoped Etienne would understand that this woman was like a second mother to her but she was much more empathetic. She listened while her mother already had her mind made up.

A mind that was never easily swayed.

"I'm so glad everything worked out the way you always wanted. When you spoke of your love, my heart always broke in to two pieces."

She turned to Etienne. "Never hurt her or you will have me to answer to, young man."

Etienne smiled, the dimple showing and at that moment, Elisa knew he'd won Margaux over. "I promise you the last thing I would ever do is hurt Elisa. She owns my heart."

"Then we will all be happy, you and me. Is anyone hungry? I've some of your father's fine wines and," she paused thoughtfully, "I believe I also have some of yours. We knew you were coming so Francoise fixed a tray of your favorite dishes. Received the message from your mother just this morning only a few hours ahead of your arrival."

They sat at the table in Margaux's dining room, the best china and silverware brought out for this occasion. For a few minutes the atmosphere seemed stilted to Elisa, the silence overwhelming. It was the first time she'd never been able to pour her heart out to Margaux since that day so long ago. Even though, she supposed, she held no secrets from Etienne.

This was different.

"I can't tell you how much I appreciate your support and love." There was a catch in her words as she thought about her mother. "It means so much to me."

Margaux leaned forward, her arms resting on the table for a second, her eyes expectant. "Tell me about the wedding. Did Angelique attend or did she stay away from your most important day in silent protest?" Margaux asked, slowly picking up her napkin before dabbing at her lips as if there was actually food that needed to be wiped away.

"She was there as was Pruitt, Etienne's father." Her gaze drifted to her silent husband who seemed content to listen and wait. She was sure he was absorbing everything that was being said and filing it away in some secret spot in his brain. He would remember everything, every spoken word, every nuance.

"I see and did she protest as everyone would have expected?" Margaux asked as she stared at her over the rim of the crystal glass holding her wine, her gaze searching for answers to questions that had not yet been asked.

"No, and that in itself bothers me. She asked to stand up for me almost as if she gave her consent seemingly, was thrilled with the marriage, which we both know she was not. In any case, I agreed hoping some of the distance between us would be narrowed."

Elisa looked at Etienne wishing to apologize but he shook his head seeming to read her mind.

"No need. I've always known exactly how your mother feels about me. She will never forgive me for taking your innocence in a brothel. It was something she tried to guard you from your entire life. Somehow, in one evening, I managed to undo all her carefully constructed plans for your life. She will never look upon me with favor but," he stopped as if thinking, "she will do nothing to put our vows asunder."

"So, now you feel differently about Angelique," Margaux focused her gaze in Etienne's direction, her lips thinning as if she might feel the same as the woman they were talking about.

"I would be lying if I said otherwise. Trusting her will be a long time in coming."

It seemed he didn't want to elaborate about that night or the myriad of consequences surrounding those moments when he broke through Elisa's maidenhead taking her innocence.

"Honest at least." She didn't look as if she was going to take her words at face value. "What are your intentions for the rest of your lives? Are you going to continue your work?"

"Margaux," Elisa said in protest. "He does not need to be interrogated and his plans are between us. Since we haven't spoken of them, I would like to be the first to know and discuss what exactly those plans are concerning his assignments."

"I'm sure your mother never sat down long enough with Etienne to ask those questions. Correct me if I'm wrong. If he hasn't thought about his plans, then he should. With a wife and a child, it is far past the right time to put his life in order."

"No, no she didn't. She might like me better if she'd taken some time to get to know me before judging. Perhaps she should have questioned me as you are."

"So," Margaux continued with an all-knowing smile, prompting Etienne to speak to her even after Elisa's protests.

Etienne picked up Elisa's hand, gazing into her eyes while holding her fingers gently. She felt his warmth along with the steadiness she was growing to appreciate. His gaze was potent and raw, filled with sincerity, his charming half-smile filling her with confidence.

"My planning, barring complications from this trip which I'm not privy to talk about, is to settle down at the vineyard and in the process raise a family. The only trips I will take from now on will be with my wife and children for leisure and her enjoyment." He squeezed her hand, his gaze focused on her, heating her from the inside out.

"What complications?" Curious, she pursued the topic he just told her he couldn't talk about.

"What I can tell you is that circumstances that were beyond my control in Glasgow have come back to haunt me. I believed, sincerely, that they were taken care of, at least legally, but individuals can always take on a motion of their own. There are a few who would like to see me brought back to Scotland for justice. Since justice has already been served, it is my thought they will try to take their so-called form of justice into their own hands thereby punishing me."

"Well, that was more than I expected you to tell me. Does Elisa know anything about this affair?"

"No, no, she doesn't. Only what I've just said. We've been preoccupied these last couple of days. If you must know, the news only came to me the evening we were wed, or at least the feeling in my gut that something wasn't right. I received an anonymous message the morning of our wedding and never got a chance to read it until later. Nor have I shared it with Elisa. Later, I will tell her what I can. We both know there are eyes and ears that people cannot see, so... she will not learn the information inside these walls."

"So, you reacted immediately."

Seconds passed before he replied. "That's why I'm still alive. I listen to my gut and counter to offset anything that could happen. What good would it do if I waited?"

"Nothing, I'm sure." Margaux tapped her fingers on the table, clearly thinking about what Etienne said.

"How does Elisa fit into all this?" Her eyes appeared concerned as she turned her attention to Elisa. "You understand that if you have to leave, she will be safe here with me."

"We both understand safety only goes so far. Last time she was here..." Etienne watched her and seemed to choose not to finish the last sentence.

Elisa stood up quickly, knocking her chair over. "Categorically! The two of you are talking about me as if I'm not in this room with you." Slipping her hand from his, she slammed her hand on the table. "I am here and I'm breathing. I also have a say in my destiny. I also know that I will be safe in this establishment. This situation is different from the one the two of you are talking about."

The air stagnated for several seconds while she breathed deeply stretching her gaze from one to the other. The ripple effect of her anger seemed to dissolve into nothingness. She knew Etienne well enough to understand he would never apologize or bring her into a conversation if he didn't want to. Perhaps the conversation had been best left between Margaux and Etienne.

Margaux's expression changed dramatically, just as Etienne's did not. Nothing about his countenance altered. The slight smile he'd been sporting most of evening remained firmly in place.

"Calm yourself, dear," Margaux said seeming to apologize for the man Elisa loved. "I'm sure he has his reasons and will tell you what he believes you should know when the time is right, just as that's all he will tell me. Now, the two of you should know that you may use whatever resources that are at my disposal. Bailey would be more than willing to help without questions. I'm understanding this is why mother doesn't like him." She sat down, crossing her arms in front of her. "He won't bend to her wishes."

"I'm sure you're right. Angelique has never liked a silent man. She doesn't trust one who doesn't run his mouth while she has this burning need to know everything. To Angelique control is everything."

"And..." Elisa prompted, hoping Margaux would shed a bit more light on the man she was wed to or her mother. To Elisa it seemed she comprehended too little about both of them.

"He took something from you, something she meant for another to have. Did you know she had a man picked out for you? Margaux asked a mischievous smile curving her lips. "What your mother didn't know was this man was or is also involved with our governmental secrets. She had absolutely no control over your choice. That fact didn't sit too well with her."

Surprise hit her clearly and she knew her expression would be readable to Etienne. "No," she said cautiously.

"Who?" Etienne asked, suddenly more eager to be a part of this conversation.

"She never told me anything about the name," Margaux said with a very noticeable twinkle in her eyes. "Suffice it to say she was not pleased at all, putting everything in motion to dissuade Etienne from seeking you out and going as far as to hide you in the bordello until he left France. I am guessing though, once it was learned that you carried another man's bastard, the man she picked for you was no longer interested."

Elisa sat back, her insides churning with the new knowledge. She thought for a moment she might lose the meal she just ingested. Sipping her wine, she willed her stomach to a calm she no longer felt as well as her nerves to steady. The task wasn't as easy as she prayed it would be. Not until Etienne enclosed her hand with his, did she begin to absorb his strength into her and release the demons that had settled into her.

"I think we should retire for the evening. I'm exhausted from the travel as I would assume Elisa is as well," Etienne said, his voice husky, ripe with emotions Elisa wanted to unravel, some she did understand though as she thought of her wedding night.

"Thank you, Margaux. Will we see you in the morning?" Elisa asked, before bending and kissing her forehead.

"I certainly hope so as I'm guessing your plans include more than one day here." Margaux rose, hugging her and nodding at Etienne.

"A room?" Elisa asked.

"The same one you had that night. Do you remember or should I have Bailey show you the way?" Margaux was standing by the door, apparently ready to call for her most trusted employee.

"No need," Etienne said looking to her and holding out a hand for her to take, his dark eyes shimmering. "I fondly remember everything about that night."

"Bailey has already stocked it with all the delicacies you might need or enjoy. I ordered a bath for each of you. The water should be hot and waiting for the two of you. It's a large tub," she said with a wink.

Etienne tossed his head back, roaring with laughter. "I can come to appreciate you, Mademoiselle Margaux. You are a woman after my own heart. *Viens.*" He tugged on Elisa's arm. "Our comforts await us." Then, bending close to her ear, "*Voudrais-tu partager un bain avec moi ce soir*? It's after all, something we have not done yet and I'm sure the experience of bathing together can be quite delightful."

A shiver of raw desire rippled through her, shimmying down her spine to heat the rest of her. Hunger grew. "If you insist," she whispered barely able to form the words as his breath continued to whisper across her neck.

"I do," he said as Bailey escorted them to their room unlocking the door then handing the key to Etienne. "Use the bell cord if there is anything else you would like."

Etienne thanked him then closing and locking the door, he turned his attention to her. She was breathing heavily, her hands clasped in front of her. She didn't have the foggiest notion what to say. The thought of taking a bath with him seemed strangely erotic, and she didn't clearly comprehend how it could be done.

She continued to watch as he slowly undid his cravat letting it fall to the floor as his gaze remained fixed on her. He was walking to her then veered off to test the bathwater. Looking at her, "It's hot. We shouldn't waste a moment."

He shrugged from his waistcoat. It too fell to the floor as he sat and wrestled with his boots. They thumped when he let them go.

Still, she stood frozen watching him disrobe as if she'd never seen him before. Her tongue ran across her lips all the while she was sure he watched the slow moment with a fascination she didn't understand.

"*Viens ice.* I will help you with your clothing," he told her, his hands resting on his thighs.

She smiled and swallowed. Her feet didn't move. His half smile slowly changed the expression on his face as his eyes darkened even more. He held his arms out for her to walk into them.

When it didn't seem she was going to obey, he rose. Striding toward her, he held her hand, pulling her toward the chair. "Sit."

"Why?" She did.

"I don't want the water to get cold. Do you?"

He walked behind her, his fingers quickly undoing the buttons of her gown, slipping the shoulders of the dress down her arms until the fabric pooled around the waist.

"No."

The laces of her corset were undone then, "Raise your arms."

Her chemise floated upward. Everything he removed he flung to one side.

His lips whispered against the nape of her neck then across her shoulders. His hands roamed down her arms. Her body shuddered at the sensations he was creating. The sound escaped her not unbidden but in surprise. Her nipples hardened when his hands lightly brushed across the tips.

He stood in front of her now, taking her hands in his and pulling her against him. She did as he wanted, mesmerized by the moment coupled with the gentle seduction by her husband. He pushed her skirt and petticoats to the floor. She stood in front of him naked.

"You're wearing too many clothes," she said, breathless as her body flamed with the desire he so easily generated.

"I am. We agree."

He rid himself of his shirt and pants. As she watched he swept her into his arms and strode to the hot water that was waiting for them in the bathing room.

When they were settled in the tub, she was straddling him. She felt his arousal hard and pulsing next to her most feminine parts. He ran his hands along her hips, sweeping across her belly then across her ribs until they cupped her breasts. His thumbs lightly swept over the tips.

Her hands rested on his chest, lending her support. When she caressed his nipples, he groaned and adjusted her so he entered inside her. She bent and kissed his lips, ran her tongue along the upper then the lower, felt the tips of her breasts against his chest. Her body clenched around him, begging him to move deeper into her. His hands at her waist, he moved her then brought her down as his hips traveled upward and further inside.

She arched her back, accepting more of him as he found the sensitive spot deep in her female parts that gave her so much pleasure when he touched her. A cry rippled from her throat as the tremors inside her grew to a fevered pitch.

"Etienne..."

Her cry brought a guttural response from him. Water sloshed over the sides of the tub onto the braided rug beneath. She closed her eyes and felt the last driving thrusts as he cried out then pulled her close against him. For several seconds she lay flush against him, her body pressed close with his hand at the small of back then venturing lower to caress her buttocks.

"*Mon bijoux,*" he whispered, his breath warming her cheek as she looked at him once before resting her head against his chest, replete.

She wanted to tell him she loved him, but she suspected he'd been told that by any number of women. He would say the words to her before she laid out her heart first.

"Perhaps we should finish the bath and move on to other things," he said before his lips brushed lightly against hers again, his fingers running up then down her back.

~ * ~

In his dressing gown he set a log on the fire, pushing at with the fire iron. She wore a silky confection Margaux left in the room for them with her name on it, calling the gown a gift for *la lune de miel*. This was hardly a honeymoon. Yet he grinned because he could see through it, every intriguing curve she possessed. If they didn't need to eat, he would remove it and make love to her again. His heavy sigh caught her attention.

"What is it? What are you thinking?"

The crystal glass that held the champagne, another gift this time from Bailey, rested on her lips, slightly swollen from their kisses as she sipped.

"We need to eat," he said, his voice low and deep.

He watched her studying him. He didn't want to tell her he would have to leave as soon as the revelry from downstairs began to fade and the couples retired for the night. Bailey was going with him this time. He needed an experienced man and Bailey had more than most, having fought alongside Napoleon and survived the battle of Waterloo among others. Bailey also knew Paris' every dark alley.

"I'm only hungry for you," she said, breathlessly but she bit into a strawberry, chewing slowly, her eyes darkening.

He groaned wondering how he would leave her tonight without telling her his plans. His smile this time couldn't be contained. "You have an evil way of changing the subject. You want this man's body, don't you? I can tell. Why Madam Dubois, I believe I've created a sex monster."

She flushed deeply at his words then tilted her head a bit sideways tempting him once again as she let the lightweight gown slip from one shoulder. The gesture didn't leave her bared but the gown rested just on top of one, milk white globe. His breath caught in the back of his throat.

Little minx.

He sat down beside her then opened his mouth for her when she placed a piece of cheese on his lips. She let her finger slide into his mouth then another. He moved onto the bed, leaning against the headboard, his glass of champagne in one hand.

"I'm still not the least bit hungry."

He watched her then as she seductively pulled the gown over her shoulder.

"You're leaving as soon as I fall asleep." Her smile didn't reach her eyes, which turned frosty with the words. "It's not well done of you, Etienne, not to tell me."

"No, when the house quiets. How did you know?"

His intuition told him he shouldn't tell her more than she already guessed, but his gut said she needed to comprehend more than he was ever willing to tell her. He never spoke of his plans with anyone but then he'd never possessed a wife before.

"I saw you and Bailey whispering. The secretive words were not about the extras that were brought to the room. Bailey never has anything to do with that."

Her long sigh was disconcerting to him. He might bring the gifts but it is Margaux who directs him.

He raked his hands through his hair displeased that she read him so easily. "Need to learn to be more discreet around my wife. You are far too astute."

Daryl MacTavish had been able to read his thoughts too. It was because of his encounter with her that trouble was once more on his heels. There were times when he closed his eyes he saw Daryl fall helplessly into the swirling ocean water.

She punched him on the shoulder. "How do you expect me to sleep when I know you're leaving?"

"Perhaps if you drink enough champagne. Maybe if I wear you out you will not be able to keep your eyes open."

He pulled her into his arms and between his legs, thinking he needed to keep her naked. Making love would be so much easier if he didn't have to remove clothing each time.

When he set her back slightly, her eyes flashed a spark of some secret he didn't like. Flashes of insight swept through, disconcerting sparks. She had better not try to follow him. He would tan her backside if she tried something so dangerous.

"I won't," she said as if she read his thoughts.

He didn't miss the lack of sincerity in her voice. "You had best stay here right where I leave you. If I thought it would be prudent of me to take you with me, I would. If you are by my side, well then I know you are safe. That knowledge would be a comfort to me." He held her by her shoulders, needing to shake sense into her. Instead, he ran his hands along her arms. "It's too dangerous. I don't want to have to worry about anyone but myself."

"Bailey can take care of himself. So, there is no argument to be had in that quarter."

"So can I."

"You've no idea," he groaned then, pulling her to him, rolling on top of her.

Her kisses were bittersweet. He couldn't get past the thought she intended to shadow him despite his wishes. She had not had nearly enough to drink to incapacitate her. Somehow, he had to extricate a promise.

Her hands were beneath his dressing gown, pushing it away and off his shoulders, as it seemed she frantically tried to touch him. One hand travelled lower. She held his sex in her small, slim hand. He groaned low and deep, husky in the back of his throat. He kept her busy then, making love to her, encouraging her to drink the champagne even though she protested until she finally drifted to sleep. The day's events should have exhausted her hours ago.

She was determined. He would give her that.

He was lying on his back, staring at the ceiling when the soft knock at his door caught his attention. She was still, her breathing easy, her hand resting on his belly. Slowly, he removed it, listening for any change in the cadence of each fragile breath. He needed to be far enough ahead of her if she did wake that she couldn't find his trail.

Needed to make sure he locked the door from the outside. He didn't like that idea. Yet that was all that would prevent her from doing something foolishly life threatening.

Quickly, he dressed before heading for the door, at the last minute slipping the key to the room in his pocket. He looked at her before he opened the door, closing it softly then securing her inside. A long slow breath of relief rippled from his lungs. Baily slanted him a reassuring grin. Only Margaux or his return could free her from the room. He didn't believe Margaux would open the door except for breakfast.

They should be back by then.

Bailey was leaning negligently against the opposite wall, his arms crossed in front of him appearing bored as sin. When he looked up, his grin was broad and his white teeth shown brightly against his dark skin.

"You ready?" he asked, his voice hushed. "Best we get on with this before your little lady wakes up and throes a tantrum loud enough to wake the entire bordello."

Etienne nodded, leading the way down the back steps to the alley where two horses waited for them. They turned their mounts toward the river, moving quickly in the direction of a tavern where they were supposed to meet an informant, someone who was sent by the king personally to aid in this situation. His gut clenched. This was all too convenient, seemed staged.

Inside, the room was dark. Only two patrons still graced the premises. Etienne's attention was directed to a man in the corner. He leaned inattentively against the wall, his hat tipped low, covering his eyes.

The hair on the back of Etienne's neck stood on end. He whirled, his hand resting on the pistol he'd stuffed in the back of his pants. His pulse raced. The energy of a confrontation surged through him. It was this kind of excited charge he lived for.

Bailey's hand stopped him. "Don't show yourself too soon. He might not be our informant or our enemy. Let's sit down at the table over there and see what happens." He nodded to a serving wench who delivered ale and bread to their table.

Etienne heard the waves of the river lapping at the beach, heard the sound of cats in the alley behind the establishment fighting over the scraps that had been thrown their way. Cries of seagulls filtered into the dim interior. He was at ease with the controversial silence as well as the waiting as it seemed Bailey was also.

He leaned back closing his eyes slightly still keeping tabs on the door as well as the man in the corner. A cup of black coffee would be nice right now. For a moment, his thoughts wandered to Elisa and the soft curves of her body, the way she responded to him so sweetly, the hunger along with the passion that seemed to be an undeniable part of her.

"Best you keep your mind on the job," Bailey chuckled softly as the man in the corner rose.

The waitress who served them stopped him with a hug and a gesture toward the stairs. They whispered something for a few seconds.

The man changed his path to the stairs and what Etienne assumed was her room.

One man was left in the tavern. He rose and sauntered their way.

He pulled out a chair and sat down. "Etienne Dubois?"

Etienne nodded as the man looked to Bailey for identification. "My friend and confidant."

"Can't be too careful you understand. As you know there are people looking for you. You're well aware of the fact that you're no longer wanted in Glasgow. Still there are people who would see to your demise. Men who don't like what you did. Your friend Gil told me you would be here."

Gil? What the hell did he know about this other than what might have transpired at their wedding celebration? "I was told that my part in the episode was forgiven." Etienne leaned forward. "Do I need to make sure that has happened?"

"No, but there has been new knowledge brought to life as well your part in some of the things the lady perpetrated. I'm sure its mere gossip by those who would like to see you pay for your complicity in the deception. There are those who would like to see you just as dead as she is."

"I'm not going back to Scotland for any reason. I've protection here but I understand I also need to be wary. It would be nice if you could identify my enemies for me. Who has traveled to France to see to my demise?"

"Leod and Troy have been the loudest voices in bringing you back for trial. I've heard they took a ship from Dover to Calais and they were headed to Paris then to Bordeaux and your winery. It's good you came here. You might have avoided a confrontation until the men can be found."

Neither Etienne nor Bailey spoke for a few seconds after hearing the revelation made by this man. This all seemed too easy and obvious. Who was going to find them and return them to Scotland?

"The Duke of Southcliff, Leslie Stewart, I believe is the name you are looking for. He has a vested interest in helping you. You met I assume?"

What to do? He'd heard the name in conjunction with Donal, Daryl's husband. If he recalled, the duke might have been present that night Daryl nearly met an untimely end, the night he began his journey back to France.

"Thank you," Bailey rose holding out his hand and when the man left, he sat down again next to him.

"What do you think?" Etienne's gaze remained on the door to the tavern.

He was focused and thoughtful, trying to decide the best course of action. An unseen enemy was not one he could fight. There were allies in play but he didn't really know them and Gil acted out some part. He did know Leod. Knew the man resented him for keeping him away from Daryl that night. Kept him from forcing her.

Friend or Foe?

The attack came from the kitchen. Forewarned by the barmaid's screech of alarm both men stood. Instantly, two men, Leod and he assumed Troy, appeared from the kitchen, brandishing guns. The weapons pointed at them. They were evenly matched if not for the weapons directed at their chests. How the devil did they know they would be here? Gil?

"Come with us."

Heavy air settled around Etienne. His pulse beat, his anticipation escalated. Waiting for an opportunity to present itself, he kept his breathing slow, modulated. He felt eager for a fight.

Bailey nodded to him and it seemed at least for now they were in agreement. For the time being they would follow the directions of these men until an opportunity arose.

One of the men motioned for them to move ahead toward the kitchen. Walking slowly, they approached the men and were quickly removed of their guns and knives. Unsaid words traveled between Bailey and Etienne. Tension radiated through his body, his fists clenching tightly as he waited for a mistake, an opportunity. He wasn't sure what was going to happen, what these men meant to do, but murder didn't seem prudent, not in the streets of Paris, not considering who they were.

The blow to the back of his head didn't render him unconscious but did make it difficult to move. He hit the ground fast and hard still aware of his surroundings. He had not seen that one coming. Bailey echoed his groan of pain. Etienne heard the big man had hit the cobblestones hard.

As the first boot hit him in the ribs, he took solace that the key to the room he and Elisa shared was safely tucked away in his pocket. No, Elisa would not turn up to help him and find herself in trouble. With the second blow his breath caught in his throat. At first count he had two broken ribs.

The pair weren't finished. One picked him up while the other pummeled his face and torso with his fists. The blows continued to rain down on him, until his eye was swollen and his ribs throbbed. He was tossed to the ground again, kicked a few more times as if the men didn't want to stop the assault. Several minutes passed after the pair left before he drifted away from consciousness. The fog in his brain could not be considered a dream. It was filled with pain and memories. Sounds came to him from time to time.

A carriage passing by in the street beyond the alley.

Horses hooves clipping on the cobblestones.

People talking.

A dog barking then a low growl.

The sound of Bailey's voice carried to him as he was lifted from the street. Then he heard another voice. Gil spoke softly to him, his voice so low Etienne could make out nothing that was said.

He heard his groan before he could open his eyes. Every part of him pulsed and ached. He tried to move his head but couldn't. Her voice came to him from what seemed like miles away. A few drops of liquid hit his swollen lips. He brushed his tongue across them, trying to absorb the water.

It wasn't enough.

"He is waking up,"

In his fog filled haze it seemed as if Elisa spoke from a distance but he sensed her presence next to him, the warmth that could only come from her. Her hip brushed against his. She touched his forehead with the back of her hand.

His tongue swept across his lips in hopes of finding more of the cooling liquid. Nothing.

"More sleep is what he needs, doctor's orders." Margaux's commanding voice was the one he heard now. "Give him a little more of the brew. It will ease the pain and help him into the needed sleep."

More liquid passed across his lips but he didn't want to taste or sleep, needed to wake up and discover what happened. "Bai..." he began but was hushed by the brush of liquid.

"Bailey is why you're alive."

Unable to help himself he tasted and drank. Elisa's hand was behind his head, lifting and supporting him so he drank more than what was spilled across his chin. He had the fleeting thought that death would take the pain away. Now even breathing hurt like hell.

Then, "Bailey is fine. He brought you back. *Mon Dieu!* Without him you would still be lying in that alley while we wouldn't know where to look for you."

In his mind he pictured Margaux with her hands on her ample hips, her bosom heaving with anger and frustration. He tried to reach out and tell Margaux that her man, Bailey, would not say no, had insisted on going with him. Bailey would have followed him no matter what he did short of locking him in his room as he did Elisa just to keep her safe. He realized his mind was adrift. Margaux said nothing of the sort. It was his guilt at the notion he put the man in danger that was eating at him.

Before he slipped away again to his dreams, he was able to open one eye. Elisa sat next to him. Her eyes were red as tears slipped from them. He never meant to create this fear in her. He wasn't used to having someone care for him to this degree. What happened in the alley was just part of the job. He had always been a lone player in the games that thrilled him and made him feel alive. Needing to touch her as well as erase the tears and fears once more, he tried to reach out to her. Margaux's brew was getting the better of him. Slowly, his eyes closed again.

Once more, the darkness his mind had been encapsulated in was fading. The fog swirling around any coherent thought he might have. Now, he was slowly waking up. The room was dark this time, one light near the bedside. He felt a soft breeze caress his face.

"Is he really going to be alright?" He heard Elisa ask.

Etienne still heard the same terror in her voice. "I didn't find him just to lose him."

"He will recover and be just as good as new. It seems Daryl and Donal Chamberlin have arrived in Paris, willing to make sure these men are returned to Glasgow and punished for their misdeeds. They will vouch for Etienne. I've also heard the Duke of Southcliff is here along with Drake Montgomerie, an English duke. If nothing else it seems that Etienne Dubois has powerful friends and they seem more than willing to help in this incident."

Perhaps the cavalry had arrived. He slipped into dreams then, wishing he could wake and hold Elisa in his arms. She needed his comfort. Needed him to erase whatever fears she might have.

The next he woke he was aware of bandages unwrapping from his ribs then more sensations. He felt her fingers brush across his back then his chest as she moved around him. The pain was not as intense as last time he'd been awake.

"He is much better. While he still needs rest, you can let him wake for a few minutes and talk to him. Maybe he remembers more than Bailey although it's doubtful. I'm sure the newlyweds would like to have a few moments alone."

He didn't recognize the voice so he assumed it was the doctor. Trying diligently, he strained to open both eyes. Still the swelling in the one kept him from accomplishing that feat. Out of the corner of one eye, he could see his wife. Saw her hesitant smile. Watched as her tongue swept slowly across her bottom lip.

"Elisa?"

He reached out hoping to find her hand. Suddenly, he felt the warmth as well as the fragility he was so aware of. He enclosed her hand in his, reveling in the texture along with the strength he discovered in something so small and delicate. Perhaps she wasn't quite as fragile as he thought her to be.

"I'm here. You should not have taken such risks. I certainly hope you discovered what you wanted to know. Hope it was worth all this pain." She was bending over now, close to his mouth whispering. "You are a very bad boy for doing these things to yourself."

You know I didn't. He assumed Bailey did not give her the information she sought. "We were." He licked his dry lips but he didn't want anything to make him sleep. He tried to sit up but her hands on his shoulders stopped him.

"Hush, you need to save your strength."

"I won't," he murmured trying to smile at the same time keep his eyes open for however long it took.

He had no idea what he was trying to deny. His thoughts were all jumbled together.

"Of course, you will take risks whenever you think they are warranted," she said turning away for a moment and sounding way too calm. "We do need to get to the bottom of this today. After all a week has passed since that horrible morning Bailey carried you through the back entrance and Francoise raced to tell Margaux. When you are quite recovered, you will have to give us some idea of who did this to you. Did you recognize them? Bailey had no idea except he wanted to blame it on Gil. I know that cannot be true. Gil would never harm you."

Gil? Why was Gil in Paris? Slowly, he was regaining his strength. He could almost manage a chuckle. "If I did remember, I would not tell you."

Somehow Elisa managed to get more of the pain medication as well as the sleep potion into his mouth despite his best efforts to stop her. His eyes slowly closed while he struggled to keep the lids open. This situation was not tenable, but he didn't seem to have the strength to do anything about it.

Sleep over took him.

Dreams filled the time, moments he didn't have any idea about how many passed. Slowly, his eyes opened. Sunlight slanted through the window in the room. Dust motes filled the space created by the sunshine. Another day had gone by or more. He couldn't be certain. When he turned his head, he could see Elisa at the window pulling open the curtains. She was standing on the tip of her toes, her arms stretched high. When she finished, she went down on her flat feet and dusted her hands across her skirts.

She turned then, a smile spreading quickly across her features as she saw he was awake. "You're not going to give me something to make me fall asleep again, are you? I'm really much better now. Hardly hurts at all."

He tried to push himself to a sitting position but with a groan he quit, falling back on the mattress with a sigh of frustration.

"No more sleeping potion," she agreed, "and I'll help you sit."

She walked to him. True to her word in a few seconds there were pillows propped behind his back and he was sitting. "You need to eat more than you need sleep."

"What day is it?" he asked, tugging on her hand so she would sit down beside him.

She plopped down, facing him. With her free hand, she reached up and tenderly pushed hair from his eyes. He smiled. Daintily she touched the dimple. "You are still just as charming even with your eye a multitude of colors. Did your nose get broken in another fight?"

"Come here."

He reached out to her pulling her closer. It seemed she wanted the kiss he was seeking as much as he did.

When she bent over him, she stayed just far enough away he couldn't reach her. "This better not hurt you. If it does, I'm not going to kiss you again for at least another week."

He laughed but stopped when his ribs told him laughing was not a good idea. "It's not the kiss. Seems I just can't laugh."

"Then you should not laugh at all."

Her indignation was obvious. She brushed his lips with hers again, smoothed her tongue along his lips as he opened for her. He returned the gesture, sweeping his along the soft underside of her upper lip then across her teeth. The sound of her delight in the back of her throat thrilled him. His hand rested on her back pulling her closer while he realized he should not tease or tempt them both with something he couldn't finish.

When he let her go, she looked very pleased with herself or perhaps it was him. "I've broth for you and all that is in it is something for the pain. While you still need rest, there is no reason to put you to sleep for your own good. If you keep it down, I'll ring and one of the ladies will bring you some stew and bread. You haven't had anything but broth for over a week and very little of that."

"I need food." At the thought of nourishment, his hungry stomach growled giving emphasis to his point.

She set the bowl in one hand and the spoon in the other then spread a napkin beneath his chin. "This will taste good. It is Francois's special recipe, and he's added a few spices to give it more flavor."

He grimaced at the thought he was so weak he needed to be spoon-fed. "I can feed myself."

She handed over the bowl. "Very well."

Surprised, he didn't expect such easy compliance to his request. She set the bowl on his hand then gave him the spoon. Just the movement of his hand from the bowl nearly sent him spinning away in pain. He groaned in the back of his throat trying hard to keep her from hearing it. She sat with her arms crossed watching him.

Trying again he was met with the same fate. With a lift of his shoulder that he instantly regretted, "You win."

Graciously, she accepted the bowl along with the spoon, feeding him a couple of times before saying, "I've won nothing. If anyone wanted you to be able to feed yourself, I did. Do you think I've nothing better to do than wait on you as if you were a child?"

He looked around the room searching for something that might occupy her time. "There is a wealth of things to do in here besides waiting on me," he told her without laughing as he valiantly fought to keep the pain away.

"Of course there are, I've taken up needle point while you've been sleeping. One of Margaux's girls is teaching me. I've a head start on Margaux's books for the year. This way she will not have to have this quarter's receipts and notes sent to me." She sounded indignant and once again he wanted to laugh but was trying desperately to keep from doing just that.

~ * ~

Gil's servant brought drinks to Leslie and Drake, the Duke of

Southcliff and the Duke of Richmond. respectively. No one seemed eager to produce information and Gil wasn't about to give up his edge. It seemed their wives traveled with them and were now sitting in another room, visiting and drinking tea.

"Etienne wasn't killed. I'm guessing that was because of your presence," Leslie said. "What makes you think the men will not return?"

"I didn't say that. I sent him to the tavern so he would know who he was fighting. In fact, all the intelligence I've gathered is directly related to the fact they will not give up easily. Once they discover he is not dead, they will be back," Gil sat on the edge of his desk in his study. His body relaxed yet very aware of the power sitting in this room with him. He'd heard tales of both men along with some of their more notorious exploits.

"And you don't think he can fend for himself," Drake said twirling the amber liquid in the crystal glass, seemingly fascinated by the changing colors. "I've heard otherwise."

Gil shrugged his shoulders, thinking about it for a moment. "He's always been vulnerable when a beautiful woman is involved. This time it's his wife. What do you think? Besides, for the past week he's not been able to get out of bed. The men left him for dead. Their mistake was allowing Bailey to live."

Gil had never met these two men but Drake Montgomerie was a legend by any standards, retired from the service after he married. The Duke of Southcliff was also rumored to be retired from the service.

Yet here they were along with more operatives than he could count on one hand.

Leslie cleared his throat, stretching out his long legs as if attempting to get comfortable. His arms were crossed in front of him. "I know how I feel when Lacie is around me. Vulnerable is a poor adjective to describe the weakness not quite defining how very helpless I find myself if she even pricks her finger in her stumbling attempts at sewing. Not really sure why she tries." He was now shaking his head, a strange expression on his face, the smile seeming nostalgic.

Drake looked just the same as Leslie. Gil was sure they were both daydreaming about their wives.

He wondered how that would feel. Having a woman, you cared

more for than life itself. Etienne found that with Elisa.

"You will have to marry before you understand what is going on here. The woman will have to have an iron grip on your heart for you to feel the same as us." Drake stood and was touring the room, his mind seeming to wander with the words.

"You will have to make sure Elisa does nothing foolish during all of this. I've a feeling she is the ultimate target. What else would make this the worst day of Etienne's life? Hmm..." Leslie said, seeming bemused by Drake's words about his wife.

Donal strode in then walking to the sideboard, poured himself a drink. "Where are the ladies?" Then as if an afterthought, "Sorry about the lateness. Some foot traffic caught me up on my way here."

"In the parlor," Leslie said, glancing in that direction as if he could see her by wishful thinking. "Having tea, I suppose."

"Laced with whiskey," Drake added, laughing. "Or they are indulging in some of your fine Bordeauxs. They've been quite spoiled on that front since one of the cousin's husband owns a winery in this area."

"What the devil are we going to do about all of this?" Gil asked, once again wishing he had found a beautiful woman to entertain him during the night and make him crazy during the day. All the ladies he'd known and been with never gave him reason to believe he could spend a lifetime with them. Except perhaps Elisa, yet he knew he didn't love her as Etienne did. As with all the others he'd known, he could not give Elisa the same dedication Etienne did and these men gave their wives.

"Kill the two men before they can do whatever they've planned," Leslie said, rocking on the balls of his feet. He turned then, "They thought they killed Etienne. Any chance of keeping him in the room at the brothel? We want these two to continue to believe he is gone from this earth."

"Not one," Gil said with a smirk. "He can pick any lock. Nothing will stop him when he decides to leave."

"You can keep Elisa in the room," Drake said. "That should not be a problem?"

"Well," Gil stroked his chin pensively. "She's friends with all the ladies at Margaux's establishment. Has free run of the place. I'm sure she could sweet-talk any one of them into unlocking the door. Even Margaux herself, given the right incentive, might let her out. Hell, Margaux might join her in whatever foolish endeavor she was planning."

Gil had never been so positive of anything before. A shudder wracked his body as thoughts took root. It wasn't like the old Elisa who did everything her mother suggested, but finding Etienne again changed her perspective on life. Changed most everything about her.

"Then we'll have to make sure that doesn't happen," Drake said appearing unconcerned about the information he gave him. "A guard for the room seems appropriate if we hope to keep these two healthy."

"I hear he left the Firth of Clyde under suspicious circumstances and was saved by your wife," Gil directed his attention to Donal who was placidly sipping his drink, his attention seemingly not focused on anything that was being said.

"He did and it was Leslie who helped him get away. I was otherwise engaged trying to keep hyperthermia from settling permanently into my wife's bones. She was tossed into the sea." His voice grew husky as it seemed he was remembering the event. "It was a frightening moment."

"She is fine now?" Gil asked his voice thickening with emotion. Memories threatened to give him away. Perhaps once a long time ago he had known a woman who captured his heart. Now, since she betrayed him, it no longer made a difference.

"Yes, indeed she accompanied me as did Lacie and Ella. Perhaps when we are done here, you could show us some of Paris," Donal suggested.

"There are sites worth seeing," Gil agreed, wondering just what had been accomplished at this meeting.

Other than a guard for the couple's room he couldn't determine anything of consequence. He supposed these acquaintances of Etienne's wanted to see who he was and if he was indeed a friend. He also suspected they had their own research to do.

Chapter Nine

Elisa was sitting in Margaux's private rooms, her mind deep in the receipts and ledgers the Madam handed over to her. The books had always been fine until now, but today she noticed some discrepancies and wondered how Margaux let anyone take advantage of her.

The sigh emanating from her was long and deep. Margaux was not getting any younger. From the numbers on these ledgers, it appeared someone had been skimming from her. She ruled out Bailey as well as Francois. They both had been with her forever, at least as long as she remembered visiting here. That had to be over twenty years. They were loyal to a fault.

What to do? She didn't want to alarm Margaux needlessly, but as proprietor she needed to know what was happening beneath her nose.

Once more her thoughts drifted to the madam. She certainly didn't want to worry Margaux any more than she already was, but this was important to her livelihood. Elisa was determined to get to the bottom of this for her. A few strategically placed questions might give her the answers she sought without alarming her or causing panic.

Elisa tapped her pencil on the table, her thoughts returning to Etienne. He would not speak to her about what happened that night nor would Bailey. They just grunted when she brought up the topic. All he would say was that she was to stay inside the brothel and not to venture out for any reason. A man's idea, no doubt thinking she could only be protected if she was not let out on the streets.

"He would keep me locked in my room if I let him," she mumbled not realizing Margaux stood at the entrance to the room watching her.

"And so would I," Margaux strode in. "But I'm not sure I would want to have to deal with your wrath. This way at least, Bailey is still nearby. You can't get outside without someone sounding an alarm."

"I didn't know you were there," Elisa laughed. "I might just try to find out if what you say is true. An efficient and quick end to this is something needed."

"Obviously," the madam laughed, sitting down beside her. "What have you found? There is a definite crease between your eyes, which tells me all is not good." she said as she poured them both a cup of tea. "Anything I should know about?"

"You expect me to find something?" Elisa asked hesitant to tell her anything just yet when she had no proof of any wrongdoing. Margaux's words surprised her. "Tell me more."

Margaux shrugged her shoulder, looking more frail and vulnerable than Elisa had ever seen her. She was a bit older than her mother, ten years or so. "Nothing I can put a finger on. That's why I'm glad you are looking at this for me. Something has definitely had me perplexed but you, better than anyone, know how bad I am with numbers. There just is something not quite right."

"I don't have anything I can identify. Simply put, the ledgers and receipts don't add up. Who has been keeping track of everything?" She was looking for a name, someone she could talk to, but Margaux looked distant as if her mind was somewhere else.

"I trust everyone who works for me. I can't give you a name. My finances are simple. The ladies tell me what they've charged their customers. I give them the required percent. They understand the guidelines. For these transactions there are no receipts involved. No paper trail. It's all under the table. You understand why of course. So, the fact that where we do have receipts, a paper trail, there are discrepancies stuns me."

Elisa nodded understanding. "Then the mistakes are derived from the products that are purchased for the brothel and it's upkeep. Perhaps even the servants who clean."

"Bailey still takes care of all that. I trust him explicably. You know that." She slathered a piece of bread with butter then added raspberry preserves. "Francois has had some issues with his grandchildren, but they never come around here anymore. I trust him too."

"I do too. There is nothing either man wouldn't do for you. They certainly wouldn't steal from you. Both men, I'm sure, know if they needed extra funds for anything you would give it to them."

Elisa had come to the same conclusion. Anyone could be threatened. Any of the ladies as well as the bouncers in the brothel could owe substantial money to someone and be asked to skim the books. There could be gambling debts. It would have to be someone with authority even if it was only a little. "We should proceed with an open mind."

"Who has hired the men here, the bodyguards?"

She supposed it was Bailey but she couldn't be sure. No one else had that much trust or influence over the madam of the house.

"Bailey is in charge of the men. I've never had any idea who to hire." She waved her hand in the air. "Actually, I don't hire the women any longer either. If there is a question, I might give an opinion after speaking with a lady. I suppose I've trusted people who I shouldn't." She held her head in her hands. A soft sob echoed in the room before Margaux straightened. "I'm getting old. You wouldn't want to take over for me? No, of course you wouldn't."

"The thought has actually crossed my mind." She laughed for a few minutes. "Not really, just the hiring of the women. They would have to travel to Bordeaux of course and meet me in the city. I've learned from firsthand experience what my mother and I assume you have always looked for. It would be a vacation of sorts to go into the city on occasion."

"I would like that but..."

"This business is yours. I don't want it nor would I presume to take anything from you. I would simply hire your ladies. In that aspect you can be confident that they will be loyal to you. If I have any doubts, I'll simply ask Angelique's opinion."

Elisa felt confident in this. The brothel had been a part of her entire life. At one time, she assumed her mother was training her to replace her as she grew older.

"You are as important to me as if you were my own daughter. If you believe you should do the interviewing then I'll make sure it happens. We can work something out."

"Do you have any idea how many ladies come here for a job? Perhaps I should interview all of them, at least all of the new girls. Do you think that would be a good idea?" She waited for an answer understanding this would be difficult for Margaux. "While I'm here I've got ample opportunity. It's not as if I'm allowed to leave even to shop."

"No, but a few years ago, I used to see ten to thirty a month. There are a lot of women who have no other means to make a living than to sell themselves. I think Bailey has taken to eliminating some of the women who have a difficult time conforming to my rules before I even see them."

"Alright then, you will need to find out who has recently come by to ask for a place in this establishment. Trust only Bailey to take the names. I understand that this cannot really be done from such distance between us unless we set up some way for the ladies to travel to Bordeaux. I think if they are truly in need of a job, they will do what is asked especially since the brothel will pay the travel expenses. If not, they'll disappear into the streets and alleys of Paris, seeking employment elsewhere. I will speak to Bailey and you will have to agree so he is sure that I'm not doing something you wouldn't approve."

"Not that he would," Margaux smiled. "He loves you as a daughter. He lost his daughter. Did you know that?"

Her heart leapt to her throat. "No, I know very little about Bailey. Only what he has been willing to share over the years. That is not very much. He seems to be a very private person."

Margaux sipped the tea. "It's cold now, you know. Whiskey can sit in the glass for hours and it still tastes fine. This is bitter. Did you have any?" Margaux's head lolled a bit to the side, her eyelids drooping downward.

"Bailey!" Elisa caught her before she fell to the ground.

"What is it?" Margaux shook her head as if trying to chase the sleep from her eyes.

"Mademoiselle?" Bailey appeared quickly from the hall outside. He turned his attention to Elisa. "What has happened to her?"

"Help me get her to the couch. I think the tea was drugged. It was bitter so I only sipped once before putting it aside. Margaux drank an entire cup."

Bailey hovered over her for minutes, his eyes watery. Then questions followed. "Who would do this to her or do you think it was meant for you? Do you think she'll be fine?"

Elisa had never seen him so worried. He appeared frantic. "You need to stay with her. I'm going to mingle with the ladies. There are some I've known forever who I would like to speak with. Then I need to talk to Francoise. Everything originates in his kitchen even if he has no knowledge of what is transpiring. He might have seen something."

"The books, were they in order?" Bailey looked up for a moment then his focus returned to Margaux.

"No, then you best only speak with the ladies you know." Bailey's voice took on an edge she'd never heard before not even when he carried Etienne into their room. "Your life could be in danger from a source other than the one who is hunting your husband. There are things going on here that are not right."

Gently he brushed hair from the madam's face and Elisa realized there was more to their relationship than friendship. Bailey loved Margaux.

She didn't believe what was happening at the brothel could have anything to do with Etienne. It would be too big of a coincidence but one never knew. Perhaps there were more elements at play than she previously guessed.

"Give me a list of women who have been hired in the last four to five years. I will talk to them one at a time. Don't know what I'll discover but in the short time we've been together, Etienne has taught me to trust my gut."

"As well you should. I'll compile the list but it will be from memory. I'm sure that as I see the ladies, I will complete the document. It's a daunting task. Margaux only hired those ladies who were sincere and needy. Most didn't even want to be in this profession but were forced into it by circumstances beyond their control. She has always let them go when they found a man or just had enough money to get out of the business."

"I understand. Mother was the same way, always willing to help a woman from the occupation if that was what she wanted."

"Some came back because they didn't know how to make it on their own or didn't have a way to earn enough money to live," Bailey said.

"It's a sad thing. I know mother would have wanted something different for her life but I don't believe she has any regrets now."

Elisa realized the truth of her words. Her mother had no regrets for herself but for a daughter who married who she considered was the wrong man. Angelique didn't know Etienne at all. She had no idea what a fine upstanding man he was.

"Do you think any of those new girls might have reason to hurt you or Margaux?" Bailey asked.

She hesitated, trying to go over all the women she'd met. "What about you? You know these women and men better than anyone. What do you think?"

"It's always possible. I rarely ask questions when someone, man or woman, asks to return to the fold. Some of the women need the protection the house gives them. They don't have it when they are working on the streets."

"Let me speak with those first. Send them to me one at time. I'll see them here if that meets your approval."

By the time Elisa was ready to stretch her legs then run to her room in order to see how Etienne was doing, clouds covered the sun. It was nearing late afternoon. She stood by the open window for a few minutes drinking in the fresh air, trying to figure out what would come next. She spoke to most of the house to no avail. No light was shed on the problem. Margaux woke with a pounding headache but it appeared she would be fine. She was now sleeping in her adjoining room.

"Elisa?" Bailey stood at the door, his body framed within, scowling. "I've a message for you."

"Who is it from?" she asked, stepping forward, expecting a written message of some sort.

"That's just it. One of the ladies said someone left it at the door. Do you want me to be looking at it first?"

"No." She tore open the envelope. "I'm sure it's harmless."

Opening the message, she read the words, blood draining from her face. She swayed slightly. When she looked up, Bailey was stepping quickly in her direction. "I'm fine, just felt a bit dizzy for a moment. Seems I've been sitting in this room all day. Tell Etienne I'll see him shortly."

Bailey watched her for what seemed like hours but was only seconds, before turning and leaving the room. She opened the letter again and reread what was written. She was to go to a certain apothecary and she would find out the truth.

What truth?

The facts about who was skimming money from Margaux or what happened to her husband? While her husband might like intrigue, reveled in secrets, it was something new to her. She tried to suck in air that didn't want to cooperate. She felt no charge of energy or excitement. He told her that was why he continued with the missions.

All she felt was dread.

Composing herself she quickly walked from the room, her steps determined but not fast enough to give her purpose away to anyone who knew her. She didn't dare stop at her room and speak to Etienne. He had this uncanny ability to figure out what she was doing before she even knew. He always discerned when she was holding back the truth.

In this case, she recognized what needed to be done and it had to be done now. At the front door, she grabbed one of the lightweight capes hanging on the pegs. Slipping it on, she pulled the hood over her head, hoping it would conceal her identity if anyone was watching. To her it seemed the brothel had eyes and ears everywhere. She doubted her departure would go unnoticed for very long.

Searching her pockets, she had just enough money to hire a cab both ways. Stopping one, she gave the directions as well as the address that was written on the piece of paper. The man helped her inside. Once there as she stood in front of the door, she wondered about the impulsive decision, which was not her usual way. The note had said not to tell anyone but in the light of the happenings lately, she was not that foolish. She left the message on the notes she'd been writing about the ladies and prayed it would be found.

Bailey, if not Margaux would discover the message, she hoped sooner, and tell Etienne. Of course, she'd been foolish. She had to count on Margaux waking up. With any luck they would be able to keep her over protective husband confined in the bedroom. Leaning against the cushioned seat, she closed her eyes, the sway and bounce of the carriage somehow soothing.

It wasn't long before the vehicle drew to a stop, the driver coming around to the side to place the stairs and help her down. For a few seconds, she held her breath before letting it out in a rush. All around her people walked, couples arm in arm, mothers with their children in hand. Everything seemed normal. Nothing was out of place. The day was still warm. She hoped whatever business she had here would be finished before the sun dipped below the horizon. If possible, she needed to be home before she was missed.

When she entered, a bell on the side of the door sounded her presence in the musty and somewhat dusty room. The scent was strange. It seemed stale as if no one ever opened a door or a window. A man poked his head out from a back room, a solicitous grin on his weathered visage.

"*Bonjour Madam*, what can I do for you on this fine day? Are you searching for anything in particular? I would love to help you out. We've a myriad of spices and herbs."

"*Non,*" she told him unsure of anything at the moment. "Suppose I will see what you have to offer. I'll just look at the shelves if you don't mind."

Nerves stretched to a breaking point, she looked around the room, searching out some of the dark corners, but as far as she could tell she was the only one in the store besides the owner, at least that's who she thought he was. Her heart raced in her chest. Her breaths rasped painfully in her lungs. A fine bead of moisture slipped between her breasts.

"Take your time," he said following her around the room, his hands clasped behind his back while seeming to watch her every movement.

"I was supposed to meet someone here. Perhaps I'm early."

Her hand shaking, she picked up a bottle of something then abruptly set it back on the counter. Leaving now seemed the prudent course of action, yet she'd come here and she was determined to see this through.

I'm in no danger.

"The shop has every kind of herb imaginable among other more potent items. Things to treat headaches, stomachaches, the gout as well. If you want I can..." he paused thoughtfully, his gaze remaining fixed on her seeming to forget what he intended to say.

Waving a hand, she interrupted him. "I'm sure you do but I've no skills in using these potions or herbs as you call them. I'm not a healer nor do I have other nefarious objectives in mind." She moved toward the door.

Her stomach churned thinking again that perhaps she should leave. This had been ill advised and too spontaneous by far. She tried to pull air into her lungs, the attempt futile. Telling Bailey would have been prudent beyond all possibilities. She was a ninny. Etienne would be angry, furiously so. Her fingers wound into the fabric of her cape as the man methodically approached. She stepped back, bumping into the counter.

"You can always learn. By the way who was it you were supposed to meet? I could tell you if they come here often and what they purchase."

When he grinned, his yellow crooked teeth sent a chill of terror down her spine. She was truly in the wrong place at the wrong time or perhaps it was the planned time. She should not be here. Etienne was going to be furious with her, more than furious if that was possible. Biting her bottom lip, she headed for the door, keeping the man in her view.

"I should leave. I don't want to purchase any herbs."

She sought a path away from him and to the blessed freedom of the street, but he stepped in her way. The sound of her heart beating roared in her ears. Her breaths, short pants that hardly brought air to her lungs.

"So soon? I'd like you to stay." His smile vanished. "You didn't answer my question. Who were you supposed to meet here?"

She tried to step around him, but he moved again to block her way. "I don't know. No one. The message did not have a name. Just to come. I'm here. Now I'm leaving. I did what was asked. Please get out of my way."

Dear lord, but she was in trouble and knew he wasn't going to give her the freedom she craved.

"Don't you think that is a bit too trusting for a lass as beautiful as you? Going somewhere on a whim? Defying her husband's wishes? I'm sure Etienne did not give you his permission. That is if he's alive."

Etienne? He knows who her husband is.

He stepped closer to her. His hand touching her cheek then withdrawing.

His touch sent her stomach churning, a sourness revolving within. For a moment, she thought she might lose the lunch she'd eaten a few hours ago. "Probably but the note was urgent and there was more to it than just to come here. It's a matter of life and death."

She shouldn't be telling this man anything. Why, was beyond her comprehension. Yet the man spoke of facts he shouldn't know anything about. How did he know Etienne was her husband? If she survives this, she deserved her husband's wrath.

He told her she needed protection.

He knew about this type of intrigue.

She didn't.

"I see." He was stroking his chin as if in thought. "Perhaps I could offer you some tea."

"*Non.*"

"A place to sit and wait? Do you want to wait for your husband although we both ken he won't be coming for you? He's dead so he can't rescue you."

All she wanted was to leave, yet she was glad this man believed her husband to be dead. He couldn't come for her. He was still too weak. It didn't seem this man was about to let her do that, leave. She looked to the door hoping someone would walk in and give her a means to exit. Short of barging through this man she wasn't going anywhere.

"No, no, I don't think you see anything at all. I've really got to be going. My husband will be expecting me soon. He will be angry if I'm not there."

"Your husband knows where you are. I thought he was dead, hoped." His voice dropped an octave as he asked, looking for a moment to the backroom. "How trusting and foolish of the man. If my wife were as beautiful as you, I would never let her out of my sight."

"Of course he knows."

She straightened her shoulders dusting off the cloak with her fingers. The entire room was dingy and filled with dirt, and she thought for a moment she would sneeze.

"I don't believe a word you've said. You don't lie well, madam. If you are going to embroil yourself in conspiracy, you should work on that problem. Lying is an art that needs to be practiced." He reached out to touch her again. This time she ducked to one side. Unexpectedly, since she heard no one, she found herself in the arms of another man. Her breath caught as she struggled to free herself, pushing at arms that seemed to have an iron-clad grip on her.

"Got her. Now all we have to do is wait for her husband to come rescue her. Shouldn't be too long before he comes barging in here. Won't be so hard to kill him this time."

"She did say he knows where she is." After raking his hand through his hair, "Not sure I believe her though."

"True, but he will discover her gone and if I haven't missed my guess, she left information for him to find her. She's not the type to follow directions."

"Then we wait."

"Yes, but I'm also sure he won't come alone. Probably bring that big fellow with him."

"Ah, Leod, don't you think we should have some fun with the pretty lady first?" Troy asked. "We do want to hurt Dubois just as he hurt us. He did share Katrina with us. He should be amicable to sharing his wife."

"You're hurting me," she said, her voice soft but filled with malice while she tugged on her arms.

She knew of men like this, understood what drove them. Growing up she'd had a wealth of information from the ladies at the brothel. This was no different than some of their stories. Use your wits, they told her any number of times, and survive. No matter what happens survive to fight another day. Their words meant nothing to her. Even if these horrid men spoke true everything had been done before they were married, before he came back from Scotland. He was in the service of the king. He had no choice. Oh, she tried not to cry.

This has nothing to do with me.

Troy loosened his hold but not enough for her to get away. "You are a pretty little thing. Not as beautiful as Katrina but nice in your own way."

"Why did you want me?"

"Didn't you hear? Waiting on your husband to come find you. He needs to pay for his part in the death of my beloved Katrina. He could have changed what happened. Had more than once chance. He didn't. Etienne made his choice. Now, he pays the consequences."

"And what part was that," she asked, hoping for time.

Bailey must have found the note she left by now. She just prayed he wouldn't tell her husband. He was in no shape for another fight or to even walk down the steps in the bordello. This man might indeed kill him. She didn't want to live the rest of her life without him. How could she tell Masson the father who he just met and loved was dead and his death rested on her shoulders?

"He sided against her with another woman. You should watch out. He is completely without loyalty. First thing you know, he'll be in bed with someone else. Just you wait."

"I suppose the woman was without fault? She was innocent of all wrong doing?" she asked even as he pulled her arms behind her back before tying them with rope the storekeeper gave him. Her heart in her throat linked to the ugliness of what they planned, terrified her. If she had not responded to the message none of this would be happening

"Katrina did not deserve the pain and fear that was caused that day. He bedded her, treated her with respect until he didn't. She expected him to be her defense against the accusations tossed her way. He wasn't."

"I'm sure there is a second side to this story," she told him, her voice calmer than she ever imagined.

At this point she didn't want to believe all the stories her mother told her about Etienne. The worst was that he would be faithless. She knew he'd not been a monk, understood there had been women before her as well as after that day four years ago. What mattered was now, the present and the future, not something that happened in the past.

"You don't know anything of what happened," the man's voice

was menacing. "Your husband is no gentleman."

Arguing with him would not be productive. "What are you going to do with me? I suppose nothing you said about the lady in question is true."

"Only that she owes me her gratitude which is why she agreed to the skimming of the books as well as the message that drew you here," Leod's voice was suddenly filled with confidence. "I own her and she will make sure Etienne never survives another night. I'm surprised he made it this long. Given his injuries, he should be dead by now."

With the information presented to her she understood they would kill her unless she could find a way to rescue herself. She inhaled a long deep breath all her senses tuned to these men and what they wanted. Hope still came in the fact Bailey might find the message.

~ * ~

When Bailey reached Etienne's room, he was sitting on a chair with his pants on and struggling with his boots. He looked up, sweat dripping off his forehead, his breathing raspy with the effort it took to inhale.

"You shouldn't be out of bed." Bailey bent down next to him and helped him with the boots he was having so much trouble with. "You know you can't do any good if you can't even get dressed by yourself."

"Have to find Elisa. She's been gone too long. She is supposed to be with Margaux, but I'm pretty sure she is not. She's done something foolish. My gut is telling me she's in trouble. Need to find her."

He knew she was doing something she'd regret. He'd regret. The feeling stretched from his head to his toes. It had been far too long since she poked her head into the room and said hello. Every instinct he possessed told him she left the bordello. All that he knew about her was that she acted impulsively. *Mon Dieu* but he didn't want her to die or be hurt in any way because of his past.

"In your condition, you're not going anywhere. You wouldn't make it down the steps before you fell on your face." Bailey helped him button his shirt and stand as if he understood nothing he told him would change his mind.

"I'm going." There wasn't anything Bailey could do short of tying him that would keep him in the room no matter how long it took him to negotiate the steps. He smiled. Even locking the door wouldn't keep him inside even if the act might slow him up.

"I know you are and I would do the same if I found myself in your place." Bailey's voice was quiet with a wealth of understanding. "I'm going to help you, but you've got to realize that you're barely able to walk. If we find her in trouble, let me take the lead. Promise me or I will make sure you can't leave for a very long time."

He nodded, with no intention of promising anything. "Just help me down the steps. I'm getting stronger with every second."

"Sure, you are." Bailey chuckled while he lifted him to a standing position. Together they made it down the steps then slowly to the front door.

"Wait," Margaux rushed to them, her voice breathless as she tried to speak. "You've got to save her." She held out the message Elisa left for her to find. "She's in more trouble than she knows."

"*Mon Dieu!*"

Etienne felt fear very real and intense. All his gut instincts proving themselves right again. He would have wished for a far different scenario. "I'll tan her backside when I finally get my hands on her. She won't be able to sit for a month." Yet he was thankful she left the message. Thankful he might see her again.

Margaux slanted him a defiant look. "Of course, you won't. What you will do is hold her and forgive her because she is doing this for you even though her actions are misguided. Then you will love her until she is breathless. First though, you have to convince her there will be no more reasons for heroics." She waved her hands in a shooing gesture. "Go find your bride. I've good reason to believe she went out the front door."

With the help of Bailey, he was able to get into a cab. Leaning back on the cushion he closed his eyes trying desperately to gain the strength he lost in the brief trek down the steps and outside. This was not how he wanted to feel. Not only did his ribs throb but so did his head. The laudanum that had been keeping his pain at bay had long since disappeared from his body.

"What do you plan on doing when you arrive at the apothecary?" Bailey asked perusing him from head to toe. "You can barely walk let alone fight a healthy adversary."

"Hell if I know," he mumbled through clenched teeth. "Guess we'll just wait and see what transpires. You don't have to look at me as if you think I'm going to crumple at the knees."

"Even if it's true?"

"Yes."

"You're not going to rush in there like a fool, are you?" Bailey sat forward, his large arms resting on his massive thighs. "You would put both of us in danger if you do such a stupid thing."

"Thought I'd let you do that. Not the foolish part but the rushing part."

He'd kill any man who hurt Elisa. His thoughts went back to the men he met at Katrina's. He'd been forced to keep his identity a secret and partake of a threesome with the men, Leod and Troy. They fancied themselves in love with the woman. Everyone did when they first met the she-devil. They did until the woman showed her true colors. He sighed softly wishing the events woven around Katrina had not spiraled so out of control. Wished they had not come back to haunt him as well as put his wife in danger.

"Doubt if you can rush anywhere and that's not my style."

Bailey looked outside for a moment, seeming to let this predicament settle in his head. He normally took his time to apprise himself of a situation before acting. This time he might not have the chance.

"Wasn't much use to you last time we got into a fray." Etienne didn't like reminding him of that fiasco, but it would do well for both of them to be more careful.

"You're useless to me today. So, what do you propose we do when we get there?" Bailey turned his attention from the streets back to him.

"That's just it. There is no telling what she walked into. What we can always hope is that it's just the two of them, no reinforcements. And pray that he doesn't want to hurt Elisa only me." He groaned as he shifted his position. When he blinked, it seemed everything hurt.

Neither spoke for a while as the time to the shop grew closer. The brief minutes in the carriage did lend him a few moments that were relatively painless. Slowly, he gathered lost strength.

"Here we are," Bailey said as the vehicle rolled to a stop. "Time to find out what's happened to your lady."

Bailey helped him to the street. He groaned again inhaling a deep breath of air, resigned to ignore the pain, Bailey's hold still keeping him upright.

"What the hell are you doing here?"

Etienne would recognize that voice anywhere. His heart sped in an instant of relief, which quickly dissipated. "Gil? Heard you might be in the city. Do you have business here or is it you Elisa was supposed to meet?"

He was angry and didn't like the fact Gil followed him when he didn't know to what purpose. For the last weeks, he doubted his old friend's loyalty. Now, he had even more misgivings.

"Bailey, you need to take him back to the brothel where he belongs, where he won't cause any more problems. He's in no condition to be here. This is going to be difficult. I don't need to worry about him along with Elisa and the rest of my men."

Gil spoke softly but Etienne heard the anger and something else he wasn't familiar with. "He's only going to get in the way here and jeopardize his wife."

"Leave him," Drake spoke up from behind having just arrived along with Leslie, "just don't let him go inside where he can cause trouble. Leslie is around the back. Shouldn't have any trouble with the rescue as well as the capture of the men we're after. When this is all done, he's going to want to make sure she's all right then he's going to lecture her. My guess though is that she'll have a few choice words to say to him too."

"No, you're right, Drake." Etienne said blandly. "I'm staying, not going anywhere until I see Elisa safe in my arms. Won't do any good to try to send me back to the brothel."

"Out of the way," Gil said, waving his hand. "You're staying out of the way," as he nodded to Bailey before stepping inside the shop his gun drawn, Drake behind him.

When they were inside, Leslie stood at the back entrance and Elisa stood on a stool a noose around her neck. Tears slid down her cheeks. Her body shook with fear she must be feeling.

"It's not as dramatic as the swirling waters of the firth but she will be just as dead." Leod waved his gun at them his smirk growing with each second. "We should have just tossed her in the Seine. It would have had more significance." He waved his pistol in the air to make his point. "I suggest you all leave. One of the men had his foot on the stool and the tiniest push would send it toppling.

Behind them all, Etienne remained in the background unable to stay outside and wait. He inhaled a gasp of air when he saw her, his fists tightening. His urge to rush inside filled him. They would figure this out and Elisa would be fine. He told himself those words over and over as the deadly scenario played itself out. Bailey's hand tightened on his shoulder silently telling him not to do what he was thinking.

"Even if you kick the stool over, neither of you will live. Is that what you want?" Leslie asked as he cautiously stepped closer. "There are three of us and just two of you."

"I'm wagering that even if you do kick it, one of us will be there before..." Leslie said as he looked to Etienne then seemed to think better of what he was about to say.

"The authorities will be here in minutes. Murder is not something you want to go to the Bastille for. A simple charge of kidnapping would serve you better. One charge, the two of you would never see sunlight again and the other..." Drake shrugged lifting his shoulders slightly, a cocky smirk on his handsome face. "A few years, ten or twenty here then you would be shipped to England to stand trial for the crimes committed there. Who knows, the court might be more acceptable to kidnapping than murder." Drake was moving his gun, pointing it at one then the other.

Etienne saw the small derringer on the floor. Good lord, but she'd tried to use the inconsequential weapon against these men. She was lucky she was still alive. Lucky, she didn't shoot herself. His gut rolled at the thoughts swirling in his head. He would just never understand a woman's thinking.

"Don't have anything to lose, but the sight of Etienne Dubois when his woman dies is something I find to my liking," Leod said his voice ripe with the pleasure the words seemed to give him. "Troy and I, well, we ken what's going to happen and decided we would finish our business even if we met obstacles. Guess you guys are our obstacles."

It happened then, Leslie lunged for the man whose foot was on the stool and Drake shot the other man who went down. Gil jumped forward, catching Elisa by the waist before the rope could tighten. Etienne watched everything as if it was a blur in his mind. His fury at his wife's foolishness grew with each second. No matter the cost, he would find a way to convince her she could not win against grown men. She could not ever again take on an opponent such as these men despite her belief she was immortal. How he would convince her, he didn't know.

He would figure something out. In the meantime, all he wanted was to hold her.

Spurred toward Elisa by Bailey he hobbled his way to Elisa and Gil. "Elisa," he whispered as Gill gave her over to him. "You will explain yourself later."

A wave of guilt swept over him for a second when he encountered her terror filled eyes. She would not put herself in danger again to help him. For now, though he held her close, tears in his eyes as he welcomed her into his heart once more.

He didn't watch the proceedings as the police arrived in order to round up the men. Bailey helped both of them into the waiting carriage then stepped back. The two dukes seemed to have everything under control despite the fact they stood on foreign ground. They both spoke fluent French.

"I'll get home in another cab. Seems the two of you have a lot to talk over then a little making up to do. Don't be too rough on her, Etienne. She was looking out for you. You've got to remember that," Bailey said softly.

"And played right into their hands."

Etienne comprehended the gist of Bailey's words but right now he needed to curb his frustration and anger with his wife. If he didn't make his thoughts and wishes clear, she might do something just as foolish again. He didn't think he could live with that fear.

He was silent just as she was while the carriage bumped and swayed its way along the cobblestones of the Paris streets. She sat on the opposite side, her hands folded in her lap, staring at him, her eyes dark with worry. Yet when he looked at her, she turned away from him, refusing to meet his gaze. He'd never felt so helpless as he had in the apothecary, and now. She was everything to him.

Ma vie.

Mon coeur.

Mon amour.

Fear for her overshadowed anything he'd ever felt before. Before, when he was the only one involved, he reveled in the fear and the excitement the assignments whipped through him. His operatives, even the females, were well trained, competent.

But Elisa...

She could have died here today, defending him, his honor. He could not have lived with such as that.

This was not well done of him by any standards, certainly not his own allowing a woman, his wife, to nearly die for him. He closed his eyes, his ribs telling him what little he did today had been overdone by him. As it was, the situation didn't sit well with his manly pride.

Pride be damned.

When they reached the brothel, the doorman helped them out. Margaux was at the door waiting for them almost as if she'd known when they were coming. Perhaps she never left the spot. She was wringing her hands, her eyes glassy with moisture.

"The two of you will never make it to your room by yourselves." She motioned for one of her other men but instead of taking them to their room, he helped them to Margaux's suite.

"What are you up to, Margaux?" he grit out, his pain escalating as he wished for privacy along with his bed.

"I'm going to get you something mild for the pain. I'm sure the others will be here soon. I'm also positive you would like to be awake for the upcoming meeting. You would like to know what happened. Rest as well as the intimacy to discuss what is on your minds, for the two of you will have to be postponed."

In Margaux's private sitting room, he was given a spoonful of laudanum and a glass of whiskey. Elisa chose a Bordeaux from his father's vineyard as they waited for the rest of the unique entourage to join them. He didn't want to begin a conversation that would have to be cut off when the others arrived so he remained silent.

Elisa sat, curled up in a large wing chair. To Etienne's way of thinking it seemed she chose the single chair so he couldn't sit next to her. Over the rim of her glass, she watched him, her eyes wide, silently questioning him. He figured sometime today she must have been confident in the path she chose, but now it seemed she was withdrawing into herself. She did come very close to dying. By the time there was finally privacy for them, she would no longer have any fight left in her. He supposed he should go easy on her. They did find her at the bad end of a noose, but the men Gil brought in to help saved her.

The thought of her hanging in front of him sent his stomach churning.

"Are you feeling better?" she finally ventured to speak, her voice weak with fatigue, perhaps even terror. The day had drained all energy from both of them. "You look as if you need to lie down. I can send for someone."

He smiled then knowing she would be fine. She was trying to get rid of him because she didn't want to hear what he had to say about her venture out this afternoon. Her yawn didn't sway him the least bit even though her eyelids were drooping. All was an act.

"I'm feeling much less pain right now and no, I don't need anyone to help me to my room. Earlier I told Bailey I was getting stronger by the second. Guess it's true."

He grinned then held his glass up in salute understanding the pain was masked for the moment by the laudanum.

Inadvertently, she pushed back in her chair as he leaned forward in his. He was still smiling at her, grinning no doubt. He was as certain as he possibly could be that she was staring at his dimple. He was so pleased she was alive and getting back to herself. Perhaps, he thought for a second, no, she needed to be told how foolish she was. She needed her bottom reddened just a bit. He didn't need rescuing and that was what she thought she could achieve by her careless decision.

"I'm tired." She set the glass down as she rose to leave. "Even if you aren't exhausted. I believe I'll forego the meeting and find sleep instead."

That wasn't tenable. He wanted her by his side when the others returned, though. She needed to know what happened afterward. This was just another ploy to get out of the trouble she put herself in. He didn't doubt for a minute if he let her leave, she would be sound asleep when he returned to the room. In that case their discussion would be put off.

"No, you don't." He was on his feet, his hand encircling her wrist. "I want you by my side." He tugged her to the sofa where he'd been sitting. She sat down with a plop and a loud whoosh of air right next to him.

"You must have hurt yourself."

He was shaking his head even while he felt tremors glide through her then into him. Pushing a way a few strands of her hair, he whispered close to her. "I didn't take you for a coward, Elisa. Stay."

She stiffened noticeably. The tiny gesture pleased him. He wanted her to give as good as she got. When they were finished, he was determined they would understand each other much better.

"More wine?" he asked as he reached for the decanter sitting in front of him on the table.

She nodded her head, still shaky but she was getting better by the minute just as he was. Holding the glass in both hands, she looked to the door. "When do you think...?"

He lifted his shoulders wishing they were here now. "Anytime soon I hope."

She tugged on her bottom lip with her teeth, "They, the men, told me you had a threesome when you were in Glasgow. I'm not ignorant, Etienne. I know what that means. You know I'm not ignorant. Because of mother, I've seen and heard a lot of things. But..."

He tried to keep his smile firmly in place but he didn't want her to think he was mocking her. "It wasn't of my choice." Quickly, he placed a finger on her lips, "Before you say anything, I heartily agree with you.

We all have a choice. It was my choice to maintain my cover. As it turns out it was a bad choice. If I could take one thing back from that assignment, it would be that and perhaps Katrina would still be alive."

"But in prison I gather."

She turned her gaze toward the window. Her face so pale it made him suck in his breath.

"In prison, yes. She did things, horrible things, not sexual deviations. She would have died in prison. Katrina was not a woman who could be confined. So, she made sure she escaped that. She also made her choices."

"What happened to her?"

"You really want to know?" he asked, tracing the line of her jaw with his fingertip. "I'm just not certain it's something we should talk about. Not convinced it's something I want to relive. What happened that day was, however, what brought me back to France. What caused me to reevaluate my duties to the crown."

"It's just they said she drowned in the Firth of Clyde."

"Yes."

"They wanted to take me to the Seine and toss me into the water. I can swim, you know. Quite well. I would not have drowned. I'm sure the water is not as cold here as it is in Scotland."

"That is good to know."

Inside he was smiling as he realized she was healing while she spoke of his misdeeds.

Etienne repeated the story to her, including his hasty retreat, the Scottish patrols following him until the Duke of Southcliff called them off. He was helped from Scotland by a series of events he could only contribute to the MacTavish clan and their extended family as their thanks for helping save Daryl a watery grave. Drake Montgomerie who helped with the necessary papers to cross the channel met him in Dover. He couldn't say how or why.

"Was Drake Montgomerie one of the men who were there today?"

"Yes, as well as The Duke of Southcliff. Leslie Stewart has a home in the Bordeaux region."

The sounds coming from the front of the house told him the others had arrived. Bailey and Margaux were the first to enter the room.

"They were taken to the Bastille," Drake said as he helped himself to the scotch before pouring drinks for Leslie and Gil.

Etienne was relieved yet the burning question in his mind was the part Gil played in all this. There was no reason he could think of for Gil to have followed him to Paris unless he was part of his earlier rescue from Scotland. This was all really passing strange.

"What was your part in what occurred at the apothecary?"

He found himself openly staring at Gil who didn't even seem to notice. Instead, Gil was staring at Elisa.

"Questions later," Drake said as Donal and the wives entered the room. "For now, we need to celebrate our good fortune." He turned to Elisa. "Everyone is alive and well."

Margaux clapped her hands, motioning for two servants to follow the others. "I'm sure, after all the escapades you are all very hungry. Francois has made a few delicacies for everyone to enjoy." She glanced in Elisa's direction.

"I've never been in a brothel before," Daryl said as she looked around, her eyes wide as saucers. "This is really quite nice. Can we have a tour, Donal? Maybe stay the night in one of the rooms. I'd truly like to wear one of those revealing dresses for you."

"Nor I," Lacie agreed, sitting down and popping one of the treats into her mouth. Then addressing Daryl, "Perhaps you can share some recipes with Francois. You could always use new goodies in your bakery."

"You never will be again in a brothel," Leslie and Donal spoke at the same time.

Then, Donal said, pulling his wife to sit down beside him. "I'm sure Justine would love to share recipes, but she isn't' here.

"I was thinking about me, you big oaf." She hit Donal on the shoulder. "Maybe he has some wonderful French pastries that would liven up the menu at my bakery."

"Gil," Etienne was finding that his exhaustion was making everything fuzzy. He needed to retire with his wife to their room. It seemed the rest of the group had other plans for the entirety of the evening. "I just need to understand what your part in all this is. There was a moment when I believed you were the enemy."

Gil cleared his throat, looking to Drake first then Leslie. With their nods he began. "It's really very simple, Etienne."

"I've found where my assignments are concerned, nothing is simple," Etienne gritted out, his fingers tightening on the glass he was holding as he stared at the man he had always thought to be his friend. Over the last months he'd had serious doubts, but most of those doubts concerned Gil's attitude toward his wife not him.

"I was assigned to follow you. One could say I was your backup if something went wrong as it did in Glasgow. We had information leading us to believe your enemies might want revenge. When you showed up with Elisa and your presence with her, well, it complicated matters."

"I see." He drummed his fingers against the crystal he was holding. One elegantly shaped eyebrow lifting in a pronounced arch. You were there when Katrina went into the sea."

He nodded, "As was Leslie. The duke understood that he should send a message to Drake and that I would be a few steps behind you, during your retreat. We didn't bargain for the two-week stay in Edinburgh. Another complication I might add."

Etienne grimaced understanding his stay in the Scottish city would be one more thing to explain to his wife before they could finally settle into some semblance of normalcy. Before he left Edinburgh, he had been waiting and hoping Daryl would change her mind about marrying Donal. He shot her a quick smile in hopes it would reassure her. Instead, her lips pursed together as if remembering the way he deceived her.

"We don't have to speak of that now. At the time it was a bit of wishful thinking on my part, which I'm quite content that what I hoped for at the time never happened."

Daryl blushed and unable to help himself, he grinned at her. She cast a quick glance at Donal whose mind seemed to be somewhere else. In any case, it didn't matter. He was positive Daryl would tell Donal about their short-lived relationship if she hadn't already. In his experience, she kept nothing from Donal. He smiled then, not even that one kiss they shared.

His attention focused again on Gil then Leslie. He'd been sent on this assignment because of the Duke of Southcliff. "So, you were never my enemy? Didn't anyone think we might have done better if we'd been working together? If I had known what you were about?"

Leslie cleared his throat, his wife's hand clearly enclosed in his. "We thought it best to keep the two of you separate. Your styles were uniquely different and in many ways, they complimented each other, but at other times you step all over each other. It was never a surprise when you found yourself in trouble because of a lady and Gil never seemed to have that problem."

The meal arrived. The conversations continued but Etienne needed to sleep. His ribs began to throb and he looked for a chance to excuse himself.

Finally, as they left the room, "I will see the two of you at the château. You will pick up Masson first, I assume." Gil nodded at them as they left. "More of your questions can be answered then."

~ * ~

Bailey pulled Margaux into his lap, her hand resting in his. *"Mon Dieu,* but I thought they would never leave. *Viens ice Margaux."* He patted his lap hoping she would come to him.

Margaux sighed softly, approaching him quickly. He pulled her onto his thighs and she responded by leaning her face against his chest. "I enjoyed their company. It was a delight. Always nice to have a hint of respectability every now and then yet I'm glad they've all retired to their separate lodgings."

"You are respectable," Bailey growled as he trailed a long slender finger along the top of her dress, dipping at the valley between them. Her fingers wound into his hair, combing through the length.

She touched his face with her hand, "You are sweet to say such things, but we both know the truth. I learned a long time ago that life was what we made of it and the only way I knew to succeed was to stay as far away from the respectable people of this city as I could get. Never had much use for that state anyway."

His lips found the sensitive spot behind her ear, touched briefly before traveling lower to stop where her pulse beat out of control. She arched slightly, wishing for more from him. He liked to take his time when he spun the vivid and very potent magic between them.

A kiss, a whisper of desire, the promise of more was all it took for her to whirl wildly out of control. No other man had ever done that to her, given her so much pleasure she could barely breathe afterward. For now, she inhaled a deep breath as he sipped his way down her neck.

"You've always known how I feel about you. Margaux, you are my world, my only world." His mouth brushed hers tenderly while his teeth worried the bottom lip. She swept her tongue across his, hearing his deep, husky groan of desire.

"You enchant me." She rose above him, straddling him as he pushed the sleeves of her gown off her shoulders, freeing her breasts.

"We should take this to the bedroom and lock the door," he told her sweeping her into his arms and doing just that.

Gently, he set her on the bed, standing back to look at her, a broad grin on his face telling her he was pleased. She reached out her arms for him as he settled her against the headboard coming between her legs. Within a few seconds his shirt was unfastened and tossed to the floor. Her fingers wandering across the broad expanse of his chest, she wondered just when did his hair start to turn silver. Not that it mattered to her.

He pushed her dress and her petticoats off, letting them all slide in a bundle onto the rug beside the bed. She trailed her fingers along the waistband of his pants thinking it would be nice to dip below the fabric just so she could see the color of his steel blue eyes darken to indigo when she touched his rod.

She reveled in their differences, sighed when he unlaced her corset and slipped her chemise over her arms. Quickly he stood, pushing the rest of his clothing off his body. They pooled on the floor around his feet.

She was his.

Would always be his.

And he was hers for all time.

It was because of Bailey she stopped seeing anyone else. At one time in her life, she thought love was a fool's paradise. Now she knew different.

She arched her back, letting the feel of his lips play havoc on her life, on her bare flesh as they closed over a nipple. She closed her eyes. A tiny of contentment sigh rippled from her.

Chapter Ten

Elisa helped Etienne up the stairs, his weight on her shoulder straining her entire body until she had to stop to breathe. Gasping for breath, she sucked in air the best she could until her breathing began to even. She'd thought he was getting better but perhaps it had all been a pretense. As it happened, they were both exhausted. All she wanted at the moment was to sleep the entire day as well as the rest of the night.

Or this damn weakness was a sham.

"You tired out now?" He turned his head to catch her eye one dark brow lifting a fraction. "What do you have to be tired about?"

A crease line appeared in her forehead. She was suddenly wary of his intentions. "What are you talking about? Of course, I'm tired. Never thought I'd have to carry you up a flight of stairs. You're twice my size."

"Nothing, just get me to the room so I can rest. My head is pounding along with my ribs. Just want to lie down on our bed, with you."

Ah ha, it is a sham.

She braced herself then and adjusted his body yet she didn't think she could take another step. He moved slightly. She fell to her knees.

"I can't do this." She breathed in deeply wishing the strength in her legs would allow her to stand.

"How will we get to the room then?" he asked slowly sliding off her shoulders to find himself sitting on the steps.

His grin was there, pleasantly assessing her with those deep dark brown eyes of his. Then he stood and sweeping her into his arms carried her to their room before carelessly tossing her on the bed.

So, the weakness was a pretense.

Elisa's smile vanished as quickly as it appeared a minute ago as she scrambled away from him. "What do you want?"

She pushed herself against the headboard of the bed, terrified by the look in his eyes. The question was redundant. She understood what he wanted now, her complete obedience. There was nothing he could do or say that would give him complete power over her, at least not the complete part.

She'd lived her entire life by her standards. She wasn't going to quit now. Giving into his directives now went against everything she believed in.

"To make sure you never do anything so stupid and impulsive again." He stood back, his gaze running the length of her. "You do realize what could have happened to you in that store. You've half the strength of a man. I believe this little episode on the stairs illustrates the facts without me having to reiterate anything to you." His hands were on his hips, his eyes growing so dark they seemed black.

"You weigh nearly twice what I do," she countered, her fingers winding into the fabric of her gown. "How dare you make assumptions such as that? Could you carry Baily up those steps?"

"Doesn't matter," he shot back.

"I won't do anything stupid or foolish again. I promise you."

He knew as did she the promise was not sincere. If either he or her child was threatened again, she would act cautiously but she would indeed act. Except her idea of cautious was so very different from his.

"*Menteuse.* Whatever you do, don't lie to me, *cherie.*"

He sat down beside her almost as if he didn't have the energy to stand. Reaching out he touched her, tenderly traced a line along her jaw. She shivered with the feather soft touch. "I almost lost you. I don't think I could have survived."

She pushed up on her elbows, her mouth a thin line. His frown grew as if he knew she would defend her actions. "I took every precaution. The note was left where I knew either Margaux or Bailey would find it. Someone would come to help me. I knew it as surely as I know I will take my next breath, as my heart will continue to beat."

She was breathing heavily, beside herself with fatigue and worry. All she wanted was to close her eyes and sleep, not argue with her husband who seemed to be having the same problem. Her laughter almost broke the ensuing silence between them.

He collapsed on the bed, one arm flung over his face as his breathing slowed. She sat up then, smiling, touching the spot where his dimple would be if he were to smile. The laudanum had finally done its job. He was fast asleep. She hoped it would help with the healing process. Even the men rescuing her saw his weakness and insisted he stay in the background.

The need to take advantage of this time sent her from the bed to the doorway. No one was outside so she rang the bell. It was only a few seconds later when one of the maids appeared.

"I'd like a bath please."

The maid curtsied and disappeared down the steps. She so needed to wash the dirt and grime from today's events from her body. She ran her hands along her arms as she paced, waiting for the hot water.

She pulled the tub from a closet and left it in the dressing room. After that she sorted through her clothing, wondering if she dared put on a filmy negligée in hopes she could dissuade her husband from the upcoming lecture if he woke up in a foul mood.

She could try.

Seduction, subtle or not, might work.

She lit several candles away from Etienne not wishing to disturb his sleep. It wasn't much later when the tub was filled and she settled into the hot water. Her muscles ached with the stress both mental and physical from today's adventure. Thoughts of the noose around her neck sent shivers through her despite the hot water.

Her fingers wound around her neck massaging where the rope had been tightened. She didn't want to remember any of the events or the evilness in the little shop of horror, glad that the men would get what they deserved. When they were in Margaux's rooms, she'd wanted to ask Leslie how those two escaped the law in Scotland. She'd not had the chance.

The lavender soap she always loved was set nearby and she put little drops of the scent into the water. Slowly, she began to lather the cloth as the water was slowly cooling. It would not do, she thought, to still be in the tub when Etienne woke. She had visions of another time and a bath they shared. Her body quivered with anticipation that would not happen, at least not this evening.

Closing her eyes, she dribbled hot water across her breasts. The sensations were doubled when his hands slipped the cloth from her fingers and gently ran it across her shoulders. She had not heard a sound.

"Do you remember...?" His lips followed the path of the cloth coaxing, enticing sensation that were better left in the background of her thoughts until he could act on them.

"Of course, but your ribs," she murmured. "Not today."

"Will be fine. Is this your way of changing the topic from the things you did today?"

He massaged her shoulders, her arms as well, knowing exactly what would ease her tension. Her eyes closed, enjoying the feelings he so easily created, his touch mercuric.

Then she realized what he'd said. She sat up suddenly, splashing water onto the floor. How dare he? "You are supposed to be asleep." She grabbed the cloth from his hands, placing it over her breasts as if he'd never seen her and caressed every part of her.

He sat back on his knees sighing softly. "Right now, I don't want to talk about today. In truth, I'm pleased you care about me enough to risk your life and terrified you might do something you are so ill prepared to deal with. Keeping you and our child safe is most important to me. You can never do anything so foolish again."

"You are?" She'd never seen that look on his face before. He really was pleased with her. "You're not going to lecture me on what you call my foolishness?"

He nodded, his lopsided smile and dimple endearing once again. "You should finish your bath now before it gets too cold. I'd like to use the water too."

She half expected him to join her but he straightened and it seemed the movement caused considerable pain. "I was just about done." She hurried then. By the looks of him he wasn't going to last long enough to take a bath.

Water sluiced from her as she stood. He handed her a bath sheet as she stepped from the water. "It's not cold."

He grunted, disrobing quickly then slipped into the water. She heard the sigh of pleasure wash through him. His bandages holding his ribs had disappeared and she wondered if that was wise. In any case after the bath, she could call for some more and take care of him.

She dried herself and looked for the prim nightgown that covered her from her chin to her toes, revealing no curves whatsoever. In his condition, she didn't want to tempt him. At the mirror she brushed out her hair, trying to untangle all the strands. He was behind her then, leading her to the fireplace and set her on the hearth where a warm fire blazed in the grate.

"I'm going to do that for you."

His voice was husky with desire, the tone she'd come to recognize. He didn't have the strength. She knew that. But...

The need to argue presented itself but she pushed it back realizing this was something he must feel he needed to do. "Alright." Her voice was soft, husky with passion and she knew seductive even though she didn't mean for it to sound that way.

He knelt down, picking up a comb then running it through her hair. "It's always so soft, even damp."

The pain in his voice left her speechless. She should tell him to go to bed but knew he would do what he wanted despite anything she had to say to him. He slipped his hand beneath her hair, brushing it to one side. She felt his lips tenderly caress her skin then his teeth grazed her there at the base of her neck.

"Are you sure you want to do this?" she asked, hearing the strain in his voice even if he didn't.

"Never surer." Yet his hand faltered for a second.

She understood it was up to her to make sure he found the bed before he collapsed. At the moment, he wore only his pants. She supposed he could go to bed in those. If he woke later, he could always remove them. Perhaps he would be strong enough to make love to her then. She hoped so. It had been quite a while, in deed it felt like months had passed and it had only been a little over a week.

Since the beating.

Missing him was too little to say about her feelings. He had become an essential part of her soul. She should tell him as much. When she turned, he grinned at her before shrugging his broad shoulders, the muscles rippling across his chest and arms.

"You should let me help you to bed."

She wanted to touch the dimple at the side of his mouth, kiss him there. It had never been so tempting or so endearing. Yet she held back.

"After you do you should join me." Over the years he'd mastered the suave tone. He'd used this not-so-subtle coaxing manner on her before but it wasn't going to work tonight simply because he still didn't have the strength.

"I'd like nothing more than to join you, but do you think you're up to it?" she challenged him even while she noticed the determined set to his mouth.

With more effort than she expected, she got him to the bed managing to turn down the covers before he collapsed on top of the bed. She stepped back, smiling. Maybe if this night passed before he could lecture her about her conduct, he would forget most of what he wanted to say.

"I'm not dead yet," he murmured closing his eyes.

"I wouldn't be smiling at you if you were." She covered him then, filling a spoon with laudanum. "I believe you need this if you are going to sleep. There will be time for us later. We do have a lifetime to satisfy each other's needs."

It seemed he didn't have the strength to fight her this time. She understood what he wanted. Sex would just have to wait. His sigh was long and drawn out. She knew he didn't want to give into her but he also comprehended he had no real choice. His body was speaking for him.

"I'll find a way," he mumbled, reaching out to her. "Did I tell you that you really shouldn't have done what you did today? The terror I felt when I read that message and Bailey, he knew I shouldn't be going anywhere but he actually put my boots on for me. You know how difficult that must have been?"

His words started fading away. In a blink he was asleep.

Sitting on the bed she kissed his forehead. Her smile reached to the tips of her toes. "I love you, Etienne. I always have ever since I can remember seeing you on that hot summer day. Maybe someday you will love me."

She walked around to the other side of the bed, pulling the covers to her chin before moving next to him and putting an arm around him. Her eyes closed then. She fell into a deep sleep, until nightmares seeped into her mind.

The scream woke her. She was afraid the rest of the house as well. She heard the footsteps pounding outside her door. "It was just a dream. I'm fine," she called out, her gaze shifting to Etienne. It seemed she woke him too. His hands were on her shoulders, his eyes filled with worry.

The candles she lit earlier were nearly burned down to nothing yet the glow in the room was bright enough she could see his eyes along with the way they darkened with worry when he looked at her.

"No." She pushed on his shoulders, fighting him, fighting what she thought he might want. "You are not strong enough."

"Don't ever tell me that. You've no idea. What concerns me now is what has you screaming in the middle of the night." He was waiting for her to explain, his features taut.

She was certain he knew. She was also sure he would wait for her to tell him, giving him an opening to lecture her. The breath of air she inhaled was shaky at best, nothing substantial seeming to enter into her lungs. Talking about her near hanging was not something she thought would be something he wanted to hear about. And yet... and yet it was why she screamed. The nightmare left her helpless, sweat beading down the sides of her face. So, clearly, she remembered the moment the man kicked the stool out from under her. Recalled vividly the way the rope tightened around her neck.

"It's nothing really." She turned over, presenting her back to him while hoping he would understand. Foolish thought.

He pulled her close, her back against him, his arms wrapped around her. Escape was impossible if that was what she wanted but she didn't. "Tell me." His breath whispered across her ear, trailed down her neck.

"Please, it was horrible. If I talk about my memories, I'll keep dreaming about them." She sounded as if she was rambling but truly, she had no other words to explain why she refused.

"Your near hanging," he prompted, his voice hard even while he held her so close so protectively. Even though his arms sheltered her, she could not speak. "If you don't want to talk about it, I will."

She nodded, assuming he would do what he wished. "Fine." The pillow she held close to her muffled her voice. As she closed her eyes, she was resigned to anything he wanted to do.

"Drake, Gil, and Leslie, they didn't want me to go inside."

He drew in a long breath of air before he let it escape. The breath ruffled her hair sending wispy pieces against her cheek to tickle her.

"But you did against their wishes."

"I did, I had to see you, couldn't let you be in there alone. I was beside myself with fear, knowing I wasn't strong enough to protect you against these cowards who would attack a woman to get revenge on a man." His voice was soft yet steady.

"You weren't strong enough. I understood," she sighed softly realizing those were the last words she should have said.

"When I saw you standing precariously on that stool, my breath caught and my heart stopped beating until I regained control. I couldn't fathom what you must have been thinking or how you were feeling."

"I was terrified." She had not wanted to say anything. Had intended to listen.

"I know you were. Your eyes are very expressive. When you looked at me, imploring me... I could do nothing. Could barely move my feet."

"For the longest time I thought I was going to die and never see you or Masson."

"I wasn't going to let anything more happen to you. You should never have gone to those men. You should have told Bailey first if not me."

The lecture was coming but if this was the extent, she could weather the storm. "You're right of course." Agreeing would be the best way to continue with him.

He chuckled then, "You are going to agree with me then do

exactly what you please. Later, when I'm well, I'll have your promise. I won't forget."

In his arms she shrugged understanding even now she could never promise what he was asking. "Something like that."

"When the stool was kicked out from under you, I tried to get to you but Bailey held me back. You were safe."

"Gil is still your friend."

"Yes. We are going home tomorrow. I don't want to stay in Paris a moment longer."

~ * ~

On their first day back, rain poured from the sky. Masson played inside with Bessy. Normalcy seemed to come in stages as they travelled from Paris to the city of Bordeaux. They spent two days with Angelique who wanted to reassure herself that her daughter was fine as well as making sure nothing horrible happened to her. Upon hearing the story of what transpired, she spent as much time as Etienne allowed, regaling him about his bad decisions coupled with the fact his actions put her daughter in jeopardy. Elisa should have stayed home. She would have been much safer.

Probably everything Angelique told him was true. He'd spent years disregarding his life while taking chances. Perhaps if she had a better opinion of him, he would have stayed and married Elisa sooner. Maybe if someone told him about his son, he would have mended his ways before he put Elisa in danger.

He reached out, taking Elisa's hand in his. "I'm glad to be home."

Masson was playing upstairs. A fire crackled in the hearth, sending merry lights throughout the room changing the dreary day into something nicer. They'd brought him new toys from Paris, which he loved.

"As am I."

"*Mon, bijoux*, it is time for your punishment." He smiled at her but it wasn't the same smile she had grown accustomed to seeing on his devilishly handsome face.

"What are you talking about?"

She was playing with her skirts, winding them between her fingers. He knew she was questioning his comment. Most probably thought he forgot about his decision to tan her backside. He didn't expect he would do that even though he wanted her to believe he would. If she gave her promise, and she would, there would be no need for a child's punishment.

However, he couldn't let this disobedience go unchecked not this type in any case. Allowing her to place her life in jeopardy again was not tenable. She would need to learn this lesson very well. He told her what he would do if she left the house without him. "You don't remember?"

She was shaking her head, her mind reeling, he was positive. "No. I thought we were done with the lecture. A punishment? That is something for a child not a grown adult. You cannot mean to..." She rose then without finishing.

He knew he would have to act quickly.

"Well, you acted as a child. So, a fitting punishment for a child is what it will be." He stood also, following her lead. "What do you think?"

"Quite frankly, that you are crazy, unfair, a tyrant because you are bigger and stronger than I am. You think you can mete out justice on a whim." She picked up her skirts, heading somewhere. She wasn't sure where. All she knew was that she needed to put distance between them, praying as well that he was still weak from the beating he took in Paris.

"You can't escape this." Under the circumstances, his voice was much calmer than he expected.

Her breasts were heaving as her focus darted from one door to the other then finding its way back to him. Her eyes turned to a deep violet-blue as realization began to surface. There was indeed nowhere for her to hide or run. "Sincerely, Etienne, this is passing strange. We've been home for a while now. You've not mentioned anything like this before. Why now?"

He lifted his shoulders, understanding this was difficult for her but by his estimation necessary. "It's prudent to take care of this before too much time has passed and you forget. When we reached our home, I had not the strength." He brought his shoulders up in another slight shrug.

"Now I do."

"I don't know what you are talking about. Take care of what?" She sat down again as if this meager amount of time could have changed her mind.

He almost laughed at her attempt at innocence. "Of course, you do. You could promise me now and avoid what you call a child's punishment."

His voice was smooth as he studied her balancing the time in her mind that it would take for her to flee versus getting caught by him. He didn't want to see her fear just acceptance along with her promise. This was something that needed to be done.

She was standing again, shaking her head and backing away from him. He understood she would bolt soon. Where would she go? There was absolutely nowhere she could go that he wouldn't find her. He saw her swallow then moisten her lips, agitated, the muscles in her neck tight. She was frightened and he didn't like that. Still, the penalty needed to be paid. Risking her life was not tenable to him.

"*Non, non*, you will not..."

"I will. Sit down for a moment so I can explain in more detail."

He held out his hand hoping to induce her to sit next to him. Where he'd have easier as well as quicker access to her.

It seemed she had no intention of doing so. Her hands were clasped white knuckled in front of her. He had not done this well and he regretted the way he began.

"What is it you've planned for me?" Her eyes were wide blue-violet orbs becoming more violet than blue while they were still darkening as they spoke.

"Remember? I told you I would tan your back side." His voice was soft belying the true emotions he was feeling. "It will hurt me more than you. I promise you that."

"You would not." Her voice held no conviction.

She turned then, pulling up her skirt and petticoats, running for the steps. He wondered if she had any idea what she would do when she reached the second floor. There would be nowhere she could hide. Oh, she could bolt the door but it would not take much for him to break it down. She must realize that. At that same moment as his thoughts were forming, she must have noticed her flight was in the wrong direction.

She would tire soon. He could wait until that time where her breathing grew ragged, her pace slow. He watched her change direction of her journey sending her catapulting into the kitchen. When he followed her through the door, his strides long, she was standing on the opposite side of the small kitchen table. It would not prove much of a barrier.

"I would." One eyebrow rose a fraction, his voice soft yet determined to see through his decision. "Don't fight me, Elisa. You cannot win. This is far too important to let it go. I will have my promise whether or not you like the method."

When he darted to the right, she managed to be quicker, putting a chair between them. "Etienne, *non*. I promise never again. There, you have what you wanted."

He stopped for a moment. By the expression on her face, he was certain she thought she'd convinced him to quit. "*Viens, ici, mon bijoux. Let me finish this and we can move on to more pleasant endeavors. We both know that promise was not heart-felt.*"

She was shaking her head, breathing hard as she searched for somewhere she could flee. Her hair was tumbling from its pins and tendrils circled around her sweat-dampened face caused by fear along with fatigue. He needed desperately to get this over with, but she seemed bent on prolonging the chastisement as well as the sincere promise.

He inhaled swiftly then lunged before she could react. His arms circled her as he pulled her against his chest. She leaned back beating him with her tiny fists and kicking his legs, doing no damage. She would not give in easily and he supposed he'd expected a bit of a skirmish before the final ending.

"*Arret!*"

"*Non.*"

She brought her knee up. He was able to avoid contact. "Madam Dub—"

Kicking and hitting she was wild and determined, her arms and legs flailing with no apparent direction. He flung her over his shoulder, not something he planned. *Mon Dieu,* nothing about this was premeditated. Truly, he was no longer sure of himself or his motives. He didn't want to cause her pain. Just needed to make a point, a very valid point.

"Do not treat me as if I'm a sack of potatoes," she cried out her small fisted hands now pummeling his back.

His hand holding her legs to keep them still, she tried to kick again, one shoe falling to the floor with a thump then the other. He needed her ready for the reprimand when they reached the room because he meant to make this fast. Afterward, he wanted to make love to her. She struggled on his shoulder, nearly slipping from his hold.

"Be still."

"You're hurting my stomach."

"If you would have come along docile, none of this would have been necessary," he told her in as calm a voice as he could manage.

He pulled in a long breath of air steadying his stretched nerves. She was testing his control to the very breaking point challenging him as no other.

She squirmed again. With one hand, he reached beneath her skirts and pulled her drawers from her, letting them land haphazardly on the stairway. When he ran his hand up the naked length of her legs, she hesitated in her struggles, gasping for air. With a few more seconds one petticoat then a second landed on the steps then the landing. He grinned thinking of the trail of clothing they were leaving.

By the time he kicked open then shut before he locked the door to the master chamber, she was quite naked underneath her dress. She quivered beneath the touch. Her anger was palpable but he expected nothing less.

"Now you will lie still while I administer your punishment. If you are good, this will go easier on you."

Truly, he didn't know how he meant to proceed. Mixed emotions swamped him and pooled in his gut as if he'd swallowed a stone.

She squirmed and shrieked. "*Mon Dieu!* How dare you? Don't even think about hitting me."

"Where your safety is concerned, milady I will dare anything. You could have lost your life. Mere words have not made an impression on you."

He sat down on a chair. She lay sprawled across his thighs, one of his large hands was splayed on the small of her back, keeping her somewhat still. He pulled her dress up until it pooled around her waist.

His mouth went so dry he couldn't swallow. She was round and smooth and so soft. He placed his hand on one rounded side of her buttocks, squeezing then the other side. Clearing his throat, he smoothed her buttocks, dropping lower to run his hand along the silken length of her leg.

All his intentions vanished to be replaced by new ones. He bent over and sipped the soft rounded flesh. Instead of squirming she froze. His teeth grazed one side then the other. He bit lightly, his tongue soothing the tiny marks he left on her flesh. The tiny rippling of her pleasure, gave him good reason to smile. She moved against him then but it was not to fight him but to get closer to his mouth. He continued to lave and kiss, nip then soothe until she quivered on his lap.

"Etienne... what do you do?" Her voice squeaked as his teeth made another contact on her derrière raking slowly across the soft skin.

He couldn't answer, his own need throbbing with no possible release at the moment. There had to be a lesson in this somewhere. She tried to look up, arching her back and turning her head so she could see him. Her light golden hair now hung in total disarray around her, blocking her view.

He ran his hand along her leg to the juncture of her thighs then down the other one. She whimpered, her body giving in to the lovemaking. He followed the path of his fingers along her legs with his lips and teeth, rejoicing in the clenching of her muscles.

"Do you like this, *mon bijoux*? I certainly hope so. I find I cannot tan your backside. There is another way to get your compliance along with the sincere promise I seek."

"Please..." Her voice, all of her quivered in the anticipation he meant to take away.

He smiled then. He knew he had her where he wanted her, needed her. She would play into his hands sweetly and she would understand the direction of the punishment to be meted out. When his kisses reached her buttocks again, he nipped and kissed as he slipped a finger inside her then another, pushing as far as they would go then holding still to enjoy the velvet soft walls surrounding him as they tightened and squeezed pleading for something more. "Your honey pot is overflowing." He whispered kisses as he pushed his fingers inside then withdrew slowly, felt her body respond so sweetly, quivering around his fingers. He lost himself in his musing and the desperate need to push the hard steel of his sex within her. Not until she gave him her promise of obedience. Her walls tightened over and over again, accepting him, squeezing against him, pulling him even deeper.

"You want me so much you are unraveling with your need." He continued, his thumb finding the erotic nub that would bring her to her full pleasure as his fingers continued their determined onslaught. He teased and coaxed until her cries filled the room then he stopped. His hand rested on the soft rounded flesh of her bottom.

"Etienne..."

He continued, his enticement patient and controlled then he stopped, withdrawing his fingers. He would stop each time just before she would find her sweet release or until she gave her promise.

"No..."

Her body was rigid with need across his knees. It seemed she reached for something he would not give. "You will not take chances with your life again, *mon bijoux*. You understand me. Promise and I will give you everything you want, all that you need," he whispered, and once again his lips and teeth touched upon her flesh, teased and tempted until he knew she was beside herself with a raw savage yearning only he could relieve.

"I cannot."

"You have to. I won't cease until you do. Your punishment or discipline whatever you wish to call it. I'll leave that up to you."

"I cannot promise something I've no control over."

"Very well." He picked her up in his arms striding with her to their big bed. Setting her down on her stomach, he straddled her. His hands made short work of her gown and corset. Within seconds they were on the floor. She tried to turn over but he held her down, bending low to explore her back and spine, laving kisses on the twin dimples at the base, sipping tender flesh with teeth and tongue until she cried out again. Her hips arched upward, twisting, searching for him, for fulfillment. She would be beyond anything she felt before. He knew it and he would have that promise. Her need was sweet and savage, uncontrollable as she arched toward him.

"What are you doing now?"

She was naked save for her stockings. Looking at her it was an erotic picture, one that was hard to ignore while his rod was also aroused beyond endurance, pulsing against his clothing. He must endure. He kissed her everywhere and she curved against him. Still, he would not let her turn over. He brushed her hair away from her and placed gentle kisses on her neck, sucking first then followed with his teeth, nipping kisses, sipping her tender flesh. She tried to push up with her hips but his weight kept her immobile. He spread his fingers and ran his hands along her back then her sides, feeling her ribs until he pulsed against his britches reminding him of his purpose here as well as the tender curve of her breasts. He needed satisfaction but more than anything else he needed to render that assurance from her.

"I'm going to come inside you, Elisa. Say the two words."

Her breaths were ragged and hard. She was exhausted if he didn't miss his guess, but she was going to be more so when they finished this afternoon. Yet he had second thoughts. He spread her swollen damp petals with his fingers, nipping again and sipping, tasting the essence of her womanhood. Then once more he pushed inside her with one finger, moving as far as he could, then slowly guided a second finger inside repeating the process from the first time.

He felt the trembling again, the deep insistent need that filled her. Her walls clenched around him once more, pulling and squeezing. "Please..." she cried out again then a tiny scream wrenched the air. "Etienne..." his name this time was on her lips.

He bent over her, touching her ear with his teeth then worrying it for a moment. "Give me your agreement and I will send you to a place of ecstasy and delight."

It seemed she couldn't talk but she was shaking her head, her hair sliding across his hand.

"No." The single word was a thin wail.

He sighed, displeased with her stubbornness. This could all be finished now if only she'd give her vow. Unfastening his pants, he grasped her by her hips, lifting her. She rose with him, her forearms on the mattress her beautiful woman's parts visible to him exposed and wet, slick, craving him, welcoming him to their mysterious depths. Then he was inside her. He waited, needing to feel the quivering as her body sucked him deeper inside with each tremor of her body.

Wrapping his arms around her he held her breasts in his hands, rubbed his fingers across the hardened tips as he kissed her again and again. He found her ear and worried the lobe with his teeth. His hands explored everywhere, arousing her to a fever pitch.

"Please..." Her voice was raspy and thin. She was beyond herself in her need, arching against him, crying out.

He drove inside then, touched her womb, again and again until his guttural cry of pleasure was the only sound in the room. His seed filled her as he remained inside, unmoving, enjoying the movement against him. Now, she was frantic in her need. It was difficult for him but he withdrew then. She was sprawled on her stomach, her hair splayed around her as she tried to breathe, deep drawn-out breaths as if she could not get enough air, still she drew this out. It seemed by the expression on her face she would not surrender.

"Promise?"

Her words came out in sobs, as she tried to calm herself. "When hell freezes over."

Then he turned her. "You really intend to keep this going? One more time? Twice more? Perhaps three?" He was shocked by her stubbornness.

She touched his chest with her fingers; his nipples then lower until she reached his pants. Her eyes narrowed before she closed them. He understood her experience in the whorehouse would tell her things he didn't feel about her. Her agile mind would go there anyway. "You did not even take your clothes off."

"You're right of course." He rose then disrobed completely. She wasn't even looking at him as he spread her legs and came down between them into her silky sultry core. "Wrap them around me over my shoulders." He whispered, sipping on the tip of one breast as he caressed the other with his fingers, pulling on the nipples.

Seemingly unable to stop herself, she ran her foot along his shoulder and arm then the other. Soft sobs, keening form her. "Please Etienne. I cannot take much more of this."

"Then promise me."

He looked at her, lowered himself so he could caress the flower of her femininity with his mouth. Her fingernails scored his back when he nipped and laved at her most intimate parts. She was moving for him, unable to stop the movements. He pulled her hips higher as he thrust into her again, not believing that she would once more withhold the promise out of stubborn pride. The ripples of her walls passed from her into him. She met each thrust with her hips seeming to need more and more until he spilled himself inside her then again, he pulled away.

He lay on top of her, nearly all of his weight pressing down upon her. She ran her hands through his hair lifting with her hips as if she could implore him to give her pleasure.

"It's your choice, Elisa. Say the words and the torment for you will end."

Tears ran from the corners of her eyes, but she didn't bat them away. She bit her lip, watching him and he saw a tiny prick of blood.

Several seconds passed. He heard the ticking of the clock, mingled with the sound of each savage breath she inhaled. His hand settled on her belly and his fingers rested on top of the soft thatch of hair shielding her women's mound.

"Say the word, Elisa."

Closing her eyes, she nodded.

"You know that is not good enough," he whispered, as he bent close his lips brushing sweetly against hers.

"I promise."

"Good then." He turned them both so she straddled him. "It is up to you but I'll make sure you find your pleasure."

He massaged the tiny velvet knot and watched mesmerized as she tossed her head back, her breasts thrusting perfections. She moved on him then as he found his ecstasy. Once more, he felt her tremors grow and grow until she cried out again and again, screaming his name as her body responded sweetly and with so much force he was left in awe.

She fell against him, replete finally, her hair spread around him. Sweeping her into his arms, he turned them so he lay atop her. He didn't believe for one second she meant her promise. Oh, she might try. In the end, however, she would do as she thought right even if it meant putting her life in danger. Truly, he accomplished very little.

Etienne braced himself, his hands on either side of her head. Lightly, he brushed her lips with his. "I know I drug that promise from you. I only wish you meant it with all your heart."

Moisture pooling in her eyes, she turned from him then. He knew the truth, knew his thoughts were right. Accepting her as she was would be hard. It was this woman, however, he fell in love with.

"Masson..."

He sucked in a deep draught of air. "Hopefully still napping."

"Our son will wonder why the door is locked in the middle of the afternoon," Elisa said avoiding further conversation about the discipline and its bizarre turn.

Watching her close her eyes gave him an extraordinary sensation, stirrings of deep unadulterated love for her. When she opened them again, she swept hair from his forehead, her lips parted.

"If I ever did nothing when you needed me, and something happened to you, I would never forgive myself," she sighed softly closing her eyes again, while she moistened her lips. "I don't want to live without you."

"You know better than anyone I can take care of myself." Softly he kissed her, brushed more kisses across her face, her cheeks, jawline, ear, as well as her light eyebrows. "You've no reason to ever think you need to rescue me."

"I realize you are better prepared for things such as what happened in Paris than I. Still..."

"Don't think it," he bent close to her, his lips gently set on her neck, then lower to the valley between her breasts.

The response filled him with love and gratitude for this woman whose faith in him changed his life.

Closing her eyes, the smile on her face telling him she enjoyed his sensuous attention to the most erotic places on her slender frame. "Do you feel this?"

"Hmm..." she sighed as he caught the small sound trapping it between his lips.

"Do you feel my love?" he asked as his lips covered hers once more, his hands roaming the length of her body.

"Etienne, please..." She arched as his hands found the swollen female petals, caressing and stroking.

"Answer," his smile embraced her body, the tips of her breasts, lower still to explore her belly. "Do you feel my love, *mon bijoux?*"

"Yes," she said softly. "I'm feeling your love. Feeling Etienne's love forever."

"As I feel your love," he murmured against her then proceeded to show her just how much.

Epilogue

Etienne, Elisa and Masson played in the vineyards throughout the summer. Husband and wife made love whenever they found privacy. It seemed neither could get enough of the other. No more trouble followed Etienne but they were ever cautious.

Masson spent many sleepovers at his grandfather's even sometimes traveling to Bordeaux to spend a few days with Angelique. It was a halcyon summer for Elisa. She was happier than she'd ever been. Etienne was not only a fabulous father and lover he was also a friend. He understood her deepest secrets along with her fears.

Tomorrow was Masson's birthday. He would turn five. They planned a big celebration. Angelique was bringing all of her ladies. Gil would be there. However, today was for them.

Elisa leaned into Etienne's arms, her back pressed against his chest as they watched a butterfly flit around the grape vines. When Elisa closed her eyes, she recalled the way Masson chased the small butterflies. He would clap his hands delightedly when he came close to capturing the beautiful winged creature. Yet, every time he would get close, the butterfly would dart away.

"Are you as happy as I am?" she asked Etienne as she held her breath waiting for the answer she hoped for.

"Of course, *mon bijoux.*"

His chin settled gently on the top her head one gruff growl of contentment rumbling up from his belly. His fingertips traced the line of her collarbone, dipping lower from time to time just to tease.

"You don't miss the old life of adventure and excitement?"

"You along with dodging Masson's questions about what we are doing behind locked doors is as much excitement as I need right now." He paused while Elisa held her breath. "Any more and I would surely be too exhausted to keep that door locked."

She turned in his arms. "What would you say if..." she wasn't at all sure if she should go on with the question.

His eyes darkened to nearly black. Somehow, she felt as if he read her mind. At that instant she was sure he already knew. Her news would not be a surprise.

"If?" He slanted a dark eyebrow mockingly, his teeth nipping lightly on her earlobe teasing her.

Desperate to tell him, yet frightened at the same time, she moistened her lips before trying for the right words. She shuddered when his lips found the pulse at her neck, sipping until she moaned. "If..."

He laughed, pulling her back then turning so he lay on top of her, his weight pushing her downward. She stroked his neck his chin. He brushed a kiss across her lips leaving them wet and slightly swollen. "Just tell me whatever it is that's on your agile little mind."

Now he was laughing harder. She hit him on the shoulder, pushing at him. "You beast. You know, don't you?"

"I was just wondering when you were going to tell me." His lips trailed softly along her jaw then back to her lips. He allowed her a breath of air before he covered her mouth with his, sipping at her bottom lip, thrusting his tongue deep inside absorbing her small sounds of pleasure.

When he looked at her again, his grin was smug all masculine. He appeared very pleased with himself and his male prowess She hit him again. "How? How did you know?"

"I'm not ignorant of a woman's body or yours as well as what happens within you. Truly, Elisa, don't ask more questions that I know will embarrass you. Just tell me."

"We are going to have another baby."

It seemed she was holding her breath now. He knew he was grinning like a besotted fool. "Yes, I'm guessing around February. What do you think?"

She gasped. "You've known that long? Does nothing ever get away from you?"

"The first month that you were not writhing in pain, I guessed. Then the next month was the same. I would have known anyway when..."

Mortified, just as he said, she buried her face in his chest only to hear more rumbling male laughter. She allowed him his mirth as she also allowed her heated face to cool.

She looked at him, "Are you happy? Another child?"

"Perhaps the babe will be a girl and look like you. Of course, I'm happy. I love you Elisa."

"As I love you," she murmured pleased with his answer.

Coming Soon by the Author
at
Rogue Phoenix Press

All I Want is Link

Virginia 1826

"Blessed hell," Link Stewart murmured. "Don't believe I've ever been this cold.

Link had never been so bloody cold in all his life. Wind whipped through his heavy coat as if he wore nothing at all. Snow poured from the sky, the white flakes piling high on his shoulders. He crossed his arms in front of him, his head down as he plowed forward through the blinding snow, heading for the alehouse just down the block from where his ship was birthed. He grimaced as a gust hit him in the face with gale-force power.

Stepping into the pub he let his eyes adjust to the darkness of the room. He found an empty table and sat down, absorbing the warmth it offered. A few minutes passed before he was willing to rid himself of his outerwear and enjoy the atmosphere the small tavern offered. A blazing fire crackled in a fireplace situated on one wall at the side of the room. He was tempted to take up a position in front of it and warm his hands.

The serving maid who stood beside his table now slowly eyed him. Ogled might be the better word. He grinned at her not wishing to encourage her attention, but the smile was natural for him when he saw a pretty girl. "What can I get you?" She looked to the upstairs then back to him, her meaning clear. She wouldn't be averse to a dalliance.

He wanted to laugh at her audacity, knew it was the way she made extra money. Ah, but he supposed things didn't change much from one country to the next. His mind was fixed however not on new dalliances with the local maids but on the rumors swirling around one Sophia Carter-Brown.

The lady was an enigma to him. She was part of why he was here. He meant to find out everything he could about the lady who did not act the role of a lady.

Link flashed the serving maid his signature grin, his smile wide understanding the affect he had on women. "A hot toddy would be nice. Might take the bite of cold away," he told the young woman casting his gaze away from the girl and to the groups of men enjoying a drink this wintery afternoon.

Nothing he read about the area prepared him for this blast of frigid weather he encountered. He loathed the idea of going outside but knew in about an hour Grayson, his plantation manager, would be at the docks to pick him up. Best he learn as much local gossip now that he had the chance.

Sophia was said to have three lovers so far. It was the so far that stopped him cold. If any of this were true, she was a harlot, willing to sell herself but for what? Why would a young lady of good breeding suddenly assume a life of prostitution? What was the price she put on her body? He heard it was quite high. Listening to the conversation in the pub, she seemed to be the main topic and just who might be her next conquest. He decided he might put himself in line for that seemingly coveted role. She would know from the start however that he didn't share. No, if she were to become his lover, she would have to get rid of the others.

Every last one of them.

He would tolerate nothing more.

The idea became more and more intriguing as he thought on taking her for his lover.

His grin widened thinking about bedding the experienced young lady. He also heard she was beautiful. Link enjoyed the experienced ones. They were usually not looking for a husband, so all he needed to do was appreciate as well as adore and pamper the ladies to his heart's content. He would look forward to seeing this woman for the first time. Wondered how she would react to him. The drink curled warmly in his belly. He would have to remember this particular concoction when he returned to Scotland. It was suitable for a cold winter night.

He sat back, his legs stretched out in front of him, felt the first moment of relaxation since he stepped off his ship an hour ago and into this frigid arctic weather. Yes, now that he knew what he intended he would proceed with his plan accordingly. He wasn't at all sure if Sophia had anything to do with the dark magic being perpetrated in the area, but she would know more than he did. Perhaps she could shed some light on the happenings as well as why.

Strangely, he was no longer bored.

By listening to the table nearby, he heard one of Sophia's lovers sold his plantation to Sophia's uncle then headed back to Scotland. He wondered to himself, thought of different scenarios that might have been the cause. Perhaps she also understood the reasons for one of her lovers suddenly moving back to Glasgow. So, now there might only be two for her to get rid of.

The hot toddy had the affect he wanted. His insides were suddenly feeling normal again. Normal until he left the warmth of the tavern to wander outside. Pulling out his pocket watch he noticed he still had about thirty minutes before he needed to head for the port.

The bar maid stood by his side again, moistening her lips while thrusting out one hip. She was plump and pretty, her breasts large enough to fill his hands. Her lips were soft pink as she moistened them. He wasn't interested though. There were too many things occupying his mind. A sexual distraction was not something he wanted or needed at the moment.

He smiled, held her hand in his. "Maybe another time, sweetheart," he murmured softly.

"You don't know what you're missing," she told him as she sashayed to another table.

Ah, but Link was sure he did know what he was missing. No, he hadn't even seen Miss Sophia Carter-Brown yet but he wanted her. No one else would do for him at least not until he learned the secrets she was hiding. She would learn quickly enough he was not a man to be played with.

If he understood women at all, he knew there were riddles to uncover. He was just the man to accomplish such a feat. He looked forward to doing just that with a resolve he didn't quite understand.

Bits and pieces of information filtered through the smoke filled air. Sophia was still the main topic. Her latest conquest was a young man, Devon Masters. His father owned a nearby plantation, but Devon had a penchant for gambling as well as whoring. He spent his father's money as if there was a never-ending supply. Perhaps there was. This plantation while still thriving could be brought down, he assumed, if the man did not concede to his father's wishes. Link decided he would have to look into the finances a bit more closely.

The third lover was an older man. The scenario did not ring true in this case. Once again Link decided he would have to learn more about the man. The rumors spoke of his longing for Scotland though. Perhaps it was innocent. Possibly Sophia was just a woman with questionable scruples, a woman who enjoyed what a man could give her. After all he would never condemn a woman for enjoying sex. He enjoyed sex, no responsibilities attached. She was allowed to be free just as any man. It was just...

Well hell, just what?

He knew what he was thinking, didn't like the gist of those thoughts either. Just then a cold rush of air filled the alehouse. The open door brought a smattering of snow as well as a man swaddled in a thick coat. A wry grin touched on Link's face as he stood to greet Grayson, the manager of the Stewart plantation. The description he'd been given fit him to a tee, salt and pepper hair included.

"A drink before we brave the weather?" Link asked, extending his hand in greeting.

Grayson shook snow off his coat before shaking his hand, "No, we need to get going. There is a break in the clouds and the snow. Should make use of the time the weather is giving us. I thought perhaps you weren't coming until I spoke to the captain who said you were the most enjoyable passenger he ever had. We should really get going."

"Very well, I'm sure you know what you're about." Link left money on the table to cover his drink. He looked at his coat, wishing he were in the south of France right now instead of Virginia then slipped his arms into the sleeves, buttoning it up to his neck. Mayhap in time he would get used to the ice and snow. Perhaps in time the weather would change and the sun would come out.

Fact of the matter was the ship's captain liked him simply because he did not sleep with his new wife a young lady making her first voyage with her much older husband. She tried to seduce him in the companionway during a storm. Evidently, the captain discovered what she was about. A solid rule of his was to never get into bed with a married woman, too many complications, way too many to make it a prudent adventure. No, widows and adventurous women were the only ones for him.

They stepped outside. Grayson was right. The snow had stopped and the sun was shining down on them. Dark clouds lined up to the south threatening more of the same in an hour or so. He hoped an hour was enough time to reach Leslie Hall. He lifted his face to the sun with every intention of soaking up as much warmth as possible now that the sun was shining. Ah, but the manor was named after his brother the duke. Until he was born it had just been a nameless place in Virginia. Their father believed naming the plantation after his first born to be a nice touch either that or they could have called it Southcliff the Second.

The wagon taking them was in front of the tavern, piled high with supplies. "Well, I can't tell you enough that I'm thanking God over and over again that you are here. We've had trouble but then I'm sure you read the letter I sent to the duke. I don't know what to do about the black magic. I'm afraid these nightly visits are escalating. Don't mind telling you they scare the very daylights out of me as well as all our slaves and free people. As to the cold, the weather will improve. By May you'll be praying for some snow before you succumb to the heat. It will also be so humid when you take a bath and try to dry off you'll still feel damp. Horrible weather."

Link wasn't sure he would still be here in May. At least he hoped he'd solve this little problem, take stock of Sophia Carter-Brown and be on his way home by May. Two months should be more than enough time to figure out all this duplicity.

"You will see to the—"

Mr. Grayson's voice broke off abruptly. He sucked in his breath. Link followed the line of sight and in turn saw a vision of his own. It was a woman... truly just a woman. He saw nothing special about her. Even from this distance, he realized who she was, yes, he was certain this was the woman who dangled three men so skillfully. When she bade them dance, they most assuredly played right into her small adept hands. A woman should never be able to wield so much power over the male species. Link grinned. He wondered what other delightful things she proposed they do. What would she propose with him? Then he sighed, too tired and cold from the weeks on board the ship to wonder about something he would discover soon enough. The intense cold was sapping his strength. He'd never experienced anything like it before in his life. He hoped Grayson's prediction was correct and either he'd adjust or the weather would improve or he'd just sit next to the fireplace and stare at the flames.

His attention went back to Grayson. The man was still staring at the woman, salivating at her, knowing she'd never be his because more powerful men coveted her. That was the kind of man it seemed she preferred. Men who owned plantations... that was an interesting thought. Perhaps, just possibly she was part of a plan to buy out other plantation owners, a monopoly of the tobacco plantations in the area. Would not be the first time a woman used her body for personal gain and greed.

"Mr. Grayson, I'd like to go to Leslie Hall now. You can tell me all about the troubles you're having on the way. Also, I'd like to hear everything you know about that lady." He nodded in the direction every male on the street was looking.

"Yes, yes Master Stewart, but that's Sophia Carter-Brown, you know." He pulled the hood of his coat over his head. "Know enough about her; known the young lady since she and her sister arrived penniless and without parents."

"Ah," said Link, his voice a blend of irony and curiosity. "Onward, Grayson. Pull your tongue back inside your mouth, if you please. We need to get myself and these supplies to warmth before the next storm hits and buries me in the white stuff." Bloody eyes but the day he arrived in Glasgow it was snowing like this, damn near lost is way when he tried to ride to Southcliff.

Samuel Grayson stuttered a few times, tried valiantly to remove his ardent focus without success. The woman in question was being helped down from her horse by a white man and had just shown a glimpse of silk-covered ankle. To render men slavering idiots with an ankle caused Link to shake his head in wonder. Her ankles were no different than any other lady's ankle. Over the course of his adult male life he'd seen so many feminine parts; many ankles, legs, thighs and everything else feminine that he far preferred a roaring fire than seeing anything the woman had to offer. At least at this moment that's what he preferred. Once he warmed up, he'd see things differently. Discovering her more feminine assets could wait.

"Back to the task at hand," Link said growing impatient.

Grayson nodded his focus still on the so-called vision. "I don't understand," he said more to himself than to Link as he urged the two horses pulling the cart forward. "Look at her, well I know you did but you're obviously not affected by her beauty. She is exquisite. One can understand why the men want her. What I can't quite conceive is why she wants them."

"She is a woman, Grayson, nothing more, nothing less. Can we go now?"

"It's nearly an hour to the plantation, but the road curves along the river. It is really quite beautiful. You will appreciate the scenery. Many of the largest farms have their own docks. The water is deep enough to handle most ships. You should enjoy the ride. The main house looks out over the river, but there is a small summer cottage close by. You might enjoy its solitary aspects. It also looks out over the river and is very pleasant during the summer months when cool air can flow from the front door to the back."

Again, Link thought he wasn't planning on being here in the summer. He would check out this cottage. It might be a nice place to get to know Miss Sophia Carter-Brown better. If the cottage was secluded, he liked the idea even better.

While they rode Grayson talked endlessly. He spoke of the weather then switched to the strange happenings, how even the slaves as well as the free-workers were terrified. The blue and yellow smoke unnerved him and everyone else. It wasn't right. It had to be something supernatural to cause all this horror. The rattling sounding like bones was even more terrifying as were the moans and groans as if someone was dying.

He didn't understand. No, he didn't understand at all. No one wanted to go outside and investigate. Leastwise, no one but his son, Edward, who didn't seem to be afraid of anything. Just last week there had been a fire set in a storage shed near the main house. Edward put it out, believed it was the work of men who were trying to scare him away. Things like that was one of the reasons why he sent for help. Then two nights ago a tree had nearly fallen on the veranda roof. The tree had been very large and very sturdy. There was no wind or anything that could have brought it down. This has been going on nearly a year now.

Link wondered when the lady took her first lover. "Did Edward find any saw marks on the tree?"

"No," Mr. Grayson said, firmly shaking his head at the same time. "No, there was nothing to indicate any man had a hand in this. It's the work of the supernatural. I tell you true. There is no reason for those things to happen. Even Edward had to acknowledge what I said. He didn't want to but he couldn't figure out how the tree fell."

Grayson tugged in a deep breath, looking over his shoulder as if something was about to attack him. "One of the slaves said he saw smoke swirling around the tree, white smoke then it turned green and red. Soon as the smoke was gone, well the tree fell."

"Ah, so this also makes you believe this is the work of the supernatural. Personally, I don't take much stock in witchcraft and the like. There will always be a scientific reason behind what takes place around man. All kinds of chemicals when mixed together can make colored smoke. It is a flesh and blood man who is causing this, nothing supernatural, no ghosts, no black magic or voodoo. All you need worry about his catching the men who are perpetrating the crime."

"Don't believe anyone around her has that kind of knowledge," Grayson muttered. "Chemicals? Not a chance. Who here would know how to mix chemicals? Never heard of such a thing."

Link wanted to laugh but carefully kept it behind his teeth. He didn't want to antagonize this man or belittle him. No, he needed his help as well as Edward's to ferret out what was really going on here. He was a man well pleased. His boredom would not return anytime soon. He looked forward to the following weeks. There would be so much to keep him entertained.

"Speaking of your son, tell me more about him. There was nothing in the letter about him."

Grayson puffed up, a grin flashing across his face. The man was clearly pleased with his son. A moment later he was fidgeting with his heavy gloves. "He is a good boy, Sir. He does a lot for me—for the Stewarts—now that I'm getting on in years. He didn't want to leave the hall unprotected so he is waiting for us there."

They passed dozens of small homes. Link wondered if these were the slave quarters or the quarters of those who'd earned their freedom. He yearned to set all of them free, but knew he couldn't go that far. He didn't understand why they were slaves in the first place even though he understood most cultures had slaves. Had been that way since the beginning of time. Didn't know why the Stewarts bought them in the first place. He decided to write Leslie for more information and a suggestion of his own as well.

Well, hell, the fact didn't make it right.

The countryside wasn't all that different from the Scottish landscape where Southcliff Manor was situated. Virginia was different though. It was completely foreign to the Bordeaux region of France where he spent most of his life. Here, instead of miles of vineyards, one saw miles of tobacco plants. He wondered if he'd see wild animals, wolves perhaps, deer maybe a bear. Perhaps not, he had enough to contend with as it was. He might see one of the Native Americans who owned this land first.

"We are nearing Rose Hall," Grayson said suddenly, his voice falling to nearly a whisper.

Link raised a speculative eyebrow.

"It's her home, Sir. Sophia Carter-Brown's home. She lives there with her uncle and her younger sister. There is one plantation between Leslie Hall and Rose Hall. As I understand, her uncle is about to buy that place substantially adding to his holdings.

Link thought that fact to be very interesting. He wondered why the man was selling.

"Charles Ewing. Some say he wishes to move to New York. It's north of here as I'm sure you know. Doesn't make a lick of sense though. He always told me he loathes the city and would never want to live there.

He has four older children who don't work, just idle away their time. His wife is said to be a trying a witch by some. It's a sad story, a real sad story."

Link was certain he heard the man's name in the alehouse earlier this afternoon. He was wracking his brain to recall what was said about the man, but he'd heard so much it was difficult to sift through all the information. What he was searching for would come to him.

Then he remembered. He spoke very slowly, "I understand this Sophia Carter-Brown has three men currently in her bed. I seem to recall that this Charles Ewing was one of them. Am I right?"

Grayson flushed to the roots of his graying hair. "You've only been here a short time. How would you know?"

"It's what all the men were talking about at the alehouse when I first arrived. The topic was Sophia. As you know, I went in there for something to warm my insides as well as my outsides. If this older man was one her lovers, why?"

"No, no, none of what you heard said is true. She is beautiful inside as well as out. She has not taken lovers. Rumors, idle rumors that's all you heard. Never take any stock in rumors. There are many men who are not gentlemen. They don't speak the truth about the young lady. She is exquisite. They want people to think she took them into her bed when she hasn't."

"It is the rumors, is it not?"

"What you heard is a viscous lie. Don't believe what you hear about Sophia. She is sweet and innocent. She has no lovers. Don't mistake me. Customs on plantations are different. Many of the white owners have black mistresses. That doesn't have anything to do with Sophia. She is a lady." Grayson was sputtering now. He was in distress over the conversation and obviously believed the young harlot was guiltless.

"Do you bow down to the local customs, Grayson?"

"Not in the beginning. Not when my wife lived. I was loyal to her. After she died, I was lonely. Yes, I took a mistress. Life here is different from Scotland in many ways. In other ways, you'll find it very much the same. You'll get used to the idea of white men bedding their salves."

Link didn't think there were some local customs he would ever grow accustomed to. He knew he wouldn't be here long enough to do so.

Nor would he be here long enough to make a difference.

Link subsided, letting his body relax and absorb the rolling, bouncing sway of the wagon. He closed his eyes a moment, breathing in the cold stinging air coupled with the smell of the nearby river. "Why is Ewing selling out then, in your opinion?"

"I really couldn't say. Never truly thought it was any of my business. So, I never asked. Once again there are rumors. It was a sudden decision I was told. He and his family are leaving next week. I have heard he lost a lot of money to Devon Masters, a wastrel but lucky with the cards. You should not gamble with him. Some say he cheats, too, but it has never been proven."

"Another rumor."

"Yes."

Link turned to face the man, his manager, a man he needed to trust. He needed information not gossip, "There is every bit as much talk here as there is in Scotland as well as Bordeaux. I don't believe I'll be the least bit uninterested. Perhaps we'll have some mysterious manifestations tonight to welcome me. Yes, I would relish a ghoulish spectacle of any type. Perhaps we can catch whoever is scaring people witless. Isn't this young Devon reputed to be one of her lovers?"

Link wondered if Grayson would denounce this rumor too. He opened his mouth then managed to keep his words behind his teeth. Then after a few moments of reflection Grayson said in a very calm manner. "I repeat Link all of this is utter nonsense. Her uncle William Brinkmeyer is a good man, solid, dependable. He is amiable, his business dealings above reproach. I imagine the vicious rumors about Sophia Carter-Brown hurt him very much. He never speaks of it because he is a gentleman of the finest type. His overseer, however, is a different story. Felix Campbell is a rotten fellow, cruel to the slaves."

"If uncle Brinkmeyer is such a fine fellow, why does he employ someone the opposite? Someone who is cruel to the less fortunate, a savage from what you say."

"I don't know. There are rumors about that too. Some believe the slaves need a stern hand or they won't do any work. Brinkmeyer doesn't have a cruel bone in his body, so the slaves would just idle away the hours if he didn't have someone with an iron fist to run his plantation for him."

"Yes, perhaps Brinkmeyer just feels pity for Ewing and is simply taking the plantation off his hands so the man can move on with his life. Brinkmeyer is the younger brother of Miss Sophia and Clare's mother. Do I have that right?"

Link wasn't really sure what was going on here. There were too many holes in the facts, too much idle gossip. It seemed Grayson took a lot for granted. "What are the girls doing here?"

"Their parents were drowned when their ship went down, about five years ago. The children were made wards of their uncle. They've been here ever since."

"Are they English?"

"Scottish. They lived near Edinburgh, a small estate that will belong to the children when they come of age. Miss Sophia is close to that age now. When she has children, a boy, he will inherit."

Link was silent going over everything that had been said as well as what had not been said. So, the girl had been raised in Scotland. Now she was here and she was a tart. His thinking turned back to the problem that brought him here to Virginia. Link strongly doubted the supernatural had anything to do with the problems occurring at Leslie Hall. Oh no, greed was the same all over the world. He said, "Did Mr. Ewing have any supernatural problems before he agreed to sell to this Brinkmeyer.

"Not that I know of. Oh, I see the direction of your thoughts, Link, but I don't credit them. As I said, Mr. Brinkmeyer is an outstanding individual. He gives to charities and those less fortunate. He is always looking after others. No, if Ewing were having financial problems or if he were being besieged as we are at Leslie Hall, Brinkmeyer certainly would not be behind it."

Link wondered if Grayson spoke as passionately about the Stewarts as he did Uncle Brinkmeyer. He'd never met a man who deserved such accolades. Well, he would soon discover the truth for himself.

Grayson turned the wagon inland away from the river. The cart lumbered up a long winding driveway before it stopped in front of Leslie Hall. It appeared much as Southcliff did. Link supposed their father had it built in the same style for good reason. He would feel at home here.

My home is beyond the main house about a quarter mile and the cottage I spoke of is just at the top of that hill. The trees surround it, except for the front and back. In the summer they provide a host of shade, cooling the building down to an enjoyable level as breezes from the river flows freely through it.

Ah, but Link didn't intend to still be in Virginia in the summer but he did intend to discover it's uses while he was here.

~ * ~

It was nearly midnight. Link thoroughly enjoyed himself in the small cottage. The fireplace blazed with logs crackling. A cozy warm glow filled the room. He stretched out on a white fur rug in front of the hearth, a glass of Bordeaux in his hand. The storm threatening to the south still had not reached them. The crisp air outside had taken on a decided chill. When he strolled outside for more logs to place on the fireplace, the snow popped and crunched beneath his feet. The scent filling his nostrils was one of impending winter and ice.

There was a half-moon shining above. He felt relaxed, ready to take on whatever real or supernatural powers that threatened the lives of these people. The night was so beautiful, the black vault of the sky overhead with the spattering of stars, so calm so silent that he felt peace flow through him. This was just how God planned life.

He wasn't a peaceful man. This newfound sensation of his was an odd feeling. He found that he didn't dislike the peculiarity, meant to soak up the moments because he didn't believe the serenity would last. Nothing peaceful ever did last. He stretched out naked on the fur wishing one of his widows from Bordeaux might have made the trip with him. Ah, Suzette, how he missed her. He did need to find a willing lady to see to his baser needs. He stretched again, relaxing even more, relishing the fur against his nakedness. Closing his eyes, he listened to the sounds he hadn't heard before. The sound of an owl came to him then the soft sound of a breeze curling around the eaves of the cottage. He thought he heard the croak of a frog, dismissed the idea. Somewhere a dog barked. He sighed when each sound became more distinct.

It was just so damn tranquil here, perhaps because he had only one purpose. He didn't have to please anyone, just ferret out the truth then go home. He was on the point of falling asleep when he heard something unusual.

The noise was too different to put a name on the sound, something he'd never before heard. Still lying on the fur, he held himself motionless while he waited. He listened hard. There it was again, that strange sort of low moaning sound that didn't sound remotely human. Although he knew it was.

He slipped on his pants and shirt then his boots, intending to discover the sound. He forgot the air was frigidly cold. Forgot everything except his quest to discover the truth. The sound became louder the closer he got to the main house. He ran lightly up the snow-covered slope toward the back of the manor. He eased around the side. The sound came again. A strange light welled up from the ground. It was a narrow thready light blue beam, and it smelled of sulfur as if it was coming directly from hell and the moans were of the souls entrapped there. Gooseflesh rose on his body. The hair on the back of his neck stood on end. This was beyond strange, bordering on ridiculous. There was an explanation. This was just a mixture of chemicals concocted by a mere mortal.

He heard a hiss. As he whirled to see who it was, he picked up snow, molding it into a hard ball, pounding more snow onto it until it was large and very hard.

It was Edward Grayson. He met the man upon his arrival at Leslie Hall. He was the estate manager's son.

Link grinned. He liked Edward. The young man had a good head on his shoulders, smart as well as possessing a great deal of common sense. Like Link he wasn't the least bit superstitious although he didn't once disagree with his father during dinner or their discussion later.

"What do you think it is?" Link asked in a deep whisper, shielding his mouth with his hand.

"Don't know but I intend to find out. Now you're here to help me. I've tried to get some of the male slaves, free men as well, but they roll their eyes and look at me as if I'm crazy. They mutter some nonsense in a different language. They won't dare go outside in the middle of the night to investigate the smoke."

"Very well," Link said resigned to the fact he and Edward were in this together with no other help forthcoming. "Go around to the other side of the light and I'll ease closer from this side."

Edward disappeared into the shadows to work his way to the other side of the smoky blue light. A trap, Link thought, pleased. Blood pumped wildly through him, thrilled by the new excitement. He thought about the two women he bedded on the long trip here. They were both charming delightful ladies but much the same. He was tired of the same. He didn't want to be bored here. This, now this was intriguing, exciting.

When Edward was in position, Link straightened, clenched his fists tight at his sides and walked directly toward the light. An unearthly shriek reverberated through the stillness then the moans followed. Gooseflesh rose again despite the fact he knew man created the mournful rendition of a ghost.

The blue light continued to rise higher into the black sky, the odor foul. Once more he reminded himself it was simply the igniting of sulfur, nothing more. Who was moaning? They were doing a blessed fine job.

Edward shouted while waving his hands in the air. He began to run following a flowing white robed figure. Ah, here we are. This is why I came to Virginia. The identity would be discovered this night. He realized he didn't want to go home so soon. No, it wasn't even May yet. Nor had he discovered Sophia Carter-Brown's talents. No, no even if he solved this puzzle, he must remain to solve the second one.

The stealthy white figured turned then and fired at him. Link felt the bullet whiz by his temple. He touched his head. There was blood on his fingers.

"Bloody hell," he yelled before racing straight toward the figure. He meant to throttle this interloper. The man was tall and large, but Link could run fast and was gaining on him. Any moment he would have him. He slipped on a patch of ice, cursed, started forward again.

Without warning a shaft of pain seared his thigh. He stopped, staring down at the feathered arrow that was sticking out of his leg.

Damnation, the man was getting away. Edward, shouting at him was at his side in another moment. "Where the hell did that bloody arrow come from? The man had an accomplice, damn him!"

"It's nothing, Edward. Go after him. We've got to find out who the devil is creating all this havoc where there is supposed to be only peace and quiet."

"No, Edward said calmly. "The men will come back. Your leg needs to be tended to. I doubt if it's going to stop you for long."

With no more words Edward ripped a strip of his shirt then turning to Link he pulled the arrow from his leg and bound the wound. "We need to get you back to the main house. It needs to be cleaned and bandaged. You'll walk with a slight limp for a while."

~ * ~

He was careful not to hit her where the bruises could be seen. The first blow hit her ribs below her breasts. Her gasp made him pause then grin. She knew this was just the beginning. He relished hurting her. Sophia understood he wouldn't stop until she lost consciousness from the pain. She closed her eyes as another blow hit her in the stomach. No bruises there.

He hit her ribs again in very nearly the same spot as the first blow. Her body jerked, the agony searing inside her as she tried not to give him more pleasure by crying out. If she could she would hit him back. He hit her temple then jabbed her twice more in the ribs. She knew her hair would cover the bruising as long as it didn't seep out to far onto her face. She cringed then sucked air, her hands trying to block each blow even though she understood the feeble gesture wouldn't stop him. He wouldn't end the relentless torment until he either grew tired or she lost consciousness.

Once again, he turned his attention to her ribcage, battering her until she was forced against the wall. She looked at him, pain excruciating, flaming though her body before she slowly slid to the floor. He wouldn't stop though. He would find a way to prop her up so he had easy access. Confused, she wasn't sure why she earned this beating, didn't know what she did wrong or didn't do.

He was so unpredictable.

He usually only attacked when he was displeased with something. When she did something he disliked. Searching her mind for the reason, she couldn't come up with any plausible motivation. He kicked her then, one more shot at her ribs. It wasn't hard enough to crack a rib.

He was truly very careful. Nothing he did would show.

"Little slut, think you can get away with acting as if you're not a slut? You aren't a lady. Stop pretending." He stood over her, his feet braced on either side of her. Slowly he bent over, pulling her to a standing position. She blinked a few times in an attempt to clear her vision. Still, she didn't understand what he was talking about.

Desperately, she tried to keep the bile in her stomach. She didn't want to lose it simply because she would have to clean it all up. Even if she spilled her lunch on his shoes, it would be fitting. He would only be angrier. Would hit her again.

"Why?" The sound of her voice surprised her. It was weak and pathetic, just the way he made her feel. She had no recourse except to obey him even though she longed to fight him. He threatened her daily with her sister's life.

"You didn't tell me. Why the hell didn't you tell me?" he was screaming at her now, shaking her until her head lolled back, until her ribs cried out more painfully than before. She heard the soft moan come from her throat.

She was standing now but only because he was holding her. She didn't know if he was going to hit her again. It probably depended on her reply, but she didn't have any notion what he was talking about. She didn't care either. As long as he didn't take his anger out on Clare, she would do anything he wanted, say anything.

"Tell you what?" she managed to say just before he jerked her close. His foul breath wafted against her cheek. Revulsion nearly sent her to the ground again. She almost lost her breakfast. His hand wound into her hair tugging her head back. She couldn't even turn away from him.

"Don't lie to me, girl. I don't like it. You know exactly what I'm talking about. You were in town yesterday. You saw him." Spittle was flying from his mouth, landing on her cheeks and lips. Once more she closed her eyes for a moment then another one, trying to soak in strength. No matter how she wanted to ignore him she couldn't.

He would go away only when it pleased him.

She swallowed hard wishing she had the answer he craved. "Who?"

"Link Stewart. You must have passed him just outside the alehouse. I know you saw Devon yesterday. Grayson saw you. Link was in the wagon with him. I gave you permission. Devon took you to lunch then brought you home. I watched from the balcony. Didn't he tell you Link was there? He would have noted a new arrival. Would have spoken of him." He was pale now, his eyes narrowed with fury. "I should have been told."

"I don't even know who that is. Link Stewart?" She was cringing again hating her cowardice yet feeling rage boiling up inside her. It was stupid of her, this temper of hers, this habit of saying what she was thinking instead of using prudence. She was going to make matters worse, but she just couldn't help herself. "I wanted him to be here, to catch you at your evil games. I prayed he would come, the voice of reason, a man who would see through the ridiculous. He wouldn't believe any of that supernatural stuff. I knew if anyone could do it, he could stop you."

She waited for the next shot to her face or ribs. It never came. Instead, she heard his laughter, saw his grin his yellowed teeth behind his lips. For a moment she saw what others in this small community saw, a man with humor and wit, a gentle man, a man of breeding. In the next moment it was gone. He was back as she knew him to be. The once pleasant grin was evil now. "If Felix hadn't shot him with the arrow, he might have discovered us. I didn't expect any of what happened last night. Here was this fellow, running at me half dressed, yelling like a banshee a snowball in his hand. Then Felix shot him."

He was going to throw the damn snowball at me. He was packing it harder as he ran.

Sophia felt the blood draw from her face. She couldn't fathom what he just told her. This wasn't possible. No, he couldn't be saying what she thought he was saying. "You killed him? You killed the owner of Leslie Hall?"

"Oh, no more's the pity. The arrow nicked his thigh. Didn't do much damage. Felix is always careful. Strange, truly strange you know. Since the man was probably having a tryst in that little cottage on the hill. Which brings me to the next part of our plan. Stewart is going to be your next lover. I want you to be the woman having the tryst in that little cottage with him. No one else, you hear me? He's a man with strong appetites. He'll play right into your lovely harlot's hands. That's the only way I'll be able to control the man. He has to fall madly in love with your sweet charms. He must be so in love he will overlook the fact that you are the town whore.

She said nothing more. Air forgot to find its way into her lungs for a moment upon moment. She should have told her uncle she'd seen Stewart in town and perhaps he would not have been shot. It was her fault. Yet, it never occurred to her the man, the owner of Leslie Hall could be in any danger. That this man's appearance in Virginia was the reason he was beating her. She'd been a fool and he'd been the one to pay for her mistake. She paid, too, but that was nothing new nor would it be the last time. She tried not to move, knowing if she did the pain would increase. It hurt her to breathe, but she had to take in air. If only she didn't.

Uncle William moved away from her. Walked around his desk to bring a chair so he could sit right in front of her, stare at her. "You're not a fool. Stupidity doesn't suit you," he said finally after staring at her for what seemed an eternity. "How many times do I have to remind you of your sister's predicament if you don't do exactly as I say? Now, think, if I had been caught, what would happen to you as well as Clare? Hmmm... Doesn't take a hell of a lot of imagination to come up with the unpleasant scenario. You won't be the only whore in these parts, my dear. Since you, my sweet niece, are underage and I'm yours and Clare's guardian, there will be no one to see to your future. No, miss, you won't lie to me or try to do me in again or I swear to you..." he paused, rose and strode back to hover over her.

She shrank back against the wall terrified he'd start pounding her again. He sank down on his haunches, grabbing her chin, his fingers tightening as he jerked her head upward. She had no choice but to look at him, his eyes simmering with hatred for her. "I swear to you, Sophia. I will kill you if you try anything like this again. Do you understand me? Then what will happen to the little sister?"

She said nothing, knew he saw the hatred glaring at him in her eyes. She also knew he saw the fear. Then his expression changed to a slow evil smile spreading across his face. "No, I don't believe I'll kill you. I'll kill your sister instead even though she would garner me a lot of money in the future just as you are doing."

He let go of her chin, standing so he would tower over her. Tell me you understand, Sophia."

Unable to help herself she nodded her head. "Yes," she finally said, "I understand everything. It's perfectly clear."

"Good." He offered her his hand. She stared at it knowing the injustice he could met out so easily, remembering the feel of his fist as it hit her earlier. She felt helpless, but she wasn't going to give him satisfaction by accepting any kind of help from this man she detested.

"You're stubborn. That's not entirely bad in a woman in your position. Means you'll pursue this until I get what I want. You can hate me too. Doesn't matter to me. I find your hate amusing, even invigorating at times. If you were my mistress, I would enjoy whipping that insolent look out of your eyes. The welts on your back would please me sufficiently to keep you alive just to whip you again. I would break you, Sophia. Ah, but I don't want you broken, at least not yet. There will be time for that." He stroked his chin, staring out the window. "Yes. The Duke of Southcliff finally reacted to Grayson's messages. He sent his brother just as I intended. Now it is time to put my plan into action. I mean to have Leslie Hall by summer.

"Ah, yes, sweet Sophia since you've seen a number of naked men you won't be disappointed with this one. He is extraordinarily built and pleasing to the eye. This man should not be too incredibly hard for you to seduce. After all, he is only a man. He will succumb just as easily as the other to your feminine wiles. This one is not a fool though. He won't be quiet so easily seduced as Devon or Charles. I will tell you in the morning what is expected of you. I'm quite looking forward to the inevitable outcome."

At eight o'clock the following morning Sophia was trying to fasten the front buttons of her gown. Every movement hurt. She tried not to groan even though there was no one there to hear her. Tried not to let the moisture in the back of her throat move to her eyes. The flesh on her torso turned all sorts of blues, greens and yellows. He wouldn't see her pain but he knew she hurt. Uncle William expertly inflicted the intended punishment. She was truly trapped here where he controlled her every action, her entire life. As she slipped another button into its hole, she felt the pain so deeply she doubled over, her breath catching in her throat. She froze for a few moments, closing her eyes to let the pain ease from her. The laudanum would take effect soon.

There was nothing to do, however. No, she had to protect Clare, do what he wanted. For her there was no end in sight. She knew if she did what he wished, he would keep his promise. At least she hoped he would. There were no guarantees. Clare poked her head around the corner, a large smile on her face. "Don't you want breakfast? It's growing cold and you know how Uncle William is. You won't get another bite until luncheon if you don't come down soon."

"Yes, I know," she said, but she wasn't sure she could eat anything. A hot cup of tea would be nice though, maybe a little lemon and milk in it.

Clare sat down on the bed, her hands clasped in her lap watching. Her blue-gray eyes seemed to see into her mind. She didn't want Clare to know how much pain she was in or why.

She finally finished dressing. She glanced in the mirror intending to brush her hair, knew she couldn't. She looked pale and disheveled, about as seductive as a cow. Some harlot she was. If Link Stewart was a man of the world as he was reputed to be, there was nothing about her he would find attractive. There were dark circles under bloodshot eyes. Only the makeup Uncle William insisted she wear would hide the circles. Nothing would hide the redness of her eyes. She wasn't sure she could put on enough makeup to hide the agony.

She finished every move, sending more ripples of pain through her body. She pulled back her dark blond hair and tied it at the nape of her neck with a black ribbon. It would have to do. "Let's go eat."

"You don't feel well do you, Sophia?"

It wasn't' a question. Sometimes Clare saw more than she should. Sophia wasn't at all sure how long she could keep the truth from her little sister. Clare was growing more intuitive every day. Soon enough she would know what was happening. "All I need is a bit of breakfast to make me feel better. Yesterday was busy. I didn't get a chance to eat. I didn't sleep well last night. I'll be fine once I get some food into my stomach."

Clare looked at her, shaking her head, clearly not believing a word coming from her mouth. No, her little sister didn't appear reassured nor did she look as if she believed her. She took her hand in hers walking with her. "If there is something wrong, you'll be sure to tell me. Promise?" Clare's wide blue eyes stared trustingly into hers.

A wave of guilt coursed through her. It was a feeling she would have to ignore. "Promise." Sophia loved Clare more than life itself. She vowed she would never let anything bad happen to her. Clare was the only person in the world who loved her. She would have to do everything he asked of her, perhaps more. She was terrified though. Link Steward was not like the other men she seduced. Even her uncle saw the difference.

Uncle William was in the breakfast room. She hoped he'd be gone, a false hope she knew. He told her last night he would explain what he wanted from her in the morning. So, she knew he would be in the room sitting on his chair, waiting, needing to see first hand the damage he inflicted. He waited here to torment her until they were alone again and he would tell her what he expected from her. She didn't want anything to do with Link Stewart, having the sinking feeling she would lose if she went up against that man.

Thirteen months since she'd become a whore, a harlot, a piece of muslin any man could use. Well, not just any man, only the ones her uncle wanted. Thirteen long months since the women in the community shunned her, whispering behind her back. It hurt her deeply yet she learned to ignore them when she was in town, learned to hold her chin high and look the other way. They didn't shun her when they came to visit at Mayfair Hall. No, they admired her uncle too much to do that.

She looked fondly at her sister, hoping somehow she would fare better when she came of age. "Sit down and eat your breakfast."

"I think I'll just have a cup of tea."

William looked up from his newspaper, the imported London Times only two months old, for English ships were regular in their arrivals. One could think they were keeping up with the current news from abroad. He seemed to study her face even as she lowered her lashes not wishing to see him.

"You and I will meet after you've eaten. You must eat, Sophia. Don't want you to waist away to nothing. Your men friends won't like it if you are skin and bones. Men don't appreciate women who are too skinny." He cleared his throat, still studying her before changing the subject slightly. "There are things we need to discuss. I know you always wish to accommodate yourself to my wishes. Ah, do not take too much time eating. Plans need to be made and put into action." He was rising, folding the paper to set it on the table before he moved to the other room, his office, where they would have the much-needed privacy.

Clare glanced between them, her eyes narrowing thoughtfully. She was smart. The little girl knew something was going on, had been for quite some time. Sophia wished Clare would stay young and carefree a bit longer. She also wished their parents hadn't died. She supposed none of her wishes would ever come true.

"Very well, Uncle," Sophia said. "In your study then. After breakfast. I'll be along shortly."

"Yes, my dear, that is exactly what I wish. He turned his attention to Clare. As for you, my fine young lady, you will accompany me into town today. It seems you've outgrown all your clothing. Don't want your ankles to show now, do we. We will get you an entire new wardrobe, one that will usher in the spring and the summer as well. Would you like that?"

Other Books by Christine Young
Available at Rogue Phoenix Press

My Sweet Broc
Bad Boys Book One

He's a bad bad boy...

Broc Wallace is a fun-loving rake who never thought any beautiful woman could melt his heart. He lives life in the present enjoying the camaraderie of his friends and the pleasures of his mistress. When Bliss races into his life, he is ill prepared to deal with her secrets or give up the tenor of his life. When the truth is revealed, he finds himself unable to forgive and forget the betrayal.

... but she's sweet for him

Bliss MacTavish knows she's playing with fire when she refuses to tell this bad boy her name. He tempts her with sweet whispers of seduction knowing her innocent nature will be unable to refuse all he yearns to give her. Deciding to follow her heart, she finds the repercussions more than she bargains for when she gives herself to this bad boy.

Crazy for Cam
Bad Boys Book Two

He's a bad bad boy...

Lord Cam MacEwen, Viscount of Rosehill, tries his best to be proper and court the lady of his dreams in the acceptable way. The feat proves impossible when the lady in question uses every means at her disposal to tempt him. He fights his jealousy for another man as well as the need to make her his own, finally giving in to her irresistible passion.

... but she's crazy for him.

Chelsea MacTavish wants the bad boy she fell in love with and kissed just before her eighteenth birthday. With feminine wiles and irresistible allure, the sensuous lady plans to best Cam at his game of hearts and make him forget his need to court her properly.

Falling for Flynt
Bad Boys Book Three

He's a bad, bad boy...

Fascinated by Hope's loss of memory yet haunted by her sultry beauty, Flynt is irresistibly drawn to the stoic miss—and into her troubles with the sultan who wants her for himself. When he discovers she is the sister of his best friend, his pride keeps him from pursuing her and making her his.

... but she's falling for him.

Raised in a harem but now penniless, alone and without her memory, Hope must discover a way to remember all that she has lost. She finds a way to continue with her life as a servant in Flynt's home. The first sight of Flynt steals Hope's breath as well as her heart. Can she overcome her fears and give herself to the man she fell in love with.

Dancing With Donal
Bad Boys Book Four

He's a bad bad boy...

Once a bad boy always a bad boy, Donal Chamberlin's carefree ways come crashing down around him when he meets the ravishingly beautiful Daryl MacTavish, the innocent little sister of one of his best friends. He is determined to win her heart as he sets his sights on marriage and an heir. His past gets in the way of his quest when a woman he once loved threatens Daryl's life.

... but she's dancing with him.

Daryl has seen the control her sister's husbands hold over them. She yearns for a life where she makes decisions for herself. No man will have power over her. But no man kisses her the way Donal does. No man can make her forget all her goals leaving her helpless to give up her dreams. Yet Donal is determined to dance through all the barriers she thrust in front of him, pursuing her until she says yes.

Loving Leslie
Bad Boys Book Five

He's a bad bad boy...

Leslie Stewart, Duke of Southcliff is stoic, set in his ways, a spy who is used to having his life well ordered. He expects life to continue on in this perfectly conventional fashion. He assumes his bad boy status while keeping mamas and debutantes at arm's length. An heir is needed but Leslie has every intention of finding a woman who doesn't covet his wealth and tittle. He is irresistibly drawn to the headstrong young lady who becomes more beautiful as she develops into a woman.

... but she is loving him.

When Leslie kisses Lacie MacTavish, she knows even at the tender age of fifteen this is the man of her dreams. Forced to wait until she comes of age, Lacie withdraws into herself. Now she is eighteen and Leslie has returned from a mission for the British Government ready to claim her as his bride. She refuses him and he must find a way to seduce her and in the process create a burning passion within her, which she cannot deny.

Pleasing Arie
Bad Boys Book Six

He's a bad bad boy...

Arie Demir has never been denied anything in his life. He takes what he wants. What he undeniably yearns for is the beautiful redheaded spitfire he sees in a restaurant in Glasgow. At every turn, she confuses him by disputing his power over her. Alison refuses to accept the fact he owns her. While Arie tries desperately with patience and tenderness to drive her wild with new sensations, his scorching kisses ignite the fires of her very soul to make her understand he is all she will ever want.

... but is she pleasing him?

Alison Fletcher never expected to find herself kidnapped and sold to a whorehouse then bought by a Turkish sultan to become his slave. She vows to never surrender to the arrogant man who believes he owns her. She is stunned by the magnificently handsome man who awaits her compliance. Unexpectedly, she finds Arie the lesser of all the evils. The hidden depths of his mesmerizing dark brown eyes hold her into their power; his muscular embrace makes her weak with desire. She is his to do with as he wishes.

Graham's Wicked Kiss
Bad Boys Book Seven

He's a bad bad boy...

Graham Chamberlin is stunned to find three young boys dangling from the trees lining the drive to Runningmead Manner. On further inspection, he is astonished at their obsession to protect a young woman who has been brutalized by her pimp. The woman he discovers hiding in a third-floor attic room is gravely injured. He takes the silver haired stowaway under his wing. Clearly, Graham's new guest is a lady with many secrets. He is determined to unlock all the mysteries surrounding her.

... But she can't resist his wicked kiss.

The years since Ria left the convent where she was raised have been a nightmare. Her secrets are dangerous—as is the powerful man determined to find her. Handsome Graham Chamberlin is clearly a gentleman with secrets of his own, but staying with him could mean the difference between life and death for Ria. With each passing day, her handsome host turns Ria's convalescence into an increasingly sensual escape. Now her greatest challenge may be imagining anything less than a future in his arms.

Foolish for Piper

The pickpocket...

Piper has spent her life surviving the streets of St. Giles Parish in London, a den of iniquity and crime. Masquerading as a boy she escapes the whorehouses the young girls are sent to as they come of age. The day she encounters Brett MacLachlan begins the same as every other one. When she picks his pocket, she has no idea her life is going to change irreversibly.

... and the mark

Handsome aristocrat Brett MacLachlan has come to London for his amusement only to find his world turned upside down by a thief and her dog. From the moment he spots her, Brett knows there is something intrinsically wrong. In his arms, Piper discovers passion and joy. Yet secrets of her past haunt her, and a scar will tell the true tale as well as her identity.

Taylor's Destiny

She traveled to another time and place to change destiny...

Enjoying a day of sailing, Taylor Maxwell never expected after a suffering a concussion she would wake up in another century. A resilient independent woman in the twenty-first century, the blond beauty is ill prepared for life in the 1800s. Her first sight of the naval captain who rescues her makes her heart stop, giving her hope for her future.

His life is transformed by a woman who appears from nowhere...

Born to a life of ease, Reid Stewart defies the dictates of those born to aristocracy and chooses a life of adventure in the navy and as a spy for the crown. When he discovers a nearly naked woman on the bow of small sailing ship, his heart warms. His love for Taylor and his need to protect her from a man who pursues her might cost him his life as well as hers.

Caitlin's Duke

She played a fiddle in an Irish pub...

Caitlin O'Shea Is the most beautiful woman Roc Leighton has ever seen. With her blue violet eyes and long black hair she captivates him. In turn he mesmerizes Caitlin. Caught in the power of his gaze as he watches her, she is wise enough to know he desires her but will never give his heart to her. Caitlin has vowed to never be any man's mistress.

And fell in love with an English Lord...

Roc knows the first time he watches her play the fiddle and dance around the pub, she will be his next mistress. Despite her protest, he will find a way to convince her that her place is with him. While Caitlin's determination to keep her vows, fate takes a cruel turn and she is forced to seek refuge with Roc.

Catching Meara
Book One in the McKenna Clan Series

Meara Thorton was a feisty, world-class computer hacker—cornered by the FBI and shockingly given the chance to be their newly acquired technical analyst. Brilliant and intuitive, yet aching with the loss of everyone she has cared about, her restless heart led her to discover a love she fought and a world she didn't know could possibly exist.

Sweet Sexy Sadie
Book Two in the McKenna Clan Series

From the first time Sadie's eyes met those of Brody McKenna in the hot Sierra Madre Mountains, theirs was a potent attraction—not gentle, slow, and easy, but hot, hard, and all-consuming. The daughter of a dysfunctional family, Sadie had dreams no man could wrench from her with hot sex and an all-consuming passion. She'd challenge this alpha male with all the strength she possessed. But her red hair, fiery temperament, and indomitable spirit obsessed Brody... and he knew he had to find a way to show her he was more than he appeared and convince her to make a life with him.

Sweet Misbehavin'
Book Three in the McKenna Clan Series

Cast adrift after fleeing the home of Jokul, the ice demon, Atantsi, a firestarter, grew to womanhood as she moved through time to keep the demon from finding her. Though stubborn and courageous, she was ill prepared to use powers she had not been taught. Her first sight of the intoxicating Carr McKenna left her breathless, and her second encounter gave her hope for a future she never thought she had.

A playboy, a second son and a shifter, a man who thought his life would be carefree, Carr McKenna was shocked to discover the woman he'd paid as an escort is a firestarter who is running for her life. He is the leader of all the McKennas around the world and that he has multiple powers. His passion for Margo and the need to defend her might cost him his life as well as hers.

Sweet Talkin' Sugar
Book Four in the McKenna Clan Series

Lyonesse McKenna, was dreaming or was she? From the instant Lyn saw Deacon McClain across a black jack table in a crowed Las Vegas casino the unmistakable attraction sent Lyn's senses flying into overdrive. Her family of shapeshifters believed in soul mates. She'd always been skeptical yet she couldn't help but question the way her heart sped when he looked at her.

When Deacon appeared in Las Vegas he knew his first job was to save Lyn from a Sea Demon, but the next order of business was to convince her he would someday mean more to her than she'd ever expected. But her stubborn nature and unbendable spirit consumed Deacon... and he had to chase away all the demons real and imagined in order to win her heart.

Sweet Surrender
Book Five in the McKenna Clan Series

Ripped from her family at the top of Infinity Cliff, Kimi McKenna finds herself thrust somewhere into the future. Dark elements threaten to destroy the earth unless Kimi can work together with the white witch to stop the destruction. Confused by her mate's role in the conspiracy, she refuses to acknowledge the connection. But amidst raging fire and attacks on the people she is coming to hold dear, she allows Maska O'keefe into her heart.

Maska O'keefe has loved the beautiful shapeshifter for years. Unable to save her life years ago, he vows to watch over her as he is given a second chance to convince her that even though he is a witch and not a shifter, they are indeed soul mates. Kimi's divided loyalties between her family and the cause she is now a part of will determine their relationship. Only the part she plays as the messiah can bring this to a conclusion in the final battle.

Dakota's Bride
The first book in the Lakota/Pinkerton Series

When Emma St. John received her brother's letter imploring her to escape her stepfather's vengeful scheme and to trust Dakota Barringer with her life, she was willing to chance it. But the handsome, brooding riverboat owner Emma found in Natchez a danger of another kind. For Emma soon found herself surrendering to an unrelenting desire.

Raised by the Sioux when his parents were killed, Dakota had been betrayed once before by a white woman. He wasn't about to trust another, especially one claiming that her stepfather, a powerful U.S. senator, had framed her as a murderess. But he couldn't let Emma's intoxicating effect on him. Now Dakota would risk his very life to protect the innocent beauty who had seduced him with her tender love.

My Angel
The second book in the Lakota/Pinkerton Series

A BEAUTY IN BUCKSKINS
When her father decided to send her to a finishing school back East, Angela Chamberlain refused to be confined to stuffy drawing rooms. Instead, the daring spitfire who could shoot like a man and ride like the wind longed for a life of adventure and romance—and she knew exactly who could give it to her. Devil Blackmoor was a hired gun with a dangerous reputation. But Angela was willing to go to the ends of the earth to capture the handsome devil's heart.

A DEVIL IN DISGUISE
He'd come to America looking for excitement, but Devil Blackmoor got more than he bargained for when he encountered a beautiful rebel who answered his kisses with a wild innocence that touched his very soul. Yet standing between them were more obstacles than either ever dreamed. For Devil had strapped on a gun for the wrong man. And that made Angela his enemy. Now he'll have to choose between his duty and the woman he loves more than life.

The Locket
The third book in the Lakota/Pinkerton Series

The year is 1894. Seeking revenge for crimes against his family, Misha Petrovich follows a path that leads straight to Ariel Cameron's boarding house in Mist Harbor, Oregon. A family heirloom in Ariel's possession leads Misha to believe she is guilty. The locket has been handed down to the oldest girl in the Petrovich family for generations. Ariel is innocent of wrong doing, but her father is not. Misha is torn by his feelings for Ariel and his need for restitution against her father. Knowing that the relationship between them is fragile, Misha does everything in his power to protect Ariel's father. His efforts are to no avail when her father is shot. Ariel comes to realize Misha's steadfast courage and determination to protect her and her father despite what has happened to his family. Ariel's love and devotion heals Misha's heart.

The Talisman
The fourth book in the Lakota/Pinkerton Series

Running from a marriage that lasted one night, Dr. Moriah McKeown discovers the land she has settled on is coveted by determined and lawless men. Yet the proud young woman who once vowed never to abandon her home has second thoughts when her adopted children are threatened. Her only recourse is to enlist the aid of a dark, dangerous gun for hire.

Haunted by the past and a betrayal he will never forgive, Ian Civanovich uses his fast gun and his reckless courage to forget the faithlessness of a woman in his past. He will trust no female—nor will he rest until the threat hovering over Moriah McKeown is put to rest.

Forever His
The fifth book in the Lakota/Pinkerton Series

Struggling to come to terms with the part she played in Jacob St.

John's death, Etta Barringer resigns from Pinkerton Agency and seeks peace and solace in a Rocky Mountain Cabin.

Jacob has vowed to discover the reason Etta has betrayed him, sold him out to his enemy and left him for dead.

Isolated in their cabin, they discover their love for each other and learn to trust. But the trust is shattered when Jacob learns she is married to his sworn enemy; the man who left him in the desert to die.

Allura's Secret
Twelve Dancing Princesses Book One

Allura McClellan is horrified by her father's decision to take out an ad in the Times awarding her to the man strong enough and smart enough to win her hand and uncover her secrets. She's an intelligent young woman who takes great delight in the freedom allotted to her by her father. She's well aware that marriage would effectively curtail the adventures she's shared with her sisters and cousins.

Hunter Gray is nothing like the other men who've arrived to vie for Allura's hand in marriage and everything that goes along with it. However, he is the first to refuse to concede defeat and pursue her despite her attempts to disguise her true appearance. It's her temperament that is of more concern to him than her looks. Hunter has worked all his life with the hope of someday owning his own land. Now that it looks like there's a very real possibility that everything he's ever wanted is within reach nothing is going to deter him – including Miss Allura's disagreeable disposition.

Amorica's Wager
Twelve Dancing Princesses Book Two

Amorica Hepburn was sent to London to find a husband. Finding a man was the last item on her agenda. With her two cousins, Amorica wagers she can dissuade her suitor before the others. Despite her efforts she discovers a chemistry that cannot be denied. Suddenly she is the arrogant man's wife, pledged to a marriage neither desire. But swept off to his ancestral home above the Dover cliffs and into his strong embrace, Amorica is soon possessed by a raging passion for the husband she had vowed to despise…

Damian Andrews couldn't afford to trust the emerald-eyed spitfire who happened upon his secret. Amorica's hatred of all men of his kind only inflames the war that rages between them. Still, he can not control the intense desire his stubborn bride inspires, or make her surrender to his will until he has conquered the headstrong beauty on the battlefield of love…

Ravyn's Marriage of Inconvenience
Twelve Dancing Princesses Book Three

A REGAL BEAUTY
When the duchess decides to wed her to a wastrel and a fop, Ravyn Grahm takes matters into her own hands and declares her engagement to another man. Instead of fessing up and telling her great aunt what she has done, she goes through with the pretense. Ariec Lakeland is the bastard son of an earl and has a dangerous reputation. But Ravyn is willing to do most anything to keep the duchess from discovering the lie.

A DEVIL-MAY-CARE SMUGGLER
He'd bought land in America, looking to put down roots and end his life of adventure, but Ariec Lakeland got more than he bargained for when he encountered a beautiful heiress who made a promise she didn't want to keep. But the promise could not be undone and standing between them were more obstacles than either ever dreamed. Ariec had made plans to spend the rest of his life in America and that was at odds with Ravyn's plan of living in England and running her father's estate. Now, he'll have to choose between his dreams and the woman he loves more than life.

Christel's Sunrise
Twelve Dancing Princesses Book Four

He Made Her An Offer...

Life has thrown Christel McClellan some experiences that could have devastated a less determined woman. Beautiful, self-assured and fiercely independent, she is trying to forget the loss of her stillborn child. But is the child alive?

She Couldn't Deny...

Life is carefree for Ryder MacLaren who loves to see what is on the other side of the sunrise. Laird of Clan MacLaren, he is wealthy, handsome and happily unencumbered... until stunning Christel McClellan enters his life. When he hears her story, he believes the child she thought dead has been sold to a wealthy buyer.

Storm's Passion
Twelve Dancing Princesses Book Five

SHE MADE A PROPOSAL...

Life strikes Storm Graham a shattering blow when she learns her father has bartered her to a man she detests. Storm is beautiful, self–assured and fiercely independent, and refuses to be a pawn in her father's schemes, yet she can find no way out of this bargain made in hell. Going on the offensive she asks the wealthiest man on the eastern coast of England to marry her, never believing she might fall in love.

HE TRIED TO REFUSE...

For Hadden Johnston life has provided everything he ever wanted, including a sanctuary for homeless children. He is wealthy, handsome and happily unencumbered... until stunning Storm Graham marches into his life and proposes a marriage of convenience. Yet this type of marriage to a woman who inflames his senses is far from acceptable. If he's going to be tied down, he will move heaven and earth to have this woman warming his bed.

Gotta Have Fayth
Twelve Dancing Princesses Book Six

A regal beauty with raven hair and piercing blue eyes, Fayth Graham is unwilling to parade herself in front of the wealthy Lords of England during the season. Seeking a means to dissuade any man wishing to wed her, she seeks a way to ruin herself for marriage. When she unexpectedly meets a man with sparkling gray eyes and an infectious grin, she decides this is the man who will keep her from agreeing to obey.

He returned from six months at sea, looking for a few nights of pleasure with a willing lass, but Jarret Kinsley got more than he bargained for when he met a beautiful debutant who responded to his kisses with a wild innocence that touched his heart. Yet the obstacles looming between them might rip them apart. Both had vowed never to marry, so when consequences of their dalliances got in the way, Jarret would have to choose between the life he's always desired and the woman he loves more than life.

Ella's Pleasure
Twelve Dancing Princesses Book Seven

A WHISPER OF PLEASURE
Ella Hepburn was an auburn haired debutant from the harsh Scottish coastline—a wild innocent to be seduced and tamed. A spirited beauty, she captivated Drake Montgomerie's jaded heart—while succumbing to the smoldering desire she felt for her unyielding suitor.

A WHISPER OF DANGER
In Drake Montgomerie's glittering world of money and privilege, young Ella discovered passion and desire could overcome everything she'd been taught to resist—entangling Drake, the heir apparent, in a lethal coil of aristocratic family intrigue. But grave peril would only nurse the sparks of a love that knew no limits and a magnificent ecstasy that would not be denied.

Eveleen's Seduction
Twelve Dancing Princesses Book Eight

A WHISPER OF SEDUCTION
A brutal attack on Eveleen Hepburn's cherished island off the Scottish coastline leaves her shattered and bewildered. Learning a man she once trusted can kill as easily as he can breathe even though the deed saves her life, creates questions that need answers. An innocent beauty, she enchants Logan Maxwell's cynical heart—giving in to the raging passion she feels for her mysterious suitor.

A WHISPER OF INTRIGUE
In Logan's Maxwell's world of espionage and privilege, young Eveleen discovers truths about herself she never expected, and a need for passion and love can overcome all her fears if she learns to accept certain truths. She finds herself entangled in a lethal battle for land that was once owned by French nobility, taken from them during the revolution and sold to Maxwell. But grave peril would unleash the flames of love that simmers, creating a magical union that cannot be refuted.

Tavia's Deception
Twelve Dancing Princesses Book Nine

WHISPERS OF DECEPTION
When her father decides to send her to London for her season, Tavia Hepburn resolves to see the world instead. The raven haired beauty decides to disguise herself as a lad and find employment on a ship bound for Barcelona as a cabin boy. But she never bargains on finding passion and love to a red haired sea captain who rescues her from certain death.

WHISPERS OF MURDER
For James Macmurra, the world is black and white until he meets a young debutante, who turns his world upside down. He's unable to deny Tavia's intoxicating effect on him. In a match tense with obstacles, unwillingness to divulge secrets, and unforeseen peril, irresistible desire

and passion grows into undeniable love. James would risk his life to shelter and protect the innocent debutante who seduces him with her sweet love.

Larena's Fascination
Twelve Dancing Princesses Book Ten

WHISPERS OF FASCINATION

Fiery, free spirited Larena Graham never wanted to marry a duke. She is thrilled to be in love with the fourth son of an aristocrat, Gavin Broon. But when it seems Gavin ignores her, she set her sights on politics and bettering human life. Unsuspecting intrigue and a plot against her, she continues her dangerous plans despite Gavin's wishes.

WHISPERS OF TRUST

Gavin has every intention of properly courting the beautiful Larena until he must leave the city in order to put his affairs in order. Returning to London, he finds the woman he means to make his own is embroiled in political protests that could lead to a prison ship. Larena must learn to trust the handsome Scotsman whose most pressing mission is to protect her and keep her from harm.

Tira's Education
Twelve Dancing Princesses Book Eleven

WHISPERS OF EDUCATION

Learning how to build ships is Tira Hepburn's only dream until she meets Jamie Lundin and her world is turned upside down. With her raven black hair and vivid green eyes, she tempts Jamie and pushes him to defy his vows. She never bargains on finding an irrevocable love and a passion to a man who cannot fulfill her dreams despite his burning desire for her.

WHISPERS OF A BARGAIN

Arrogant and self-assured Jamie is brought up short when Tira captures his heart. All his carefully made plans are put to the test when he decides to teach her the art of ship building if she will spend a week with him alone on his ship. He is unable to deny Tira's intoxicating effect on him. When Tira leaves him behind unwilling to live with him without the benefit of marriage, he races after her. Jamie will risk everything to shelter and protect the innocent debutante who seduces him with her sweet love.

Aidan's Love
Twelve Dancing Princesses Book Twelve

Whispers of Love
Aidan McLellan has loved since she first set eyes on him as a young girl. Spontaneous, wild and eager to grow up, Aidan haunts his waking thoughts day and night, insinuating herself into his life. With her fiery red hair and sparkling sapphire eyes, she seizes Blade's heart even while he tries to resist the innocent child until she becomes a woman.

Whispers of Courage
Blade has waited what seems a lifetime to claim the woman who captures his heart as a little girl. Claiming his inheritance before his younger brother takes what is rightfully his, Blade must convince Aidan of his sincerity after years of avoidance and wed her before his father dies so he can return home, securing his rightful place. Everything is put to the test when his life as well as Aidan's is threatened by the man who once called him brother.

Twelve Days to Love

When Archer Steele shows up at Calanthe Durand's failing plantation with an alligator over his shoulder, Cali thinks she's never seen a more handsome man. During the war she had to defend herself and her servants from both union and confederate soldiers. Independent and self-sufficient, she vows to never marry.

But Archer Steele has different ideas. The first time Archer sees Cali in town, he feels an instant attraction. He decides he will do everything and anything to convince the beautiful Miss Durand he is worthy of her love. During the weeks leading up to Christmas, he gives her twelve gifts in hopes she will fall in love with him. Yet they are faced with challenges they must overcome before Cali can commit to a marriage.

Door to Heaven

Jessica Lawrence is the stepdaughter of a woman born in the twentieth century transported back in time to the year 1868. An acclaimed suffragette, she raises Jessica to believe in the equality of women. Jess Law believes everything she was taught, and when the time is right she becomes a private investigator. Courageous and impetuous, Jess finds danger in her quest to save all women from white slavery. Her passionate mission results in a wedding to Roc Newman, a man she knows can steal her heart...

Roc can't trust the sapphire-eyed spitfire who invades his home in search of secret papers and knocks him flat with her karate moves. Jessica's refusal to obey his wishes serves to inflame the war between them. Still, he cannot control the intense desire his reluctant bride inspires, or make her surrender her independence, until he has conquered the headstrong beauty on the battlefield of love...

Rebel Heart

HER REBEL SPIRIT DEFIED HIS OUTSIDERS SOUL... She was velvet and silk, eyes the color of a summer storm and amber hair. Victoria DeMontville, because of a promise and a codicil to her father's will, was forced to marry one man to protect her from another. She hated Cameron Savage with a fierce passion. But to hold on to her genetic research and find a cure for the deadly Signe virus, she must pretend to love the enemy at her door, come with weapons of fire to melt her icy heart...

HIS OUTSIDERS TOUCH IGNITED RAGING PASSIONS...
[SEP]He wore a mask, disguised as the Phantom, a true legend come to life. Even as war and debate over new genetic research engulfed them all, he would find his greatest adversary in the beauty who'd branded him an outsider and barbarian, the woman he was born to possess, his soul mate.

Safari Moon

Solo St. John, a wildlife photographer, is preparing for a trip to Alaska. Suddenly, Solo finds women of all sorts invading his privacy, his home and his office, all cooing nonsense words and blatantly throwing themselves at him. Solo doesn't know why, and he has no idea how to rid himself of the persistent women. He finally decides to beg a favor of his best buddy Nyssa Harrington.

In love with Solo for the past ten years and knowing he doesn't return her feelings Nyssa doesn't want to talk to Solo. She knows if she accepts his phone call, she will not be able to resist the temptation to hope again.

Straight to Heaven

Running from demons, Alexandra McMurdie stumbles into Forbidden Ground where up is down and elements of nature are contested. Though a strong independent woman in the twenty-first century' she is unprepared for life in the 1800s. Her first site of the formidable James Lawrence makes her heart skip a beat, giving her cause to reconsider her desperate need to find a way home.

Born with a silver spoon, James' life was torn apart during the War Between the States. Moving west he vows to put the life he once knew in the past. When he discovers a half-frozen woman near Gold Hill, his heart begins to thaw. His love for Alexandra and his need to keep her from a man who has pursued her through time might cost him his life as well as hers.

A Valentine's Anthology

The Lending Library-a fantasy by Christie L. Kraemer
Faeries try to fit into the human world when the forest where they make their home is destroyed by a mysterious enemy.

Chasing Rainbows-a contemporary romance by Genene Valleau
An eccentric aunt, an inventive uncle, a mother who wears poodle skirts, and a brother who wears pearls provide a hilarious backdrop for the courtship of a young woman who yearns for a "normal" family.

The Gift-an historical romance by Christine Young
A man and a woman on opposite sides of the Civil War get a second chance at love after one final battle returns soldiers to their war-torn homes to rebuild their lives.

A St. Patrick's Day Tale
Christine Young, C. L. Kraemer, Genene Valleau

Tumble through time…
…to Ireland in 1817, when tensions are high between Protestants and Catholics and fae people guide the fate of villagers. A lovely Catholic lass stumbles upon the weakly ritual fisticuffing between Irish lads. She falls into the lap of a handsome young Protestant. Family ties, grudges, and two conniving faeries threaten their budding love. But the faeries outsmart themselves when they hijack a time machine that has mysteriously appeared in their forest and are whisked to…
…Eugene, Oregon in the 20th century, amid a property feud between the local faeries and night elves. The conniving faeries from Olde Ireland try to stir up more mischief. However, a warrior gnome convinces the magic folk to control their own destiny, and forces the intruding faeries to take refuge in the time machine again, spinning their way

toward…

…A modern day castle in western Oregon. An eccentric inventor is determined to reclaim his wayward time machine and save his beloved wife from her latest misadventure. If only they can travel safely past the black hole…

a May Day Anthology
Christine Young, C. L. Kraemer, Rosemary Indra, Genene Valleau

Highland Miracle — Christine Young
HURTLED THROUGH TIME, Sean Michael Sterling, landed in the midst of a May Day celebration he didn't understand, assuming the role of Laird Sterling.

ILLIGITAMATE CHILD OF NOBILITY, Reagan Douglas searches for a way out of her half brother's house.

Defying the Odds — C.L. Kraemer
The night elves on the hill aren't happy without their magic. They concoct a plan to punish those who were involved in the act that rendered them almost human. Meanwhile, Uther, the rogue night elf, has returned to woo the Librarian to be his eternal mate.

Love in Bloom — Rosemary Indra
When childhood friends reunite it takes two fairies and a matchmaking daughter to help them admit their true love for each other.

No More Poodle Skirts — Genie Gabriel
After drifting for years in the innocent age of the 1950s, a woman struggles to join today's world by finding a career and a new love, with some help from her zany family.

Once Upon a Christmas Moon
Christine Young, C. L. Kraemer, Genene Valleau

TWELVE DAYS TO LOVE

When Archer Steele shows up at Calanthe Durand's failing plantation with an alligator over his shoulder, Cali thinks she's never seen a more handsome man. During the war she had to defend herself and her servants from both union and confederate soldiers. Independent and self-sufficient, she vows to never marry. But Archer Steele has different ideas. The first time Archer sees Cali in town, he feels an instant attraction. He decides he will do everything and anything to convince the beautiful Miss Durand he is worthy of her love. During the weeks leading up to Christmas, he gives her twelve gifts in hopes she will fall in love with him.

BOOTS AND BLADES

An ancient evil from the old country has arrived in the high desert of Oregon. Gnome children are vanishing then re-appearing, showing various stages of traumatization. Tiamoon, warrior gnome, will put her skills to use alongside Killian, a handsome warrior, also in need of a cause.

CHRISTMAS PAWSIBILITIES

With their world destroyed and their space ship malfunctioning, the dogizens of Planet Canid have little choice but to crash land on Earth. They face tortuous experiments at the hands of the Geeks in Green... or they can trust an eccentric inventor and his zany family to deliver the Canine Queen's puppies and help them celebrate new lives.